Fiona was born in a youth hostel... ...e started working on teen magazine *Jackie* at age seventeen, then went on to join *Just Seventeen* and *more!* Fiona has three grown-up children, writes for many newspapers and magazines and lives in Glasgow with her husband Jimmy.

For more info visit www.fionagibson.com. You can follow Fiona on Instagram @fiona_gib.

By the same author:

Mum on the Run
The Great Escape
Pedigree Mum
Take Mum Out
How the In-Laws Wrecked Christmas: a short story
As Good As It Gets?
The Woman Who Upped and Left
The Woman Who Met Her Match
The Mum Who'd Had Enough
The Mum Who Got Her Life Back
When Life Gives You Lemons
The Dog Share
The Woman Who Took a Chance
The Man I Met on Holiday
The Woman Who Ran Away from Everything

Fiona Gibson
The FULL NEST

avon.

Published by AVON
A division of HarperCollins*Publishers* Ltd
1 London Bridge Street
London SE1 9GF

www.harpercollins.co.uk

HarperCollins*Publishers*
Macken House
39/40 Mayor Street Upper
Dublin 1
D01 C9W8

A Paperback Original 2025
1

First published in Great Britain by HarperCollins*Publishers* 2025

Copyright © Fiona Gibson 2025

Fiona Gibson asserts the moral right to be identified
as the author of this work.

A catalogue copy of this book is available from the British Library.

ISBN: 978-0-00-849447-6

This novel is entirely a work of fiction. The names, characters
and incidents portrayed in it are the work of the author's imagination.
Any resemblance to actual persons, living or dead, events or
localities is entirely coincidental.

Set in Sabon LT Std by HarperCollins*Publishers* India

Printed and bound in the UK using 100% Renewable
Electricity at CPI Group (UK) Ltd

All rights reserved. No part of this text may be reproduced,
transmitted, downloaded, decompiled, reverse engineered,
or stored in or introduced into any information storage and retrieval
system, in any form or by any means, whether electronic or mechanical,
without the express written permission of the publishers.

This book contains FSC™ certified paper and other controlled
sources to ensure responsible forest management.

For more information visit: www.harpercollins.co.uk/green

*To my newly empty-nester friends
(It'll be okay . . . honestly!)*

'Missing the kids? Feeling bereft now they've left home? Remember your life is about you now – and what you want. So let's celebrate your fabulous second act.'

The Empty-Nester's Handbook: Living Your Best Life When the Kids Leave Home

PROLOGUE

I can't remember the last time I was out past sunrise. And now my heart is beating hard as I creep guiltily into our house.

'Carly! Where have you been?' My husband appears before me, looking aghast.

I tell him where I've spent the night.

'For God's sake,' he thunders. 'Have you gone completely mad?'

Quite possibly, yes. I wince at the volume of his voice. Does he always talk so loud? 'I didn't plan it,' I start. 'It just sort of happened, Frank. Can we talk later? I have to get ready for work . . .' I hurry upstairs, but he catches up with me on the landing.

'Carly, what's going on with you?'

'I need a shower,' I announce, relieved to be able to close and bolt the bathroom door. But when I emerge, swathed in a towel, Frank is waiting. He looks distraught now, and I'm hit by a rush of remorse.

'Frank, I'm really sorry,' I say. 'With everything that's been happening here, it just got too much. I had to get away, only for a little while—'

'Is our home really so terrible to you?'

'No! Of course it's not . . .' *Actually, yes. Yes, it is!*

In our bedroom, I dress quickly and head downstairs with Frank still in pursuit. We can't even talk because my dad is installed at the kitchen table, and Eddie – our son – is moaning about something or other; I don't even know what it is. There's an altercation between him and his dad, and it strikes me that we're really not designed to all live together – isn't that why adult children leave home? Then something is happening and I can't quite believe it's real. Frank is hastily packing a bag.

I stare at him. 'What are you doing?'

'I've had enough. I can't stand it here anymore.'

Minutes later he's out the front door, with the bag slung over his shoulder.

'Frank!' I shout. 'Please—' I break off. As he storms off down the street, away from us all, a single thought rings loud and clear in my head.

Frank and I have fantasised about being empty-nesters. *It'll be our time,* we kept telling ourselves. And we couldn't wait.

How has it turned out like this?

CHAPTER ONE

Six months earlier: January

Living at Kilmory Cottage: Carly, Frank, Eddie

Carly

My son is lying on the sofa as I make my approach. *Be casual,* I tell myself. *Keep it light.* The open Quality Street tin rests on his stomach, and a few gleaming wrappers are scattered around on the floor.

'Eddie?' I start.

'*What?*' He jolts, as if electrocuted.

'I saw this job advertised. I thought you might want to—'

'Not-qualified-for-it,' he snaps.

I exhale slowly, trying to remain patient. 'It's not head of ICI, Eddie. It's not Secretary-General of the United Nations. It's just an admin assistant role with HMRC—'

'What's HMRC?'

'The tax office—'

'Oh my *God!*' he wails, interrupting me again. 'You think I want to spend my life doing that? Going round taking money off people?'

I blink down at him, sprawled there at 6.27 on a Monday evening. He's been lying there all day, I can sense it – festering in that terrible brown hooded robe. Marketed as a dressing gown (foolishly, I bought it for him) it now looks as if it was peeled off a dead shepherd and seems to permanently swathe his body these days. I fear that my son and his robe will eventually merge with our sofa, in the way that a stain disappears into the carpet if you leave it long enough.

'You wouldn't be personally taking money off them,' I explain. 'It doesn't work like that.'

'It's the government taking money, isn't it?'

'Yes, but they don't *go round*, Eddie. They don't turn up at people's houses and wrench it out of their hands. And this is just an office role.'

'*Urrrr!*' He shudders.

'Y'know, general admin-type stuff.'

'Oh no. No thanks.' As if I'd said, *You'd be extracting worms out of cods' intestines, with your teeth.*

'It wouldn't have to be forever,' I add. 'It'd just be something to have on your CV.'

'My CV's fine, thanks.'

'Is it, though, Eddie? Really?'

He shrugs, exhales forcefully and dunks a hand into the tin. He grabs a sweet at random, as if making an active choice would be way too much effort.

Does Eddie's CV even exist? Or is it a mythical thing, like dragons and mermaids and home-made hummus that doesn't turn out looking and tasting like clay? If there is such a document it would read something like this:

Eddie Silva, aged 22
Left school at first opportunity despite being extremely bright.
Tried college, hated it, left.
Sat at home for a year, arse scratching.
Eats too many takeaway pakoras in bedroom.
Leaves pakora cartons, with pointless salad garnish untouched, under bed.
Doesn't seem to register his sister Bella (a year younger) upping sticks for London, or his other sister Ana (three years younger!) heading off to art school in Dundee.
Resists parental cajoling/nagging to get a job.
Drives parents to drink.
Tried college again. Hated it again. Left again.
Currently engaged in further arse scratching and advanced studies in using all the mugs in the house but never putting them in the dishwasher.

Is it us? Is it him? I drive myself crazy going over it because this boy – this *man* – could do anything he wanted, if he'd put his mind to it.

Eddie lets out a soft burp and unwraps the chocolate.

'I thought you didn't like those ones,' I remark.

'Now you're deciding which Quality Street I like?'

'For God's sake, Eddie! Why are you being like this?'

Orange Cremes are the devil's work, he used to announce, when he was funny and sweet and beavered away at his homework without even having to be asked. As a little boy, he was often right there at my side, clutching my hand. A mummy's boy, I suppose; my funny little buddy.

I'd have to coax him to walk into a birthday party. 'Mummy, I want to go home with you!' he'd announce tearfully. Turned out he was scared of balloons. So, maybe I've mollycoddled him, and this is why he lies around in a fug, while Frank and I are out all day, earning money to keep him.

However, Eddie's sudden tolerance of Orange Cremes suggests that things have taken an even darker turn.

He sighs and tosses down the sweet wrapper to join the others on the floor. 'Can you *please* stop dropping wrappers?' I ask.

'I'll pick them up later.'

'Well, you say that but you never do. You just leave it all, Eddie. A trail of litter for me to—'

'I said I'll do it later,' he snaps.

'No need to speak to me like that!' It's another mythical thing – this 'later'. When is that exactly? In fifty years' time when, presumably, he'll still be lounging in his robe, the only difference being that his father and I will no longer be around to buy Quality Street, pick up his wet towels from the bathroom floor and the roll-up butts he leaves scattered around by the back door? (He's long since shed any discomfort about us knowing he smokes.)

His best friends Calum and Raj left home straight after school, both heading for Edinburgh University. It's not that I compare Eddie to them, or believe that he should have gone to university too; of course I don't. He reckoned it wasn't for him and, beyond making gentle suggestions for courses, his dad and I weren't going to pressurise him. However, four years have spun by and throughout that time, he's seen his old mates less and less. Soon Calum and Raj's holidays were no longer spent back here in Sandybanks but travelling with girlfriends or groups of new friends. Or they'd stay in Edinburgh, which had clearly become 'their' city, working at the Festival or in various clubs and bars.

Then straight after uni, both of the boys landed grad-scheme roles at the same company, so now they're proper professionals. Their parents aren't braggers but whenever we run into each other around town there'll be an update. 'He's not earning heaps,' Raj's mum told me recently, 'but he's getting by and loving his job. What's Eddie up to these days?'

'Not an awful lot,' I replied with a grimace.

'Aw, I'm sure it'll all work out. Give him my love, won't you?'

Wouldn't Eddie like to nip over to Edinburgh to see his oldest friends? Whenever I've suggested it, he's snapped *Yeah-maybe* and stomped away.

I can't understand why he's allowed his closest friendships to drift. It's not as if the boys had moved to Alaska; Edinburgh is only two train journeys away, each one less than an hour. And his sisters aren't like that. They've always maintained contact with old friends, despite the physical distances now. Eddie still has a few mates here but their numbers are dwindling as, one by one, they move away too. Soon, I fear, there'll be no one left. And then what will he do?

He's glaring at me now, willing me to leave the room. 'Can you stop looming over me? It's freaking me out.'

Mechanically, like a robot programmed to follow instruction even under intense provocation, I lower myself on to the arm of a chair. 'So, if that job's not for you, then maybe you could—'

'I don't need you to plan my life for me, Mum.'

A terse silence hangs over us. 'All right. But how about going back to college?'

'College wasn't my thing.'

'So, what *is* your thing?'

'I don't know!' he announces. 'I don't have one. I mean, I haven't decided what it is yet.'

'But, love, everyone needs a *thing*.'

'Well, I don't. I'm not like you, happy to trundle off to the library every day of my life for years and years and *years*—'

'*Eddie!*' It's like a punch to my gut. 'D'you realise what it's done? This job of mine that you seem to think of as so tragic?'

'I didn't mean that.' He looks away. 'I just meant—'

'I'll tell you what it's done,' I cut in. 'It's kept this family together. How else d'you think we paid the mortgage and bills and bought food when your dad's schemes went tits up?'

'What's that got to do with anything?' he cries.

'I'm just *saying*. I'm making a point.'

'Well, don't!' he shouts. 'Don't make points!'

'But I only—'

'—And don't suggest jobs for me because I'm *never* going to be tax inspector—'

'But I never said—'

'—No matter how much you want to see me in a suit and a tie with a briefcase—'

'A *briefcase*? When did I ever—'

''Cause I'm *just not doing it,* all right?' He leaps from

the sofa, sending the Quality Street tin flying and clanging onto the floor, its contents scattering all over the room.

'Eddie!' I exclaim as he charges out, robe flapping behind him, and thunders upstairs. His bedroom door bangs, rattling the house.

I stand there for a moment, pressing my hands over my hot, smarting eyes. *Don't cry,* I will myself. *You only suggested a job! You were trying to help. But was that wrong? Are you too controlling? Should you just let him flump about in that disgusting robe for the rest of his life?*

I gaze round at the scattered sweets and wrappers, picturing the six of us – me and Frank, our three kids and my father – dipping into the tin when we were all together at Christmas. Paper crowns, mince pies and rowdy games of Pictionary and Boggle. Frank and I were so happy to have the girls home, albeit briefly. Bella and Ana have gone back now, keen to return to their flats and their friends and their New Year's Eve parties.

And now my heart seems to crumple like one of those discarded wrappers on the floor.

CHAPTER TWO

I know I'm lucky to be a librarian. I love books and reading and the fact that our beautiful Victorian library serves as a much-needed community hub in our town. I especially love my colleagues, who've become great friends. However, the next morning, as I *trundle* to work, I don't feel lucky.

Eddie's remark still smarts as I march along the seafront. Tiny snowflakes skim my face and a sharp wind stings my cheeks. Apart from a sole dog walker in the distance, the flat, wide beach is deserted.

I'm not like you, Eddie announced. Meaning, *you think I'd want your shitty life?* And maybe he's right! He's seen his dad and me struggling and arguing, unable to pay bills. We'd planned to do so much to Kilmory Cottage, but the years have whipped by and nothing's come to fruition. At least, not to the house itself. In between raising three kids and working full-time, I've managed to create a beautiful cottage garden, filled with roses that bloom all summer long. But apart from that, what mark have I actually made?

The trouble is, I've never had a grand life plan. So can I really expect Eddie to have one?

His dad and I were twenty-one when we met and fell in love. Frank was a bartender, working the summer season at a resort on the Algarve. I'd gone on holiday with friends, never intending to peel away from the group, but I couldn't help myself. I'd met boys who were cute, or even handsome – but not *beautiful* like Frank. Not wild and brimming with life and schemes and daring, in the way that he was. His face was all cheekbones and angles, his eyes the darkest brown. His big beaming smile melted my heart like ice cream under the hot Portuguese sun. When my holiday ended, he skived off work to see me off at Faro airport where we hugged tightly, and I cried.

As we pulled apart, I saw that Frank's face was wet with tears too.

'It'll be okay,' he insisted and somehow, I knew he was right. Somehow we'd make it work, despite the hundreds of miles between us, and the fact that we were virtually broke. Back in Glasgow, I was working in a soon-to-be-defunct bookshop, while Frank would be expected to go home to work on his family's farm after the summer season.

Why would we let any of *that* stand in our way? At that age we believed that anything was possible. Had anyone urged us to work at the tax office, we'd have laughed in their faces.

So I blotted my wet cheeks and boarded my plane home to Glasgow, clutching the piece of driftwood on which he'd carved *Carly + Frank Forever.*

We started writing to each other. A torrent of impassioned scrawlings, with Frank's wonky English always making me smile. The way he said *foot finger* for toe, or *Get a plane for coming to see me soon!* There were calls and occasional visits, and every so often we'd decide together that maintaining a long-distance relationship was too hard. Yet we couldn't give each other up. It took my mum's illness to make us realise that we had to be together. At first things had seemed hopeful. But when her cancer spread and she was moved to the hospice, Frank turned up in Glasgow with a rucksack and his dark hair all wild, to be with me.

I fell to pieces when Mum died. Thirteen years younger than Dad, she'd always seemed so young and vibrant. He'd left her suddenly for another woman when I was fourteen – I'm an only child – and although heartbroken, she was also furious and determined that we could manage just fine by ourselves.

Mum never wanted another man. She didn't need anyone. It had been the two of us, thick as thieves, and I'd never imagined a world without her. And she'd loved Frank, and admired his free spirit, his love of life.

Within weeks of Frank moving to Scotland we found out I was pregnant. That certainly wasn't planned. We were living in my tiny rented flat, and only just finding out how to be with each other in normal life – rather than those heady reunions when we'd barely emerge out of bed.

Yet we were delighted too. We just had to figure out how we'd manage a future together, and what we'd *do*. With baby Eddie's arrival, we were propelled into a house-hunting mission.

Having grown up on a farm, Frank had been driving a tractor virtually as his milk teeth fell out, and worked the land along with his father and brothers. He wasn't a city person at all. Plus, he loved the sea – the farm was close to Portugal's wild south-west coast – and we started to wonder if the west coast of Scotland might be the place for us.

A sleepy Ayrshire town called Sandybanks had been a childhood favourite of Mum's. She'd taken me there, although I could barely remember it. But one day I suggested to Frank that we hop on a train for an exploratory look around.

We strolled along the seafront and stopped at a house with a For Sale sign nailed to its garden fence. At twenty-seven, and still trying to come to terms with losing Mum, I stared at Kilmory Cottage and squeezed Frank's hand. The house was battered by salt winds, the garden a tangle of thorns. The town was pretty faded too, having once been a bustling holiday destination. Now the few remaining guest houses badly needed a lick of paint. The birthday cake roundabout on the seafront had probably looked jolly at one time, with its icing swirls and candy-striped candles jutting up from the seats. But now rusting and splattered in seagull poo, it clearly hadn't moved for years.

However, the place still had plenty of olden-day charm, and the glorious sweep of Sandybanks Bay captivated us. Although Eddie was snoozing in his carrier against my chest, I pictured him a few years on, running delightedly along the beach. *This* was what we needed, I decided. A new start by the sea to raise a family of our own.

And there was our perfect cottage, for sale, facing the

sparkling bay. The Isle of Arran a purplish smudge on the horizon, and the ferry cutting its way towards the quay.

'Shall we do it?' I asked Frank, willing him to say yes. He did.

With my inheritance from Mum, together with every other penny we could scrape together, we had just enough for a deposit. And so we bought Kilmory Cottage. Our daughter Bella was born a couple of months after Eddie had turned one, and Ana came along two years later. Frank and I never had the urge to get married. After being left as she was, Mum had been resolutely anti-marriage – 'No need for it, Carly!' she'd insisted, and I guess that message had stuck. And Frank was – and still is – a fantastic dad. I've never doubted that he loves us all very much. But he wasn't easy back then. There was still that wild impetuousness there; the boy who, at twenty-one, had grabbed my hand at two in the morning and we'd run, screaming with laughter, into the sea. That young man who'd jumped feet first into a life with me, in a foreign country, because he'd wanted us to be together and have a good life. To have more, certainly, than he'd had on the farm.

However, Frank wasn't an employee type of guy. There was a restlessness in him; an insatiable urge to throw himself into a thrilling new project. And soon, this father of three was insisting that taking over Sandybanks' failing ice cream parlour was 'too good an opportunity to miss'.

'I know you want to do your own thing,' I'd reasoned, 'but it feels too risky, Frank.'

'Yes, but the rent's reasonable and the location's great.'

'If it's so great then why does nobody go there?'

'They will,' he insisted. 'I'll brighten it up and drag it into the twenty-first century. I'll completely transform it. And we're at the seaside, Carly!' His dark eyes beamed excitement and I tried to swallow down my guilt at not sharing his enthusiasm. 'Who doesn't want a delicious ice cream at the beach?'

At the time, Frank was working crazy hours as a delivery driver while I was a full-time mum. I could see how passionate he was, and told myself that he deserved this chance if he could secure a loan. Next thing I knew, funds had been raised and there he was, master of a malfunctioning commercial freezer that the previous proprietor – now disappeared, leaving no contact details – had assured him was 'in perfect working order'. Frank plundered his funds to rent a replacement freezer but still the shop failed. Somehow, this man from southern Portugal hadn't factored in our long Scottish winters and the fact that ice cream sales dwindle to virtually nothing when the cold weather bites.

Next came a tiny bakery, tucked away down an alleyway, where he planned to wow the west of Scotland with Portuguese custard tarts. '*Everyone* loves pastéis de nata,' he'd insisted. 'It can't fail.'

Well, yes – maybe in Lisbon or even London, they did. But the craze was a long way from reaching our little corner of Ayrshire (in fact it still hasn't arrived).

Then there was the food truck project, embarked on with wild enthusiasm one spring. He'd planned to sell sizzling garlicky steak sandwiches – which proved popular – but still he never managed to turn a profit and the venture was dead in the water by the end of the year.

I'd feel terrible for Frank, to see his dreams shattered. But then he'd blunder into the next thing, and I was more often furious about the perilous financial position we'd find ourselves in. It wasn't just the two of us anymore, free as birds. We had three children depending on us. As soon as Ana started nursery I went back to work, doing various office jobs – *and I didn't think it was beneath me, Eddie! Sometimes, I even enjoyed it!* Then a decade ago, the library job came up and I leapt at it.

These days Frank works as a mechanic at his mate Dev's garage. He'd never been a mechanic before, but he can turn his hand to virtually anything, when he puts his mind to it. And somehow we've scrambled through. But on this, my first day back at the library after the Christmas break, something hits me hard in the gut.

I stop abruptly on the seafront. Snow is still falling, dusting the birthday cake roundabout like icing sugar.

I'll be fifty this year. My birthday's in September – nine months away. My mum died at fifty. My life is speeding by and Eddie will be still lying there, posting Orange Cremes into his mouth. Or maybe it'll be those hard round toffees that are always left at the end?

That's me, I think wildly, marching on now, past the bandstand and the faded town map on a big wooden board. In the Quality Street tin I'm the Toffee Penny; the one that cements itself to your teeth. Why do they even put it in? It's just there to be annoying – like a mother haranguing her son to find a job.

I veer away from the seafront and towards the town centre, passing the fishing tackle shop and the beauty salon. The library is in view now, the jewel of our town with its turrets and spires and stained-glass windows. A leaky jewel, as it happens, as there's no money to fix the roof and guttering. Just enough for an array of buckets that we rearrange to catch the ever-changing locations of the drips.

The snow has stopped falling and way above the library, in the sky, a tiny dark speck has appeared. The speck is a plane and it shocks me to realise how much I wish I was on it.

Like all those times I flew out to see Frank, desperate to be together again. When he'd spot me at Faro airport arrivals and we'd fall into each other's arms.

'Ahh!' I'd often hear people exclaim in pleasure at the sight of us. Same in Glasgow, whenever Frank arrived. 'Love's young dream!' I once heard a stranger announce fondly, and we laughed as my cheeks blazed.

'We *are* love's young dream. You're my dream, Carly!'

Now, taking care not to slip on the icy ground, I head for the yellow salt bin at the side of the library. As I grab the shovel and start digging out salt, I replay Eddie, shouting at me yesterday and flouncing upstairs. Later I'd lain awake in bed, worrying about whether I'd handled him in the right way.

'Just leave him be,' Frank had said. 'It's not worth getting upset about.'

Maybe Frank has the right attitude, I reflect now as I scatter salt rather aggressively around the library's entrance. Eddie's a fully fledged adult and if he's not going to start living his life – well, I damn well am!

Like Mum did, when Dad left her. Working two jobs and seeing her friends and doing wonderful things with me, like baking and making fancy dress costumes, and taking me out to our favourite Italian café. But also never mollycoddling me. And certainly never picking up after me at home. I'd no more have thrown my dinner on the floor than dropped a sweet wrapper in the house.

I'm *far* too soft with Eddie, I decide, as I unlock the library's heavy main door.

And from now on, things are going to change.

Inside the library, I turn on the lights with the ancient brass switches that make a definite *clunk*. I breathe in the aroma of thousands of books, mingling with a tinge of furniture polish and something else – the smell of learning and study and history.

When our three kids were all home it felt as if Kilmory Cottage might burst at the seams. Our home really wasn't big enough for the five of us. So, as one of the library key holders, I started coming to work early, just to enjoy the calm and quiet and stillness.

The habit stuck, and I still do that now. In fact, Frank probably thinks the library opens at eight-thirty a.m. I make an instant coffee and wander over to the 20p box, where we sell off books that have been removed from the lending shelves. There's a few novels and a small selection of non-fiction. A book about Clyde shipyards and wildlife guides about seabirds and coastal flora. And something else that I hadn't noticed before. One of the others must have put it there.

I pick it up and sip my coffee as I examine the cover. *The Empty-Nester's Handbook: Living Your Best Life When the Kids Leave Home.*

I can't help chuckling dryly as my gaze lands on page one.

Let's celebrate your fabulous second act!

What if Eddie never leaves home? If Frank and I are never empty-nesters? Could turning fifty count as the start of my second act?

Think of it as a thrilling new chapter, the author urges. *How do you want it to look?*

I have absolutely no idea – although after Eddie storming upstairs last night, I know how I *don't* want it to look.

With my fully-grown, size-eleven-footed son flinging my 'helpful' suggestions back into my face.

With me picking up his sweet wrappers and damp, stinky towels and mouldering takeaway cartons.

With me picking up anything at all! Or doing any of that shit!

Or feeling in any way responsible for the fact that Eddie wants to do nothing with his life!

Or letting my 'second act' slide by without having adventures!

What kind of adventures do I want? Fun ones, with Frank, if he's up for it. Why don't we do fun stuff anymore? Why do we just *trundle* on?

My birthday's nine months away, I figure as I switch on my computer at the main desk. So what am I waiting for really? For Eddie to miraculously figure out what he wants to do with his life?

The front door opens and my friend Prish appears, armed with a transparent tub of home-made cakes, swiftly followed by Jamie and Marilyn. There are hugs and cries of 'Happy New Year!' and the cakes are cooed over and devoured. There's no occasion Prish won't bake for: our last library day before the holidays, and our first day back, plus everyone's birthdays. Over the Christmas break, when she could peel herself away from her huge family – four grown-up kids and seven grandkids, all descending on her for the holidays – she brought home-made brownies for our blowy beach walks. Now the rest of us catch up on each other's news, delighted to all be together again.

'I'm *so* relieved to be back at work,' announces Jamie, and I know he really means it, as his home life is complicated.

'How did it go?' I hand him a mug of coffee.

'Oh, the usual story. Lewis went to his parents and I went to mine.' A shrug and a wry smile. 'But what about you, Carly? All the gang home?'

'Yeah, it was lovely,' I say. 'But the girls left the day after Boxing Day. Desperate to get away from us,' I joke.

'That's how it's meant to be,' Prish remarks. 'That's our job, to set them up for leaving us and breaking our hearts.'

'Hey, I've still got one at home, remember?' I smile.

'Not for much longer, I bet.'

'Well, let's see.' Having dropped a coin into the honesty box, I've stashed *The Empty-Nester Handbook* into my bag. Soon, our first lenders arrive, and weak winter sunshine ekes through the stained-glass windows.

I'm still not sure how I want my second act to look, as our beautiful library flickers back into life. But somehow, I'll figure it out. After all, a lot can happen in nine months.

CHAPTER THREE

On the walk home I vow to myself not to react if Eddie behaves like he did yesterday. *Don't rise to it,* I tell myself. However, as soon as I step into the house, it's apparent that something is different. Eddie isn't lying on the sofa or shut away in his room. No, my son is upright – devoid of hooded robe and actually in motion! Most bizarrely of all, Eddie is *smiling* as he bounds into the hallway to greet me.

Greeting me, as if I am an actual human, with feelings!

'Hey, Mum,' he says brightly.

I gawp at him. Has he broken something? Is this cheery display a way of buttering me up before imparting bad news?

'Hey, love,' I say, hanging my jacket on the hook. I'm naive enough to expect an apology over yesterday's shitty behaviour. 'Everything all right?'

'Great, yeah. I'll just put the kettle on, shall I?' And off he goes.

Suspicion rears up in me as I follow him through to the

kitchen. Normally, he opens the fridge and glares into it, announcing, 'There's nothing to eat.' But not today. Today it's as if another, extremely pleasant person – who looks *exactly* like my son – has taken his place.

Has the real Eddie been abducted by aliens?

'Here you go, Mum.' My body fizzles with tension as he hands me tea in my favourite pale pink china cup. What's going on?

He leans against the sink and looks at me. Like his dad, Eddie is strikingly handsome: brown-eyed, with defined cheekbones, having recently grown into his looks. His hair is dark and glossy, rarely cut or washed – or even combed – but somehow still the hair any young man would want.

'Dad back soon?' he asks with studied casualness.

'Yeah, should be,' I reply. 'Why, love?' Normally, our movements don't even register on his radar. We could be at home, or out – even *dead*, I've sometimes thought. It's all the same to Eddie as long as meals appear, miraculously, at dinnertime.

'Just wondered.' He places his mug on the worktop and grins at me in an odd way. As if he's holding something inside him. Something that's bursting to come out.

'You seem very perky today,' I venture with a smile.

'Perky?' He chuckles.

'Well, yes.' And his deathly pallor has gone, I notice now. In fact he's more like the old Eddie. The *younger* Eddie, I mean, who'd hug me for no reason at all, before this interminable malaise set in, like a mould, that no amount of forced jollity, or trying my damnedest to be kind and patient could shift.

'It's nice to see,' I add, 'but you seem, I don't know . . .'

'Well, I have news!' he blurts out.

'News?' My heart clangs. 'What kind of news?'

He rubs his hands together and pushes back his hair. 'I'm moving out.'

'You're *what*?'

'Moving out. Leaving home.' He laughs. 'It's what people do when they're adults, Mum. They break free of parental constraints. They fly the nest and forge their own independent lives. They grab opportunities . . .'

'But . . .' I catch myself. *Be pleased! This is good news, right?*

'Aren't you happy for me?' Eddie arches a brow.

'Yes! Yes, of course I am!' I sip my tea, scalding my lip. 'But where are you going?'

'Well, there's this room in a flat in Edinburgh.'

'Edinburgh?' I repeat. 'Wow!'

'Yeah.' He nods. 'In Raj and Calum's place. Their other flatmate moved out. Their landlord had someone who wanted the room but that's fallen through. So it's mine if I want it. So of course I said yes.'

'Wow, that's great news . . .' I'm trying to remain positive. 'But how will you afford this flat, love?' Surely he doesn't think his dad and I will pay his rent?

'It's really cheap,' he announces. 'Like, *so* cheap you wouldn't believe it. Some friend of Calum's dad owns it, so he's done them a deal on the rent.'

'But it must cost *something*,' I remark.

'Yeah, but I'll work, Mum. I can work, you know!'

'Oh, I know, darling,' I say quickly. 'Of course you can. But what kind of work?'

'In a restaurant. I have a job already. Don't look so shocked!'

'But how . . . ?' I start.

'Someone Raj knows works there and said they really need staff. So I emailed them and we spoke on the phone. They want me. They're really keen. So they're going to try me out.'

'Waiting tables?' I ask.

'No, *kitchen* work.' Oh God, last time Eddie fried an egg he set off the smoke alarm and the incinerated pan had to be thrown away. And aren't people always cutting and damaging themselves in kitchens? Eddie is *terrified* of blood. As a little boy every cut or graze was a major drama. 'It's kitchen portering,' he continues cheerfully. 'But if they're happy with me, they're gonna train me up to be a chef!'

I blink at him, remembering the time he was grating some cheese and somehow grated his thumb. I'd found him bleeding, traumatised, lashed in sweat. 'Will you be okay, doing that?' I ask.

'God, Mum, yeah.' He laughs in disbelief. 'D'you think I'm incapable?'

'Of course not!' I clear my throat. 'So, what's the restaurant?'

'It's this amazing place, just opened. Called Bracken – have you heard of it?'

'Um, no, love.'

'. . . They do those tasting menus, y'know? Like, ten courses of totally amazing food?'

'Wow!' I blow across my tea, remembering how uninterested he was when Frank bought the food truck.

How he'd flatly refused to learn even the basics and do the festivals with his dad. 'So you really like the idea of working in a professional kitchen?'

'Yeah.' He grins. 'It'll be fun!'

'And . . . you don't think it'll make you queasy? You know, with your fear of blood and all the butchering and offal and—'

'Mum, that's just *meat*.' He shakes his head at my idiocy. 'I'll be fine.'

I muster a broad smile. 'That's great then. I'm so happy for you. So when is this happening?'

He grins, cheeks flushed with excitement. 'My first shift's on Saturday.'

'Saturday? You mean *this* Saturday?'

'Yeah!'

'But that's . . . that's three days away. How are you going to pay your first month's rent if—'

'Paid it,' he announces. 'Used all my Christmas money and savings.'

'Oh, Eddie.' I stare at him, emotion surging up in me like a wave. 'I wish you'd said. We could've helped with that.'

'Well, you *can* help. Could you or Dad give me a lift?'

'To Edinburgh? Of course, darling!'

'Can we do it tomorrow?'

'Tomorrow?' I exclaim, then quickly gather myself. 'Yes, if that's what you want. As long as you're sure.'

'I am sure.' He grins.

'We'll drive you over after work then,' I say, deciding that this really *is* good news. At least, he seems to have thought it through.

'So you're getting rid of me at last.' He chuckles.

'Oh, Eddie.' My eyes prickle with unexpected tears. 'I don't want to get rid of you. But I'm happy for you. I really am. Wait 'til Dad hears about this!'

He beams at me and then, unexpectedly, he throws his arms around me – my big, tall, handsome boy who's barely found it in himself to be civil to me for months now. Years, even. My heart seems to splinter as he pulls away. 'Sorry I've been . . . y'know,' he murmurs. 'Like I've *been* lately.'

'Oh, love,' I start. 'You don't have to apologise.'

He shrugs, looking down at his feet. 'It's just, Bella and Ana are so clever and amazing and they're getting on with their lives and doing so well. And you and Dad are always going on about that. About how proud you are . . .'

'Eddie, that's not true,' I exclaim. 'We are proud but we've *never* compared you. We don't "go on".' Have we, though, unwittingly? Guilt twangs at me, deep in my gut.

'. . . And I've felt left behind,' he continues, 'like I'm this failure, this massive disappointment to you both—'

'Honey, you're not! Please don't say that. You're not at all.' Tears escape now, trickling down my cheeks. As Eddie looks up at me I see that he is welling up too. 'You have so much going for you,' I add. 'You're clever and popular and kind and I'm *so* proud of you.'

He smiles then, and rubs at his eyes and hugs me again. 'Thanks, Mum. So you can stop worrying about me now, okay? 'Cause everything's gonna be all right.'

CHAPTER FOUR

In truth, I'm a little on edge once the news has settled. Eddie has never even seen this Edinburgh flat, and what if he can't handle working in a restaurant kitchen? He insists that it'll be 'easy', but he has no idea what it's like. At home he takes exception to being asked to put the milk back in the fridge. How will he cope with being barked at by chefs and slogging away on gruelling shifts? From lying on the sofa, mindlessly slotting Quality Street into his mouth, to holding down a demanding job and paying his rent every month. It feels like a heck of a leap.

However, it's what he wants so of course I'm happy for him. And when Frank comes home, still in blue overalls and smelling not unpleasantly of oil and graft, he's clearly delighted. 'That's brilliant, Ed! Great news.' He catches my eye and grins. *Can you actually believe this is happening?* his look says.

'Let's go out and celebrate,' I announce. 'We'll invite Granddad too. He'll be so pleased for you.'

Eddie smirks. 'Oh, d'you reckon?'

''Course he will,' I say, brushing off his remark with a smile – because we all know how hard it is to please my father these days. While Frank showers and changes, I call Dad with the news, and then set off to pick him up from his harbourside flat a few miles further along the coast. And later, as the four of us settle around the table at our local Italian restaurant, I'm determined not to let his spiky presence dent the mood.

Our pizzas arrive and wine is poured – just water for me as I'll drive Dad home later – and I make a toast. 'To you, Eddie! To a whole new start.'

'To Eddie!' Frank grins as we all clink glasses.

'Thanks.' Eddie beams with pleasure.

'About time too,' my father remarks. 'I was starting to think you'd never leave home, Eddie. Fifteen, I was, when I started full-time work in the shipyards—'

'Oh, I thought it was nine?' Frank murmurs with a mischievous twinkle, and I have to suppress a laugh.

'Yes, Granddad,' Eddie says dutifully. 'But things are different now.'

'You can say that again.'

'Eddie was just waiting for the right opportunity,' Frank remarks, ever loyal to our son.

'Working in a kitchen?' Dad frowns.

'Yeah. Food's the big thing now,' Eddie assures him.

'Really? It's a new invention, is it? This *eating* thing?'

'Dad!' I glare at him.

'What'll be the next big thing?' my father muses. 'Breathing?'

'Yeah, probably, Granddad.' Eddie smirks.

'Well, I think it's great,' I insist.

'Although you did try to force him to work in the tax office,' Frank teases, nudging my arm.

'I did not! It was a suggestion, that was all . . .'

'Wanted to buy him a briefcase for Christmas,' he goes on, fibbing wildly. 'I had to wrench it out of her hands in John Lewis—'

'Frank,' I cut in, laughing now. 'I did not.'

'There's nothing wrong with honest hard work,' Dad remarks.

'But Eddie *will* be working hard,' I say firmly.

'Yeah, I will.' Eddie grins. 'And I didn't want an office job, Granddad. That's just not me. And I think this will be. At least, I'm going to give it my best shot.'

Dad seems to soften at that, and he nods in approval.

'Well, I'll drink to that!' Frank announces, and there's more clinking of glasses and wine is topped up. And so the evening goes on, with good-natured teasing and Eddie chatting excitedly about how it'll be to flat-share with Calum and Raj, his oldest mates, who I suspect he's missed more than he's admitted. Eventually, after a couple of large red wines, even Dad relaxes a little, and by the time we step out into the bitterly cold night, my worries have subsided. It was a bit sudden, that's all. Coming home from work today, this was the last thing I expected.

'So you really think he's up to this, do you?' Dad glances at me as I drive him home.

'Of course he is.' It's a reasonable question but it still irks me.

'The girls just seemed a lot more organised, that's all,'

he adds. 'This has all happened in a bit of a rush, hasn't it?'

'Well, the opportunity just came up,' I say, trying to remain patient. 'But yes, Bella was organised. We all know what she's like, Dad . . .'

'Yes, she's a sensible kid with her head screwed on,' he remarks – the implication being that Eddie's isn't. That the minute he's out of parental jurisdiction, it might topple off. He's right, though, in that Bella had planned her move to London with military precision. It felt as if she'd barely unpacked in her new house-share before she'd found a gym, a local food market and signed up with a dentist. I can't imagine Eddie doing that unless all his teeth fall out.

'Ana was more chaotic,' I remind Dad. 'She was still cramming clothes into bin bags on the day we were driving her over to Dundee. And she stole our cheese from the fridge and her dad's old denim jacket!' I'm trying to lighten the mood, to make the point that his three grandchildren are all different, and all equally wonderful in their own ways. His blatant favouring of the girls always riles me. But he merely grunts, and as I turn off the main road and into his cul-de-sac, I realise there's no point in discussing it any further.

As I park up, I remember the day Ana moved into halls in Dundee. We'd stopped off at a supermarket en route, as I'd wanted to make sure she had plenty of nutritious food in, to start off her new life as an art student. But she showed zero interest in the fruit and veg I was loading into our trolley, and I suspected it would all wither before being thrown away. Ana seems to exist on cheese on toast and Pringles – yet somehow I always know she'll be okay.

She hugged us cheerfully as we were about to leave her in halls, announcing that she'd forgotten her DMs and could I post them to her?

'I'm sure Eddie will be *fine*, Dad,' I say as I see him upstairs to his flat. It's not ideal, a man of eighty-four living alone on the second floor with no lift. But he loves his little flat, so who am I to argue?

'Let's hope so,' he says gruffly.

I muster a smile and hug him briefly, which he tolerates, and then trot lightly downstairs and back out into the night.

The moon is shining pearly bright. Before climbing into my car I stop for a moment, just to take it all in: not only the silvery reflection on the calm sea, but the enormity of what's happened today.

Tomorrow will be the start of something wonderful, I can feel it. Not just for Eddie – but also for Frank and me. Perhaps this really is the beginning of my second act.

CHAPTER FIVE

And the next day he's off. When Eddie asked for 'a lift' he actually meant, 'Move the entirety of my possessions all the way across Scotland after a full day's work.' But of course that's fine. We'd have driven him to Finland if it meant assisting our son on his first rung of proper independent living. And now, as we park as close as we can to Eddie's new Edinburgh home, I'm grateful that Frank and I are doing this together because, actually, I feel quite choked and emotional as this is really it. Our last child is finally moving out.

Dad wasn't involved when I left home. He hadn't offered to help, and Mum and I hadn't wanted him there. Although I was only moving from Glasgow's Southside, where I'd lived with Mum, to a house-share with friends in the West End, it still felt like a momentous occasion. The unspoken message was that the two of us wanted to tackle – and savour – it together. Mum was a tiny, bird-like woman and her many admirable qualities hadn't included physical strength. However, together we'd lugged my numerous boxes upstairs to the top flat, and afterwards we'd cracked open the bottle of cava she'd bought as a celebration.

'It's lovely around here,' I enthuse now as Frank and I help to carry Eddie's worldly goods along the street. We're close to The Meadows, in what looks like a charming neighbourhood on this sparkly, snow-dusted evening.

'Yeah, it's great,' he enthuses. We pass a cosy-looking bistro, an independent bookshop and a grocer's specialising in French delicacies. *Delicious salted butter from Brittany*, reads the chalkboard in the window.

'Is it much further?' I ask, my arms starting to ache now.

'Next street,' replies Eddie. In fact, my box – with a skateboard balanced on it – is becoming heavier by the second. Even Frank, who's strong and muscular, lets out a groan over the weight of his load.

'What's in this? House bricks, Eddie?' he calls out to our son, who's marching ahead – carrying only a pillow, I notice now.

'Just stuff! Not much further!'

Frank catches my eye and we smirk, exchanging a silent message: *This is it. Finally, this is it.* Although it turns out that Eddie's flat isn't in the next street; somehow he misread Google Maps. And now, instead of bistros and French delicatessens there's a deserted chippie with a smashed window and a shabby takeaway with two men arguing loudly inside. Finally, just as it feels as if my arms are ready to pop out of their sockets, Eddie stops abruptly and announces, 'This is it!'

'Thank God for that.' Frank exhales loudly as we set down the boxes at the shabby front door. Beside it, the entry system has numerous buttons and handwritten stickers denoting flat numbers and multiple surnames. Eddie peers at it and jabs at a button, and a moment later we're buzzed in.

Lit by a grubby sealed wall light filled with flies, the hallway is cluttered with bikes and packing crates. Flyers are scattered all over the chipped floor tiles. 'Top floor,' Eddie tells us, and obediently we lug the boxes upstairs.

The flat door opens, and here's Raj, clearly delighted to see his old mate. 'Hey, come in!' he enthuses, and there's a flurry of hugs and backslaps as we all step into the musty-smelling flat, grateful to dump Eddie's possessions in the hallway.

As if Kilmory Cottage hadn't been full enough already, Raj and Calum were near-permanent additions for meals and movie nights when the boys were younger. I loved that stage, before teenage hormones kicked in – when our kitchen was full of young people, all chatting happily around the table while I dished up lasagne from a giant tray. The kids had so many sleepovers that sometimes it felt as if we were running a small hotel.

'Let me show you around,' Raj enthuses.

'This is great, Raj!' I say, my gaze skimming the hallway's peeling wallpaper and cracked ceiling. Posters have been tacked up haphazardly, and an assortment of trainers have been kicked off in a corner.

'Yeah. We love it.' Raj beams. 'This is your room, Eddie.'

He opens a door off the hallway and Eddie pokes his head in, but doesn't invite us to see. Instead we're ushered through to the open-plan kitchen-cum-living room. A clearly ancient sofa is strewn with faded throws. There are more posters, and a shrivelled spider plant trails from a wonky bookshelf. It's like an extension of a boy's bedroom – although the only plant life in Eddie's bedroom has been the mould in his abandoned coffee cups. But endearingly, the boys have obviously tried to personalise the place, and make it homely. Candles in wine bottles are crammed onto the mantelpiece and a large embroidered floor cushion dominates the centre of the room.

'Welcome, man.' Raj grins. 'Your new home!'

'Brilliant,' Eddie says, and I can see how happy he is to be with friends of his own age, just as he should be.

'Calum'll be back soon,' Raj tells him. 'We'll go out for a few beers later.'

'Great!'

'Sure we can't help you unpack, Eddie?' I ask.

'No, no, it's fine.' He shakes his head. Then Calum appears, and as they're lovely, well-brought-up young men, there's the offer of tea or coffee before we head home.

'No, they'll need to get back,' Eddie says quickly.

'Actually, I could do with a cuppa.' I shoot him a quick look. '*Thank you*, Calum.' Eddie looks as if he's in actual physical pain as tea is made, and we drink it. Then relief floods his face when I say, 'Okay, we'd better get going.'

'All right, Mum. Great!' So we get up to leave, and as we head along the hallway I can't resist peeking into his room. The walls are dingy magnolia and marred with various scuffs and stains. There's a melamine chest of drawers, a small wardrobe leaning precariously to one side, and a lumpy bare mattress on the single bed. My heart squeezes as Frank and I exchange a quick look.

'Shall we get you a few things,' I start, 'just to make it more homely?'

'No, it's all right.'

'Honestly, I don't mind, love. I could order some stuff, have it sent here—'

'There's nothing I need. *Nothing*,' Eddie says firmly.

I eye the tall, narrow bedroom window. In lieu of a blind or a curtain, a faded bath towel has been nailed up. 'How about a curtain, Ed?' his father suggests.

'No thanks, Dad.'

'Or a blind?' I add. 'We could easily order a—'

'It's all *right*,' Eddie insists, in a tone that says *Stop fussing, old people!*

Then he virtually manhandles us downstairs, like a bouncer dispensing of undesirables, as I implore him to take care in the restaurant kitchen (I can't stop thinking about his grated thumb) and to set an alarm so he's not late for work and to at least try and get *some* sleep before he starts.

'Yeah-yeah,' he mutters.

Outside, on the pavement, I will myself not to cry as I pull him in for a hug. 'Look after yourself, darling,' I gush.

'Yeah, take care, son,' Frank says, his voice cracking a little. He hugs Eddie too.

'I will. 'Course I will.'

'. . . And if you need anything, Eddie,' I add. 'Anything at all—'

'Mum, please stop worrying,' he says, grinning and shaking his head now. 'You can trust me, y'know.' Then he steps back into the scruffy hallway and firmly shuts the door.

CHAPTER SIX

Eddie

Eddie thought he'd never get rid of them. His parents, that is, yacking away to Calum and Raj: *I saw your dad on the beach, Calum. He's looking well. Oh, and your mum was in the library the other day, Raj! I was saying we do miss you boys being around. Eating us out of house and home, haha! D'you miss my apple crumble? I was thinking the other day, remember that time I took you all out trick or treating? And Raj, you were so polite, taking one of Brenda Murray's nasty muffins and feeling obliged to eat it. You spat it out into a bush—*

Actually, that had been his mum (Eddie's dad tends to stand there, waiting for her to finish). On and on, she'd gone – for weeks, it felt like. And then, just as she was winding up, Calum had offered them a cup of tea, the traitor! Couldn't he see that Eddie was desperate for his new life to start? And how long did it take to drink a cup of tea?

Another age, it felt to Eddie as he watched his mum sip-

sip-sip. Seasons changed, devices slipped into obsolescence and still she was clutching that chipped red mug, firing questions about Calum's mum's poetry writing. At one point she'd stopped and gazed happily around the room. 'They're amazingly spacious, aren't they, these flats?'

Actually no, Eddie thought, clawing at his scalp. *This one's feeling awfully crowded right now with you and Dad in it!* Finally his mum seemed to remember that they had a home to go to, and they left.

Dizzy with relief now, Eddie stretches out on the somewhat lumpy mattress in his little room. So this is it. Freedom to do whatever he likes. Admittedly, he was a little taken aback when he saw the single bed; for years he's been used to a double. Plus, his bedroom window back home had an actual curtain – something he'd taken for granted. But this flat's still brilliant, Eddie decides.

He is an independent man now and this is the start of a thrilling new chapter in his life. It's been long overdue. Eddie will never again have to live at Kilmory Cottage, and endure his dad going on about how he's rebuilding some wrecked old truck at the garage, and have his mum sharing gossip she's heard at the library about people he doesn't even know.

Parents! They're okay, he surmises. And his are good people and of course he loves them. But Eddie's family has always done his head in a little bit, and he's never felt as if he's truly fitted in. There's his sister Bella who's so precise about everything, and stuck a line of tape across the carpet to divide the girls' shared room into two. Ana's stuff had spilled over it constantly, and there'd been perpetual squabbles until finally Bella flounced off to London and then it had felt weird at home without her.

It felt weirder still when Ana left for art college. Ana, his baby sister, moving into halls! It was embarrassing really. Eddie felt like the spare school dinner languishing in the canteen – that rank slice of broccoli quiche that no one wanted. Maybe he was being hypersensitive but he felt that a kind of sadness settled over the house then, with the girls both gone. He knew his parents were missing his sisters and now his mum's full focus was on him. Or rather, on the state of his room and how many hours he spent wearing his dressing gown. Eddie didn't like being the only one left at home. He felt too conspicuous – like he was under constant surveillance. He and his parents are definitely not designed to all live together anymore.

Happily, those days are over as Raj calls Eddie out of his room and hands him a chilled bottle of beer. 'You'll need to down it quick,' his friend says, 'if we're gonna have time for the pub.' Then off they go, with Eddie hoping he's acting like a normal person as they trot downstairs. Because what he really wants to do is gallop down, three steps at a time, whooping and punching the air.

FREEDOM!!

As the trio step outside he could scream it from the top of his lungs it into the wintry night. Virtually his whole life, he's lived in Sandybanks – since he was a baby. *Thanks, Mum and Dad,* he's often thought, bitterly, *for taking me out of Glasgow before I could even voice an opinion and forcing me to grow up in a boring seaside town where nothing ever happens!* And by God, he's been looking forward to having some fun without his mum breathing down his neck, commenting on his persistent low-level cough, asking if he wants a cup of tea (no, he doesn't want a cup of fucking tea!) and dispensing 'helpful' suggestions, like working at the tax office.

He'd literally rather plunge his face into boiling water than do that.

Eddie, Raj and Calum step into the pub. A thrilling Edinburgh pub, with a long, curved wooden bar and hundreds of bottles glowing invitingly on the shelves behind it. Not like The Cross Keys in Sandybanks, with a couple of old men with dogs and Barry-the-barman who'd laughed in Eddie's face when he'd tried to get served under-age. *I'll tell your mother, mate. Works in the library, doesn't she?*

Here, no one knows him so he can do what he likes. The sense of liberation is as intoxicating as the two vodka shots he's just necked. 'Right,' Raj announces, setting his glass down. 'There's this party.'

A party on a Thursday night? 'Oh, whose party?' Eddie asks, trying to appear blasé.

'Just these people,' Raj replies, declining to elaborate further. And off they go.

Eddie's been to Edinburgh plenty of times. As kids, he and his sisters were ferried over by their parents for trips to the castle (which he'd loved), and museums and art galleries (he hadn't loved that at all). That was the Edinburgh Eddie knew: all battlements and cannons and old stuff in glass cases, plus a trip to Winter Wonderland, the Christmas funfair, when Princes Street Gardens were decked out in multicoloured lights. Not taking a bus that seems to crawl along forever, leaving the bustling city centre behind. Here, the quiet street is bordered on both sides by concrete houses. There's barely a soul around, and Eddie's chest tightens with unease.

He feels even more out of place than the one time he'd visited Calum and Raj during their freshers year at university. They'd been in student halls then, a chaotic flat crammed with excitable teenagers going on about semesters and essays, bemoaning their 'deadlines' and, it seemed to Eddie, trying to outdo each other with their cleverness. 'What are you studying?' a ginger-haired posh boy had asked him.

'Nothing at the moment,' he'd replied. 'What about you?'

'Economics. So you're not at uni then?'

'Not right now, no . . .'

The boy was starting to look uncomfortable. 'So you're on a gap year?'

'Sort of, yeah.' Eddie willed his interrogator to fuck off and leave him alone, and couldn't wait to jump on the train and escape back to Sandybanks. It was the dullest hellhole ever invented, but at least back home it was only his mum who fired questions at him.

'This is it,' Raj announces now, checking his phone, and they all hop off the bus. Eddie looks around, trying to appear casual and entirely comfortable with where they've landed. They cut across an expanse of flat scrubby grass, heading towards what looks like a vast estate. Then they're *in* the estate; all hard-edged grey concrete and some skinny guy yelling at them incoherently and clinging onto a wire fence.

For a moment, Eddie panics for his safety. Kilmory Cottage springs into his mind. His safe, warm home, with his familiar bedroom with the big soft duvet and his favourite dressing gown that he forgot to pack.

The three friends arrive at the entrance to a block of flats. As the entry system is broken, they just walk right in.

'Sure this is the right place?' Eddie asks as they ride up in the lift.

'Yeah, 'course it is,' Calum says, and Eddie realises how different his friends are now, after finishing their degrees and landing jobs virtually the minute they'd graduated. Edinburgh is their city now. They jump on buses and go to parties in far-flung estates. This is normal to them. It doesn't faze them one bit. Eddie must stop being sweaty and nervous and wanting his dressing gown!

The lift doors open and they step out of the stinking metal canister with their carrier bag of beers. Then a flat door opens and they're in the smoky fug of the party, surrounded by people shouting over the pounding music.

Raj and Calum seem to disappear instantly, taking their beers – thanks, guys! Eddie glances around desperately for someone to latch onto and wonders what to do now.

He looks down at himself and is hit by a terrible realisation.

Christ, his clothes. In this crammed and smoke-filled flat, he feels conspicuously small-town and completely out of place. Weirdly, he hadn't felt small-town when they'd loaded up the car and driven away from Kilmory Cottage early today. They were just his *clothes*. Clothes that had seemed perfectly fine in Sandybanks, for lying around in his room and having a smoke at the bandstand. But now he realises that even his jeans are wrong. And so is his hair and his trainers and even his face – what the hell has happened to Eddie's face in the few hours since he left home? With no one to talk to and nothing to drink, Eddie has escaped to the bathroom in this overcrowded hovel that reeks of weed, with an undercurrent of bleach and bins. And now he notes with horror that his skin has erupted.

He rubs at the smeary mirror above the cracked washbasin and leans in closer. These aren't tiny, insignificant spots. They're angry boilers, protruding from the lower parts of his cheeks as if he were fourteen years old again and not twenty-two!

Only one thing for it, he decides. For a few years now, Eddie has been able to enjoy a few drinks without making a fool of himself. At parties back in Sandybanks, he was never the one puking on someone's bathroom floor. He might not have many notable talents – not like Bella, wowing the marketing agency in London and getting a job there at twenty-one. Or Ana sailing right into art school. But what he *is* good at is pacing himself, when it comes to alcohol. 'You hold it together, man,' Raj always says.

Well, stuff that. Never mind pacing himself tonight. He strides out of the bathroom, making straight for the kitchen where he glances around stealthily, picks up a vodka bottle and pours a generous shot into a plastic cup. He gulps it and pours another. No one notices the small-town boy stealing their drink and so he has some more. And as he drinks, Eddie starts to feel less awkward and more like he belongs here. And next time he goes – actually wobbles – to the bathroom, he is amazed to see that the terrible spots have simmered down and are barely noticeable now.

Forget skincare, he decides as he studies his face. The thing to do with a spotty outbreak is to annihilate it with vodka. It's obvious to him now! He should market it as a miraculous cure and make a fortune! Eddie takes another swig from the cup he's brought into the tiny bathroom with him, wondering briefly if his vision is blurred, and that's why his skin seems to have improved. But no matter, because if Eddie is viewing the world all fuzzily now, then so is everyone else. Clinging onto that thought, he bounds out of the bathroom.

And that's when it happens. Eddie literally crashes into a girl who's standing there. And not just *any* girl.

She's the most beautiful girl Eddie has ever seen in his life.

'Oh, I'm so sorry!' he exclaims.

'It's okay,' she says, touching his arm lightly. As she smiles, Eddie feels as if all the bad stuff that's happened tonight has ceased to matter.

Raj and Calum abandoning him. His clothes and hair suddenly being all wrong, and having no one to talk to and feeling so very lost.

Everything is fine now – no, it's actually brilliant. Because this beautiful girl, who's obviously made from sunshine, is smiling at Eddie. The empty plastic cup crumples in his sweaty grip. And his heart seems to stop.

And although he can't possibly know it yet, at precisely 11.27 on a bitterly cold January night, Eddie Silva has stepped out of his old life forever, and into a new life that nothing could have prepared him for.

And nothing will ever be the same again.

CHAPTER SEVEN

Living at Kilmory Cottage: Carly & Frank

Carly

'So we've done it, darling,' Frank announces.

'We have.' I smile at him, lying beside me in bed.

He chuckles and touches my cheek. 'Bit of a shithole, wasn't it?'

'Oh, it's not too bad. My first place was worse.'

'Yeah. I remember *that* dump very well,' he teases.

'Anyway, it's better than being stuck here with us, isn't it?'

'Yeah. Anything's better than that.'

'So it's just me and you now,' I remind him. 'How d'you feel about that?'

'Fucking terrified.' He squeezes my hand.

'So you should be!' Although bone-tired from all the box lugging, I can't settle tonight. But Frank is already drifting off at just gone midnight, so I slip quietly out of bed and pace around downstairs, wondering what Eddie's doing now, and knowing I'm being ridiculous.

He's twenty-two! What do I think he's doing on his

first night in Edinburgh? Celebrating of course – with his best mates.

I still can't quite believe it's only the two of us now, in this house where there were three, then four, then five. I click on the kettle and hunt around for my favourite bone china cup – a gift from Prish. Tea just isn't the same in anything else. But there's no sign of it here and I've already gathered up all the disgusting bacteria-incubating mugs left in Eddie's room.

Settling for a substitute cup, I carry my tea through to the living room. *The Empty-Nester's Handbook* catches my eye from the bookshelf. Thinking it might settle me – to read about this being a perfectly natural stage – I pull it from the shelf, stretch out on the sofa and flick it open.

The trick is to focus not on what your adult kids might be up to, because your work there is done. Instead, think about this thrilling new life stage you're embarking on . . .

I smile at that. Frank doesn't believe in life stages. To him, it's just life. But now I'm thinking we should mark this somehow. Do something to celebrate the fact that, at long last, our firstborn has got his act together.

I fetch my laptop and settle back on the sofa, excited now as an idea starts to form.

Frank will think it's mad – I know that – because we don't have much money. However, I do have a small amount squirrelled away. Since his failed business ventures I've had to, for my own sanity.

My just-in-case fund, is how I've always thought of

it. But never mind just-in-case. We are empty-nesters – finally! – and on top of that, Frank turns fifty next month. He's already announced that he doesn't want to make a big deal of it as he hates any kind of fuss. But this won't be 'fuss'. It'll be fun – something just for us. By God, after raising three kids we deserve it.

My heart quickens as I start to browse hotels and apartments. The choice is dizzying and I'm so out of practice at this, I'm not sure how to narrow things down. When the kids were old enough to be left for a night, Frank and I would manage the occasional overnighter, staying with friends in Glasgow. But we've never been away together to a hotel without Eddie and the girls. We didn't even take them abroad – apart from the occasional trip to visit their Portuguese grandparents, now long gone. Calum and Raj's families seemed to be forever nipping off to Greece or Italy or Majorca, but we could never afford that.

At just gone one a.m. I send a message to Dev, Frank's mate, who owns the garage where he works.

Hey Dev, could you manage without Frank for a few days in early Feb? It's his 50th. Thinking of taking him away as a surprise.

Of course I don't expect a reply until morning. I was too excited to wait. But then to my surprise, when I look again there's a message.

No probs, Dev has written. *Can get one of the lads to do extra if I need it.* His sons, he means. Hard-grafting boys who are always willing to pitch in.

Excitement flurries in my chest as I browse accommodation again, plus flights, and reply to Dev.

Great, thanks so much!
Going anywhere nice?
Thinking Paris but please don't mention it to Frank.
Excellent idea! Not a word, I promise.

The last time we had an overnighter, we came home to find Bella, Ana and Eddie suspiciously cheery and happy to see us. And we soon noticed that things had been repositioned in odd places. Lamps, framed photos, *sofa* – all having clearly been 'put back'. And things are only 'put back' when an illicit party has happened. On top of that, my beautiful apricot 'Bathsheba' climbing rose was splattered in vomit and the living room curtain rail had been pulled down.

'It just fell!' Ana protested, while her big sister Bella – who's never been comfortable with subterfuge – squirmed in the background.

There'll be none of that this time, I reflect as I find what appears to be the perfect little hotel. Not too pricey, but *so* Parisian with curly wrought-iron balconies and blue and white striped awnings in a beautiful tree-lined street. I book it, plus our flights, and then go back to the hotel's website to gaze at it some more. I'm so engrossed that I don't hear Frank coming into the room.

'Hey, how come you're up?'

'Oh!' I try to hide the screen with splayed hands. 'I couldn't sleep so I thought I might as well come downstairs. Didn't want to disturb you.'

Looking bemused, Frank runs a hand back over his mussed-up hair and steps closer. 'You up to something there, honey?'

'Oh, Frank . . .' I shake my head and laugh, knowing

there's no point in trying to keep it secret. Because his gaze is on my screen now and he can see exactly what I've been looking at.

'What's this?'

'Oh God,' I groan. 'It was supposed to be a surprise for your birthday!'

'What?' He bends slightly and blinks at the screen. 'Where's this?'

'Paris,' I reply.

'*Paris*?'

'Yes, love,' I say with a resigned smile.

A pause. 'You mean, *we're* going to Paris? You and me?'

'Yes, darling. You and me!'

'But . . . can we afford that?'

'I can, Frank. I've booked it. We're going away for five days—'

'Five days in Paris? I'd love that. You know I would. I've always wanted to go there—'

'Me too!'

'—But I can't just assume it's okay,' he cuts in. 'With work, I mean. With Dev . . .'

'I've already cleared it with Dev,' I explain. And then I get up and turn to face him, sliding my arms around his waist.

'And he's okay with that?'

I nod. 'He is.'

'Oh, darling,' he murmurs. 'Thank you. I can hardly believe you've done this.' His hair is flecked with silver now, and crinkles have gathered around his deep brown eyes. But age suits Frank. He's fit and strong and strikingly handsome. Infuriatingly – even at his most maddening moments – I've never *not* fancied him.

'So, you think you'll enjoy it?' I ask.

'What, being together, just us?' He laughs softly. 'God, yes. I can't think of anything better.'

I smile and kiss him on the lips. So we've made it. Plenty of times, I thought we'd never get this far. I pull back and take his hands in mine. 'D'you realise what this trip is, Frank? Apart from your birthday treat, I mean?'

He chuckles. 'A completely mad but brilliant thing to do?'

'Well, yes – it's definitely that. But it'll also be the first time we've been away together since those first trips of ours. You know, in our early days when you and I were long distance . . . d'you remember?'

He blows out air and grins, and now I see that his eyes are shining. 'Of course I remember, Carly. How could I forget?' He holds my hands tightly. 'So, what're we going to do with ourselves in Paris?'

I smile, filled with love for him and feeling so very, very lucky. 'Don't worry about that, Frank,' I say, kissing him. 'I have a few ideas . . .'

CHAPTER EIGHT

Eddie

Suddenly, Eddie feels like the luckiest man on earth.

No matter that a mere few hours ago his mum was still in charge of his laundry and cooking and nagging him to bring the collection of dirty glasses and mugs out from his room.

Eddie, there's virtually none left in the kitchen! Am I supposed to drink my coffee out of a saucepan? Or a jug? And are you absolutely sure you haven't seen my pink china cup?

Thank God that's all over. Now, at just gone two a.m. on a freezing Edinburgh night, he's a different person entirely.

He's no longer Eddie from Sandybanks in the wrong clothes, but a properly functioning adult, with choices. And this new, urban, carefree Eddie finds himself able not merely to converse with this beautiful girl, but to also make her smile and laugh and actually enjoy herself in his company. It feels as if it's no longer a shabby flat that he's found himself in tonight – but an alternative universe.

And in this thrilling new universe, Eddie is wildly entertaining and attractive to a beautiful person like Lyla.

That's her name. *Lyla*. Already he's regaled her with his life story, omitting to tell her that the past few years have been mainly spent sitting around getting stoned and eating chips on the bandstand. He's also – despite all the vodka and beer sloshing around inside him now – remembered to ask her lots of pertinent questions and really listen to her replies.

Obviously, she's extremely smart. He's learnt that she runs her own copywriting business (whatever copywriting might be). However, no matter how much Eddie tries to focus on her obvious intelligence and career success, it's her beauty that's consuming his attention. Her long, gleaming hair, like actual gold, and her big pale blue eyes. She's wearing a plain black top and jeans and a fine gold necklace. No make-up, he thinks. She's so natural. And perfect. He's never met a girl who'd be confident enough to go to a party just as she is.

Now Raj has appeared. Proudly, Eddie introduces – no, *presents* – Lyla to him, and waits for Raj to be impressed.

'Hi,' Raj says. Then to Eddie, grinning: 'You could've thanked your mum and dad for bringing your stuff over today!'

'Oh, have you just moved out from home?' Lyla's eyes widen in surprise.

'Um, yeah, I was staying there temporarily,' Eddie fibs, sensing his cheeks flushing.

'As in, temporarily-for-your-whole-life,' Raj teases.

Eddie glares at him, projecting a powerful telepathic message to Raj to *leave them alone*.

'Your friend seems nice,' Lyla says as he saunters away.

'Yeah, he's okay.' Eddie grins and rolls his eyes. 'Still writes thank you letters to his aunties . . .'

'Does he? I think that's sweet!'

'Uh, yeah. It is,' Eddie blusters, sensing that he's dug himself into some kind of hole, as now it's Raj she wants to talk about.

'So, you two are old friends, are you?'

'Yeah.' He nods. 'We grew up in the same town.'

'He's very good-looking,' she ventures.

'Is he?' Eddie blinks. 'Oh, I dunno . . .'

She laughs then, and he realises she's playing with him as she adds, 'And so are you.'

Eddie has no idea how he should respond to that. By insisting he isn't, or saying, 'Thank you'? Neither option seems right. But then he realises he doesn't have to respond – at least not in words – as Lyla is kissing him. As in, she instigated the kiss. He'd have been no more shocked if she'd suddenly turned into a unicorn. But within a blink he's relaxed into it, and now, as they kiss, all the people and thumping music and bin smells fade away. And then she's taking his hand and somehow her jacket is found and pulled on, and she's leading him out of the flat and into the not especially fragrant lift.

They kiss some more as the metallic box descends to ground level. Then out they tumble and everything goes hazy, and now Eddie realises how very drunk he is. Should he have told Calum and Raj that he was leaving? No, he's not answerable to anyone now! Too late anyway as now they're in an Uber, leaving the estate. Lyla must have called it; Eddie doesn't even have an account.

He must get an Uber account and be a city-dwelling adult man! But at least he has his own set of keys to his new home, so everything's fine. He delves a hand into his jeans pocket, reassured by their metallic presence there.

Now they've stopped outside a building. Eddie has no idea where they are, but they're stumbling out of the cab, and Lyla has taken his hand as they climb the short flight of wide stone steps to the front door. They're inside the building now and clattering upstairs. The stairwell is far nicer than the one at Raj and Calum's place. *My place too,* Eddie reminds himself. He lives there too now. It's his home. It hardly seems possible.

They reach a landing where Lyla stops. Eddie takes in the shiny brown floor tiles that remind him briefly of those Toffee Pennies in the Quality Street tin, the ones that are always left at the end. Then Eddie is no longer thinking about Toffee Pennies as they are inside a flat. A huge abstract painting dominates the wall above a fireplace. The living room is beautiful in an extremely tasteful way, like a hotel room almost, with tall, multi-paned windows. Eddie has never been in a flat like it before.

Where *are* they? He doesn't care because now he and Lyla are kissing on a sofa that seems to be made out of velvet. Eddie's so happy, and Lyla is so beautiful, and her skin is like, like – what do they say? Like porcelain? Yeah, that's it. She has skin like his mum's favourite cup, the one he knocked off the kitchen worktop the other night, after they'd come back from the Italian restaurant and his parents had gone to bed. He'd quickly swept up the pieces and buried them at the bottom of the kitchen bin, a guilty secret. 'Has anyone seen my pink cup?' he heard his mum asking next morning. 'Eddie, love, is it in your room?' He'd feigned sleep.

Now Eddie and Lyla stop kissing and curl up together on the sofa in silence. It doesn't feel awkward, not talking at all. In fact, it feels completely right. And in the stillness of this unfamiliar room he tries to make sense of the amazing discoveries he's made in the few hours since he left home.

That people have parties on Thursday nights.

And he can go to such a party and be abandoned by his so-called mates and it'll be fine.

In fact, *better* than fine. Because he's met a beautiful girl who seems to really, really like him.

And leaving home – something Eddie had worried might never happen – is more thrilling than he could have imagined.

For one split second, as Lyla reaches for a glass of water and takes a big swig, he thinks about that smashed pink cup again, which funnels his thoughts to his mum and dad. They're going to miss him so much. But they'll cope, he decides. Maybe they'll get some hobbies? Isn't that what old people do?

Then Eddie's not thinking about his mum and dad anymore as Lyla has put down the glass, and she's smiling and her eyes are sparkling in the darkened room as she pulls him up by the hand.

'Where we going?' Eddie croaks.

'Where d'you think?' They go into another room – is it her bedroom? Yeah, the clue's in the fact that there's a bed in it. And they fall onto it, and Eddie's entire being seems to split into billions of shooting stars as she winds her arms around him and their clothes seem to dissolve into thin air.

This must be Lyla's place, Eddie decides. It's somewhere in Edinburgh – he has no idea where, but right now, as she wraps herself around him, he doesn't care. Because the place Eddie Silva has landed in is actually Heaven, and in his drunken haze he could happily stay here for the rest of his life.

CHAPTER NINE

February

Carly

Six weeks have passed since Eddie left home. Now, I'm not saying it's great being empty-nesters.

No, actually, I am! It's bloody *brilliant!* There's been no gathering up dirty plates and bits of crust from Eddie's room. No constant veering between frustration and worry at the sight of him rotting away in that robe – which, incidentally, he forgot to take to Edinburgh. I offered to bring it over when we visited, but he politely declined. I took this to mean that he can now exist quite happily without it, which had to be a positive sign.

On top of that, a blissful sense of calm has settled over the house. There's no muttering and whispering when we hope he's out of earshot – and now Frank and I can happily stroll about in our pants, simply pleasing ourselves. The sense of freedom is almost *dizzying*. All that trying my utmost to be patient and supportive, because maybe Eddie was depressed? I love my son dearly but Christ, it was exhausting by the end.

Plus, for over two decades Frank and I have managed to *just about* keep our sex life going, albeit hanging by a thread at times. Because the kids have been here, and Eddie's room shares a wall with ours, we've learnt to be incredibly quiet. Not that we're yelling the house down now, or throwing each other around the room – but we're certainly freer and, frankly, it's more fun. A knock-on effect is that we're more affectionate, even as we're doing ordinary things like cooking together or watching a film. It's almost like being a new couple again, when those passionate reunions were all we had.

My God, how I loved Frank then. I *yearned* for him. If I could have jumped into the sea and swum to Portugal, I would have.

Of course I still loved him once we'd tumbled into a world of nappies and night feeds and daubings of baby sick on our shoulders. But somehow, it was never quite the same again.

Until now.

Now Frank comes home from work, and the sight of him all oily and mussed up gets me going again.

Or I'm about to head off to work in the morning, and our goodbye kiss quickly turns into something else. And I no longer head off to the library early, just to snatch that little bit of peace for myself.

I want him more than I want to be in the library alone.

Frank Silva, you crazy man, taking over an ice cream shop with malfunctioning fridges. I still love you so very much.

Then one bright, crisp Friday morning we are that

speck in the colourless winter sky. We are on a plane heading for Paris, a city we've only ever seen in films. It's not quite noon, yet Frank and I are drinking wine. 'This is all right, isn't it?' He smiles.

'It is,' I say. 'So, d'you think we're managing on our own?'

'It's hard,' he teases, 'but yeah, just about.'

In fact, I've stopped fretting that Eddie will sever a finger in that restaurant kitchen. I've learnt how to let go – and about time too, Frank reckons. It's just taken a little getting used to as, unlike Ana and Bella, Eddie never calls. It's me who's been keeping in touch, mainly through messages, and Eddie's replies are brief:

Yeah all good Mum.

Or, more often: *All fine.*

He hasn't come home yet and we've only visited him once, when he could squeeze us into his packed schedule. In his flat, while he and his dad chatted over coffee, I snuck into his room and speedily measured the window so I could surprise him by ordering a blind. The nailed-up towel just seemed so depressing. Then we took him out to a café where he wolfed a panini, a slab of chocolate cake *and* a doughnut, as if he hadn't eaten for a week. But he also seemed happy, and I realised, *this really is it*. Eddie moving out wasn't a mad experiment that was bound to go terribly wrong. Frank and I really are on our own now.

And as the days unfold in Paris, it's no longer Eddie who's at the forefront of my mind, but the two of us. All the years seem to fall away as we stroll around the Musée D'Orsay and the Petit Palais and a delightfully ramshackle flea market. Some afternoons, instead of sightseeing, we nip back to the hotel and fall into bed.

A middle-aged couple having sex in the daytime? I'd never imagined that that would be me and Frank. But something has reignited in us. Afterwards, we lie together in a tangle of crisp white sheets in our little top-floor room with the wrought-iron balcony and the whole of Paris going about its business below.

On our last night we celebrate Frank's fiftieth birthday in a cosy bistro. The girls have called, and Eddie managed to fire off a text (admittedly, I sent him a firm reminder). Five days have whipped by in a delicious whirl, and all too soon we're up at dawn to catch our flight, and touching down at Glasgow airport.

Coming home from a trip can be a real downer. Maybe the house smells bad, as if it's soured, like milk. *Does it always whiff like this and people are too polite to say?* However, this time there are no nasty surprises, because it's only us. Nothing terrible has happened to my Bathsheba rose. Nothing 'just fell', or smells terrible, because I did a thorough clean before we set off. Seeing that everything is as we left it triggers a surge of happiness in me, and I kiss Frank on the lips.

'Hey, what's that for?' He grins.

'I'm just happy, Frank. Paris was wonderful, wasn't it?'

He nods, smiling. 'Yeah. It was brilliant, darling. I had the best time with you.'

After dumping our bags in the hallway, we head through to the kitchen where I fill the kettle. This kitchen – in fact, this house – seemed so poky when there were five fully-grown people here. Now it feels perfect.

'Never mind tea,' Frank announces. 'How about a glass of wine?'

I set down the milk carton we picked up at the airport. 'In the daytime? You are feeling wild, Mr Silva!'

'Well, why not?' He lifts out the bottle of chilled sauvignon that's been sitting there untouched. *We've been away for five days and no one's guzzled our booze!* My God, I reflect, as he pours two glasses, and we head through to the living room. We've entered the era when we can trust that a bottle of alcoholic beverage hasn't been topped up with water.

We sip our wine and snuggle up on our saggy old corduroy sofa. 'I loved our family holidays,' Frank says, 'but I think this trip's been my favourite.'

I smile. 'Mine too. You know what that book would call it?' I indicate it sitting there on the coffee table.

'No, what?'

'"An empty-nester marker trip".'

'What on earth's that?' He laughs.

'You know! To celebrate a new chapter in our lives.'

'Right.' He smirks, bemused. 'But I thought we just . . . *went to Paris?*'

'Oh, we did,' I say quickly. 'We absolutely did. We just went.'

He grins, squeezing my hand. 'So what else does your book advise, now we're all washed up and redundant?'

'Hang on.' I reach for it and flick through it, stopping at a random page. '"Redecorate your house,"' I read aloud. '"Splash new colours around to cover the scuffs and scrapes of family life. It's time to reclaim your home as your own personal space . . ."'

'Can I just unpack my bag?' He chuckles.

'. . . Or how about this? "Now you'll have time to pursue your own interests, why not take up a new hobby or plant a rose garden?"'

'You have a rose garden already,' he points out.

'Yes, and now I'll be able to lavish *all* of my maternal love and care onto it . . .'

He winds an arm around my shoulders, pulling me close. 'We don't need instructions, do we? On how to survive without the kids?' Frank doesn't turn to books for answers. Ideas simply ping into his head.

'No,' I say, setting the book down, 'we don't. In fact . . . d'you fancy coming up to bed?'

He laughs. 'What, at four o'clock in the afternoon?'

'Well, we did in Paris.'

'This isn't Paris,' he says in a mock-stern voice. 'You're wearing me out, Carly. I'm fifty, remember? An old man now—'

'Hardly!' I laugh and jump up, pulling him up by the hand.

'Is this in your book too?' he asks as we scamper upstairs.

'Might be . . .'

'"Keep the flame alive by seducing your man in the middle of the day when he's been up since six"—'

'Hey, I was up then too!' Then we're in our bedroom, tugging off our clothes and laughing at how deliciously naughty it feels, to be slipping into bed together. I still love

Kilmory Cottage, but all the graft and struggles of our family life are embedded in these walls. Maybe we just needed a little break from the everyday, to remind us that we still love each other.

My phone trills, cutting into my thoughts. 'Shit,' I mutter.

'Leave it,' Frank says, and it stops. We kiss some more, and his body feels so good against mine; warm and taut, smelling delicious. And now his leg hooks over mine, and I want him so much, deep inside of me, and it makes me so happy that we still feel this way, even though we're gnarly and old and he leaves beard trimmings in the sink and wears flattened old leather slippers that are frankly hideous and—

My phone rings again. 'Oh, God. I'd better get it.' I peel myself away from him and reach for it on my bedside table.

'Your dad?' he suggests.

'Probably.' It stops ringing as I pick it up. The two missed calls aren't from Dad, but Eddie. Eddie who *never* calls. Bolt upright in bed now, I call him back. 'Hey, love. Everything okay?' Instinctively, I tug the duvet up to my neck as if he might be able to see his parents naked together – in the daytime! – and this'll make it less disgusting for him.

'Yep. I'm all right.' His voice is tight. 'How're you?'

How am *I*? He never enquires about my wellbeing. 'Fine,' I start, uneasily. 'We're just back from Paris. It was lovely, really beautiful—'

But my son jumps in, cutting me off.

There are some things a parent never wants to

hear. *Mum, please don't be mad,* is one – usually when something's been broken.

Eddie doesn't say that now. Because it's not about a broken thing or anything that can be fixed. I know him well enough to be sure of that. My heart is thumping hard as he clears his throat and says, 'I have something to tell you.'

'Oh, what's that?' The silence stretches, chilling my blood. He makes a terrible gulping sound and, oh God, I think he's crying. 'Eddie!' I exclaim. 'Are you okay, love? What is it?'

'Just . . . this thing, Mum. This thing that's happened. Are you sitting down?'

CHAPTER TEN

I don't think I heard him properly. I can't have because this is my son – my *kid*. I realise he's a fully fledged grown-up on paper and could pass for an adult man on the outside. But what does 'on paper' actually mean? His passport looks as if it's been fished out of a septic tank. He still carries a skateboard at any opportunity, as if it's some life-supporting device – and he still hasn't replaced his lost debit card.

'No time,' he'd announced, when I asked him if he'd spoken to the bank.

Yet he's had time to get someone pregnant!

That's what Eddie's just told me – I think. *Hang-on-it-doesn't-take-very-long-to-make-someone-pregnant*.

No, I must have misheard him. Having spoken perfectly clearly until around the age of thirteen, Eddie suddenly developed a muffled diction, as if speaking through a cushion, and it's stuck.

'I said I'm going to be a dad,' he repeats.

I grip onto the duvet, as if that'll help me. 'Oh my God, Eddie,' is all I can say.

'What is it?' Frank asks, alarmed. 'What's wrong?'

'Hang *on*.' I swivel to cut him out of my vision. 'Eddie, are you sure?' I'm trying to keep my voice light, as if asking, *Has a bird just shat on my head?*

'Yes, Mum. I'm sure.'

For a moment, I simply try to take this in. Frank is asking repeatedly what's going on, but I can't bring myself to tell him. 'What I mean is,' I start, straw-clutching now, 'are you sure it's your—'

'Yes!' Eddie announces. 'Why d'you even ask that?'

'I'm only asking. That's all.' *Because I know, from what you and Bella and Ana have told me – very sharply, on occasion – that ancient people like me aren't meant to assume that people are exclusive. They might just be hanging out, or 'talking', whatever that means – and what-do-I-know-anyway-he's-only-been-in-Edinburgh-five-bloody-minutes!*

'Carly, what *is* it?' Frank demands.

I still can't say it out loud. Right now, I can barely breathe. I fix my gaze on the little green cut-glass vase on the chest of drawers that used to belong to Mum. 'I'm just trying to figure out how it happened,' I say.

'In the normal way,' Eddie mutters.

My heart is thumping against my ribs. 'I didn't know you were seeing anyone.'

'I'm not.' He clears his throat. 'It was just . . . a *thing*.'

'Right. Okay—'

'Carly, I need to know what's going on!' Frank is out of

bed now, still naked but grabbing at the clothes he tossed all over the floor in expectation of an afternoon's session. He stumbles as he tugs on his boxers. 'Can you please tell me—'

'Someone's-having-a-baby!' I blurt out.

'*What?*'

'Oh, have you told Dad?' Eddie snaps accusingly.

'Well, yes, love! He's right here.'

'*Who's* having a baby?' Frank thunders.

'I didn't think you were going to tell him *right now*,' Eddie complains.

'Does it matter? He's going to find out—'

'I just thought you could . . . build up to it,' Eddie says. How does he imagine I'd do that?

Frank, I need to break it to you that our firstborn is sexually active.

Darling, our son has been somewhat cavalier with contraception.

Frank, honey, sit down a minute. How does the idea of being a granddad feel to you?

I watch bleakly as Frank pulls on his jeans and T-shirt.

'There isn't really a way of building up to this,' I start, then turn to Frank: 'Eddie's going to be a dad.'

He stares at me, frozen for a moment. Then his entire being seems to sag as he lowers himself onto the edge of the bed. 'Oh, Jesus,' he breathes.

'I met someone,' Eddie is explaining now, 'on a night out. I know what you're thinking but *please* don't start lecturing me because I know it's a real fuck-up . . .'

'Eddie,' I start, 'I'm not going to lecture you but—'

''Cause I know it was stupid,' he barges in. 'It just

happened. I was drunk and didn't think much more about it. Then she got in touch and said she's pregnant and I thought, God, right. Okay. And *then* she said she wants to have the baby . . .'

Tears flood my eyes. 'Oh, love. Is she really sure about that?'

'Yeah.'

'And . . . how old is she?'

'Dunno. About the same age as me . . .'

I breathe out slowly. 'And she's absolutely certain, is she? I mean, does she need time to think it over—'

'Nope,' he says firmly. 'She's definitely going ahead.'

A silence hangs between us. Last time we saw Eddie he gleefully told us that, after just two weeks, his boss had taken him off kitchen portering duties and was training him up as a commis chef. A vacancy had come up and Eddie had proved himself to be eager and hard-working. 'He said I've got potential,' he announced, 'and I'm picking it all up really fast.'

'I wish you'd been this keen when we were doing the food truck,' Frank had teased him.

'Yeah, but this is real cooking,' Eddie retorted. 'It's like, *proper* food.'

Frank spluttered and I thought: *well, at least our boy's found something*. And maybe this could be his 'thing'? He seemed so happy and confident and my heart swelled with pride. Now he sounds like a boy again.

'Eddie,' I start, 'have you both really thought about this? I mean, d'you realise what it's going to entail?'

'Well, yeah! It's going to entail a baby being born.' *Obviously, thicko Mum!*

I swallow hard. 'That's just the start of it. The easy bit! This is massive, d'you realise that? You need to talk it all through with her. Have you discussed it at all?'

'Not really,' he says defensively, as if that's another of my ridiculous suggestions. Like getting a proper window covering for his room!

'Well, might that be a good idea?'

'Don't shout at me.'

'I'm not shouting!' I take a moment to try and steady myself. 'Sorry, Ed. I'm . . . shocked. That's all.'

'I'm sorry too,' he mumbles. And now my tears spill over because, even though he's been stupid, he's still my son. Still the boy who loved my banana pancakes and wrote a story at school about a candle-shaped man made of 'wacks', as he spelt it. And right now, all I want to do is hold him close.

I wipe away the tears, telling myself to be calm, and wondering when Frank might think of doing something more useful than sit there staring at the wardrobe.

'So, what's her name?' I ask flatly.

'Lyla,' Eddie replies.

'And . . . what's she like?'

'I don't really know.' His admission hangs in the air. Get it together, I tell myself. *Do* something.

'Okay,' I start, 'so me and Dad'll come over . . .'

'What for?' Eddie asks, alarmed.

'To see you!'

'When?'

'Well, right now if that's okay? Not at work, are you—'

'Yeah, I am. I'm on a break—'

'Tomorrow, then?'

'I'm working in the afternoon.'

'We'll come in the morning then. First thing—'

'You can't come in the *morning*,' he exclaims.

'Why not? We want to see you—'

'I'm going out tonight and it's gonna be a late one.'

'Oh, right,' I exclaim. *Go clubbing as if everything's normal and you haven't made a baby!*

'Mum, honestly,' he says firmly. 'There's no need to dash over here like it's an emergency.'

'But it *is* an emergency!'

'Well, I just wanted to let you know,' he cuts in sharply. 'I'm not up for a family conference, okay?' I start to protest that it won't be a conference; only me and his dad, coming over to show our support, because we love him. But Eddie wraps up the call, and I'm left feeling hollow and sick and battered, all at once.

So that's what happens when you think, *At last our son's got his shit together.*

I swivel out of bed, pull on my clothes and look at Frank. He's standing at our bedroom window now, staring out to sea. Then he swings round to face me, dark eyes beaming hurt and disappointment as he says, 'I thought you gave him the contraception talk?'

CHAPTER ELEVEN

How dare he say this. How dare he blame me, as if I made the girl pregnant!

Oh, I've failed at plenty of things. My driving test twice. I never remember to engage my core, the way Pilates Wendy is always telling us to: 'It's the area where your six-pack would be, Carly.' (Note: 'Would be'. Not: 'is'). And I've never managed to cook a meal that my dad has actually enjoyed. At least, shown any pleasure in eating.

But Frank is wrong in implying that this is my fault. Yes, I tried to tell Eddie about contraception. But saying I 'did the talk' makes it sound as if it was delivered effectively with major points all clearly communicated. *Congratulations, Carly, on your excellent keynote speech!*

What actually happened is, I'd got wind of the fact that they were doing sex ed in Eddie's school year, and I wanted to make sure he'd understood things properly.

However, with five of us here it was tricky to talk to any of the kids on their own. Then one afternoon, Frank and the girls had gone out. At last, my big chance!

I'd rounded on Eddie, trapping him like a rat in the kitchen. 'Erm, I know you're covering sex ed with Mrs Telfer,' I started.

'Er, yeah.' He backed up against the fridge.

'I just . . . y'know. Thought we could have a chat . . .' Damn, I was sweating already. The girls had accepted some basic information from me – albeit tersely, in Bella's case, as she'd stood there with arms folded, waiting for it to be over. Ana had giggled and made jokes throughout. But at least there'd been some communication. Eddie had always been more resistant.

'No-it's-fine-thanks,' he squawked, then bobbed down to tug open a freezer drawer with unnecessary force.

'Eddie,' I carried on, addressing the back of his head as he burrowed noisily among its contents, 'this is important, love. I want to make sure you're clear about things that really matter, okay? Things like condoms and safe sex—'

He leapt up, pulling out a Magnum ice cream but also dislodging an open packet of frozen peas, which tumbled out, sending little green bullets shooting all over the floor.

'Eddie!' I cried.

'Sorry. Gotta go. Meeting Raj.' He gave the scattered peas a cursory glance and legged it out of the house.

'Frank,' I say now, as I follow him downstairs, 'are you saying this is my fault?'

'Of course not. I meant—'

'Why didn't *you* do the contraception talk?' We are

facing each other in the hallway now. 'I asked you to, so many times—'

'I was going to. I just didn't get round to it.'

'Were you planning on waiting until he was forty-five?'

'Don't be ridiculous!' He marches through the kitchen and storms out to our back garden that overlooks the sea. It's dark already, and I stand there shivering at the door.

'Please come back in, Frank.'

'In a minute.' He's pacing around the lawn, back and forth.

'You don't have any shoes on. Just your socks . . .'

'I'm fine!' he snaps.

'Can we stop being like this?'

He places a hand on his forehead and turns to me. 'What's he thinking, throwing away his life like this? The flat, the job, the new life in Edinburgh . . . he's only getting started, Carly. After all this time. It's fucking crazy.'

'I know. It's a disaster. But let's not be like this—'

'Like what?' he exclaims. 'What am I s'posed to be like?' He marches towards me and barges back into the house.

I shut the door and reach for his hand. 'I know it's upsetting and shocking, Frank. Don't you think I'm upset too? But being like this, it's not helpful—'

'I'm not trying to be *helpful*.'

'No, well, that's obvious!' I let his hand drop and glare at him, this man I woke up with in Paris this morning, in our little white room, where we kissed and giggled that we should really get up, and there wasn't time to do it. We still had to pack and check out and set off for the airport.

We had a quickie anyway, just like in the olden days,

when we used to do it all the time. Afterwards, we hurried downstairs to the hotel's front desk – a dishevelled middle-aged couple, giddily happy and flushed in the face. We were convinced the thin-lipped receptionist would know exactly what we'd just done.

We laughed and kissed in the street then, and strolled to the Metro station hand in hand. A fresh start, the holiday felt like. A thrilling new chapter for Frank and me.

And what is it, now we're home again? I have no idea. What I do know is that right now, I'd rather kiss a goat.

CHAPTER TWELVE

March

Eating, sleeping, going to work. In the ten days since Eddie's shock announcement, Frank and I have been doing all the normal things. I've actually preferred being at Pilates to home, even though Wendy seems to be making the class harder, by stealth – and my core *still* isn't fully engaged. I've certainly been grateful for having a job to go to, because at the library I'm among friends. Whereas Frank and I have been going around in circles about the whole thing – and achieving nothing – Prish, Jamie and Marilyn have helped to distract me and lift me out of my gloom. And of course they've listened without judgement, and reassured me that everything will be okay.

'Maybe they'll make it work in their own way,' Jamie offered one morning as he made our coffees.

'I just don't know. Eddie hardly gives me any information at the best of times.'

'All you can do is be there if he needs you,' Prish added, and I figured she was right.

Some evenings, instead of heading straight home, I go for a stroll on the beach to grab some time to myself. It doesn't matter if Frank's still at the garage or not; I find myself putting off even the possibility of the two of us being stuck in the house together. And when we are both there, a simmering ill humour pervades. But mostly, I haven't even seen Frank in the evenings because he's taken himself off to our rickety old garden shed – the shed he rarely ventured into before all this happened, but now he remains there after I've gone to bed.

It's like Paris never happened. When I look through our photos, all happy and laughing on a boat trip on the Seine, it's all I can do not to cry. Because Frank seems to have gone into himself, in a way I've never seen before.

However, at least our son has agreed to see us, finally. Somehow, the boy who is always frantically busy has managed to take a Saturday off.

We are here now, at noon as arranged, outside his flat. I press the door buzzer and wait. Frank is standing grimly beside me, arms folded across his chest.

We wait, but no one buzzes us in. I press it again, thinking that at least we'll be able to have a reasonably helpful and productive talk today. The three of us, like a proper family.

By now, we've gathered that Lyla did the pregnancy test a couple of days before we came back from Paris. But when I asked Eddie when the baby is due, he started babbling, 'I think in late autumn or winter or something?' As if I was a teacher springing a difficult question on him in class. However, whatever's happened, it happened bloody quickly. He only saw her once – that first night in Edinburgh, after we'd dropped him off, presumably before he'd even unpacked his stuff. Fast work, Eddie! Whenever I asked him to empty the dishwasher at home he'd take at least three days to get around to it, if he did it at all.

We must be supportive, I remind myself. We're not here to make him feel worse. I won't throw frozen-peas-day in his face.

More importantly, his dad and I must show a united front. 'Frank,' I start, glancing at him, 'can we please show Eddie that we're on his side?'

'Yeah, of course,' he mutters.

My chest seems to tighten. 'And can we *please* cheer up a bit?'

'Oh, am I not being cheerful enough?' he snaps.

'You know what I mean—'

'Sorry, should I be wearing a clown's outfit and juggling balls?'

'Don't be silly—'

'Want me to pull a rabbit out of a hat?'

'Frank, don't be like this!' Anger surges up in me now. 'It's been horrible lately, the way we've been with each other. You're barely speaking to me as if this is all *my* fault. In fact I've hardly seen you. You've been hiding away in the shed every night . . .' I look at him imploringly, but it's like talking to a brick. 'Please, Frank. Stop being so, so—'

'I'm just standing outside our son's house,' he announces loudly, 'waiting to be let in so we can find out how he thinks he's going to cope with a baby, with this girl he doesn't even know, and what's going to happen when it's born and how's he planning to make enough money—'

'Frank—' I clamp my hand on his arm.

'—and will he even see the child and have anything to do with it? And what about his young life that was supposed to be so brilliant and now it's all *fucked*!' Angrily, he jabs at the button multiple times.

'Stop that!' I swat his hand away.

'He's not answering, is he?'

'No, but you'll enrage him, doing that—'

'Oh, *he's* the enraged one, is he?'

I stare at him in shock. 'Is *that* what you are then? Enraged, rather than being supportive and caring and—'

'I didn't say that.' He turns away as if something fascinating has caught his attention up the street. Without warning tears flood my eyes. *Don't cry,* I will myself. *What will Eddie think if he opens the door to find you blubbing?* A tear escapes as a man in a tweed jacket saunters by. Then along trots a woman clutching the lead of a tiny velveteen dog.

I blink away more tears, trying to pull myself together. 'Maybe he's forgotten we're coming,' I murmur, now recalling the last time we visited. Like today it was almost lunchtime. It had taken Eddie ages to buzz us in, and he'd appeared on his landing with his hair all rumpled and a pillow crease imprinted on his cheek, clearly having just rolled out of bed.

Frank mutters something under his breath.

'What?'

'I said we've really messed up, haven't we?'

'No,' I exclaim. 'No, of course we haven't.' I inhale deeply, trying to think of how to lighten things between us. 'That rabbit-in-hat-thing you said?' I start. 'It's magicians who do that. Not clowns—' I break off as a young woman in a billowing overcoat sweeps towards us. She stops at Eddie's building, and we step back dutifully as she fishes out keys from the depths of a pocket.

'Hi. Want to come in?' She flashes a smile.

Not really, no. I want to be at home, foolishly thinking that everyone's doing fine instead of standing here, together but not together because it feels as if we're falling apart. 'Yes please,' I say. 'Our son lives on the top floor.'

'No problem.' She unlocks the door and as we follow her inside, Eddie stomps down towards us.

'Oh, you're in,' he says accusingly. As if we should have waited obediently outside.

'*Hello*, Eddie.' I force a hug on him as the girl heads upstairs.

'Hey, son.' Frank and Eddie embrace awkwardly.

'So, d'you want to go straight out?' I start. 'Or shall we—' I cut off as Eddie bounds out into the street. Okay, so we're *not* going up to the flat. What did he think we'd do up there? Talk to his friends? Dare to accept a cup of tea? It's only as we head away from his building that I notice his unusually smart attire.

'You look good, Eddie,' I venture, scampering to catch up with him. 'New clothes?'

'Uh, yeah. Yeah.' He nods.

'Wow.' *What brought this on?* I wonder. Eddie tends to wear clothes until they disintegrate, virtually hanging in tatters off his body. Yet today his mid-blue shirt looks neatly pressed, and in place of his usual jeans he's wearing smart black trousers. I'd be no more startled to see him wearing jodhpurs. And I've never seen his blazer-type jacket before. I've never seen Eddie in *any* jacket, other than a puffer or various sports-related items, apart from when we attended a Portuguese cousin's wedding. Then he looked like he'd had a gun put to his head to force him into a suit.

Today, as we round the corner, I also notice that his hair looks unusually clean. He's shaved too. And do I detect a gust of fragrance?

'So, where d'you want to go?' I ask.

'There's this place,' Eddie replies vaguely. His flat's a tip, I decide, and he doesn't want us to see it – as if we'd care, with everything that's happened. That still doesn't explain why he's dressed for court.

We cut across the grassy expanse of The Meadows. It's a grey, chilly day and it seems to be mainly populated by runners and a group of dads and children playing football. 'Where are we going, Ed?' his father asks.

'Just this *place*.'

Frank throws me a curious look.

'What kind of food is it?' I ask, as if it matters. It could be cat food for all I care, because we're not here to enjoy lunch. We're here to show a united and supportive front.

'Just normal food,' Eddie replies distractedly, and soon we're in the melee of Princes Street, virtually breaking into a trot as Eddie swerves past tourists consulting their phones and taking selfies with the castle as a backdrop.

I glance at my son as he powers along. He normally employs a slow, loping walk, checking his phone constantly and puffing on a roll-up. Perhaps he's quit? Is this the start of a new, wholesome Eddie, preparing to be a dad? I'd ask, but am afraid of being accused of 'getting on' at him.

'Anywhere will do, love,' I remark, catching my breath. 'Shall we just find somewhere—'

'We're going to this *place*,' he announces with more force than seems necessary.

'All right, Ed.' His dad frowns, clearly baffled – as I am – by the lengthy march. Since puberty kicked in, our firstborn has avoided unnecessary movement.

'You haven't . . . booked somewhere, have you?' I ask.

'Uh, yeah. I mean, no. Not me. But somewhere's booked.' I exchange another look with Frank. We'd be no more shocked if he'd booked opera tickets.

It dawns on me now: he's taking us to Bracken, where he works! This is a major step forward. With its tasting menu it'll cost an absolute packet but, on the positive side, this would suggest he's not ashamed of us after all. 'Eddie,' I start, 'are we going to *your* restaurant?'

'*No!*' He looks appalled, and my heart seems to drop as we find ourselves in the New Town. The Georgian terraces look so elegant in sunshine, but today seem rather bleak under a buff-coloured sky.

Eddie swerves into a cobbled side street. It's one of those streets where you don't really know what happens inside the buildings. There are brass plaques and discreet signs saying things like J Pritmarsh Associates and The Onyx Society. I imagine middle-aged men in suits, Chesterfield sofas and whisky in cut-glass tumblers.

Eddie stops abruptly, mouth set in a grim line. 'We're here.'

'What d'you mean, we're here?' Confused, I glance around. There's no café or restaurant as far as I can see.

'I mean, this is it.' He indicates the nearest doorway.

The outer door is open, and beyond the glass inner door I glimpse dark wooden panelling, a deep red patterned carpet and a huge, glittering chandelier.

'What, this?' Frank asks, frowning. Two small topiaried shrubs in zinc containers flank the doorway. But nothing tells us what kind of place this is.

'Yeah. It's a club,' Eddie mutters, peering down at his feet.

'You belong to a *club*?' I stare at him. His hair is so clean, I can smell apple shampoo coming off him.

'What kind of club?' Frank asks. Does this explain the eerily pressed outfit?

'Just a club. I don't belong to it,' Eddie says quickly. 'I'm not a *member*—'

'Could've fooled me,' Frank remarks dryly, his feeble attempt at a joke offering a glimmer of hope that he might be softening, and perhaps the Silvas might even be able to enjoy a pleasant lunch?

'Look, I'm sorry I didn't tell you.' Eddie winces. 'It's a bit awkward. I wasn't sure how you'd react.' He rakes back his dark hair and glances furtively up and down the street.

'React to *what*?' I ask.

'This, uh, this thing today. *Please* don't be mad at this—' there it is, the line no parent ever wants to hear '—but we're, erm . . . I mean, it's not just us.'

I frown at him. 'I don't understand.'

'I mean there's, uh . . . gonna be *other people*.'

Shit, we're going in front of a tribunal because my contraception talk failed to communicate the basic facts.

'What d'you mean?' I stare at him.

'I mean, urr . . .' His mouth twists. 'We're meeting Lyla today.'

'Who?' Frank barks.

'*Lyla!*' Eddie repeats.

'We're meeting her today?' I exclaim. 'What, here? *Now*?'

'Yes, now.' He nods grimly.

'Who's Lyla?' Frank looks baffled.

'Lyla-who's-having-a-baby.' I glare at him. *For God's sake, keep up!* It's astounding how he's coasted through the raising of three children without bothering to remember the name of a single person connected to their lives. Not me, obviously. Frank just about remembers *my* name. But the kids' teachers and friends and their friends' parents? Or the Scout leader who'd called me in for a ticking-off after Eddie had mooned through the coach window on the way back from a trip? To Frank, it was a sea of random faces – or, if forced, *that pointy-nosed woman*, or *the guy with the beard*.

He exhales forcefully and shakes his head. 'No, Ed. Sorry. We're not meeting her now—'

'No, we are,' Eddie insists. 'And her mum's going to be there too—'

'Her *mum*?' I choke out.

Eddie nods. 'Yeah.'

'No way,' I say firmly. 'Sorry, Eddie, but I'm with your dad on this. We're not doing this today. We've come to see you and we need to talk as a family. *That's* why we're here—'

'Please, Mum. *Please!*' Eddie's voice wavers and he grips my arm. 'They're in there. They're waiting for us now . . .' A pause, then: 'I thought I'd be able to count on you.'

His gaze locks with mine, and something sparks between us; the fact that our son really needs our help and support, like never before. Are we really going to refuse to go in?

'All right. We'll meet them.' I press my hand briefly over my eyes, as if that will imbue me with special powers. Then I turn to Frank. 'You okay with that?'

He shrugs extravagantly as if acknowledging that he no longer has any control over his destiny. 'And another thing,' Eddie adds, hand already on the glass inner door. 'She's told her mum that we've been together for six months and are solid together. So that's the story, all right? That's what she's got to think—'

'Absolutely no way!' I cry out, horrified. 'If you want to lie then that's up to you but—' I cut off and look around helplessly at Frank. Because Eddie has already marched in.

CHAPTER THIRTEEN

'Eddie!' I stumble after him across the foyer. 'Hang on. Wait! STOP RIGHT THERE!'

He spins around to face me. 'Stop shouting,' he hisses.

'I'm not shouting.'

'You are! You're embarrassing me, Mum. Stop it.'

'But no one's here!' I look around the otherwise empty foyer. The gleaming wood panelling is hung with formal portraits of men in plumed hats and full tartan battle wear. None look especially friendly.

'You can't do this to us, Ed,' Frank announces. 'It's not fair.'

'Sorry, I know it's not *ideal* . . .'

'Not ideal?' I splutter. 'You could say that. Why didn't you warn us?'

'I couldn't! I didn't know it was happening 'til yesterday—'

'But we've just walked halfway across town,' I point

out. 'All that way, you let us think we were just going for a panini—'

'I never said anything about paninis!'

'You've basically *tricked* us,' I announce.

'And we're supposed to go along with this lie,' Frank exclaims, 'that you and, uh – this girl—'

'—she's called Lyla, Dad—'

'—That you're *together*?' Frank says in disbelief.

As Eddie shrugs, looking helpless, I realise how wrong I was, to believe he'd properly grown up. I was fooled by the flat-share, the job in a fancy restaurant, and his bewilderment when the blind for his window turned up at his flat. 'I don't need you to order things for me, Mum!' But was the towel still pinned up? No, the blind was in place. He'd put it up himself, he assured me. It was *easy*. Did I think he couldn't operate a screwdriver?

'I didn't know what else to do,' Eddie admits now, unable to look at us. 'Lyla arranged it with her mum, soon as she knew you were coming over to see me.'

'So you *are* in touch with her then?' I venture.

'Not really. Yeah, a bit.' He bites his lip.

'And they're here now?' Frank says, as if he still can't believe it. Eddie nods gloomily.

My heart feels heavy, like a boulder in my chest. 'I'm not really up for this, Eddie. Let's just go.'

'We can't just not show up!'

'Yes, we can,' Frank insists. 'Say we couldn't make it. Something happened. Your mum fell ill—'

'Why me?' I retort. 'Why am I ill?'

'You just *are*—'

'What's wrong with me?'

'I don't know. Anything. Your sciatica's bad—'

'I've never had sciatica—'

'Lyla's mum *really* wants to meet you,' Eddie cuts in, desperation in his voice now.

'But why?' I ask, genuinely confused. To berate us for our shoddy parenting? *I tried to tell him about contraception but he was too busy burrowing for Magnums in the freezer!*

'To see what you're like, I s'pose.' Eddie seems to cringe as he looks at us, clearly finding us lacking. And admittedly, I can't imagine that anyone would mistake us for members of this presumably private members' club. Frank always looks good – and I often see other women checking him out – but today his ancient denim jacket, black jeans with a small rip in one knee and a yolk-coloured T-shirt with a cartoon bear on the front, plus the slogan 'I prefer their earlier stuff', don't seem quite right.

Not that I look any better. This morning I'd been too preoccupied by Frank's brooding ill humour, and whether we'd be able to present a united front, to be able to even think about putting an outfit together. I'd simply grabbed an old stripy sweater plus jeans, scruffy Chelsea boots and a jacket that's definitely tipped over into the realm of gardening wear. My face is bare, my hair unwashed.

Now an immaculate woman in a charcoal trouser suit has appeared from a back room. 'Can I help you?' She flashes even white teeth.

'We're meeting, uh, Lyla Balfour and, ah . . . Mrs Balfour,' Eddie blurts out.

'Ah, *the Balfours*.' She stations herself behind the reception desk. 'They're through in the restaurant. Just along there.' She indicates a corridor leading off the foyer. 'Like me to take you through?'

'We're fine, thanks,' Eddie says quickly. We follow our son towards the convivial sounds of chatter and clinking crockery, passing a glass cabinet housing a display of what look like ceremonial swords. But what if they're not? What if they're real and we've been lured here for our execution?

'What's her name?' I whisper to Eddie, grabbing at his arm.

He shakes me off irritably. 'Lyla!'

'I mean her mum.'

'Uh, Shelley, I think . . .'

That's a friendly name, I try to reassure myself. A Shelley won't have a list of questions ready for our interrogation – or a gun.

We step into the bustling restaurant and stand close together, like small woodland animals huddling for safety. 'I'm too ill for this, apparently,' I murmur. '*My sciatica's so bad . . .*'

'Mum, don't start,' Eddie says through his teeth.

'I need to go to hospital. Get an ambulance, Eddie. Call 999—'

'*Mum!*' His sharp nudge shuts me up, and I gaze bleakly around the restaurant. There's more polished wood panelling, lit by glowing wall lamps with tasselled shades. Although the room is sizeable the effect of all this copious dark wood is making me feel like I'm trapped in a box. Or a coffin, more like. A coffin with the lid just put on. There are windows, but they're almost obscured by drapes and swags, like giant tartan knickers. It's all very posh, old-school Scottish and somewhat overheated. Or is that just me?

I tug off my jacket and glance down at my sweater, noticing with horror how bobbly it is. Did this happen suddenly as we power-marched here? It must be ninety-five per cent bobble. I can't take it off and stuff it into my bag, as I have a rank old T-shirt on underneath, unfit for public display. Maybe, I think wildly, Lyla and her mother aren't here after all. The receptionist got it wrong—

'There they are,' Eddie announces in a tone more suited to, *There's a parking attendant. Look, she's sticking a thing on our car.*

'Where?' I ask, heart thudding.

'Over there.' He nods towards a tiny blonde girl in a distant corner. She's raised an arm to attract our attention, and my mouth's interior is as dry as toast as we make our way towards her. Now an older, equally beautiful – also blonde – woman is waving too. Then they're both up on their feet, and we're greeted in a blur of introductions and unexpected hugs and artfully dishevelled hair.

'Hi, hi!' I say, inanely. How to act? They say I'm unflappable in the library, and despite what Eddie might think it's not all stamping books and tidying shelves. The odd drunk person blunders in, mistaking us for the kebab shop. We've had people falling asleep in the poetry section, vomiting by the kids' books and one crazy man shouted at Jamie for apparently 'looking at' him. Whatever happens in the library, I know what to do. And now I *don't* know.

'Lovely to meet you, Lyla, Shelley,' I start.

'It's Suki actually.' Lyla's mother beams, dismissing my apology with an elegant hand. I can see now that she's quite a bit younger than me – possibly early forties. Or maybe she's just better preserved.

'Don't worry! It's a silly name—'

'Not at all! It's a lovely name,' I insist.

'—A nickname from back in my teens. But it stuck. Please, sit down . . .'

I glance at Eddie as we take our places at the circular table. Panic is radiating from him as he lands next to Lyla. He looks as if he's realised he's in the wrong exam hall; the one for final medical exams when he's only done a day's workshop in cake decorating.

'Really nice to meet you both,' Lyla says, echoing her mother's easy charm. 'I've heard lots about you.'

I take a moment to register her calmness and poise. So we're plunging headfirst into the lie. 'We have too,' I manage. 'About you, I mean. We've been *so* looking forward to meeting you . . .' I glance at Frank in panic and he shoots me a warning look. Am I talking like a terrible actress, struggling with her lines?

'Well, you're lucky!' Suki casts her daughter a fond glance. 'All this time and she'd never even mentioned you, Eddie. Not until last week. And now this. Such a dark horse!'

He chokes out a dry snigger and twitches in his seat. 'You don't need to know everything about me, Mum,' Lyla chuckles.

'No. Obviously.' A wry smile from Suki. 'Hope you didn't mind coming here,' she adds.

'Not at all,' Frank says with forced enthusiasm.

'It's my ex's club.' Suki grimaces. 'Used to bring all his girlfriends here . . .' She chuckles again and I glance at

Lyla, wondering if that's her father she's referring to. 'Not Lyla's dad,' Suki clarifies. 'Jonathan was far too dull for that. Left him down in Gloucestershire with his hunting, shooting, fishing buddies. And Sebastian never comes here anymore because I'm never out of the place...'

She laughs again huskily. Everything about her suggests old money and ponies and a house in the country with soil-encrusted wellies lined up in the porch. And now she's telling us, 'I bought Lyla a little place just round the corner from here when she came up to study. And I was so jealous, because it's such a beautiful city, that I ruined it all for her by renting out my house down south and buying myself a place five minutes away! Didn't I, darling?'

Lyla nods and laughs. 'Absolutely ruined it,' she jokes. 'Mum would've enrolled on my uni course if she could.'

'So are you still studying, Lyla?' I ask because clearly, neither Frank nor Eddie are planning to say anything.

'No, it wasn't really my thing,' she says breezily.

'It's not for everyone,' I concur.

'Lyla was keen to get out in the real world,' her mother goes on. 'Wanted to start working and earning, didn't you, darling?' Lyla nods. '... So she started a freelance copywriting business, all by herself. Does all the marketing, client liaison, everything. Inundated with work, aren't you?'

'Yes,' Lyla agrees. 'It's crazy hours sometimes.'

'I'm so, so proud of her. She's so driven—'

'Mum, you're *embarrassing* me,' Lyla announces, looking pleased and not embarrassed at all. And I wonder how Eddie would react, if I were to gush about his achievements like this; how apparently he can pan-fry scallops perfectly and make a roulade. How just weeks ago he was sweeping the kitchen floor and how very proud we are.

I flick my gaze towards my son who's supposed to be familiar with Lyla's life and her wildly successful freelance business. How will a baby fit into all of this? Will Suki sweep in and take care of everything? I'll help, of course, if they'll let me. But what about Frank? How will he slot into a granddad role? I glance at him now, sitting there mutely in his yellow bear T-shirt, as if carved out of rock.

'I hear you're from Glasgow, Carly?' Suki says.

'Yes, that's right.' So Eddie and Lyla have exchanged a few basic facts as well as the other stuff. 'We live on the Ayrshire coast now,' I add, thinking: isn't it glaringly obvious that they're not a couple? They're both attractive young people but there's no chemistry, no spark between them. They could be strangers sitting together on the bus.

'And you're Portuguese, Frank? Is that right?'

'Yes. Yeah, that's right.' He nods grimly.

'My ex, Sebastian, has a place on the Algarve. A beautiful part of the world . . .'

When are we going to talk about the baby? Not yet, as now Suki is telling us about her childhood in rural Gloucestershire ('So, so, dull, I basically spent my first ten years swinging on a farm gate'), and how her current boyfriend – 'an *incredible* plumber' – is refitting her Edinburgh bathroom. 'Finally, a regular guy. Isn't he lovely, Lyles?'

'So lovely,' Lyla agrees.

'Nightmare, though,' Suki declares with an eye-roll. 'I know which taps I want. It's only *my* flat, *my* bathroom. But no, Tom knows best. But he's a sweetie really, I shouldn't complain, should I, Lyles? After all the duds I was due a good one . . .' All of this is delivered in a breathless stream while Frank watches her, agog, as if he's never encountered anyone quite like her before. Admittedly, there aren't many Sukis in Sandybanks. While sweat pools on my chest beneath my second-hand sweater, she looks as fresh as a daisy in a pale blue linen dress.

Finally, she stops to draw breath. 'We should order, Mum,' Lyla remarks, glancing around for a server.

'Yes, darling,' her mother says. 'They're awfully busy today, aren't they?' As if all this is normal and no one is pregnant and Eddie are Lyla are madly in love.

'So, um, Suki,' I start, grabbing at my chance to jump in. 'I wondered . . . I mean, I've been thinking, with this situation with Lyla and Eddie . . .' I catch a wave of horror crashing across my son's face. *Well, it's happening,* I transmit back to him. *We might as well face it instead of pretending we've all been thrown together to discuss Suki's bathroom fittings!* 'So I was thinking,' I go on, my heart thumping as I look around the table, 'that we should probably talk about how we're all going to—'

'—How we're going to celebrate?' Suki cuts in. 'Yes, of course. Excellent idea!' She cranes her long, slender neck and waves to a young waitress. 'Nina, love? When you have a minute?'

'Oh, Suki.' The girl hurries over. 'Sorry, it's nuts in here today . . .'

'No worries, darling. No worries at all. But when you have a minute I think we'd all *love* some champagne.'

CHAPTER FOURTEEN

Bollinger arrives and glasses are poured for Suki, Eddie and me. 'Have a tiny glass, Lyla,' her mother urges her. 'I drank all through my pregnancy and look how well you turned out.'

'Oh, okay then.' Lyla smiles.

Acknowledgement of why we're all here today – *finally* – gives me a mental shake, and I catch Frank eying the bottle with blatant regret. Not because of the cost – if he has money he's happy to blow it, and he's always been a generous man. No, I can see in his eyes that he's gasping for a proper drink, and perhaps I should have piped up, 'You have some, Frank. I'll drive home.' But I'm sorry, right now I need alcohol like air, and by the time we've learnt that Lyla is an only child – 'I'd have loved more but my marriage was over by then' – I have already guzzled a glass.

'So, what d'you do, Carly?' Suki asks.

'I'm a librarian,' I reply.

'How lovely. Such an amazing service and terrible that so many are shutting down . . . and you, Frank?' She turns to him.

'I'm a garage mechanic,' he says, mechanically, and it strikes me that we're acting like particularly unconfident contestants on my dad's favourite quiz show – stiff and awkward, hardly our *best selves*. I haven't built up the courage to tell my father about the baby yet. I can only imagine how he'll react, and I'm putting off the conversation for as long as possible.

'A practical man!' Suki beams. 'Fantastic. The best sort.'

She chatters on, barely drawing breath, wanting to know how we met: 'A holiday romance? How romantic! A proper love story . . .' She should have seen us an hour ago when Frank was shouting about pulling rabbits out of hats.

Our food arrives, by which time I'm sweating like a racehorse. Recently, I've decided I must be perimenopausal. At night I often lie awake, clammy and churning over people who wronged me twenty-five years ago. Not to mention recent events: Eddie's shock announcement and Frank pulling away from me, refusing to discuss anything at all.

I look down at the entire fish on my plate. It seems to be gawping at me with its dead eye. Having picked the first thing on the menu that jumped out at me, I've never felt less hungry in my life. I couldn't face breakfast either, and now, unsurprisingly, the champagne has rushed to my head as I hack at my bream or turbot or whatever it is. Gills, tail, *eyes* – the inedible bits seem to have taken over the plate. I'm making a hash of it as if I've only encountered fish in the form of fingers before. Meanwhile Suki removes her fish's entire skeletal system in one slick move, and Frank is stoking his mouth with hand-cut chips, as if trying to fuel himself through this crisis.

'And I hear you're a chef, Eddie?' Suki rests her fork on her plate.

'Yeah. Uh-huh.' His first words at the table.

'Which restaurant?'

'It's called Bracken,' he starts.

'Oh, I know Bracken! A gorgeous place and the food's amazing,' she enthuses, clearly familiar with tasting menus and wine parings. 'We must go soon, Lyla,' she adds. 'But I guess you two go there all the time?'

'We haven't actually,' Lyla says, addressing Eddie directly for the first time today.

'Um, no, we haven't.' He affects surprise, as if it's been an oversight. 'We should, though. Yeah.'

'Great.' I catch her shooting him a look: *could you act a bit more enthusiastic?* Although just twenty-two, like Eddie – apparently he's now managed to confirm that much – Lyla is a world away in terms of confidence and poise. Yet there's something fragile about her, physically. She's so pale and delicate, like a china doll in a simple long-sleeved pink top, her long hair loose, barely any make-up apart from a touch of lip gloss. I can't imagine how that tiny body will cope with a baby growing inside her. But then, that's what women's bodies are designed to do.

Eddie forks in a broccoli spear. So he's tolerating green vegetables now! That's nearly as surprising as the washed hair and smart trousers. Just as I'm thinking, perhaps he *is* mature enough to handle night feeds and colic and surviving on forty minutes' sleep a night, he coughs and splutters, seemingly uncontrollably, his face reddening and eyes filling with panic and tears.

'Are you all right?' I exclaim across the table.

He nods, still spluttering and coughing. He grabs wildly for Lyla's napkin, knocking over his full champagne glass and flooding the table as he presses it to his mouth. 'Shit!' he cries.

'Oh, Eddie—' I start.

'Sorry,' he croaks through the thick linen.

'Eddie, are you all right?' Frank barks as I jump up from my seat. To do what, I don't know. Wind him like a baby? Am I going to have to do the Heimlich manoeuvre today on top of everything else?

'I'm fine,' Eddie manages, waving me away. As I sit back down, he removes the napkin from his face, gulps some water and wipes dribble from his chin. Finally, the coughing subsides.

'Oh, Eddie. Are you okay now?' Suki asks kindly.

Eddie nods, still flushed a violent pink.

'Poor Eddie,' Suki says, obviously trying to defuse his embarrassment with humour as she turns to Lyla. 'Does he always do this in restaurants?' she teases.

'Yeah, all the time,' Lyla says, with an indulgent eye-roll. *Can't take him anywhere!*

The waitress glides over to blot the sodden tablecloth. We finish the champagne, and Suki chatters on, ordering a bottle of Chablis now as if this is all perfectly normal; five unlikely people thrown together for lunch.

She pauses and leans forward. 'I'm so glad you're both

happy with the situation,' she announces to Frank and me. Hang on, did we say that? 'See, you two met when you were young,' she adds, beaming now. 'And sometimes it's best to dive right in when you're full of energy and life.' So she's not putting on a brave front. She's actually thrilled about the baby. 'And you two are *so* young and beautiful,' she goes on, turning to Lyla, who's remained remarkably composed throughout, while Eddie now looks as if he is awaiting root canal treatment. 'Okay, you've only been together six months,' she adds. 'But that's long enough, isn't it, to know if someone's right for you? Don't you think, Carly?'

'Er, yes,' I manage, nodding. 'I suppose it is.' What else can I do?

'It's the best time of your life,' she enthuses, 'before you're bogged down in responsibilities...'

That's what a baby is, I want to cry out. *The biggest responsibility of all.* But perhaps I'm being a killjoy and overthinking everything, and it'll all be fine? Suki seems to think so.

'So,' I start, 'with the baby coming...' I glance down at the remains of my fish on my plate. It looks as if it's been torn apart by dogs. 'I wanted to say,' I continue, clearing my throat, 'to both of you—'

'Mum-it's-fine!' Eddie says sharply.

'No, Eddie, can I just say this please?' I blink at him, trying to transmit the message: *You're twenty-two and a dad-to-be so can you stop acting like you're twelve?* 'I just wanted to say,' I press on as Frank watches me expectantly, 'that this *is* a bit of a surprise. But if you're happy, Lyla, and Eddie is too, then me and Frank—'

'Oh, I'm so glad you're positive about it,' Suki interjects. 'And isn't it gorgeous, the way they met? Have you ever heard anything so cute?'

'Erm no,' I bluster, flushing instantly. 'I haven't.'

'I mean, what are the chances?'

'I *know!*' Eddie's gaze is boring into my forehead like a dentist's drill. I tip the rest of my wine down my throat.

'And we're all going to help you guys,' Suki announces.

'Yes, we are,' I say firmly. 'That's what I wanted to say. That we're here for both of you, and we'll do everything we can to help and support you.' I pause and catch Frank's eye. 'Won't we, Frank?'

'Yes!' he blurts out, voice croaky from underuse.

'I was a young mum,' Suki explains, when our table has been cleared. 'Just twenty when I had Lyla. And that didn't turn out too badly, did it, darling?'

'No, Mum,' she agrees with a smile. 'You did amazingly.'

Will Eddie and Lyla 'do amazingly' too? I look at my son, reminding myself that he's a grown man now – *on paper*. Then there are desserts, which Suki insists we all have. And when we're done, stuffed with nursery puddings and custard, she insists, squiffily, on paying the bill, despite my and Frank's protests: 'No, it's my treat. Absolutely.' Then we all tumble out into the bright March sunshine, which seems to sear my retinas as she hugs me, and then Frank, and says, 'Don't know about you but I'm in the mood for some shopping!'

'Mum, remember last time?' Lyla chides her playfully.

'*What* last time?' She giggles, linen jacket not worn but draped over her shoulders.

'You said you'd never go shopping again after wine!'

'I did, didn't I? Too many rash decisions. Never mind. You up for it, Eddie?'

'Oh no,' he says quickly. 'I'd really better—'

'I think we'll head back to Eddie's,' I cut in, thinking that we need time alone together, as a family. That's what we came for, after all: to speak to our son! To find out what's going on inside his head! But Suki is already saying, 'Come on then, Eddie. You're coming shopping with us. Bye, Carly, Frank. It's been absolutely lovely meeting you. A real pleasure.' Then she links one arm with her daughter and another with Eddie, who looks at us, eyes wide in alarm.

'I'm not sure Eddie wants to go shopping!' I start as if he can't speak for himself.

'Mum, it's *all right*,' he mutters, and Suki laughs.

'C'mon then!' As she leads them away, tottering slightly in her heels, I'm hit with a wave of panic that I may never see my son again.

CHAPTER FIFTEEN

Whatever I'd hoped to achieve on Saturday, it doesn't feel like I managed it. 'But you did,' Prish insists. 'You wanted to show Eddie that you're fully supportive, didn't you?'

'I guess so. But it didn't seem like I *did* anything. I just sat there and slugged wine and ripped a fish to pieces—'

'Oh, Carly.' Jamie squeezes my arm as we step down from the seafront onto the beach. Whatever the weather, we try to fit in a quick lunchtime walk, taking it in turns to man the library desk. Today we've left Marilyn on duty.

'You went along with the story,' Jamie reminds me. 'Pretending they're a couple, I mean. Most people wouldn't have done that.'

'We didn't have much choice,' I explain as we make our way across the flat, wide beach. 'Eddie just sprang it on us. I can't understand why. So he and Lyla had a one-night stand? Her mum seemed nice, y'know. Kind and supportive, not judgemental. I'm sure she'd get over it. And Lyla – well, she's young, but she's an adult. Surely you reach the point where you stop lying to your parents?'

'I don't know about that.' Grinning ruefully, he wraps his woollen scarf more snugly around his neck.

My heart squeezes. 'Oh, Jamie. I'm sorry. I didn't mean—'

'It's okay. But people can be weird.' He smiles and shrugs, his gaze following a gull as it soars overhead.

'I know, love. It must hurt so much.' I touch his arm. 'Still the same scenario at home?' Prish asks sympathetically. With his boyfriend, she means. In their late thirties, Jamie and Lewis have been together for several years, and are happily settled in a rented cottage a little way inland. We've had numerous gatherings in their beautiful garden on balmy summer's days. Yet whenever Lewis's parents visit from down south, Jamie has to decamp to the spare room and Lewis to the sofa bed, while Lewis's parents share their double bed. And for the duration of their stay, Jamie and Lewis act as if they're just housemates – although Jamie tends to make himself scarce as much as possible. I don't blame him. It's a ridiculous pretence and, understandably, Jamie finds it hurtful and ridiculous that Lewis can't find it in himself to be honest to his mum and dad.

'Yep, no progress there,' Jamie replies with a shrug.

I look at him as we turn back towards the steps. Reasoning, pleading, delivering ultimatums that he's never followed through; he's tried everything to persuade

Lewis to tell his parents that they're a couple. It seems blindingly obvious to me, and crazily out of time to perform such a charade when everyone else knows they're together. A cottage in the country, for goodness' sake, with a vegetable patch and an adorable brown and white collie! It all says cosy coupledom – but somehow, Lewis's parents don't register this, or resolutely choose not to.

'D'you think you can carry on like this?' I ask tentatively.

'Forever?' Jamie grimaces, stuffing his hands into his jeans pockets as we make our way back towards the library. 'Honestly, I don't know.'

'Maybe he's just scared,' I suggest.

'Scared of being written out of the will?' He smirks.

'You don't really think it's that, do you?' Prish exclaims.

'Sometimes I do,' he admits. 'I mean, they're a bit pompous and stuffy but they're not *that* scary. And even if they were—'

'You'd tell them,' Prish suggests, 'if it was you.'

He nods. I know Jamie's parents don't merely accept Lewis, but love him, as the son-in-law that he is. 'Anyway, how's your dad these days?' he asks, turning to me.

I smile. 'Oh, you know, his usual charming self.'

'Told him about Eddie's baby yet?' Prish crooks a brow.

'I'm . . . sort of building up to that.'

'The girls know, right?'

'Yes, they do.' At twenty-one Bella likes to assume the role of the most sensible one in our family – and to say she was shocked is an understatement. 'Does he realise what he's getting into?' I'm sure he doesn't, I'd replied. 'Has he even met a baby before? Does he know which way up they go?'

Ana had a different take. 'D'you think it could actually be the making of him? He might surprise us all!'

'And what about you, Nana?' Jamie teases. 'Got your head around being a granny yet?'

'Not really,' I admit. 'I still can't believe it's happening.'

'You're going to love it,' Prish says with a smile. 'Let me tell you, having grandkids is the most wonderful thing.' At fifty-eight, Prish is divorced and sporadically 'swimming optimistically in the sea of dating', as she puts it, on rare occasions when it's fun. More often, 'sea' is switched for 'cesspit', and she and Jamie often rib me about how lucky I am, being with Frank. But they see him only at barbecues and parties, chatting and laughing, at his sunniest.

Later that evening I look out from our kitchen and glimpse the feeble light at the shed's window. Tucked away at the bottom of our back garden, the shed has been quietly decaying for years. There's a workbench in there, but mainly it's been used only for storing my garden stuff. Until Eddie's announcement, that is. Since that day, the man who ravished me so deliciously in that Parisian hotel room seems to have been spending every spare moment out there.

Tonight I venture out and knock lightly on the shed door, hoping to coax Frank back into the house. 'Come in,' he calls out. Then: 'You don't have to knock, y'know.'

It feels as if I do, but I let it go and step inside. 'What are you doing in here?' I ask, hoping it doesn't sound accusatory.

'Just stuff,' he replies with a shrug. He's sitting at the old workbench with various bits of wood and tools and scraps of paper scattered all over it.

'Making something?'

'Just thinking really.'

'Couldn't you come inside and think with me?' I ask lightly.

'I'm all right.' *I'd rather be out here alone,* is what he means. It's hard not to feel rejected – but maybe it's me who's being needy? He only wants a bit of space, I tell myself, like all those times I've gone to the library early, simply to be alone.

'Oh, I thought that was lost years ago!' My gaze lands on the smooth stick he carved, when we'd just met. Our *Carly + Frank Forever* driftwood. It's sitting there on the bench in the dim glow of my old anglepoise lamp. I reach for it and trace its smooth curves with a finger.

'Yeah. It was in a box of old stuff.'

'Oh, right. A box of junk?' My chest tightens.

Frank nods, and I set it back down, realising now that I could cry. It's only a stick, for goodness' sake. Maybe I should take it and throw it for a dog on the beach, as it obviously means nothing!

'Night then,' I say quickly, and head back into the house. Let him hide away out there with the earwigs and spiders, and let Eddie resist communicating with me, bar the absolute minimum. He's made it quite clear that he doesn't 'need' any more visits from us at the moment.

He doesn't need *anything* and, seemingly, Frank doesn't either. Bella and Ana are living their lives, fiercely independent – and of course that's great. I wouldn't want them to be any other way. But still, it's strange to realise that no one wants or needs anything from me now. As if I don't matter. As if I might as well be a piece of driftwood myself, floating away in the sea.

There's nothing in *The Empty-Nester's Handbook* about that.

CHAPTER SIXTEEN

April

The days grow brighter and warmer and the daffodils come out, punctuating my borders with splashes of butter yellow. Scottish winters can be bitter and linger on for way too long. So I'm usually happy and grateful when spring finally shows its face. But this time, everything is different. Seven weeks have passed since Eddie's baby announcement and there's still a terrible feeling of distance between Frank and me.

One evening I sense my heart growing heavy as I march home from work along the seafront. On my back, my rucksack contains a selection of 20p books I picked out for Dad, plus some groceries for him, and his prescription that I collected at lunchtime.

I turn into our street and spot Frank's old banger parked outside our house. It doesn't mean he's back from work, as he often walks to Dev's garage; it's just on the edge of town. But now the light from our living room window tells me that Frank is definitely home.

I stop suddenly as my heart seems to snag. Kilmory Cottage has always felt like home, even when there was barely enough room in the living room for us all to sit comfortably. I thought I'd love it even more, when Frank and I finally had the place to ourselves. But something's changed, and now it feels hollow. Empty, really. I can hardly bear it.

Dad's expecting a visit this evening. Normally, I'd pop home for a quick cuppa first, and a catch-up with Frank, but now it hits me that I don't want to do that.

I don't want to see my own husband.

Another chilly reception is more than I can stand tonight. So instead of popping into the house, I climb into my own car, parked next to his, and I drive away.

I pull up at Dad's rather stark modern block at the edge of a smaller town than ours, seven miles along the coast. It's the home he shared with Maggie, the woman he left Mum for when I was a teenager – and who left him three years ago. Dad won't let me have keys to his flat. 'What would you need them for?' he asked, radiating surprise and suspicion in case – what exactly? I let myself in while he's sleeping and rummage through his private things?

'Just in case something happens, Dad,' I explained. But no – nothing will ever happen to Kenny Munro, and why on earth would I worry? At eighty-four he's *fine* living almost exclusively on tinned soups and stews, apart from the meals I make him, as has been the situation since Maggie walked out.

Things had been tricky between us in the early years. Naturally, my loyalty had been to Mum rather than Dad's new, younger and more glamorous girlfriend. But over the years I discovered how kind and sweet Maggie was, and how she'd loved Dad absolutely – until she'd had enough.

'I'm sorry, Carly,' she told me tearfully. 'I can't cope with him anymore.' I felt sorry for Dad, finding himself suddenly alone, but unable to admit that he was in any way hurt or upset. They'd been together for over three decades and yet he'd seemed more perturbed when a seagull had crapped on his living room window. But I understood why Maggie had left. It was Dad who'd bought this place, so she walked out with nothing. And, actually, I admired her courage.

Now Dad buzzes me in, and I carry up the shopping he always insists he doesn't need, but which I always bring, in addition to ingredients for dinner. 'What's all this?' he exclaims.

'Just a few bits,' I say, unpacking it in his tiny galley kitchen.

'All this food! How will I get through it all?'

We're talking a small selection of fruit and some posh vintage Cheddar, which he loves – although he only buys himself value-range industrial cheese, and only then when it's reduced.

'I'm sure you'll manage. And I was in the shop anyway, Dad.'

'Hmm. Well, that's up to you,' he says grudgingly, and I can't help noting the lack of thanks as I quickly wipe away a spillage of something sticky on the worktop. His somewhat functional flat has grown increasingly musty and unloved since Maggie's departure, despite my best efforts to clean it without him noticing. *I can do it! Why d'you think I can't take care of myself?* However, I can see why he fell for this place. The living room's sliding glass door leads onto a balcony, offering a spectacular view over the marina, and the sight of the bobbing boats and the glittering sea beyond is soothing, even in Dad's presence.

I unpack the books I've brought him, which he examines noncommittally, as if not sure what they are. 'And what's in *this*?' He glowers at the large paper bag as if he's never seen such a thing before. A bag with the pharmacist's logo clearly displayed. What does he think is in it? Turnips?

'I picked up your prescription, Dad.' *Don't rise to him,* I remind myself. *Don't rise, don't rise, don't rise!*

'Why do they think I need all this stuff?' Huffing, as if the medications are foisted on him for no reason, he starts to pull out the various packets. Always robustly fit – he worked as a high-ranking electrical engineer at a shipyard – Dad experienced his first ever health crisis last summer. He collapsed, alone, right here in this flat.

Still just about conscious, what he *didn't* do was call me – his daughter and sole offspring, living a convenient fifteen-minute drive away. He didn't call an ambulance either. Instead he somehow navigated all those stairs and climbed into his car. And then – a silly old heart attack won't stop Kenny Munro! – he *drove himself to hospital.*

It was the talk of the acute coronary ward. Once Dad was out of danger, Frank expressed surprise that he hadn't stopped by at the supermarket to see if there were any yellow-stickered bargains to be had.

And I was shocked to discover that my father had a heart at all.

So now it's all packets of pills – seven kinds a day –

which Dad is unpacking slowly, suspiciously, as if they may be radioactive. Reluctantly, he has also stopped driving, and I suspect this has only served to crank up his ill humour.

'What's *this*?' he barks.

Something thuds inside me as he glares at the yellow box. 'Don't worry about that,' I say quickly. 'It's Citrolax. That stuff you mix up with water to make a drink—'

'Yes, I can see that. But why have they given me it?'

'I did tell them, when I left a message on the surgery answerphone. I said you definitely don't need any more—'

'I've *never* needed it!' As if the presence of laxative powders in my father's home is a personal affront.

'No, I know that, Dad.'

'So why do they keep giving me it?' He glares as if I'm in cahoots with them – the mysterious 'them', who are convinced he can't poo without help.

Don't-rise-don't-rise-don't-rise. 'It's a mistake, obviously. Just throw it away,' I say lightly.

'What, and waste it?' Dad hates waste. On my last visit, suspecting that danger lurked, I quickly checked the bottom shelf of his kitchen cupboard. There sat a whole stash of vintage tinned steak and kidney pies, dented and rusting and emitting the threat of death. I made a mental note to deal with them next time.

Sure, he'll go mad, if he notices. But better than him being poisoned by prehistoric offal, surely? How would I live with myself if Dad died after eating that? Today – daringly – I plan to smuggle the tins out of his flat.

Right now, he's still rumbling on about the Citrolax. 'Keep it then,' I suggest, 'in case you need it one day.'

'Why will I need it?'

'Well, you might have, y'know, bowel trouble—'

'I *won't* have bowel trouble,' he says, aghast.

'Great! Fine! Throw it away then.'

'But these things cost money.'

'No, Dad. Prescriptions in Scotland are free.'

'It's taxpayers' money, isn't it?'

I open my mouth to reply but find myself staring mutely at the box. *Throw it over your balcony for the seagulls for all I care! Or sprinkle it over your toast and then see what happens—*

'Can you ring them and tell them to stop sending it?'

As far as communicating with his GP is concerned, Dad will at least permit my involvement. But only because the surgery's call queueing system drives him to fury.

'Yes, no problem, Dad.' I inhale slowly and fully, like Pilates Wendy is always telling us to. At the same time you're supposed to 'expand' your ribs, although I've never quite grasped this. *Push out your ribs at the sides, Carly. Picture your body flooding with oxygen.*

'Something wrong with you?' Dad frowns.

'No, no, I'm fine.' *Just, you know. Your grandson's about to become a father when he's not yet mature enough to be able to walk down the street with me. Instead, he charges ahead as if terrified that anyone will see us together. And, as far as I'm aware, he still leaves a trail of possessions wherever he goes: jacket, bank cards, ID. How will he manage with a baby? Will he leave it on the bus?*

Of course I don't say any of this, as I still haven't broken the news to Dad. Instead, I start to make dinner. Being windowless, his kitchen is pretty gloomy, but at least I can escape him for a short while, and give the surfaces a more thorough wipe-down. And now, as I try to wipe a film of gunk off a shelf crammed with spirit levels and old chipped mugs, an image of Suki pops into my mind.

Suki ordering Bollinger to toast an unplanned pregnancy.

Suki being so effusive and positive over me being a librarian, Frank a mechanic and Eddie starting out as a chef.

Such sunny positivity. God, I could do with a sprinkling of that, I decide as I chop an onion with unnecessary force. Dad and I should be quaffing champagne to celebrate the fact that his bowels are in perfect working order, and will continue to be until the end of time, because he's immortal, apparently!

I start to fry the onion and garlic, and as I add spices and chicken, a delicious aroma starts to fill the room.

I should be more Suki, I decide.

'Not too much for me,' Dad calls through. 'You always give me those ridiculously big portions.'

I don't, actually. I serve normal portions and, without fail, Dad always guzzles it all. Sometimes he even wants seconds.

He appears in the kitchen doorway, a little stooped now, although he's made a remarkable recovery from his heart attack. 'Managing all right in here?' he barks, as if unsure that I possess the skills to knock a meal together.

'Yes, I'm fine, Dad.'

I catch his gaze and something seems to twang inside

me. He can't help it, I remind myself. When I'm feeling together and strong, and I'm remembering to breathe properly as per Wendy's instructions, I can accept that this is just Dad; it's the way he's made. And in his own way he loves me, just as he loves Bella and Ana and, yes, Eddie too, even though he's hardly the cuddly granddad.

Will Frank be a cuddly granddad? I wonder as I take our bowls of chicken curry – Dad's favourite – through to the table by the window.

'Enough for a horse!' he announces, proceeding to tuck in with gusto. When we're finished I make a pot of tea and we watch the yachts bobbing in the marina. Above them, a cloud of starlings appears, swooping en masse above the spindly masts.

I put down my fork, noticing that Dad is watching the starlings too. 'I wonder why they do that?' I remark.

'What, the birds?'

'Yes. They keep swooping back and forth, not landing or going anywhere. All in a huge cloud like that.'

My father nods and his face seems to soften. I do worry about him, living here on his own. His friends seem to have all fallen away – or died – and he's not one for joining clubs or societies. But I catch a spark of something in his eyes as he says, 'I think they do it for fun.'

'You think so? Really?'

'Yes. Yes, I do.' I leave him still sitting at the table, watching the birds intently as I wash up. Then, while he's settled at the window, I bob down and inspect the tinned meat pies at the bottom of the cupboard. There are eight in all, and they went out of date before mobile phones came into popular usage. They pre-date Dad buying this place. Pre-date it being built, even! He must have brought them with him when he and Maggie moved here from their last place.

Stealthily, I pack the tins into my rucksack. And I send out silent thanks to the starlings for holding Dad's attention as I zip it up.

'That looks heavy,' he says later as I hoick it onto my back. 'What's in it? Bricks?'

'Just some work stuff,' I fib.

'What, books?' He frowns.

'Yes, books. Really heavy books.' I laugh awkwardly. Dad's a smart man. It wouldn't surprise me if his X-ray vision could spear right into my rucksack, to the pies that expired in 1998.

His clear blue eyes glint with suspicion. 'Thanks for those books,' he says, a little belatedly.

'You're welcome, Dad. They were just out of the 20p box in the library.'

'Quite right. No need to spend money on me.'

I smile, and as I hug him goodbye he says, 'Remember I don't need those bloody powders!'

'Don't worry! I'll remember!' Then I escape down the fifty-six steps Dad managed to navigate while having a heart attack, and step out in the cool evening.

The starlings are still swooping in the dusk, simply for fun. That's what I need, I decide. To do something that's not about earning money (I love my job but it's still work), or keeping Kilmory Cottage and Dad's flat to a standard that won't alert the authorities – but for myself. 'I need some fun!' I announce loudly to the birds above.

My God, after all that's happened lately I could do with a little light relief.

Then, as I'm walking to my car, my phone pings with a text: an unknown number.

I glance back at the flats. Dad has appeared at the top landing window, as he always does when I leave. I wave and he raises a hand in response. He'll be wondering why I'm standing there rather than climbing into my car. God forbid he should see me checking my phone. *It's all phones, phones, phones these days! People gawping at them like they've had their brains removed. Are they born with them glued to their hands?*

Rebelliously, I stand there, still clutching my mobile in full view of my father. Yes, Dad, I'm gawping at it like I've had my brain scooped out! I'm tempted to start walking while staring at it, and deliberately smack into a lamppost just to rile him.

Instead, I turn away, conscious of Dad's gaze spearing the back of the head. And I read the message:

Hi Carly, hope you don't mind, I got your number from your lovely son . . .

Suki. My heart crashes in panic. Is Lyla okay? And the baby?

. . . A group of us are going away to my little cabin up north this weekend. Just me and some girlfriends. It's a little place in the woods, lovely and secluded with a hot tub. I know it's short notice but bathroom renovations are doing my head in and I have to get away.

I stop, letting the information settle, and glance back at Dad. Although he's silhouetted against the landing light, I can sense him frowning. *It's all phones, phones, phones!* I smile broadly and give him another wave.

   . . . *Wondered if you'd like to join us?* Suki's message goes on. *With the baby coming I'd love to get to know you better and there's plenty of room. Please say you'll come. I'd say bring Frank but it's girls only, hope OK! Love Suki xx*

CHAPTER SEVENTEEN

Normally I wouldn't dream of saying yes. I don't know these women – I barely know Suki – and if I were to plan a weekend away without Frank, it'd be with Prish, Jamie and Marilyn. Occasionally we book a Travelodge in somewhere like Liverpool or Manchester and have a ball.

Plus, what about the whole ridiculous Eddie-and-Lyla-are-together charade? What if *that* came up? However, I can't help picturing Suki's cabin somewhere way out in the wilds. And being there, away from everything is sorely tempting.

I lug my rucksack out of the car and step into the empty house. Funny how the things that drove you mad about a person can become the very things you miss. Like the way Frank would always hang around, every time I was cooking, and give the pan a perfunctory stir – as if to 'help'. Then he'd taste it: 'Does that need more salt?' *If it needed more salt I'd have put some in!*

And the way he'd show me videos of golden retriever puppies on his phone, when I was trying to read in bed.

And insist on doing DIY projects in the kitchen, spraying sawdust everywhere, rather than tackling the job in the shed.

None of those things happen anymore. There's no unasked-for pot stirring now. No foisting of cute animal videos on me. These past few weeks – as our grandchild has grown from the size of an apple pip to a grape to a plum – I've craved the warmth of Frank's body, wrapped around mine. Is he depressed? Or angry with me? He's the one with the penis around here! Surely *he* should've had a chat about the facts of life with our son? It was his job, as a father. His contractual obligation, like dragging the wheelie bins out onto the street which, I have to say, he's also often neglected to do!

Having dumped my rucksack in the hallway, I go and open the back door and glare out at the shed. Its door opens and Frank steps out. 'Oh,' he says. 'You're back.'

Clearly, yes. 'Yep, just in.' No, *How was your day? How was your dad tonight?*

He trudges towards me and follows me back inside and into the living room where I snap on the TV. 'Everything all right?' he asks.

'Not really,' I say.

He frowns. 'What is it?'

I turn and glare at him. 'Frank, why are you spending so much time out there? In the shed, I mean?' After Dad's rant about the Citrolax, I don't care about sounding accusatory.

'No reason,' he replies with a shrug.

My heart is thumping now. 'There *must* be a reason. Why are you being so secretive? You're not usually. At least, you weren't before all this happened . . .'

'I'm not being secretive,' he exclaims.

'You are, Frank. Is it because you want to stay away from me? Because if you are—'

'Of course not!' Frank declares.

I glare at the TV. Prish has often reminded me how lucky I am, enjoying simply hanging out with my husband. Although we could rarely afford to go out, that never mattered because, on the rare occasions when it was just the two of us, we always cherished our cosy evenings together.

Now Frank comes in when I fetch him – when dinner's ready – and guzzles it like a starved teenager before sloping off out to the shed again. Some evenings I'm tempted to carry out his plate and set it on the ground outside the shed door. Let the gulls get it, for all I care!

'Frank . . .' My voice cracks, and I clear my throat. 'I feel a bit . . . lonely at the moment.'

He looks confused. 'Lonely? What d'you mean?'

'You know what lonely means. It's that kind of . . . hollow feeling. When you feel . . . alone.'

He shrugs infuriatingly, as Eddie might have done. Frustration rears up in me. 'Well, it was going to feel a bit weird, wasn't it, with Eddie leaving home?' he remarks. 'The empty-nester thing. You even bought a book about it—'

'It's not about Eddie or the girls being gone,' I say sharply.

'So what—'

'It's *us*!' I exclaim. 'It's me and you, Frank. That's why I feel lonely.'

'But why? I'm here, aren't I?' He looks genuinely baffled.

'It feels like you're not really.' My eyes prickle with tears, and I quickly blink them away. 'People can feel lonely in a marriage,' I add. 'They can feel shunned and pushed away and—'

'I'm not shunning you, Carly.' His forehead crinkles. 'I'm just . . . doing stuff. I'm fine—'

'Oh, I'm glad *you're* fine!'

'Carly!' he exclaims, placing a hand gently on my forearm. 'What's wrong?'

'Nothing,' I say firmly. And then, realising this discussion is hopeless, I thrust my phone, displaying Suki's message, at him.

Frowning, he reads it. 'Jesus. That's weird, isn't it?'

'It's a bit out of the blue, yeah . . .'

'Why d'you think she's asked you?'

Maybe my hormones are raging tonight, or I'm still all out of kilter after seeing Dad. Sometimes, the colossal effort of maintaining my cheery daughter act knocks me off-centre for hours afterwards. 'Maybe because she liked me?' I venture.

'Really?' His eyes widen in surprise.

'Well, yeah! I'm thinking that's probably the reason. Because some people – even people who hardly know me, Frank – aren't totally appalled by the idea of spending time with me!'

'Hey!' He tries to grab my hand.

Irritably, I shake him off. 'What's brought this on? I don't get it—'

'What I said, Frank. Just what I said—'

'Okay, okay! But obviously, you're not going, are you? On this weekend thing with Suki?'

I blink at him. 'Aren't I?'

He shakes his head in disbelief. 'I wouldn't have thought so. It's not exactly your kind of thing, is it?'

'What, having fun? Doing something spontaneous and making new friends? Spending time with the woman who's going to be a grandmother to Eddie and Lyla's baby? Because like it or not, Frank, they're having a child—'

'For God's sake!' he snaps. 'I do know that, Carly. I can hardly think about anything else.'

We fall into a grim silence. Then, as I'm about to get up and leave him simmering away on his own, he murmurs, 'She's a bit odd, though, isn't she? Didn't you think so, that day at the lunch?'

'What, Suki? Not especially,' I say, contrarily.

'Come on, you must've thought she was a bit bonkers. Didn't you?'

I glare at him. 'I thought she was nice, actually. You know – positive and supportive, unlike—'

'Okay,' he cuts in, eyes flashing. 'Say yes then, if you want to!'

I stare at him. So he's giving me permission to go away to Suki's cabin? Did Frank ask for my permission when he bought that food truck, with plans to spend the summer doing the festivals? 'It can't fail,' he'd insisted – but he tried one event and made a loss. He hasn't been able to sell the van either. It's still rusting away like a giant version of one of my father's tinned pies on the scrubby ground behind Dev's garage.

Still simmering with irritation, I put off replying to Suki's message for now. I don't want to say yes simply because I'm mad at Frank. That would be no reason to go. Later that night, as the wind rattles our ancient sash window, I try to figure out what to do.

My alarm trills just before seven, but Frank is up already, getting ready for work. He never used to set off before me. These days he rushes out with only a hasty goodbye. No kiss.

A little later I set off for the library. Its ornately carved tower comes into sight, red sandstone against a clear blue sky. My phone rings and I pull it from my pocket, expecting it to be Suki, wondering if I'm planning to come. But it's Dad.

'Everything okay?' I ask. He rarely calls me, and these days I know he enjoys a lie-in.

'Well, it wasn't *books* in your rucksack, was it?' he starts.

My heart seems to clang. 'What d'you mean?'

'My pies!' he announces.

'What pies?' Holy fuck.

'Those steak and kidney pies. You know what I mean. In the cupboard. Where have they gone?'

'Uh . . . Dad . . .' I exhale, realising someone is waving from the bus stop across the street. Helen, the family tree researcher, one of our regulars at the library. I smile brightly and wave back. 'I'm sorry. I should've said something. I just thought I'd clear out some space—'

'Clear out space? They were *my* pies, Carly! Where are they?'

In my wheelie bin, Father! 'I, um . . . moved them,' I mutter.

'You mean you threw them away?'

I take in a deep inhalation as I stride onwards, as if that way I'll feel strong and purposeful and unafraid of Dad. But it's not working. Because now, instead of being a fully-grown adult woman heading to work, entrusted with library keys, I'm flung back to being ten years old, and frankly scared of the man who presided over our little family of three.

Yes, I'd deserved it. For some mad reason I'd stuffed a Caramac bar into my pocket in our local corner shop.

I didn't mean to take it! I was going to pay! Having spotted my despicable act, the shop owner, Mr Blyden had cornered me and phoned my dad. The two men played golf together. I was sent home to face my father; he wasn't a hitter but, God, he could shout. How I'd wished for brothers and sisters, not just to absorb some of his wrath but to huddle up with, when I'd been sent to my room. That's why, once we had Eddie, I knew I wanted to have more children, if we possibly could. It's why I loved Raj, Calum and all of the kids' friends cramming around our table and filling our kitchen with laughter and noise.

A full nest. How I loved it.

And now, as Dad insists that those ancient pies are perfectly fine, I sort of phase out and let him rant.

Suki's message. An invitation to a weekend away.

'. . . No idea why you decided to do that. What on earth were you thinking? You know I hate waste . . .'

Someone who actually wants to spend time with me, even though I sat there sweating in the restaurant in a bobbly old sweater I bought off Vinted.

'. . . And to not even say anything to me!'

A luxury cabin in the woods. It sounds like a fairy tale.

'Carly?' Dad barks.

'I threw them out.' I say it quickly, like ripping a plaster off. Better to get it over with.

'Why?'

'Because they were old and rusty and—'

'Tins don't go out of date.'

'They do, Dad. They *do*. Otherwise why would they put dates on them?'

'That's a new thing, sell-by dates.'

Not that new, I think, *considering the pies expired around the time Take That broke up*. 'No it's not. They've been around as long as I can remember—'

'It's all this woke nonsense. The world's gone mad—'

'Sell-by dates are *woke*?'

'Tins are fine until they blow!'

Still gripping my phone, I pull out the big bunch of keys from my pocket and unlock the library's main door. 'They blow when there's a gas build-up, Dad. Is that what you want? So the contents are actually fermenting—'

'You're trying to take over my life,' he retorts.

'No, I'm just trying to stop you getting food poisoning,' I shoot back. 'But I didn't mean to upset you. And okay, I probably overstepped the mark. I realise that now and I'm sorry.'

The door opens and I step inside, inhaling the still, cool air that's lain undisturbed all night. Heading for the kitchen, I pull off my jacket and fill the kettle and click it on. 'I'll replace them,' I add. 'How many were there again? Eight?'

I exhale slowly, certain that I can sense the oestrogen leaving my body. No one warns you about this: that sometimes it goes quietly, like a neighbour leaving after a cup of tea. At other times it's like a crowd surging out after a gig, spilling out onto the pavement and having a brawl.

'Oh, don't bother with that.' Dad's tone softens.

'If you're upset I will. I don't mind. I'll bring them next time I come over—'

'No, it's fine,' he mutters, and the silence stretches between us. *I do my best, can't you see that? I bring you groceries and books and your medication, and cook for you and clean your flat. I sit and watch* Cash or Crash *with you, when you shout at the TV and mock the contestants who get seemingly simple questions wrong.*

It feels cruel, when you do that. You can be cruel, and so can Frank, although it's a different kind of cruelty. Two men, whom I try to keep happy.

Well, fuck that, I decide as the kettle comes to the boil and switches off.

'Well, I'm sorry anyway,' I say briskly. 'But I'm at work now, Dad. I'd better get on.'

'Are you? All right.' He clears his throat. 'So, I'll see you at the weekend, will I?'

I pour boiling water over the teabag. 'Actually, not this weekend,' I reply.

'Oh.' He sounds taken aback. 'Look, Carly, I was

just upset,' he adds gruffly. 'It was a bit of shock to see everything gone. But I didn't mean—'

'It's not about the tins, Dad,' I cut in quickly. 'That's not why I won't be over to see you this weekend.'

'What is it then?'

'Something's come up. I'm going away, so I'll see you next week, okay? Bye, Dad.'

And then I finish the call and reply to Suki's message: *That's so kind of you! Thank you. I'd really love to come. Cx.*

CHAPTER EIGHTEEN

My ten-step preparation plan for Suki's cabin weekend:

1. Shave legs, underarms, bikini line, knees. (I had hairy knees! How had this escaped my notice?) Marvel at how much fuzz there was to remove from my various areas. Enough, if it was gathered in a bucket, to carpet a hutch. Is that why Frank's gone off me – because it's like being in bed with a guinea pig?
2. Select outfits for a weekend of – what exactly? Not knowing what we'll be doing makes it especially tricky to pack. A few weeks ago, fired up by *The Empty-Nester's Handbook* – 'Now's the time to freshen up your look!' – I ordered a couple of items from the dog-end of the Boden sale. Trouble is, things look lovely online, but seem to come to me via the Frumpification Plant: what I picture as a vast, faceless factory where all of their loveliness is

obliterated. Dismiss dowdy items in favour of jeans/sweater old faithfuls.
3. Hunt for swimwear. Discover that my sole swimsuit has been quietly decaying to the point of almost total transparency at the bottom of a drawer. Which means a replacement must be bought.
4. Order new swimsuit online, opting for next-day delivery. Pray that it fits.
5. Do nails (hands & feet).
6. ENGAGE CORE!!!
7. Leave what I hope is an extremely clear voice note on Dad's GP's message service, giving my father's full name and date of birth. *It's about his repeat prescription. Can you please take Citrolax off the list? He's never needed it and, uh, he's quite agitated that every month there's a big box of it and—* The message cuts off with a piercing tone, and I'm loath to go through all the options again.
8. Panic that I should take a present to Suki's cabin. But what? Aided by Jamie's keen eye, I scour the charity shops in our lunch break (that's one thing Sandybanks has an abundance of), homing in on a wicker hamper in perfect condition. *Is this enough?* I wonder as I fill it with treats from the posher reaches of our local supermarket. When we had lunch that day Suki was all, 'Let's have champagne!' I know better than to bring Blossom Hill. But are the wines I've chosen classy enough for her group?
9. Picturing these women – gorgeous and glamorous with 'places' dotted around the globe – I panic some more and add a bottle of champagne.

10. Pack a bag. I can't help remembering how different it felt, to be deciding what to take to Paris – so thrilling! This time Frank seems to be taking zero interest in the fact that I'm going away.

And so, by the time Friday comes, I explain to Frank that I'll be eating later up at the cabin, and can he knock together something for himself?

'Of course,' he says. I leave him pondering the options as I carry my bag and the hamper to the front door.

Finally, he seems to take notice of what's happening. 'Have a nice time then,' he says lightly. As if I'm going to Pilates and not for a weekend away with a woman I barely know, yet with whom we are about to become entwined – forever – by Eddie and Lyla's child.

'Thanks,' I say.

He leans in the kitchen doorway, observing me in an oddly detached way. 'Think it's going to be all right then?'

'I hope so.' I pause, trying to read his expression. 'Why, d'you think it's mad that I'm going?'

'No, no. You *go*,' he says with unnecessary force.

I frown. 'Frank, is something wrong?'

'No,' he says, with emphasis. Then: 'I just think it might be a bit awkward, y'know?'

'Why's that?'

'Well, with all this pretence about Eddie and Lyla being a proper couple, or whatever—'

'I'm sure that won't come up,' I say. Infuriatingly, he only shrugs, as if he doesn't care one way or other. 'Bye then,' I add.

'Bye.' No coming towards me for a hug. He just stands

there, arms folded, like another time recently when he'd fished out a cluster of bra underwires and my long-lost back door key from the bowels of our washing machine. Helpfully, he'd set out the whole lot on the worktop, like museum exhibits, for me to see.

What did he want me to do? Apologise for the wires breaking free from my bras? As an act, it seemed terribly petty. I couldn't help thinking, what's happened to the man who moved hundreds of miles to be with me, because my mum was terminally ill? *Of course I'd come,* he told me, holding me close. *Did you honestly think I wouldn't?*

Frank was always a little crazy and impetuous but I knew he loved me. I could depend on that. Yet since Paris he hasn't touched me once. He's certainly not been 'put off' by my hairy legs or even those bristly knees. These days my entire body could be swathed in luxuriant fur and I doubt he'd notice.

I turn towards the door and finally, he moves. 'D'you want a hand with that?'

With the hamper, he means. 'No, no, I'm fine.'

'Carly, let me carry that,' he says. But clearly it's more sensible of me to shun his help, and to struggle to open the front door while gripping the hamper and my overstuffed weekend bag. 'Give me that!' he commands, trying to take the hamper off me.

'Frank, I'm fine!'

'Don't be silly, it's too heavy—'

'I can manage!' I snap. Am I turning into Dad now, angrily shunning offers of help? Frank grabs for the wicker handle, and as I tug it away the hamper slips from my grip.

'Hey!' he shouts as it tumbles to the floor, the lid flying open and cheeses and crackers and chocolates scattering and bottles clanging. At least the wine bottles don't smash. But the champagne bottle does, shooting liquid and shards of glass all over the hall floor.

'Oh God!' I cry.

'Fucking hell, Carly.' We gaze down at the broken glass and the fizzling lake we're standing in. 'Champagne?' He grimaces.

I nod. 'Yes, champagne.'

'Jesus.' Then: 'You were taking it to the cabin?'

For a moment I absorb what he's just said. 'Yes, Frank. I was taking champagne to the cabin.' He gives me an inscrutable look, and then stoops to pick up the biggest pieces of broken glass. I try to reassemble the hamper as best as I can, and then sweep up the glassy splinters and mop the hall floor. As he stands there, watching me, I think: *I'm really not sure anymore.*

The ice cream shop and bakery and food truck all made me angry, at the time.

But I still loved Frank. There was never any doubt about that.

I take the dripping mop back to the kitchen and wash my hands. Then we head out to my car with Frank carrying the hamper.

'Was it a problem, me taking champagne?' I ask as he places it on the back seat.

'Of course not.' A pause, then: 'But it does seem like quite a lot.'

I look at him, realising it's not just Frank who clearly feels differently now.

It's me too. Something has clicked in me, deep in my gut.

'Well, I'm not taking it anymore, am I?' I say. Then I climb into my car and drive away.

CHAPTER NINETEEN

At first, as I head north, I can't help wondering if I've made a terrible mistake in accepting Suki's invitation. But then, if I'd stayed at home how would the weekend be? I really need some space away from Frank. Perhaps he's relieved, too, that I'll be out of his hair for a couple of days.

Dusk is falling and a bright moon shines above, triggering something in me. It's a flicker of excitement, sparking through my body now. I spot them then, silhouetted against the darkening sky: starlings swooping in a glorious cloud, back and forth, just for fun. I smile, reminding myself that this is exactly what I've needed. To do something spontaneous, just for myself.

It's properly dark as the satnav tells me to come off at the next junction. I drive through a sleepy village where the whitewashed pub and a cluster of single-storey cottages look so cosy and inviting. Now the winding road leads me away from the village and high up into the hills. To my right the land scoops down towards a loch, illuminated by moonlight in a clear night sky. In the distance there's a castle, perched on a mound, silhouetted against the gleaming water. It's a ruin, the kind Eddie loved as a kid – the crumblier the better, as far as he was concerned. He and Bella and Ana would run wild, shrieking that the castle was under attack, and they'd defend it with imaginary bows and arrows.

As children the three kids got along extremely well: a little gang, usually organised by Bella even though she was the middle child. But as they grew older Eddie seemed to pull away from his sisters, and no coaxing on their part could persuade him to join in with their games. 'Why won't Eddie play with us anymore?' Ana asked me on holiday once, looking hurt.

'He's maybe just a bit too old now,' I said, aware of a pang of sadness. I wondered if it was a gender thing, and that he felt left out with his sisters sharing a bedroom, doing virtually everything together. Soon the girls stopped asking and left Eddie to do his own thing.

The road has narrowed now, and as it twists and turns sharply, my confidence starts to ebb away. What was I thinking, coming here? Is the hamper acceptable or will they notice that the cheeses are a little dented from the 'incident' back at home? What will they make of a librarian who buys ninety per cent of her clothes second-hand? Not to mention the fact that Suki thinks Lyla and Eddie are madly in love! Although I hate to admit it to myself, perhaps Frank was right to be dubious about me coming up here.

The road takes me through a thick, dense forest. I

emerge, high above the valley, then plunge down again, braking suddenly as a deer appears on the road. It stops and looks at me, then canters away, long-limbed and graceful, into the woods. I pass a hand-painted sign at the roadside. It reads 'Red Squirrel Watch', which reassures me a little. Hopefully, this weekend will be all about being in nature, rather than discussing Eddie and Lyla's loving relationship that doesn't even exist.

And now, as I round a bend, the satnav tells me I've reached my destination. But there's nothing here on the narrow lane, bordered on both sides by thick pine forests. Briefly, I pull up at the roadside to check Suki's last message. Glenfail Cabins, the place is called. Although she sent directions, I have no signal now and Google Maps won't work. Plus, my phone's down to seven per cent. In my haste to leave earlier I'd forgotten to charge it. And now I'm cursing myself as the road seems to lead me deeper into the forest, in the dark.

I pull over again and look around for anything that might count as a landmark. There are only trees, forming a bank of darkness with the road cutting through. An owl hoots and light rain is spattering my windscreen. I check the time: almost eight. I'm running late already. Suki was expecting me at around half-seven. I climb out of my car and try Google Maps again. No luck there – but at least now there's one bar of signal. I don't want to call Suki for directions. What I really want is to spirit myself back home, where I'll learn to accept that Kilmory Cottage feels horribly empty now, and somehow figure out how to live with it.

That's okay, I decide. I'll adjust, but if Frank and I

carry on like this, who knows? Perhaps it was only the kids who were holding us together, throughout our ups and downs and financial disasters. And now they're gone, there's nothing left.

Prish left her husband after the last of their kids had moved out. 'My second act,' she called it – just like it says in the book. She took up running, and has chalked up three marathons and seems to have shed a decade from her face; she is *ageing in reverse*. And what have I done? Driven north for two and a half hours and got myself lost in the woods!

I look around wildly for something to pin my location on. And then I spot it, through the steady rain. A wooden gate to what looks like a farm. I stride towards it while calling Suki, relieved that the farm has a name, so at least I'm *somewhere*.

She answers straight away. 'Thornyhill Farm? Oh, you're so near us! Sorry you got lost, Carly. I should've sent clearer directions . . .'

'No, it's my fault,' I say. 'I really am hopeless at finding places, even with satnav . . .' Frank has always been the one who knows the way, I reflect with a twang of shame. And I make a mental note to be self-sufficient from now on – to not need him for anything as Suki says, 'Hang on, Carly . . .' Then, to someone else: 'She's down that forestry lane, the one just past the phone box in the village, you know?' It's a male voice that seems to respond. 'Yes, *okay*,' Suki says impatiently. 'I'm trying to explain. She's taken a wrong turn . . .'

'Suki?' I start. 'Don't worry. I'll set off again now. I'm sure I'll find you—'

'No, just wait there,' she insists. 'Stay where you are. He's coming to get you now.'

'Er . . . who is?'

'Oh, I should have said. Sorry! It's my brother, Oliver.' So not a girls' weekend after all? 'He gatecrashed,' she adds, lowering her voice. The sound quality has changed, as if she's stepped outdoors. 'He has stuff going on. But it'll be fine, I promise . . .'

'Okay, if you're sure,' I start.

'Absolutely. He'll be with you in ten minutes so sit tight.'

So I wait as rain spatters my windscreen. And when a Land Rover pulls up I spring out of my car like a dog being released for a walk. 'Thank you!' I exclaim, bounding over to the driver's side window.

Suki's brother seems to pause before lowering it. It feels like a reprimand; a light tap on the wrist. 'You must be Oliver? I'm Carly. Honestly, I thought I knew where I was, but then it all went wrong and I lost signal . . .'

'No problem,' he remarks in a tone that says, *It actually is*. I take in the cool blue eyes behind black-framed spectacles, and the resigned expression. He is regarding me like a beleaguered teacher dispatched to round up an escapee on a school trip.

'Anyway, sorry,' I bluster, pushing back my damp hair. 'And thank you.'

Oliver nods. 'Let's get going, shall we?' The window closes, and I scamper to my car and we set off.

As I follow, Oliver makes no concession for the fact that I don't know the roads around here. It takes intense focus to keep him in sight as the Land Rover whips around corners and bumps along narrow lanes. By the time he slows down, and a scattering of golden lights comes into view, I have already decided that coming here was lunacy on my part. I only said yes because Frank assumed I wouldn't come, and Dad was mad about the pies. 'I'll show them!' I decided. Show them *what*, exactly? They'll barely notice I've gone.

Oliver turns into a clearing where several A-framed log cabins are clustered at the edge of the woods. All is quiet and still as we park and climb out. 'Thank you *so* much,' I gush again as I lift my bag and the hamper from the back seat.

'Here, I'll take that,' Oliver says, and I hand the hamper to him.

'Thanks.' As we make our way towards the cabins I glance at this tall and slim, rather stern and reserved-looking man. It's hard to reconcile that he and Suki are brother and sister. Physically, there are clear similarities: the fine features, the clear blue eyes and rangy build. But of course there's no reason why he'd be all bubbly and gregarious, all 'Let's have champagne!' like his sister.

'What an amazing place,' I announce.

'It is, yeah,' Oliver agrees. The cabins are all uniquely beautiful, each decking area immaculate with potted shrubs and hanging bird feeders. Some are occupied, their lights glowing invitingly. Strings of lamps, placed high up in the trees, bathe the settlement in a pool of golden light. Now the rain has stopped and the heady scent of pines pervades the cool night air.

'D'you come up here a lot?' I ask.

'Not really.' No further information supplied. He's probably just arrived, I tell myself. The last thing he wanted was to be dispatched to rescue some woman he doesn't even know, and then be expected to make small talk. However, walking together in silence feels awkward, so I plough on.

'So, whereabouts are you from?'

'Gloucestershire,' he replies.

'Oh yes, of course. Suki told me . . .'

'But I'm in the process of moving,' he adds vaguely, and I stop myself from asking where from, and where to. Because clearly, he's interested only in ferrying me to Suki's cabin; job done. 'That's the one,' he adds, indicating a cabin set a little away from the others, tucked into the woods.

'It's beautiful!' I gush, and now Suki has appeared on decking strewn with twinkling fairy lights.

'You made it! Hi!' The grin lights up her face as she hugs me, and Oliver and I follow her into the cabin.

'Yes, finally. I'm so sorry about getting lost. And thanks, Oliver,' I reiterate as he places the hamper on the counter top.

'Ooh, what's that?' Suki asks.

'Only a few things I brought . . .'

'You needn't have. You *are* lovely.' She unbuckles the hamper's leather straps and gasps in delight at the selection of wines and cheeses and chocolates as if everything is box-fresh. 'How lovely! You're so kind.'

'Honestly, it's nothing . . .' I look around the cabin's spacious open-plan living area. A squashy pale grey sofa and comfy chairs, strewn with fluffy sheepskin throws, are arranged around a flickering wood-burning stove. The sleek kitchen has an island unit with chrome stools neatly lined up. At the large window, looking out onto the clearing, a rustic oak table is set for dinner.

'This is gorgeous,' I announce.

'Thank you.' She beams.

'How long have you had this place?'

'Couple of years now. Little present to myself. I do love it. I've tried to make it a little sanctuary.'

'Oh, you've done that.' I smile, soothed now by the wood burner's orangey glow, and the fact that Oliver has disappeared, presumably to his room. *Just forget about how weird this all is,* I tell myself. *Forget about what it is that's brought you together.*

'Let me show you your room,' she says, leading me off the main space and into a short corridor. She indicates the various doors: 'Oliver's in there. Dinah's there. She and I are sharing . . .'

'Dinah?'

'My friend.' She drops her voice to a murmur. 'Having a nap, I think. Amazing person. Pretty intense. Can't wait for you to meet her. Anyway,' she adds, 'bathroom's at the end there, and this is yours . . .' She opens a door into a compact but cosy single room and follows me in.

'This is lovely!' I say.

'Sorry it's not en suite,' she adds, as if I'd mind.

'Honestly, it really is lovely. Thanks so much for inviting me.'

She smiles, but tension flickers around her blue eyes as she gently closes the bedroom door. 'I'm just happy you could come. And I'm glad you like it. We can do walks or go for drives, if you like? I can show you around the area tomorrow . . .'

'Great,' I enthuse.

She seems to hesitate before going on. 'Honestly, I'm so glad you're here, Carly. I can't tell you.'

I look at her quizzically. 'Why, is everything—'

'Oh, it's fine,' she says quickly. 'It's just, this isn't exactly Dinah's thing. Being stuck out in the country, I mean. She likes being near – you know. Facilities. Goes all funny if she's outside a five-mile radius of a branch of Cos . . .'

I splutter. 'Oh dear.'

'Yes, exactly. And then I thought, Carly! She's easy-going and friendly. You know how it is, with a group?' she goes on. 'How people balance each other out?'

'Er, yes,' I say, still not quite grasping the situation here.

'. . . And I invited Oliver because he's had a tough time lately, since the break-up. *Wife-left-him*,' she mouths.

'Sorry to hear that,' I say, and she grimaces.

'Making it all sound rather grim, aren't I?'

'Not at all!' *It sounds like loads of fun, absolutely . . .*

'Anyway, everything's going to be okay. It'll be great,' she says brightly. With that – and a sudden, 'I'll get supper started!' – she breezes out.

I start to unpack, still reeling from the flurry of information. So Suki thinks I'll somehow 'balance things out' between two guests who, I gather, don't want to be here? Seeing that my phone has died, I plug it in and perch on the bed, waiting for it to come back to life, and hoping that Frank might have messaged to check I arrived safely. But there's nothing. So I get up and take in the view of the velvety night sky, filled with glittering stars. The only sound is a faint rustle of wind through the trees. Then there's movement from the main room, and a woman – presumably Dinah – pipes up: 'So, is she here, finally?'

'*Yes*,' Suki says, her agitation palpable.

'Well, I don't know how I'm going to sleep a wink having dinner so late . . .'

So late? How old is she – six?

'It's not that late,' Suki reasons. 'Only a quarter to nine. And we're just about ready, if you could grab some glasses please, Dinah . . .'

Keen not to delay things further, I quickly check my face in the oval wall mirror and tug my brush through my hair. Then, trying to rally myself, as I do whenever I climb those stairs to Dad's flat, I take a deep, fortifying breath and stride through to join the jolly gang for dinner.

CHAPTER TWENTY

Kenny

Kenny is still a little stung that his daughter had better things to do than pop in to see him at the weekend. But at least he won't have her going on at him. About taking his pills, that is, and eating fresh food. Fruit, she keeps bringing him. What does Kenny Munro want with *fruit*? Not to mention her obsession with sell-by dates. What was she thinking, throwing out those pies? He's still reeling with the shock and wrongdoing of perfectly good food going to waste. 'Young people,' he mutters out loud. Not like his generation, born in wartime, with rationing, his mother baking cakes with dried egg.

'Granddad's *always* talking about the war!' He remembers Ana giggling about this with her mum some years ago.

'Well, it was a pretty big deal, love,' Carly remarked.

'But so long ago,' she added, always the cheeky one. 'Things have moved on!'

Unable to settle on the war documentary he's currently

watching, Kenny flicks over to watch *Cash or Crash* on catch-up. It's his favourite quiz show. However he's feeling, it always lifts his mood.

'How many legs does a tripod have?' the quizmaster asks.

The middle-aged man looks nervous in his tight grey shirt. 'Seven?'

Kenny guffaws in derision. He loves it when contestants show themselves to be idiots. Too busy poking at their phones, that's the problem. Thus cheered by the lunacy of today's world, he realises it's nearly nine o'clock and he hasn't had any dinner.

Stomach growling now, he wanders through to the kitchen. He doesn't head for his usual cupboard where he stores his tins – but the other place. The secret place where he'd stashed some of the overflow. These other tins, he'd tucked away in a different cupboard, behind the half-used cans of wood varnish and paint stripper and a dented flask that probably still has the residue of decades-old tea in it.

It's not tea he wants now as he pulls out various items to reveal the treasures hidden within. It's the tinned fish he bought when it was on offer at some weird little grocers, close to the last place he lived. The shop was closing down and, unable to resist a bargain, Kenny had bought the dozen tins for mere pennies. Maggie had teased him for packing them up when they were moving to this place. 'We're not taking those with us, are we?'

'*Yes*, we're taking them,' he retorted, and she'd let it go. She was an easy-going sort, kind and attentive and treating Kenny like a lord. Cooking, cleaning, shopping, arranging their holidays and dragging home the Christmas tree from the bloke who sold them out of his garage; all of that was Maggie's area.

Until that Christmas, over three years ago now, when she'd gone out for the tree as usual. But instead of buzzing the intercom so he could go down to help her to carry it up, she'd burst into the flat like a hurricane, having dragged it up the fifty-six stairs all by herself.

'Here's your tree!' she'd announced, flinging down the five-footer in the hallway and promptly bursting into furious tears.

Why hadn't she asked for help? And it wasn't *his* tree; it was Maggie who insisted they had one. The only reason it had to be carried home on foot was because Kenny wasn't prepared to have his car littered with needles. Surely that was reasonable?

That afternoon, Maggie packed her bags and called her sister, who drove over to whisk her away. And Kenny has never seen or even heard from her since that day. It was pretty shocking, to discover that the woman he'd assumed was perfectly fine, boiling his eggs for the requisite six minutes and pairing up his socks for all those years, wasn't fine at all.

Why hadn't she just said?

Women! They are a complete mystery to Kenny Munro.

Anyway, he's not bothered about Maggie anymore because it's easier really, living alone at eighty-four years old. He can please himself – at least when Carly's not here, forcing laxative powders on him and telling him off about his tinned food. And this weekend, knowing she's far away with someone or other, he can do – and crucially, eat – whatever he likes.

This stuff's fine, Kenny tells himself as he extracts a can of pilchards in tomato sauce from the very back of the shelf. It's rusting and bulging a bit, but it's what's *inside* that counts. That's the canning process for you, he thinks, still smirking at that idiot man who didn't know what 'tripod' meant. Tinned food lasts forever.

He opens the cylindrical can with some difficulty, as his ancient tin opener – also speckled with rust – has almost seized up. But finally, with no small degree of grunting and determination, he manages to tear off the lid.

This is the life, Kenny reflects, dropping two slices of stale white bread into the toaster. As it toasts, he forks the pilchards in their blood-red sauce into a small saucepan. They smell pretty strong but then fish does smell; that's the point of it. If it didn't you'd think something was wrong. Kenny feels satisfied now that he's using up his stores and that Carly isn't here to interfere. Because he isn't one to waste things. Food, for one thing. And time, for another. So while he waits for his toast to toast and his pilchards to heat up, he fills a large tumbler with scotch and knocks it back in two gulps.

Multi-tasking, he reflects with a smile. At the shipyard he was always excellent at that, juggling numerous projects at a time.

Things are working out perfectly tonight. All alone in his little flat, as rain batters the windows, he carries his pilchards on toast and a refill of scotch to the small table by the window. He tucks in with gusto, his pleasure enhanced by the whisky and how he imagines Carly's reaction to be, if she could see him now.

'Dad, you can't eat that! You'll kill yourself!'

'Young people today.' He chuckles, forgetting for a moment that his daughter is in fact fifty this year and has raised three children to adulthood herself.

'Call me if you need anything,' she'd said before she swanned off on this mysterious weekend. As if he would!

Kenny shovels in the warm pilchards and toast and takes a big swig of scotch. What would he possibly need her for? As the alcohol floods his veins, he congratulates himself on the fact he doesn't need anyone for anything. Not Carly or Maggie or *anyone*. Then, leaving his fishy plate on the table, he settles on the sofa for another episode of *Cash or Crash*, laughing heartily at some brainless woman who thinks the capital city of Mexico is bloody Calcutta!

CHAPTER TWENTY-ONE

Carly

'No I don't,' Dinah exclaims across the table. As if I'd asked, *Do you suffer from incontinence, Dinah?* I'd only wondered if she had any children, and it's not the first thing I asked tonight. I mean, I didn't dive right in, presumptuously, as Suki dished up perfectly cooked spaghetti with garlicky prawns, plus a watercress salad and delicious sourdough and posh deli butter and the cheeses I brought, all accompanied by lashings of chilled white wine. The children issue surfaced only after a somewhat stilted exchange of all of our background information, during which I felt as if I'd been grilling both Dinah and Oliver, although it wasn't intended that way. But there's something about awkward pauses with strangers that triggers a need in me to fill them.

'What d'you do, Oliver?' I'd asked.

'I work in nature conservation,' he replied. Again, no further info supplied.

'He's doing amazing things with beavers,' Suki

announced with a little laugh. And in any other situation I'd have had a giggle about this too.

'What kind of things?' I asked.

'We're reintroducing them to the area,' he replied, sending the clear signal that he didn't want to go into it all now.

I was about to ask more but the tiny spark in me fizzled out like a damp firework, and I sank a little in my seat. A whole weekend with this bunch. How was I going to survive it? Then Suki topped up our glasses again and put on some music, clearly trying to rev up the atmosphere to above that of a morgue. And she started to tell Oliver and Dinah about my *lovely* son, and how delighted she is to see Lyla so happy. On and on she went, gamely keeping things going and topping up glasses.

Now, as I help Suki to clear the table and wash up, Dinah settles by the fire as if tonight has been exhausting for her. 'So many carbs,' she announces, tight-faced in a snug grey sweater and slim black trousers, her tiny feet poked into olive-green leather slippers. Her short dark hair is cut close to the scalp, streaked with a little grey. I've gathered that she and Suki are book group friends, meeting fortnightly to discuss literary works that Suki admitted, as a whispered aside, 'are a bit of a struggle sometimes. But I needed new friends in Edinburgh and they were happy to welcome me in.'

Not much evidence of welcoming vibes now as Dinah opens a book, making a cursory effort to allow a little room for me on the sofa. Meanwhile Oliver has been busying himself by stoking and poking at the wood burner.

Suki darts around, trying to refill glasses that don't

need refilling, and urging Oliver to 'stop poking, Ols. It's fine!' Finally she settles on a chair by the stove.

'That was a lovely dinner,' I start. 'Thank you, Suki.'

'A *lot* of carbs,' remarks Dinah again, who I've learnt is a psychotherapist. Is she as chilly as this with her clients?

'Dinah, you must show Carly your art,' Suki enthuses, swivelling towards me. 'She absorbs all of her clients' fears and traumas and distils them into these amazing—' She breaks off. 'How would you describe your art, Dinah?'

'I don't really talk about it,' Dinah says, still gripping her book. 'I prefer the work to speak for itself.' She purses her lips and, as Suki shifts uncomfortably in her seat, I prickle with annoyance on her behalf. Really, there was no need for that.

'Sounds fascinating anyway,' I remark.

'Oh, Lyla loves Dinah's work,' Suki says, having recovered her sparkle. 'Maybe I'll buy them a painting, Dinah? To celebrate the baby, when it arrives?'

Dinah blinks at her as if this is an insane suggestion. 'They're very young, aren't they? To be starting a family?'

Suki blanches and Oliver swings round from the fire, still gripping the poker. 'They're twenty-two,' she says levelly. 'Not *that* young . . .'

'And you're okay with this, are you?' Dinah asks, in a neutral tone, turning to me.

'Well, I er—' I start, but she leaps in.

'How many kids d'you have?'

'Three,' I reply. 'Two girls and a boy.'

Dinah nods as if this confirms something for her. 'All grown up?'

'Well, yes,' I say. *Obviously.* Considering I probably look – and certainly feel – ancient.

'The thing I don't understand,' she announces, sitting up pertly now, 'is why parents can't let go of their kids when they've actually grown up. You know?'

I blink at her. 'What d'you mean?'

'The way they keep fussing, running around after them. Worrying about them constantly, even though they've left home—'

'They still exist even when they've left home,' Suki says with a bright smile.

'Like you, following Lyla up to Edinburgh!' Dinah exclaims. It's impossible to tell if this is good-natured teasing between friends.

'Oh, I know.' Suki laughs and shakes her head. 'I *am* ridiculous, I realise that . . .'

Dinah's mouth has set in a flat line. 'I know people who send their adult kids food parcels, as if they're incapable of going to the shops!'

'Oh, I do that,' I say before I can stop myself.

'Do you?' Dinah peers at me.

'Well, yes. One of my daughters is at art college, so she's broke all the time and a bit scatty anyway. I know she basically survives on Pringles and beer. And my other daughter's in London and it's so expensive, so I send the odd parcel of treats—'

'I don't really see the need,' Dinah interrupts as I realise I've committed the cardinal sin of going on about my kids to someone who – fair enough – has no interest in them. Best not to mention that I ordered Eddie that blind for his window, plus a new duvet cover and matching pillowcases. She'd probably slap me down for that, for *caring* about my son. Instead, I start to calculate how soon I can possibly slip off to bed without seeming rude. Because now, as Dinah launches into a tirade about 'overindulgent parents', while Oliver regards her mutely, something hits me.

Eddie, and the way he is. I must have spoilt and mollycoddled him for things to have turned out this way. Bella has accused me of this – of treating him differently because he's the boy. I've denied this strenuously, and honestly believed that she'd got it wrong. That if I fussed less over her and Ana, it was only because they were always fiercely independent. There was no choosing their outfits or packing their lunchboxes, even when they were little. The girls always wanted to do it for themselves and I had to back off.

Meanwhile, through his whole childhood, Eddie just seemed to *need* me more. But actually, now I'm thinking Bella was right. And if I hadn't run around after him, doing his laundry and burrowing under his bed for takeaway cartons and mugs growing fur, then maybe things would be different. Perhaps, if I'd been tougher, as delightful Dinah here is insinuating, then my son would have left home as a fully fledged adult, instead of only being one *on paper*. And then he would've just gone for a few drinks with Calum and Raj and come home and unpacked this room and not made a baby!

I touch my clammy forehead. The cabin, which seemed so delightfully cosy when I arrived, now feels stuffy and oppressive, and I'm seized by an urge to escape. On top of this, all this talk of adult children reminds me that at any moment, Suki might mention Lyla and Eddie's supposedly rock-solid relationship. How would it go down, in present company, if I leapt up and announced, 'I'm sorry to tell you but actually, they just had a drunken shag on a pile of coats!'

I won't, of course. I'd no more destroy Suki's illusion than go to Dinah for therapy. But now my reserves of politeness are running critically low, and although I'd love to know more about Dinah's digestive troubles and Oliver's beavers, I'm done for the night.

'Is there another bottle of wine?' Dinah asks Suki. 'Did you open the good stuff I brought?'

Rather than the not-good-enough stuff Carly brought, is what I think she means.

'I'll get it.' Suki springs up and fetches it from the fridge. She returns and goes around the room with the bottle.

'Actually, that's enough for me tonight,' I say quickly.

'Oh, are you sure?'

'Yes. Thanks – and this has been lovely – but I think I'll head through to bed.' I get up and say goodnight, aware that ducking out of the fun at 10.40 is perhaps a *little* rude, but fuck it. Oliver turns briefly from the fire he's been poking at again, as if it needs constant attention, like a risotto.

'Goodnight,' he says.

I smile tightly and scurry through to my room, hoping that the several glasses of wine I've downed will knock me into unconsciousness the moment my head hits the pillow. Then, in the morning, I'll make my excuses and leave.

I can't face a whole weekend with this lot. I just can't.

However, sleep won't come, even when the voices dwindle and everyone seems to be heading to bed.

What shall I say in the morning? I'll be ill! That's the best thing. But I'll need an illness that doesn't have visible symptoms. What could that be? It comes to me as, tucked up in bed now, I glance through the window at those twinkling stars.

Sciatica! That's it, I decide, as sleep folds over me in the silent room. I'll have an attack of the sciatica that Frank tried to make me have at Suki's club. And then I'll be out of here.

CHAPTER TWENTY-TWO

Kenny

Kenny loves his little flat. He's never happier than sitting at the window, watching the birds and the gently bobbing boats. But he's not loving it now as it seems as if the sea has somehow washed right through the glass and into his living room – because his entire body is drenched. And now a wave of nausea surges over him and he vomits, loudly and dramatically onto the carpet.

The sea hasn't really burst into Kenny's flat. It's sweat that's soaking his tartan pyjamas, and somehow he's roasting and teeth-chatteringly cold, both at once. Kenny is an electrical engineer, a logical man who knows that this is impossible. Yet it's happening right now. It's as if his body's internal systems have been rewired incorrectly and all he can do is sit there, shivering and gazing miserably at the dirty plate from his pilchards on toast, waiting for it to stop.

Kenny woke up an hour ago, at three-thirty a.m., feeling woozy and sick. Thinking it would help to walk around a bit, he fetched a glass of water from the kitchen, even though he never drinks the stuff normally. That's another thing Carly nags him about. *Try to drink more, Dad!* Kenny drinks plenty, he always tells her. Plenty of whisky and beer, at any rate.

Unsteadily, he gets to his feet and takes his plate and water glass to the kitchen, wincing at the terrible stench that's coming, he realises, from the empty pilchards can sitting by the sink. Christ, that's bad. He drops it into his bin, trying – and failing – not to get any of the saucy residue on his hands.

Maybe he just had his dinner too late. Normally, if Carly's not coming over, he'll have it done and dusted by five-thirty, all the better for a long, uninterrupted evening of jeering at the TV. But occasionally, like last night, he forgets.

He also had a fair few whiskies, come to think of it. One wee dram led to another, and it all went a bit hazy towards the end. Another wave of nausea surges through his body and he clings onto the sink for support. Cramps follow, gripping his torso and triggering a fresh bout of the sweats. Kenny lurches out of the kitchen and along the short hallway towards the bathroom where, just in time, he manages to yank down the tartan pyjama bottoms Maggie bought him in Woolworths' closing down sale and collapse onto the lavatory, where terrible things happen from the other end.

What the hell's going on?

Kenny sits on the loo for a few minutes, leaning forward with his sweat-dowsed head in his hands.

That stuff! That's what it'll be, he decides. Those

bloody unasked-for powders that the doctor keeps foisting on him! Of course they're the culprit – and not the pilchards he consumed six hours ago that went out of date before these flats were even built. Then, as he gets to his feet unsteadily and pulls up his pyjamas, Kenny remembers that he's never actually eaten/drunk/whatever the hell you're meant to do with the powders. So it can't be that. As he washes his hands, then splashes cold water onto his pale and sweating face, he tries to figure out what to do.

It'll be fine. He just needs to stay calm and it'll subside eventually. Slowly, Kenny makes his way to his bedroom where he lies down on top of his ancient bedspread. He knows he should go through and clean the living room carpet, but he can't face it right now. How will he do it anyway? Whenever he allows it – i.e. the carpet is crunchy underfoot – Carly runs around with his hoover. But he can't hoover up *that*.

A fresh wave of nausea sweeps through him. Should he call her now to tell her he's sick? She's always telling him to, if he needs anything. But Kenny's default setting is to shun help/interference of any kind. Recently, she offered to do his laundry on a regular basis. Was this her way of saying there was something wrong with the trousers he'd been wearing for a full fortnight and which, admittedly, were splattered with salad cream and chicken soup?

No, he won't phone, he decides. If he does she'll come running and it'll be all, 'Oh, Dad! Can you really manage here on your own?' Then she'll be urging him to look at sheltered accommodation – a ground-floor flat, she's mentioned that before, with an alarm bell and a warden (significantly, the only other place with wardens is prison). Or, worse, she'll be on at him to move in with her and Frank. *That* hasn't been mentioned – yet. Just as well, as Kenny would rather saw off a hand than do that.

It occurs to him that maybe he should call *someone*, as now it's not only the nausea but his breathing too. There's Ian and Sandra, who he and Maggie used to meet for drinks, but they never call him now, and he can't focus as he's finding it hard to breathe.

This is scaring him. He wants to breathe normally – he knows it's essential for life – but something seems to have gone wrong with his throat and chest. Terrified, and feeling horribly alone, Kenny lets out a faint moan as his entire abdomen seems to cramp. He manages to climb off the bed. From his trouser pocket he retrieves the fifteen-year-old mobile phone that he bought for £10 and which does him perfectly well – what's the point of these stupid smartphones? People photographing their dinner and filming themselves doing silly dances?

He grips it, wondering who he could call. Carly's away, he remembers now, and the doctor's surgery won't be open yet. He can't think of a single friend he could call for help, apart from Myra next door, and she's not a friend, she's a neighbour, and even in this sorry state he doesn't want her muscling into his life.

Kenny is shivering. He's frugal with his heating but it's not that. This coldness seems to be chilling the core of him – his heart and bones. With another groan, he dumps his phone on the bedside table, registering briefly on his 1980s digital clock that it's 6.47 a.m. The sun is a ball of gold rising over the marina. The water is sparkling, as if sprinkled with the tinsel strands Maggie always insisted on scattering all over their Christmas tree.

A nuisance, they were, getting everywhere. But Kenny isn't thinking of Maggie or anyone else right now. And he's *fine* on his own. He really is. He just needs some peace and quiet and for everything to be dark and very, very still, until he's better.

So Kenny crawls into bed, beneath his thin faded bedspread, and prays for sleep.

CHAPTER TWENTY-THREE

Carly

I left the curtain open last night so I could see the stars. And now, as the sun rises, the room is filled with golden light. I sit up and look out, pulling the fleecy blanket around my shoulders as I gather my thoughts.

Oliver. Dinah. And Suki, doing her utmost to jolly everyone along. As the events of last night slide into place, I slip out of bed and pull on a sweater over my pyjama top. I couldn't help feeling sorry for her, going to all this effort and being met with ungratefulness and downright rudeness. Still best that I leave, I figure. The thought of a repeat performance tonight – with Dinah especially – is more than I can stomach. I'm not worried about shooting off without saying goodbye to her, or to Oliver. I can't imagine either of them being exactly chirpy over their muesli, or minding that I'm leaving. But I won't head off without thanking Suki.

At just gone seven I pull on my trainers, figuring that it'll only take me a few minutes to pack and be ready to leave. There's no sign that anyone else is up yet, and I don't want to disturb them by moving around too much. So, carrying only my phone, thinking I might take some photos outside, I creep through the cabin and quietly open the front door and step out onto the deck.

The sight before me makes me gasp.

We have incredible sunsets at Sandybanks but I have never seen a sunrise like this. Dawn is streaking the sky with vivid orange and pink. Never mind that I'm not even properly dressed; there's still no one around. I step down off the deck and tread lightly along the path that skirts the forest. It feels so good to be out, and alone. It's more peaceful, even, than those early mornings in the library. Because here there are no traffic sounds, no rumble of the twice-hourly train. Just the cry of a bird and the breath of a light wind through the trees.

I pause briefly and send a quick message to Prish. She was all for me coming up here, saying the 'change of scene' would do me good. *Trapped with bizarre group in the middle of nowhere,* I type, with a gone-bonkers emoji. *Send help!* Then I stride onwards, feeling better already as I mentally rev myself up for my 'sudden sciatica attack' performance, back at the cabin.

Finally, about to turn back, I perch on a sawn-off tree trunk and check my phone. I'm not expecting a reply from Prish yet. Rather, I'm hoping that a message from Frank has miraculously appeared. But there's nothing. I want to be with him now, to pour it all out – how I miss how we were together. So I start to type out a message. *Hope all good. Hate to admit but you were right. Strange group here so I'm thinking of—* I look up with a jolt, tapping 'send' accidentally. 'Oh!'

'Sorry,' Oliver starts. 'I didn't mean to scare you . . .'

'It's okay,' I say quickly. 'I just didn't hear you there.' So much for the peace of the morning.

He steps back as if keen not to encroach on my space any further. In a dark green jacket and jeans and a black beanie hat, he's more sensibly dressed than I am for the crisp early morning. His boots look as if they're designed for serious walking, and a small rucksack is slung over a shoulder. 'I really didn't mean to creep up on you like that,' he adds.

'Honestly, it's okay.' I jump up, glancing at my PJ bottoms. 'Look at me, not even dressed!'

A smile crosses his mouth. 'Aren't you cold?'

'I'm not actually.' I shrug, feeling awkward now. 'I came out to see the dawn. Woke up early, you know.'

He nods. 'Me too. Thought I'd have a stroll before – well, before it all gets going in there.'

'Right,' I say, realising I should probably start to conjure up my terrible back pain right now, if it's to be believable. But somehow I can't bring myself to put on an act. Oliver slips his rucksack off his shoulder and unzips it, pulling out a metal flask.

'Don't suppose you fancy a coffee?'

'Erm, I was just going to head back to the cabin. But actually, that sounds good—'

'I only have one cup,' he adds apologetically. 'But I can pour you one, if you like?'

'No, no. You have it.'

He fills the cup. 'Here. Have this. I can drink from the flask. Hope black's okay for you?'

'Yes, perfect. Thank you.' We both sit on the tree trunk where I sip the coffee, grateful now for the warmth of the cup in my hands. 'It *is* a bit chilly out here.'

'Yeah. Beautiful though, isn't it? And a good time to see who else is around.'

'Who else?' I ask, puzzled. He seems to be scanning the area around the forest's edge. 'Not a *bear*, is it?' I smile.

'Not as far as I know.' He smiles too and sips from his flask, seeming so different from the terse, stove-poking man of last night. 'Let's wait,' he suggests. And so we do just that, and as the sky lightens from pink and orange to a wash of pale blue, it strikes me that I have no urge to fill the silence now. Because it feels anything but awkward as we sit and wait and watch.

And then it happens. There's a small rustling noise as, from out of the woods, a red squirrel appears. It stops, looking around in jerky movements.

I glance at Oliver. 'Wow,' I mouth silently.

He nods, eyes widening. This squirrel is smaller and leaner than the plump greys that frolicked around our Glasgow garden when I was a child. Its coat is deep rust-red, its eyes beady bright as it scampers in short bursts, stopping to scratch among the leaves and pine needles on the ground. Having found some kind of snack, it clutches it with both paws like a child gripping a hot dog. Then another squirrel appears, and then another.

We watch, transfixed by the spectacle. And as the sun rises and the squirrels enjoy their breakfast, I sense something happening to me.

All the stress and worry about Eddie and Frank – and Dad too. That's always there, a niggling undercurrent of anxiety over whether he's *really* okay, stuck in that second-floor flat all alone. But all of that seems to blow away now like a dandelion seed on the breeze. Sitting here, with a man I barely know, I feel entirely at peace.

Time passes. I don't know much because neither of us want to make a sudden move that might scare the squirrels away. Then something startles them – another animal or bird – and they flee.

'That was amazing,' I announce as we get up.

'Quite something, aren't they?' There are no beleaguered teacher vibes now. Oliver's blue eyes are bright, his demeanour relaxed. Clearly a little older than Suki, I'd put him at late forties. He's pulled off his beanie now. There's a hint of grey around his temples, and his face is lightly tanned and slightly weathered around the eyes. He seems like a man who's happiest outdoors.

'I've never seen red squirrels before,' I tell him. 'Thanks for showing me.'

'We're lucky they came out,' he says, then seems to hesitate. 'Erm . . . can I just say I'm sorry?'

I look at him in surprise. 'What for?'

He exhales, running a hand back over neatly cropped hair. 'I owe you an apology, Carly. The way I was when I came to pick you up – and the rest of it. I want you to know how sorry I am about last night.'

CHAPTER TWENTY-FOUR

I tell him it was my fault for getting lost but Oliver won't have it. 'It's easily done around here,' he says. 'One wrong turn and there's no signal or landmarks . . .' He pauses. 'Anyway, I wasn't in the best frame of mind. But that's no excuse.'

'Really, it's okay,' I insist.

He shrugs, looking genuinely sorry. 'Bit awkward last night, wasn't it?'

I hesitate, wondering how to put it tactfully. 'It seems like a bit of an odd mix, that's all . . .'

Oliver nods. 'I think my sister had some kind of agenda.'

'What kind of agenda?' I ask, intrigued.

'Oh, Suki means well. I mean, she's great. Really. But, uh . . . since my wife and I split she's made it her mission to fix me up—'

'You mean, matchmaking you?' I cut in.

'Yeah.' He chuckles. He seems like a man who's got it

together, with an air of easy confidence. I can't imagine he needs, or wants, anyone to organise his life.

'Does she think you can't manage on your own?' I ask.

'Uh, not exactly. At least I hope not. But Suki's always had this thing of wanting everyone she cares about to be all settled and happy, in their cosy little unit.'

I take a moment to absorb this. Could this explain why Lyla won't admit that her pregnancy is the result of a one-night stand? Would that upset Suki too much? 'You mean,' I add hesitantly, 'Suki wants to fix you up with *Dinah?*'

Oliver nods, grinning now. His blue eyes catch the morning light.

'And that's why she invited you both this weekend?'

'Reckon so, although I gather that that wasn't her original plan. But I think a couple of her friends – her so-called friends – dropped out . . .'

'Ah.' I smile. 'So you and I were late additions?'

He grimaces. 'Sorry. I didn't mean to put it like that.'

'No, it's fine,' I say firmly. 'I kind of guessed.'

'Yeah, I did too.' Oliver chuckles. 'Because Suki told me not to make any snap judgements about Dinah. To give her time, to get to know her, as she's a wonderful person underneath . . .'

I smile. What had Suki said about me, I wonder?

'She said you seemed great, that one time she'd met you,' he adds, as if reading my thoughts. 'That you're obviously so supportive of your son.'

'I try to be,' I say, slightly taken aback. 'I'm just doing my best really.' I pause, keen to veer away from the topic before Oliver asks how I *really* feel about the baby situation. I had quite enough of that last night, from Dinah. We gather ourselves up and start to stroll back slowly, crunching twigs and brittle leaves underfoot.

'Does Dinah know Suki's trying to get you two together?' I ask.

'Uh, no. I can't imagine she does.'

'So,' I add carefully, 'Dinah's here for you, and I'm here to balance things out—'

'Are you?' Oliver looks bemused.

'Yes. That's what Suki told me. She said this kind of place—' I look around at the dense forest '—isn't really Dinah's thing. But now you've told me this, I reckon I'm here to make the matchmaking project a little bit less obvious. You know, to sort of dilute things. Make things less intense . . .' I can't help smiling at the irony.

Oliver looks at me quizzically. 'What is it?'

Well, things weren't exactly un-intense when I was grappling with Frank over the hamper and smashing the champagne . . . 'I was, um . . . a bit apprehensive about coming here,' I admit.

'And I was so rude to you.'

'No.' I shake my head. 'You just seemed preoccupied.'

'I thought I'd made a big mistake in coming,' he admits. 'That's all.'

We walk in easy silence for a few moments. 'I hope it all works out,' I say as Suki's cabin comes into view. 'I mean, I hope this weekend's not too awkward or difficult for you.' I stop and look at him, registering the vivid blue of his eyes, and wonder what Dinah thinks about him really. He's attractive, certainly. But I can't imagine the two of them hitting it off. 'Now you've told me all that, I feel a bit bad actually,' I add.

'Why?'

'Because . . .' I push back my windblown hair, wondering how best to put it. 'I won't be here to dilute things. I'm sorry. It probably seems a bit off, and Suki was so kind to invite me. But I'm not sure about being the balancing-out person this weekend, you know? After last night—'

'You mean you're going home early?' he exclaims.

'Yeah, I think it's best.' I nod.

'You're planning to leave me here with Dinah and my sister?' Oliver feigns horror, and I laugh.

'I'm sure you'll survive!'

'Yeah.' He nods. 'Guess I'll have to. It seems a shame, though, after you've come all this way. Why not see how today goes?' He looks up at the searing blue sky. 'Weather looks promising.'

'Yes, it does.' And now, as Suki appears on the decking, clutching a coffee pot, I glance at Oliver again.

'Where have you two been?' she calls out.

'We went to see the red squirrels,' I reply.

'Oh, aren't they gorgeous? There are red kites too. You know, birds of prey—'

'I'm sure Carly knows what they are,' Oliver cuts in with a grin.

'Er, yes. I do.' I smile too, aware of a tiny spark of happiness flickering inside me. I'm not sure where that came from.

''Course you do.' Suki laughs. 'So if you like, we can go up to the hide later and watch them. The farmer puts out food for them. It's amazing – isn't it, Ols – to see them diving down for it?'

'Yeah, it really is something special.' He catches my eye with a bemused glance, and his sister pats his arm fondly as we step into the cabin. By the time I've come back from getting properly dressed, warm croissants and bowls of fresh berries have appeared. In between carrying them to the table, I quickly check my phone.

Nine-forty a.m. and still no reply from Frank to the message I sent accidentally. And now the thought of driving back, to the house that no longer feels like home, causes an ache deep in my gut.

'Dinah, breakfast is ready!' Suki sing-songs. Then to Oliver and me: 'Sit down, tuck in. Oh, Carly! Lyla just sent me some gorgeous photos. She and Eddie were at a party last night. Look!' She grabs her phone from the worktop, pulls up a photo of the two of them and hands it to me.

My heart seems to clench as I take it from her. Their young faces are pressed together, cheek to cheek. Lyla is wearing a cream sleeveless top, or maybe a dress, with delicate beading around the neckline. Her blonde hair is scooped up with loose tendrils floating at her flushed cheeks. She looked lovely that day at the private members' club. But I was too shocked, from having that lunch forced upon us, to appreciate it fully.

Here, she looks like an angel. And Eddie looks . . . well, I don't know *how* Eddie looks. Kind of frozen there, and helpless. My son, playing a part.

Something snags in my throat as I hand back Suki's phone. 'Lovely picture,' I say, as if everything's normal.

'Don't they look great together?' Suki enthuses as

Dinah wanders in, rubbing her eyes sleepily. 'Look, Dinah! Aren't they cute?' Suki rushes over to show her.

'Very nice,' Dinah says curtly. It's like someone who doesn't like dogs being forced to admire a chihuahua.

I glance over at Oliver and we seem to exchange a silent message as we all take our places at the table. *This is all so weird. But it'll be okay.* And, stranger still, even the party photo and Dinah's terse presence don't propel me into feigning illness at the breakfast table.

Oliver offers around the coffee pot as sunshine slices into the bright and airy room. And as Suki chatters happily about all the wonderful places she plans to show us today, I figure that perhaps I'm not ready to go home just yet.

CHAPTER TWENTY-FIVE

Eddie

At ten-thirty on a cool, bright Edinburgh morning, Eddie looks at the photo of him and Lyla on her Instagram and feels as if his heart could break.

That party. God. He plonks his phone face down on the duvet and glares at the towel pinned up at his window. Obviously he can't draw it, like a curtain. But the concept of taking it down every morning and pinning it back up again at night is too much to wrap his head around. There's the blind his mum ordered for him, still in its packaging, propped up in a corner of his room. *Your Blind From EasyBlinds has arrived!* reads the yellow sticker on the hefty cardboard tube.

Nothing easy about installing a blind, Eddie reckons. Nothing easy about life when you're having to fend for yourself, without the comforts of home. In this miserable room Eddie exists either in the unforgiving glare of the room's centre light, or the meagre amount of sunlight that struggles through the towelling layer.

Neither option creates the ambience he'd envisaged when Raj and Calum had told him about the vacant room. Edinburgh with his best mates! Finally, Eddie's adult life would properly begin. No more getting stoned at the bandstand and watching the Arran ferry chugging back and forth as the years slid away. No locking himself in the bathroom at home just to glean a bit of privacy from his parents. Moving out, he'd decided, would be *bliss*.

Eddie had pictured his friends' flat as being scruffy but relaxed and fun, with impromptu gatherings and late nights sitting up, having a smoke and a few drinks and long, hilarious conversations.

It hasn't quite turned out that way. Okay, there was that first night when he'd just moved in. The party and meeting Lyla *and look what happened then!* But since that night, Raj and Calum have been too busy to go out beyond the occasional quick drink. Too busy with work, that is. Eddie had never realised how *serious* they are now; proper corporate types, working for the same company and forever going on about systems and targets and 'awaydays' with 'the team'. It's as if they went straight from being normal teenagers to being instantly forty-five. While Raj is single, Calum has a girlfriend, Zara, who also seems oddly mature for twenty-three with her sensible blazers and curled-under brown bob and talk of how she and her flatmate want a modular sofa. What's that all about?

Not only that, but these days Raj and Calum are up at dawn and heading off to their workplace's gym together. They even go there at weekends! They'll be there now, working out on a Saturday morning when they should be lying around the flat, drinking coffee and nursing hangovers like normal people. Eddie's suggested finding a skate park they could all go to, but they looked at him as if he was mad.

Now Eddie mooches through to the kitchen in the otherwise empty flat, cringing at the sight of the huge, pearly-white helium balloon that's hovering at the ceiling. Zara brought it round for Calum – she 'stole' it from a work event, this is what counts as rebellion these days! – and Eddie couldn't admit that he still fears balloons.

Trying not to look at it, he fills a greasy pint glass with tap water. It tastes as if it's come out of a rusting tank with a dead pigeon floating in it. Maybe it has – who knows? He saw a rat running along their street with a bit of battered sausage in its mouth the other night. At least, he thinks it was sausage. He didn't exactly get up close to inspect it. Anyway, nothing would surprise him around here.

He glugs down the stale water while glaring at another appalling object in the kitchen. Sitting there on the worktop is a ridiculously huge, clear plastic bottle with a spout and measurements marked down the side. Eddie knows it's to encourage you to guzzle water all day long. He faintly remembers a time when life was all about messing around and laughing with your mates. Now it's about staying *hydrated*. All the same, he's desperately hungover and needs liquid before he can function. He drank way too much at that party last night. It was the only way he could handle it.

Please come to Josh's thing, Lyla had messaged him. *We can do some photos. Mum'll like that.* Obligingly, he said he'd go. But it wasn't like the party where they'd first met. It was a fancy thing in a hotel suite, full of braying people with loud, confident laughs. And the loudest and brashest was Lyla's uni friend Josh.

Of course he was a *Josh*: holding court with his big white teeth and expensive shirt and a job at the Scottish parliament. 'What d'you do, Eddie?' he asked.

'I'm a chef,' Eddie replied, and Josh looked at him as if he'd said, 'I shovel shit'. There were loads of Joshes last night. Joshes and Bens and Millies and Tillies and even a Dilly, he remembers now. Under the feeble dribble of the shower, he replays it all like a terrible movie as he tries to wash the mint-scented lather off his skinny body. It's like standing under a dripping leaf.

At least no one seemed to care about the nature of Lyla and Eddie's relationship last night. He was just *there*, like some amusing random she'd picked up and made a baby with. And everyone seemed cool with that. They kept teasing her, calling her 'Mama', and she lapped it all up while Eddie was basically ignored. Apart from being called upon to do photos, that is.

Eddie dries himself on a fraying towel and gets dressed. As he pulls on battered trainers he tries to push away how weird it all is, acting this part. As weird as his mum going away with Suki this weekend.

They're going to be best mates, Eddie decides as he steps out into the musty hallway, shuts the flat door behind him and heads downstairs. It's all too much. It feels like a tangled web he's in – trapped, with no means of escape.

As he steps out into the chilly morning, trying to rev himself up for his shift at the restaurant, what Eddie really wants to do is call home. Or, more specifically, his mum. His dad's great, and Eddie loves him to bits but it's his mum he wants to talk to now. But he can't do that because she's away with Suki. And even if she wasn't he couldn't bear to admit what an almighty fuck-up he's made of everything, and that the girl he's having to pretend to be in love with – well, he really is in love with her.

Lyla is amazing. She's so incredibly beautiful he can hardly bear to look at her face.

So, in a bizarre tangle Eddie is having to pretend *not* to be in love with the person he's pretending to be in love with. Right now, with the hangover steadily crushing his brain, Eddie can't make sense of that at all. It feels like the time his little sister Ana tipped out a whole load of jigsaw puzzles onto the living room floor and all the pieces were muddled up. Occasionally, his sisters message him: Bella being all: *I'm here for you, give me a call sometime when you're free?* and Ana sending him jokey videos that have nothing to do with babies or the mess of his life. Eddie appreciates it, that his sisters think about him sometimes. But his replies are brief. *All fine yeah talk soon.*

Eddie's running late for work now. Even so, he stops to roll a cigarette. Why does he go along with this crazy pretence that he and Lyla are together? Because he'd go along with anything she asked of him. He lights his roll-up and looks at that photo again, of the two of them at the party last night. Now he's really scrutinising it, deciding that anyone would think they were together and in love. Then he can't see it properly because something shocking is happening.

Tears are falling out of Eddie's eyes. He's crying, right there in the street, with people going about their business all around him. People carrying books, whizzing past him on bikes and striding along with takeaway coffees. They're all so *normal* – just regular people who've got their lives together.

Eddie should be rushing to work now. But he can't. He can't go to the restaurant and pretend everything's okay because he's crying, and the hand that's holding his skinny roll-up is shaking, so how could he possibly work with knives? So he messages his boss, Marius, who's been so great with him, teaching him how to make the perfect reduction and sear a fillet of fish to perfection, rather than lightly poaching it and turning it grey.

Sorry can't make it in today feel really ill.

Immediately, his phone buzzes into life. 'Hey, what's up?' Marius asks, clearly busy. There's clattering and urgent voices in the background as the team prepares for lunchtime service.

'Um, I just feel really bad,' Eddie croaks, hoping Marius doesn't pick up on all the outdoor sounds around him. The traffic, a dog barking, the ding of an approaching tram.

'Don't give me that,' he booms. 'We need you here on prep today. Remember we've got that big party coming in? The table of ten? They booked two months ago!'

'Yeah, I know,' Eddie starts as an ambulance siren shrieks.

'Where *are* you?'

'In bed—'

'Don't give me that. I can't be one man down, today of all days. What've you got? A Hangover? Take some fucking ibuprofen and get yourself in right now—'

'Honestly, Marius, I can't,' Eddie protests. 'I'd be no use. Really. I'm going to have to go. Sorry. I'll be in tomorrow—'

'Oh, so you'll be better then, will you?' his boss snaps.

'I think it's just one of those twenty-four-hour things,' Eddie starts. But Marius has already ended the call.

CHAPTER TWENTY-SIX

Carly

'So we could pack a picnic and drive up into the hills,' Suki suggests. 'Or take a boat trip across the loch, or watch the red kites from the hide. What d'you think?'

'I think I'll stay here and use the hot tub,' Dinah announces at breakfast. 'I came here for a rest, Suki. You all go out.'

'I'm not leaving you here all alone,' Suki protests.

'I'll be fine! Honestly.'

I glance at Oliver and we seem to transmit a look. It hardly seems believable that Suki's been hatching a plan to get her brother and Dinah together. 'No, I'll stay with you, Dinah,' she says with a trace of regret. 'We'll have a lovely time chilling out together.' She musters a bright smile and turns to Oliver and me. 'But what will you two do?'

'I'm happy to amuse myself,' I say quickly, hoping my relief isn't obvious. I wasn't *loving* the idea of a whole day with Dinah, extolling her strident views on the correct way to parent adult kids.

'I can show you around, if you like?' Oliver ventures. 'I've spent quite a bit of time up here.'

'I'd love that,' I enthuse, 'if you're sure.' And so we set off in Oliver's Land Rover, with the picnic Suki insisted on packing for us. 'I'm not really a hot-tub person,' he remarks as we leave the cabins behind.

'You *do* surprise me.' I smile, and he chuckles. There's been no discussion of where we might go today. I have a feeling we'll just see where the winding lanes lead us on this bright and sunny spring morning. I glance at Oliver as he drives – calmly and steadily, rather than barging around corners, as he did last night – suspecting that he is as relieved as I am to be heading out for the day.

Come home! Prish messaged earlier, in response to my message. *You don't have to stick it out. We can go out tonight if you like, if you need to spill it all out?* I felt a little foolish replying that the situation had 'improved' and that I was planning to see how things panned out.

Now we're climbing higher, cresting the hill where the landscape spreads out before us like the spectacular opening of a film. Way down below, a loch glimmers in the bright morning sunshine. 'Oh, this is incredible,' I exclaim.

Oliver smiles. 'So you're glad you stayed after all?'

'Yes, I am,' I say truthfully. We settle into a comfortable silence as the road ribbons back and forth down the hillside. And as the loch grows closer, I sense Oliver turning something over in his mind.

'So, that photo Suki showed us last night,' he ventures, giving me a quick look.

My heart jolts. 'You mean the one of Lyla and Eddie?'

'Yeah,' Oliver says. 'It can't be easy for you, all of

this . . .' What does *he* think, I wonder, as Lyla's uncle? I can't imagine he's overjoyed either.

'No, it's not,' I say carefully. 'But it's not really about me, and what I think, is it?'

'Well, it kind of is,' he remarks, and I'm not sure how to respond.

'I just . . . hope they'll be okay,' I say, taking care not to let anything slip out. Because it feels as important to keep up the pretence with Oliver as it does with Suki. 'I mean, I hope Lyla's well and healthy and that everything's fine with the baby,' I go on. 'That's all that matters really. And afterwards, when the baby's born . . .' I break off, suddenly overcome by emotion. 'I can hardly get my head around that part,' I admit. 'That Eddie will be a dad. It just seems crazy and impossible, you know?' I glance at Oliver, hoping he doesn't think I'm rambling. But I've barely talked about the fact that, virtually every moment of every day, all I can think is that a baby is growing. My grandchild, who I know will change all of our lives forever. I haven't even shared this with Prish or Jamie, as I haven't been able to put it into words. And I still haven't told Dad.

'I know what you mean,' Oliver says. 'They *are* young, aren't they? There's no getting around that.' He glances at me. 'I guess it's one of those situations where it's affecting you hugely but you actually feel a bit powerless.'

'Yes, it's exactly that.' I pause, surprised by his understanding. That's it, I decide. This new life is happening – never mind that the situation is a mess – and I simply don't know what to think or do. It's left me flailing, with Frank and I falling apart.

'D'you have children?' I ask now. After my faux pas with Dinah last night, I've hesitated to broach the subject.

'I do,' Oliver replies. 'Two boys, all grown up now.'

'They've left home?'

'Yeah, yeah, a few years ago. And you have three, is that right?'

'That's right,' I reply. I tell him about Bella in London, and Ana loving her art student life as she carouses around Dundee.

'You must miss them a lot,' he ventures.

'Oh, I do. They come home on visits of course. And their dad and I see them when we can. We've had a couple of trips to London to visit Bella. But I'm happy, you know. They grew up in a sleepy little seaside town and were desperate to get out there into the world. Not like Eddie. He hung on the longest, only moved out in January—'

I stop myself. Oh, Christ. When the pregnancy was announced, he and Lyla were meant to have been together for six months. My brain whirs, calculating how long the great love affair should have been going on for now. Eight months? Don't panic, I tell myself as we pull up at the lochside. Oliver won't be doing the maths. We climb out, and I'm relieved as he points out a ruined castle perched on a rocky outcrop. We head towards it with the picnic stashed in Oliver's rucksack. Thankfully, he seems more interested in enjoying the day than delving into whatever might be going on with my son and his niece.

'My kids were obsessed with castles,' he says.

'Mine too. The more ruined the better. That way, they knew there'd be no boring exhibits to look at inside them . . .'

'Just crumbly old walls with plenty of climbing potential,' he says, and I laugh.

'Exactly.' We reach the castle and perch on the softly worn wall overlooking the loch. 'So, how was it for you when your kids moved out?' I ask.

'Um . . . it seemed okay at the time.' A wry smile and a shrug. 'But then their mum and I got divorced. Patrice decided her work was done—'

'Oh, I am sorry,' I say quickly.

'No. It's fine. Well, it wasn't fine at the time. Far from it. But . . . you know. We'd had the boys pretty young, and it turned out that it was them who'd been holding us together.' *Is that me and Frank too?* I wonder. *Is our work done too?* 'We're okay now,' he adds. 'We're . . . cordial.' Another wry smile.

'It's a big change when the kids go,' I admit. 'Not quite what I expected. I mean, Frank and I . . .' I pause, wondering how to put it. 'I suppose we're still adjusting.'

Oliver nods. 'You crave all this time and space, and then you get it and don't know what to do with yourself.'

'Exactly. So, you mentioned you're moving?' I prompt him.

'Yeah. I've been working on some projects down south but there's something up here I really want to get my teeth into—'

'The beaver project?' I cut in, and he nods.

'That's it. We've reintroduced them to other areas really successfully. A family near here hope to do the same on their land—' He stops, catching himself. 'God, don't let me get started on the project . . .'

'I'd love to hear about it,' I say truthfully.

'Really? I can show you the site if you like. I mean, where we've build the lodge—'

'The lodge?'

'A home for beavers, built from sticks and undergrowth.'

'Oh, I see!'

He chuckles. 'Honestly, enough about that. So, Suki mentioned that you're a librarian?'

'Yep, nothing as exciting as reintroducing threatened indigenous species . . .'

'See, you do know about beavers!'

I smile. 'We have a natural history society that meets up in the library. Sometimes I sidle over, just to make sure that's really what they're up to with their hushed conversations and intense minute-taking . . .'

'They're not out and about, discovering nature in the wild?'

'They do that too, but we have a brilliant natural history section. Lots of rare out-of-print volumes on wildlife and ecology and . . .' I cut off. 'Now listen to *me*, going on!'

'Sounds great,' Oliver enthuses. 'I should meet them, if I'm ever in the area.'

'Oh, they're terrifying. Mostly in their late seventies – even eighties, some of them – but they reckon they run the library. We moved their table once because there was leak above it. "Carly,"' I start, mimicking Thelma Campbell's strident tone, '"we're really not sure about the repositioning and the strong consensus is that it should be put right back where it was!"'

Oliver laughs. '"Natural History Society outraged by table move."'

'Exactly. You'd think we'd put it in the toilets for all the furore it caused.'

'So it *all* goes on in your library,' he suggests.

'Like you wouldn't believe,' I say as we make a start on our picnic, looking out over the loch. And so the hours pass. We drive on for a while, stopping at any spots that take our fancy. Eventually, we enter a country estate, where we park at a stable block and then step carefully along a narrow path through the woods.

Finally we arrive at the river. The late afternoon is cooling now, the sky darkening as heavy clouds gather. We finish the remains of the picnic and perch on a fallen tree at the water's edge. Here, beavers have dammed the river to create a pool of still, calm water. We sit and watch as dragonflies skim across it, their iridescence catching the light. And finally a beaver emerges from the mound of sticks – the lodge – and plops into the water.

'Oh, wow,' I breathe, transfixed.

'We're lucky,' Oliver whispers. 'They usually only start to come out at dusk.' We watch as the beaver glides majestically, head slicked wet, held just above water. Another emerges, and I feel as if I am barely breathing as we take in the scene.

My head is swimming with the sights of the day as we pick our way back through the forest. 'So, did you enjoy your day?' he asks later as he parks up at the cabins.

'It was wonderful,' I say truthfully. A small pause settles as we climb out of his Land Rover.

'Look, um . . .' he starts, seeming suddenly awkward. 'I don't want to pry, but . . .'

'What about?' My chest seems to tighten.

'You, uh . . . you mentioned that Eddie moved out in January, didn't you?'

Oh God. Here it comes. 'Er . . . yes.' I nod, waiting for it to follow. He knows, I realise, as we make our way towards Suki's cabin. He knows the whole Lyla-and-Eddie thing is a lie.

'But,' he starts, 'Suki said they've been together for—'

'Yes, I know,' I say quickly. Her cabin is in view now, fairy lights twinkling in the dusk. 'It's what Lyla wants her mum to think,' I explain, my cheeks burning as if I'm the one who concocted the lie. 'Eddie told us that's the story, and that we had to go along with it. But actually . . .' I look at him, grimacing. 'They just had a fling – a one-night thing, I think. And that was that.'

Oliver holds my gaze for a moment. 'I kind of wondered,' he says gently.

'It's crazy really,' I add. 'I don't know why they're lying and it's bound to come out. I mean, they're not even together. It's all an act. But would you please not say anything to Suki? I'd hate it all to come out, and for her to be upset, especially this weekend—'

'Hey,' he says, touching my arm. 'Of course I won't say anything.'

'Thank you. It seems really important—' I break off as Suki appears on the deck.

'Back at last!' She grins, welcoming us into the cabin and pressing glasses of wine into our hands.

'Hey, let me get my jacket off,' Oliver says, laughing, and glances at me. Perhaps it will be okay, I reassure myself, as Suki spins off, a blur of tousled blonde hair in her pink cotton dress, to put the finishing touches to dinner.

Dinah has yet to appear. I think about everything Oliver and I have seen today – the beavers and the dragonflies dancing on the still water, not to mention the castle and the gleaming loch. She's missed so much. Frankly, I can't understand why she came here. Yet my spirits remain high, even when Dinah finally emerges from her room to join us at the dinner table.

Of course Oliver won't tell. I just *know* that. And who cares if our resident psychotherapist seems intent on putting the damper on the weekend? Employing the bombard-with-enthusiasm approach, I tell her all about our day.

'Sounds great,' she says noncommittally.

'Did you have a nice time?' I ask.

'Yes, very nice,' she says. 'Though I'm not really a hot-tub person.'

'You could've fooled me,' Suki teases. 'We were in there for hours, shrivelling away.'

Dinner is more relaxed tonight, and when we're finished Suki looks around at all of us, eyes sparkling. 'Maybe we can all come up here when the baby's born,' she announces.

'Oh. That would be lovely,' I manage.

'Lyla loves it here,' she adds. 'She's a nature girl really, like me.' I catch Dinah studying me and take a big swig of wine. It's as if she *knows*, I realise. As if she's well aware that Lyla is spinning her mother a yarn. And that I – bringer of substandard wines – am in on it too.

'So, Carly,' she starts, spearing me with a look across the table, 'how *did* Eddie and Lyla meet?'

Sweat beads on my forehead as all eyes are on me.

What do I do now? Feign illness? Conjure up the sciatica I've never had and stagger off, groaning in 'pain'? I glance at Oliver as if he might be able to help me wriggle out of this. 'I, er . . .' I start. Then something happens and I can only think of it as a *double* miracle.

One, my phone must have come within signal range because – *two!* – it starts ringing in my pocket. Someone's calling me! It's probably a scam call, but I'm already dispensing silent thanks to the scammer as I leap up and snatch it from my pocket. 'Sorry, I'd better take this . . .'

Striding away from the table, I blink down at name that's displayed. Dad? Why would he be calling? I step out of the cabin and onto the deck.

'Dad, is everything okay?'

'Carly . . .' His breathing sounds ragged and my heart rate accelerates in panic.

'Dad! What *is* it?'

'I – I'm probably making a fuss about nothing. But I'm feeling bad. Really bad. And I don't know what to do. Sorry. I didn't want to call and spoil your trip.'

'What's happening? What are you feeling, Dad—'

'Please, just come and help me, Carly. *Please* help.'

CHAPTER TWENTY-SEVEN

May

Kenny

Botulism. That's what he had – or what they kept saying in the hospital when it all happened. Kenny can hardly believe a month has spun by since that terrible night when there was nothing he could do but call Carly and have her rush home and phone an ambulance. Even as he was being loaded into it, Kenny was ranting to the paramedics that he couldn't go anywhere – not when there was vomit on his living room carpet.

'Dad, never mind that,' Carly had snapped, more firmly than he'd ever known her to be before. 'We'll get you to hospital and then I'll go back to your flat and clean it up – which means I'll need your keys.'

'What for?' he asked, delirious.

'To get into your flat! Unless you'd like me to break in?'

He'd stared at her helplessly then. His keys! He was in no mood to put up a fight, but as she wangled them off him it felt like having an organ ripped out. A load of fuss about nothing, he reckons now, even though things were a *little* bit tricky when he couldn't breathe or see properly or even walk, when his muscles seemed to be paralysed and he was vomiting and couldn't keep anything down, not even water, and they had him on a drip – what's the obsession with staying hydrated these days? Sip-sip-sip, young people with their phones and those great big water bottles with the spouts, big water-bottle-sucking babies—

Kenny's thoughts break off as the kind nurse with shiny auburn hair sets a covered plate on the small moveable table beside his bed. 'Here you go, Mr Munro. Your favourite.'

'Thank you, love.' He readjusts his position in bed and removes the plastic cover with a flourish, as if it's a silver dome in a swanky restaurant. There's a Jenga brick of unnamed white fish in white sauce. Beside it sits a small globe of white mashed potato, scooped like ice cream. It's *all* white, like the plate – none of the rabbity salads Carly tries to force on him – and Kenny finds this soothing. He had hallucinations, during the worst of whatever it was. Terrifying nightmares with violent nurses holding him down on the floor while trying to force drugs into his mouth. Even in his dreams Kenny rebelled, secretly storing the pills hamster-style in his cheek.

Throughout it all, Carly's been popping in pretty much every day – not in his nightmares but in real life. And Frank appeared, and his granddaughter Bella came all the way up from London, even though there was no bloody need! Travelling four hundred miles just because he'd had a stomach upset? The expense of it! More money than sense.

'Oh, Granddad,' she exclaimed at his bedside. 'Of course I'd come. Did you think I wouldn't?'

Kenny huffed at that, embarrassed by the concern of a child – because his grandkids will always be children to Kenny. Even daft Eddie who's going to be a dad. But he had to admit that Bella did seem very grown up these days as she listened gravely to what had happened, and told him what she'd been up to in London. 'I'm going for a promotion at work,' she said. Got her head screwed on properly, that one. And then Eddie was here, seeming concerned but also somewhat relieved when visiting time was over.

And then Myra, his neighbour, bowled up with homemade fruit scones, for God's sake. 'To build you up, Kenny!' It was like Glasgow Central Station at rush hour with people crammed around his bed, even though it's only meant to be two visitors at a time.

For a short time there, Kenny felt almost popular. But mostly it was exhausting, and thankfully things are a little calmer now, and his appetite is returning and he is almost feeling like his old self. 'You could be out of here tomorrow,' said the doctor this morning. Although what did he know? Another child, commenting on Kenny's health. 'We just need to finalise your care plan, Mr Munro.'

Care plan? What care plan? What do they think he is – geriatric? Kenny does *not* need a care plan or fruit scones or people fussing around him, filling his water jug and reminding him to *drink-drink-drink*. He needs to be left alone to recover quietly in his flat. And he's definitely ready. Very soon, he'll be back home and everything will be normal again.

'Hi, Dad.' As soon as dinner is over Carly reappears in the ward. She plonks herself down on the chair next to his bed.

'Where's Ana?' he asks. She'd waltzed into the ward earlier, all pink hair and smiles and jangling jewellery. She didn't seem to think he'd notice the new tattoo on her wrist (he misses nothing). Dutifully, she and Carly had left the ward during dinnertime.

'She's just calling a friend,' Carly replies.

Kenny frowns. More like having a cigarette outside, he suspects. He smelt it on her earlier. 'So, you're definitely coming out tomorrow,' Carly explains. 'I spoke to the nurse at the desk . . .'

'Oh, that's good news,' he says.

She seems to hesitate as she bites at a fingernail. It was a moment of weakness that caused Kenny to call her that night. He'd panicked, that was all. He had no one else to phone and he wasn't about to bother Myra next door, who's always asking if she can pick up some sausages from the butchers for him. Once Myra's in, there's no getting rid of her.

'The thing is, Dad,' Carly starts, shuffling in the seat, 'they're saying you've refused the care plan. That you don't want any help at home.'

'No, no.' Kenny shakes his head. 'I don't need any of that.'

A small groove appears between her eyebrows. 'But why not?'

'Because I'm perfectly fine now.'

She rubs at her eyes. She looks tired, he thinks, and a little pale. He knows about Eddie getting some girl pregnant. Ana blurted it out by accident earlier today. Carly nearly fell off her chair. *Ana! Granddad doesn't know!* As if it should be kept from him. Did she think he'd make a moral judgement or what? Eddie doesn't seem mature enough to be a father. But what does Kenny know about anything anymore? The boy could have mentioned it, though, when he was here. *That* would've been some news to share. As it was, all Eddie said was, 'Nothing's really been happening, Granddad.'

'Dad, I really think a care plan's a good idea,' Carly says now, pressing her palms together, as if in prayer. 'It's just people dropping in to see you three times a day—'

'Three times?' he exclaims. 'What for?'

'To make sure you're okay—'

'I told you, I'm okay now!'

'Mr Munro?' Having overheard, the auburn-haired nurse arrives at Carly's side. 'We've been through all this, haven't we? They'd just pop in to make sure you're up and dressed in the morning—'

'I'm perfectly capable of dressing myself.'

'And then they'd pop back at lunchtime to make your—'

'Why do I need this?' He stares at Carly. 'All this popping! I'm not having people poking around my flat—'

'But Dad, they *won't* be poking around,' she insists.

'They don't have time for that.' The nurse chuckles. 'They'll be in and out in minutes, Mr Munro. You'll hardly see them. They'll be a *blur*—'

'Absolutely no way,' he says firmly.

Shaking her head in disbelief, the nurse strides away.

Carly's gaze is steady, meeting his. 'It's free, you know,

Dad. The carer service, I mean. You won't have to pay for it.'

'All the more reason,' he mutters. 'I don't want to waste resources—' He breaks off as Ana reappears, carrying teas from the cafeteria. She's a bit wild, that one, and he's not keen on the silver nose ring or, for that matter, the tattoo. But despite this Kenny gets on well with his youngest grandchild. She's always had an easy way about her, chattering happily about her art, and college, which he finds interesting. Kenny used to paint a little himself – mostly watercolours of the marina from his living room window. But since Maggie left, he's lost his enthusiasm.

'So I hear you won't have carers, Granddad?' Ana chides him. She places his tea on his bedside table.

'No, I don't need anyone looking after me.'

'I know you don't.' She smiles knowingly. 'So, are you going to miss the hospital food?'

'I am, as a matter of fact. They serve just the right-sized portions here.' He glances at Carly, detecting a subtle eye-roll from her, and then at his granddaughter. Even with her crazy pink hair, Ana seems to have grown up suddenly, in one huge jump. Maybe he hasn't been paying attention.

'So you're going to take notice of sell-by dates now, then?' Ana teases.

'Hmm. We'll see.' His mouth twitches and he allows the smile to escape. 'I'm not sure *what* caused all of this . . .'

'No, we can't imagine,' Carly remarks. And then Frank appears, and there's a kerfuffle as chairs are moved to allow space for him.

'More visitors!' Kenny retorts.

Frank smiles, leaning forward in his seat. 'You're looking much better, Kenny. That's great to see.'

'Thanks. I feel better.' But now the less friendly nurse comes over, the one with the silver spectacles who's always bustling past his bed as if he's not even there. She reminds them sharply of the two-at-the-bedside rule, and Frank jumps up.

'I'll wait for you in the cafeteria,' he tells Carly and Ana. 'Bye for now, Kenny. Sorry to be rushing off. We'll come to take you home tomorrow, okay? If you let us know when you're ready to leave?'

'Thanks.' Kenny nods his gratitude, briefly.

The nurse frowns at Kenny. 'So it's not ideal, discharging you without a care plan in place. But it's your choice—'

'I know that,' Kenny retorts.

She is clutching a sheaf of papers in a cardboard folder. His notes, he assumes. What have they been writing about him? 'I'm not happy about it,' she adds.

He catches Carly looking at Ana again, who's sitting at her side. The sideways glances, the notes; it all goes on around him and Kenny isn't having this. 'I'm perfectly capable of looking after myself,' he tells the nurse firmly. 'And I'm not having any carers—'

'Dad, are you sure about this?' Carly leans forward.

'I've never been more sure about anything!'

'Right then.' Carly stands up, quickly followed by Ana. 'We're just going to nip downstairs and find Frank . . .'

'Oh. All right.' Another look passes, this time between his daughter and granddaughter and the nurse. All this silent communication! Why doesn't anyone just spit out what they want to say?

'We'll be back in a bit, Dad,' Carly says, touching his hand lightly. 'Don't be running off anywhere, okay?'

CHAPTER TWENTY-EIGHT

June

Living at Kilmory Cottage: Carly, Frank, Kenny

Carly

'I won't be here long,' Dad announces as Frank clears the table after dinner.

'Kenny, you can be here as long as you like,' Frank says. 'Honestly. Just treat it like your home.'

'Yes, Dad,' I add. 'Don't worry about anything at all.' I glance back at the supermarket order I'm doing on my laptop.

'Don't get anything special in for me,' Dad says, looming over me now, peering at the screen. 'I'll be gone by the weekend.'

'There's no rush, Dad. You don't have to make any decisions yet—'

'I'm just saying.'

'Okay,' I murmur wearily. 'I'm getting the normal shop.'

'Just don't go mad.' He hovers there, breathing in my ear and observing me 'going mad' by ordering wildly extravagant potatoes, bread and butter. Would he prefer margarine? Or lard? Still, it's fine Dad being here. Right now, it feels like the right thing to do because, when we went to collect him from hospital, a young nurse who looked a little like Eddie quickly pulled Frank and me aside.

'We're relieved he's going to stay with you,' he said. 'He lives in a second-floor flat, doesn't he? With no lift?'

That's true, I told him, adding that we were happier too, considering the trauma he'd been through. And if Frank wasn't exactly delighted, then to his credit, it didn't show.

'Thanks for all this,' I murmur now in the kitchen. Since his arrival Dad has commandeered the TV to binge-watch *Cash or Crash*. Old episodes, featuring spectacularly dumb-brained (his term) contestants are rewatched to his immense enjoyment. But at least they keep him occupied, and for now, with *The Empty-Nester's Handbook* stuffed away on a shelf, we seem to have settled into this strange new routine.

'Thanks for what?' Frank asks lightly.

I turn and look at him. 'For being there for us, all that time Dad was in hospital. All the visits you did and keeping things going at home.'

'God, Carly,' he exclaims, 'what else was I going to do? Of course I'm here for you. Honestly.'

But I wasn't sure you were anymore, I want to say. *And now I know you are. It took a can of rotten pilchards to show that you still love me, and that when all this is over, and Dad's ready to go home, we'll be okay.*

Frank wipes his dishwater hands on a towel and hugs me. 'We'll get through this,' he adds, and I nod.

'At least he doesn't steal chargers or leave takeaway

boxes under the bed,' I remark. And as I've told Suki – who very sweetly has been texting to see how he's doing – Dad seems to have not only settled into Kilmory Cottage, but is actively enjoying ruling the roost. We've given him the biggest and brightest bedroom, with a sea view. The girls always shared it, then when Bella moved out it was Ana's, and when Ana left home Eddie commandeered it before Frank and I even had a chance.

'I've waited all my life for this room!' he announced, a little unreasonably, considering the fact that Eddie never had to share a bedroom. But in he went, fouling it up within days, thinking we didn't know about him smoking out of the window. For weeks on end it felt as if the curtains were barely opened. So much for the sea view! Then when Eddie moved to Edinburgh, our plan was to make it *our* room. But the baby announcement knocked the stuffing out of us, so the move was never made.

Anyway, now it's my father's domain. And so, it would appear, is our sole bathroom. 'Can I please get in there!' he calls out, with a sharp rap on the door if Frank or I dare to occupy it for longer than five minutes.

Meals are different too. My father, refuser of fresh food, favours the plainest of fare: fried fish, oven chips, pies. With the TV blaring, because isn't that what you want as you eat your dinner after a day's work?

Quizmaster: 'What's the capital of Finland?'

Tense-looking woman, visibly sweating: 'Er . . . Stockholm?'

Dad: 'Oh-for-God's-sake-fools!'

We tolerate all of this because his body is healing after being racked by botulism. Being so utterly poisoned at eighty-four could have killed him. So I cook the meals he enjoys, and we bring him endless coffees, made with Nescafé (Dad regards real ground coffee as a crazy extravagance, and it simply isn't worth the fuss). We speak in whispers when we don't especially want him chipping in because, although Dad's hearing isn't great, when it's a personal matter it's suddenly as sharp as a whippet's. And of course I do his laundry and buy his daily newspaper and pick up his prescriptions, steeling myself when the Citrolax keeps on coming.

Occasionally, Dad insists on going to the shops, which is good for him, I suppose – a bit of exercise. He returns with a carrier bag of reduced food: pineapple slices turning brown, and a pack of cooked chicken that I can hear screaming 'Danger! Danger!' before it's even come out of the shopping bag.

And then the days turn warmer, and our garden bursts into full bloom in the bright June sunshine. Bella visits again from London, fussing over her granddad and telling me that she can't get her head around being an auntie yet. 'How d'you think Eddie will be?' she asks. 'As a dad, I mean?'

'Honestly, I have no idea,' I say.

'They're so young. It seems such a lot to handle, doesn't it? I can't believe I haven't even met her yet.' We're sitting in the back garden together, making the most of the late afternoon sun.

'I know, love. And who knows how they'll manage? We'll just have to wait and see.' It seems trite but it's the best I can come up with. I've given up trying to discuss the situation with Frank, because what is there to say, really?

'So, um . . .' Bella hesitates. 'How long d'you think Granddad'll be staying here?' She loves him, but over the past few days she's been party to the hefty dinners, the mocking of quiz show contestants and the banging on the bathroom door. On her first night home, she had the audacity to have a bath. Four minutes, she managed, before Dad was rapping loudly, needing the loo.

'I'm not sure,' I tell her. 'We're just sort of seeing how it goes. It's fine, Bel. Honestly.'

'But he seems all better now, Mum.'

'He does, yes.' She's right, I think – but I'm no doctor. It's only when she's about to leave that I sense that things aren't one hundred per cent rosy in Bella's world. We've taken the local train to Glasgow together, as we usually do, with a plan to have lunch in the city before I see her off onto her London train. It's not that Frank doesn't want to see her off too. But he understands that we need a little time together.

However this time, towards the end of our lunch, she goes quiet. 'Is everything okay, love?' I ask.

She nods, fiddling with her spoon that's resting in the residue of melted ice cream.

'Bella, are you sure?'

She looks up at me, my daughter who seems to breeze her way through life. 'It's just a few little things with the house,' she says quickly.

'What kind of things?' I ask, alarmed. I've been to her terraced house in Bethnal Green. It's a bit battered around the edges but homely enough, with a tiny garden. But it transpires that one of her housemates has moved her boyfriend in, 'and he's playing his guitar on the stairs at all hours because he says it has the best acoustics and I can't sleep, Mum. I can't sleep!' And on top of that a new girl has moved in, a colossally messy party girl who leaves the sink piled with dishes and uses Bella's crockery that she bought herself, leaving food-encrusted plates in her bedroom. 'Honestly, Mum. She's worse than Eddie!' And if that wasn't enough – and this is what's really bothering her – Bella didn't get the promotion she was hoping for. She has always set incredibly high standards for herself.

'Oh, love, you've not been there long,' I say, resting my hand over hers. 'And you're only twenty-one.'

'What's that got to do with anything?'

I swallow. 'Just that you've achieved so much already, building a life in London, all by yourself without any help from us—'

'It just feels like such hard work sometimes,' she blurts out, eyes filling with tears. She fiddles with her long dark hair, tucking it behind her ears.

It is, I want to tell her. Just living can feel like carrying a boulder sometimes. But of course I don't say this. 'You know, you don't have to go back to London today,' I say, squeezing her hand. 'You could stay a bit longer, have a bit of a break—'

'But I've got my train ticket and work tomorrow—'

'Yes, I know.'

She sniffs and rubs at an eye. 'Sorry, Mum.'

'Bel, you've nothing to apologise for, sweetheart. But I wish you'd said something. There's so little time now. Why didn't you tell me any of this before?'

'There's been no chance!' Her sharpness startles me, and immediately she seems to check herself. 'Sorry. I don't mean to be horrible, and this is going to sound awful. But it's so hard to talk properly at home with Granddad there . . .'

Now I'm starting to understand. Kilmory Cottage wasn't the same for her this time – and isn't that what we want from home, even when we're all grown up? For it remain the same forever? It wasn't just her granddad jeering at the blaring TV, and somehow making our house feel rather small again. I suspect it's been more the way her dad and I are together, and she's picked up on that.

'Well, I'm glad you've told me,' I say gently. 'So, can we help at all? You have to tell me if we can. D'you want to move? If it's money you need, you only have to say—'

'I'd never ask you and Dad for rent money,' she says firmly. We fall silent for a moment.

'Honey,' I say eventually, 'you do know, if London's not for you—'

'I'll be all right, Mum.' The waitress comes over and I pay the bill and we wander towards Central Station. The thought of saying goodbye to her is crushing my heart.

We stop on the concourse and check the departures. 'I just want to say you can come back home any time,' I start. 'To live, I mean, if you'd like that. To have some home comforts for a while.'

She nods mutely, lips pressed tightly together. We hug then, and she seems to brighten. 'Oh, Mum. Of course I can't come back to Sandybanks. That would be like going backwards, wouldn't it? I'm just feeling a bit emotional, that's all.' Then we see that her train has arrived at the platform, and I'm rushing to buy her a bottle of water and a sandwich for later, even though water and sandwiches are readily available on the train. And we're hugging again tightly before she leaves, promising me that everything will work out, of course it will.

It's a little blip, that's all.

*

The fact that home didn't feel right to Bella sets me thinking that maybe Frank feels that way too. And perhaps, now we're sort of empty-nesters, it's time for a big change? So one Sunday evening, as I'm starting to cook dinner, I say, 'D'you like it here, Frank?'

He looks at me in surprise. 'What d'you mean? In this town or this house or—'

'In this house,' I clarify.

'Why d'you ask?'

'Well, we've been here an awfully long time, haven't we? Twenty-two years. And we chose it because we had a baby. It was to be our family home. But now everyone's gone and—'

'I still like our house.' He looks puzzled. 'Of course I do.' Dad is napping on the sofa but we're keeping our voices low, just in case.

'But are you truly happy here, Frank?' I go on, unable to let it drop now because something is wrong – I can sense it. And I need to know what it is. 'I mean, d'you like being here in Scotland? Or d'you ever, I don't know . . . wish you were back in Portugal?'

'Of course I like Scotland.' He eyes the groceries on the worktop that haven't yet been put away. Tinned soup, peaches, baked beans and pork sausage, all bought at

Dad's request. 'I'm just not sure about living in Scotland in 1952,' he adds.

I smile, grateful that he still has it in him to make a joke. 'It won't be for much longer,' I murmur.

'No, it's fine,' he says with a shrug. However, we both know what we really want to say, but can't quite say it.

My father keeps saying he 'won't be here long'. However, it's been over a month now, and he seems fine, health-wise – yet there's been no mention of when he might actually want to go home. Prish keeps saying I should broach it with him: 'Maybe his confidence has taken a knock? And all he needs is a gentle nudge?' But how to do that without implying that we want him to leave?

Naturally, Frank and I have done nothing more thrilling than drink cups of tea in bed since Dad's arrival. Not that I *mind*, of course – sleeping at opposite sides of the bed with the Gulf of Mexico between us. But really, it's no easier than when Eddie was here. The only difference is, I'm not perpetually worried about my father finding a job.

'I think,' I murmur, 'he might not want to go back to his own place, Frank. And we might need to accept that.'

I study his expression as the realisation settles. 'Right. Okay.' He blows out air.

'I'm sorry. I mean, he was always so fiercely independent. So I can't understand it . . .'

'He must like it here,' Frank suggests.

'Yeah.' I nod. 'I can't ask him to leave, Frank. I just can't.'

'No, I know, honey—'

'Carly! CARLY!' Dad yells from the living room.

'Yes, Dad?'

'Is dinner on the way?'

'Jesus,' Frank mutters.

'Yes, Dad,' I call back, although I have barely started it.

'Not too big a portion for me!' he retorts from the command centre. 'You always give me way too much.'

'All right!'

I look at Frank, and he groans. 'Is there any need for that?'

I throw out my arms in a gesture of helplessness. 'What can *I* do?'

'You're giving me *far* too much,' Dad hollers through the house. 'I'm putting on weight—'

'This having to eat at six on the dot,' Frank exclaims. 'I don't see why—'

'It's just the way he is.'

'Okay,' he huffs. '*Fine.*'

However it's not fine, and both of us know it. Another weekend comes and goes, and I wrestle with frustration over our new living regime, and guilt over not feeling one hundred per cent delighted about it. After all, the doctor did say Dad had a lucky escape. 'He's made of strong stuff,' he told me.

I lost my mum young, and I know I'm lucky that Dad is still here, rankling us. It should be an honour to look after him.

Yet I can't help thinking: is this it? This really is my second act?

CHAPTER TWENTY-NINE

Eddie

'We've got to be really on it this next couple of days, guys. New menu rolling out tomorrow. I think we're all au fait, right?' Near the end of a hectic shift, head chef and proprietor Marius is addressing his team in the restaurant kitchen. A bearded bear of a man, he is perpetually red-cheeked with jet-black hair slicked back, his chef's whites immaculate.

'Yep, we're all set, boss,' says Kim, his second-in-command.

'Excellent.' He beams around at the team. 'And now I have some exciting news for you all . . .' A respectful hush settles. All eyes are on Marius.

'Spit it out then,' Kim teases.

He grins. 'Well, we've got someone very special booked in for lunch on Friday. Using a fake name of course. But we know who it is.' He pauses, building the tension. 'It's *Jill Gilbert*—'

'Oh my God!' Kim gasps. 'How exciting!'

'Yeah.' Marius nods, brown eyes shining under bushy dark brows. 'So tomorrow's a trial run if you like. Five new starters, six mains. Not that I expect less than your best on *any* day. But Friday lunchtime I need you all to be absolutely on it . . .'

'Jill Gilbert,' murmurs Paulina, the pastry chef.

'Wow,' Eddie breathes, trying to look as if he knows who they're on about. But he's bluffing again. Living a big fat fib, like he's had to since Lyla's announcement. Will this go on forever? Eddie wonders. Will his entire life be a lie until the day he drops dead?

'. . . Need everything to be slick and on the money,' Marius goes on. 'No one shambling in late. No sneaky breaks. This is a big deal for us, I think you all know that . . .'

On and on he goes with the half-dozen team members all paying rapt attention. Apart from Eddie, that is. Eddie's attention is wandering. *Who's Jill Gilbert?* He'll have to google her and get up to speed. But right now, as Marius starts on about their new supplier of fresh herbs – 'You've never seen chervil like it!' – it's Lyla who is infiltrating Eddie's mind.

They've started meeting up now and again, always on her instigation. And Eddie obliges, because he wants to see her and this is a way for it to happen. He doesn't feel *he* can suggest meeting, because it might sound like he's asking her out on a date and they're not dating.

How mental it all is, he reflects as Marius homes in on Paulina, suggesting a small finesse to her signature chocolate tart. Eddie and Lyla are having a child together, yet he doesn't feel he can just call her, to ask how she's feeling, and to check what size the baby is now and what it's *doing* in there, inside her. Because he should know this, shouldn't he? He should know if his unborn child is the size of a pea, an egg or a Starbucks muffin. What he does know is that her belly is growing, her body softening in a way that causes an actual pain in Eddie's heart.

Because pregnancy is making her . . . *bloom*, is that what they say? She is glowing, all soft and pink cheeked, her golden hair lustrous and shiny. And he wants to kiss her, every time they're together. That's what he's thinking about now at 10.27 p.m. as Marius starts to wrap up his pep talk.

The first time Eddie kissed Lyla, when she'd slid a hand around the back of his neck to pull him close, rockets had gone off in his head. Because in all of his twenty-two years he had never been kissed like that. The actual sex part is a bit blurry now, and next morning Lyla had made it clear that she needed him to leave. She wasn't rude exactly, just direct. *I've got stuff to get on with, okay?* She took his number, saying she'd text him – but she never did. Not until a few weeks later, when he'd given up hope of seeing her again.

'I have something to tell you,' she'd said. 'Don't freak out.'

Eddie freaked out.

'Eddie!' Marius fixes him with a hard stare. 'D'you have any idea who we're talking about?'

'Er . . . sorry, what?' He snaps to attention, sensing his cheeks blazing.

His boss's shiny round face breaks into a grin. He's not

a bully, not at all. Marius took a shine to the new kitchen porter, teasing him when he went all pale and clammy at the sight of a bowl of liver and a side of beef, dripping blood. 'Get used to it, mate!' He did too, working hard and rising to the challenge. From day one, when he still couldn't quite believe his luck, all Eddie wanted was to impress his boss. And now, in turn, it feels vital to impress the girl he's besotted with. He's going to be a dad, for fuck's sake. It's time to make something of himself.

'*Jill Gilbert*,' Marius announces. 'She's a critic, Eddie. You should know that. Don't you read restaurant reviews?'

''Course I do,' Eddie fibs. He'd no more read the ingredients list on a packet of Wotsits.

'Then you know who I'm talking about, right? And the influence she has? I've met her, she's bloody terrifying—' Marius breaks off and laughs. 'But we needn't be scared 'cause we'll be prepared, won't we, guys?'

'Yeah, 'course.' Eddie nods as the team all murmur in agreement.

'So make sure you all get your beauty sleep tonight,' Marius commands. 'We need everything to be absolutely slick tomorrow, and then by Friday we'll be a hundred per cent up to speed.' He widens his eyes at Eddie. 'No twenty-four-hour bug crap, okay?'

'Definitely not,' Eddie says, meaning it. Because this time he won't let Marius down.

*

And this thought is burning fiercely in Eddie's mind as he wakes at eight on a crisp, bright Thursday morning. He sits up in bed, propped up by a flat pillow – he's known naan breads that are puffier – and reaches for his phone.

Two messages. The first from his mum: *Remember it's Granddad's birthday on Saturday! Did you send a card?*

No, he didn't send a card because that would have involved going to the shops and buying one, and a stamp, and then posting it – in an actual postbox – which feels like a logistical nightmare to Eddie. He doesn't even know where any postboxes are.

I'll text him, he replies.

Could you send a Moonpig e-card?

For fuck's sake, Mother! He doesn't bother replying to that.

The second message is from Lyla. *Can you come to a PV with me tonight?*

Eddie blinks at it. He doesn't know what a PV is, any more than he knew who Jill Gilbert was until Marius told him. So he googles it. How would he survive without Google? He can't understand how his granddad manages with that ancient phone.

Eddie frowns. 'Photovoltaic' is the top result, something to do with converting sunlight into electrical energy. He's assuming Lyla didn't mean that.

Surely PV isn't short for PVC and she's taking him to some kind of sex club? He wouldn't have thought she was the type. But then he doesn't know what type she is, not really. Eddie rubs at his face, under pressure now.

Fuck it, he'll just call her.

'It's a *private view*,' Lyla says, with emphasis.

'What?'

'An art opening, Eddie.' Oh, of course. He goes to them all the time! (He doesn't really. She might as well have asked him to the ballet). 'Mum'll be there,' she adds. 'The artist's a friend of hers. She likes seeing us together. It'll be nice—'

'Sorry, I can't do it,' he says quickly. 'I'm starting work at twelve. I won't finish till midnight . . .'

'It's only a couple of hours,' she protests.

'I can't just take a couple of hours off in the middle of a shift! We've got a new menu—'

'—Dinah's an *amazing* artist,' Lyla goes on, as if he hadn't spoken. 'She's a psychotherapist. Like a really top one. And she channels her clients' traumas and it all pours out into these amazingly powerful, intuitive works.'

Eddie wonders if he could actually do with some psychotherapy. It feels like it sometimes. Would this Dinah woman do him a special rate?

'Eddie?' Lyla prompts him. 'Can you come, or—'

'Are we going to keep this going?' he blurts out, shocking himself with his directness.

In the pause that follows he can tell he's shocked her too. 'Keep what going?' she asks.

'Pretending to be together, like a normal couple?' His left eyelid is flickering now, through stress.

'Uh, I don't know . . .' For once, she sounds hesitant. 'It's . . . difficult,' she murmurs. Talk about understatements. Then: 'Are you going to work right now?'

He checks the time. 'No, I've got a couple of hours before I start. Why d'you ask?'

'You don't . . . fancy coming over, do you? For a quick coffee?'

Eddie frowns. Of course he wants to. He wants that more than anything – but what does Lyla want?

'You really want me to come over?' he says hesitantly.

'Yeah, I'd just like to see you,' she says. 'That's all. Would that be okay?'

It takes Eddie a moment to digest this. 'Right. Yeah, of course.' His heart is lifting now. Then something occurs to him. 'I . . . don't actually have your address.'

Lyla emits a small laugh. 'This is so mad, isn't it?'

'It is, yeah.' His mouth twists into a smile.

'I'll text you it. See you soon.' And with that, she's gone. Eddie lies there, grinning, for a moment. Then he scrambles out of bed, deciding this is it. He must seize the day! He remembers Mr Crowther, his English teacher, barking at him when he was having a little nap on his desk.

'Wake up, Mr Silva! Carpe diem! Know what that means?'

'Something to do with carpets?' he'd wondered aloud. The whole class laughed, including Mr Crowther – and now Eddie is going to do just that.

'Carpe diem!' he announces out loud in his dismal room. Grinning now, Eddie reaches up to his window, rips down the faded bath towel and blinks, joyously, as sunlight streams in.

CHAPTER THIRTY

Eddie feels super-charged as he strides along Princes Street. No lolloping walk now. He bounds along as if he'd guzzled a whole tub of Raj and Calum's vitamins and his hourly quota of water according to the markings on the giant plastic bottle. He isn't smoking a roll-up because he's trying to stop smoking, as of forty-five minutes ago when he woke up.

Already it's making him weirdly sticky-eyed and hyper-aware of every nerve in his body, but he just needs to ride through it. Can't be smoking around a baby, he's decided. Can't be all stinky with Rizlas, filters and lighters stuffed in his pockets when he has his newborn son or daughter in his arms.

The irony of having to ask Lyla for her address isn't lost on him as he walks past a bagpiper, the squawks and drone so discordantly awful, it sounds as if the pipes are being reversed over by a truck. But it feels good, like some kind of progression. Of course he'd been to her flat before – on the night it happened – but he'd never have been able to find it again. And now he knows where she lives!

He is smiling as he rides the escalator down to Marks & Spencer's food hall. Because he's decided to pick up a couple of gifts for Lyla. He rushes around the store, piling a basket with chocolates, posh biscuits and a showy bunch of brightly coloured flowers. He baulks at the price tag – is that how much flowers cost? He's never bought anyone any before, apart from a tiny bunch of supermarket daffodils for Mother's Day on strict instructions from his dad. And they were only two quid. Still, Lyla's worth it, he tells himself. Then he's back on street level and bounding along with his wares.

Still an hour and a half before he's due to start his shift. The restaurant's nearby. Maybe he'll take Lyla there sometime soon. Really, he has no idea how things are going to pan out. But now he's allowing himself to believe that they might be . . . *something*. Like partners. Co-parents. Not in an intimate sense, but as two sensible adults who created a child and are somehow going to manage the whole business with ease and maturity and everything will be *fine*.

He reaches the main door to her building and, a little nervous now, presses her bell. She buzzes him in and he hurries upstairs. Bizarre how they conceived a child in this building and he has no recollection of the place at all. Then her door opens and she's standing there, wearing a fresh white T-shirt and black sweatpants, her bump clearly visible now and a big smile on her face.

'Oh, flowers!' She beams. 'That's so sweet of you. Come in. I've got some coffee on.'

'Great. Thanks.' She takes the gifts from him and he glances at her bump. *A bun in the oven!* Marius had teased him at work, when word got out. It seems a bit crude now and Eddie is all on edge, wondering what to do with himself as she goes off to fetch their coffees.

'Sure you can't come to Dinah's thing tonight?' she calls through.

'Sorry, I really can't,' he replies, although now he wishes he could. But after Marius's talk yesterday he's determined not to put a foot wrong. He's checked out Jill Gilbert. She not only writes for a prominent newspaper, but glossy magazines too, *and* she's a guest judge on a cookery show. He's inspected pictures of her, forensically. With her short black hair and red lipstick – like a slash of blood – she looks pretty scary. Eddie is relieved that he'll be in the kitchen rather than having to interact with her face to face tomorrow.

His gaze skims the pale grey walls, the expensive-looking lamps and the porridge-coloured sofa. He perches on the edge of it, afraid of sullying it. Unlike the sofa at his place, it's not covered by a throw. This, he realises, is because there aren't any stains that need hiding. When will Eddie have furniture that doesn't need shrouding in pieces of cloth?

Lyla reappears with their coffees in posh-looking china mugs that remind him of the one he smashed back at home, which belonged to his mum. She places them on the low table in front of them, and sits beside him. 'Funny this is only the second time you've been here,' she remarks with a smile.

'Yeah.' He nods. 'So . . .' He picks up his cup and takes a sip. 'How're you doing? How's your work and stuff?'

'It's good,' she says lightly.

Eddie doesn't know what else to ask about her job because he doesn't really know what it is. 'And are you . . . you know?' His gaze drops briefly to her bump.

'I feel good,' she says with a nod. 'Bit tired sometimes but that's normal.'

'I'm sure it is,' he says, although he has no idea.

Lyla smiles. 'It's kicking, you know.'

'What, right now?' he asks, astounded.

She laughs as he stares at her bump. 'Not right now, no. But come here, put your hand *here* . . .' His heart jolts as she takes his hand and places it on her bump.

He waits, his entire body tense as if the baby might suddenly burst right out of her. Suddenly there's a flicker of movement – 'Whoa!' he yelps, and his hands shoots away. They look at each other and laugh.

'Was that it? The baby kicking?' He is trembling slightly.

She nods, grinning. 'I'm looking forward to it, y'know.' She seems to catch herself then, and chuckles. 'Sounds a bit mad, doesn't it? Like it's a holiday or a birthday or . . .' She stops, pushing back her hair. As she turns to face him, her gaze fixed directly on his, Eddie is aware of a thudding in his chest.

'Yeah.' He nods. 'I'm looking forward to it too.'

Lyla looks at him in surprise, and Eddie is surprised too because until he said it, he didn't know *what* he was feeling. He's been scared and sometimes he's found himself plunging into a deep well of desperation. He's also been furious with himself for his part in this: for having unprotected sex, for being carried away in the moment. Ashamed too, for not knowing the best thing to do. He can hardly talk about it with Raj and Calum, because what is there to say really? Besides, he hardly sees them these days.

But now, as clear morning light beams into Lyla's living room, this new sensation has landed on him like sunshine.

He's going to be a dad.

They're going to have a baby.

A little boy or girl and he's going to be the best dad he can possibly be.

And right now Eddie knows that, whatever happens between him and Lyla – and really, he knows that *nothing* is going to happen, because she is way out of his league – he will love this child with every cell of his being, until he takes his last breath.

'Eddie?' Lyla's voice is gentle, her blue eyes wide. 'Are you all right?'

'Yeah,' he croaks, rubbing at his eyes.

'Oh, you're upset . . .' She takes his hand and sparks shoot through him.

'Yeah. No, I'm not. It's not that. It's only . . .' He squeezes his eyes tight shut for a moment. *Get it together, idiot!* 'I s'pose it's only really just hit me,' he admits, blushing.

'Bit of a delayed reaction?' She smiles teasingly, sunlight dancing in her eyes.

'Yeah. I'm sorry—'

'No need to be sorry. This isn't your fault, y'know. It was both of us, wasn't it?'

He nods mutely and she takes both of his hands in hers. Then her lips are on his and he anticipates a quick kiss, just to say *It's going to be all right.* But it's not quick.

The kiss carries on, growing deeper and making Eddie's head spin like the roundabout at Winter Wonderland. For a split second he thinks, *New menu today! I can't be late!* But the thought disappears like a popped bubble, and then Lyla is getting up from the pristine sofa, and they're in her bedroom, and she's pulling off her clothes and Eddie is too, and he's kissing her beautiful soft, rounded pregnant body all over and it's actually *happening*.

He's scared at first, in case it does anything to the baby. 'Is this okay?' he whispers.

'It's fine.'

'You'd say, wouldn't you? If it was going to hurt—'

'The baby's fine,' she reassures him. 'Don't worry.' For a moment it feels all wrong, as if a third person is here; a tiny person that they definitely shouldn't be having sex in the vicinity of. But Lyla pulls him close and into her, and as she gasps in pleasure, Eddie feels his worries floating away like dust particles dancing in the morning sun.

*

'OH MY GOD WHAT TIME IS IT!' Eddie shoots out of bed and scrambles for his phone. Where *is* it?

'What's wrong?' Lyla asks, blinking in the light.

'We fell asleep! I've got to go to work! What time is it?'

'Oh. God. Hang on . . .' She pushes tangled hair from her face and clambers slowly out of bed. Normally Eddie would be transfixed by this. By a beautiful naked girl strolling casually around her bedroom, looking for something. But now he's filled with panic and already pulling on his clothes.

'Fucking hell . . . he's going to kill me . . .'

'Who?' She frowns. Finally her own phone is extracted from the pocket of her discarded sweat pants.

'Marius! My boss!'

She looks at him, nonplussed. Of course Lyla doesn't have a boss. She doesn't have to go out to a restaurant and prep vegetables and fillet fish and make sauces as per Marius's precise instructions, which is what Eddie should be doing seven minutes from now because Lyla has just announced, 'It's eleven fifty-three. What time d'you—'

'Gotta go!' he cries. 'Where's my phone?'

'I don't know! Hang on, we'll find it—'

'There isn't time!' Then: 'Can I see you tomorrow? I'm on an early shift. I'll be finished by four—'

'Okay,' she says, smiling. 'I'll see you tomorrow. Why don't I come over to yours? I don't even know where you live.'

A wave of alarm crashes over him. 'Shall I just come here?'

'Are you ashamed of your place?' She laughs. 'Is it a boys' hovel?'

'It's a bit—' He stops. No time for negotiations now. 'It's fine. Come over.' He rattles off the address and she taps it into notes on her phone. She beams at him and he plants the briefest kiss on her beautiful full mouth before hurtling out of her flat, down the stairs and out into the bright morning sunshine.

Now he runs, already feeling the benefit of having quit smoking, what, three hours ago? He sprints through the New Town, swerving around corners and almost colliding with a street sweeper truck – 'Steady on, pal!' the man yells – and clattering onwards until the restaurant is in sight.

Scooting up the alley now, Eddie flies in through the side door to the bank of lockers. By some miracle of God or something – suddenly Eddie thinks there might be a God after all – he locates his key in his pocket and kicks off his trainers and then, not caring if anyone sees, he pulls off his jeans and yanks up his chef's trousers and tugs on his slip-on kitchen shoes and hurries through to the kitchen.

'All right, Eddie?' Paulina throws him a bemused look.

'Yeah.' Eddie tries to steady his breathing as he unpacks his own kitchen knife. Only now does he dare to look around at the kitchen clock. He is eight minutes late.

'Is Marius about?' he asks Paulina.

'Nah, he's gone to meet a supplier or something . . .'

'Great. Fine.' Eddie positions himself at his station, his whole body flooding with relief as he gets to work.

The shift is long and hectic, but it goes fine. Better than fine, as Eddie is propelled along by sheer happiness and exhilaration. He isn't even upset about not having his phone right now. For what feels like the first time in his life, he feels fully alive.

Him and Lyla. He can hardly believe what happened this morning. It was better – *far* better – than the first time as, for one thing, there wasn't a river of beer and vodka sloshing through his veins. He was fully present and sober and it was wonderful. Falling asleep afterwards, and the ensuing panic, wasn't quite so great. But it's all fine now. Marius didn't even know he was late.

At eleven-thirty, the shift is almost over. Eddie's boss is

jovial as he grabs a cloth and dabs at his shiny forehead. 'Great effort today,' he announces, looking around at his team. 'New menu's rolled out really well. You pulled it off and I'm proud of you all.' He pauses, fixing Eddie with a look. 'Nice work, Eddie. You're really coming on, mate. Must be impending fatherhood. Found out how to change a nappy yet?' He guffaws.

'I'll figure it out,' Eddie says with a grin.

''Course you will. Nothing to it.' Then he looks around at the others who are launching into the final clean-up at the end of the night. 'So you all remember Jill Gilbert's in tomorrow? She's here at one. Table for two. Remember, guys, I need you all on it and no messing about.'

CHAPTER THIRTY-ONE

Carly

The house is so quiet at night now. When the kids were here there'd be constant chatter and music playing. Maybe some clattering in the kitchen as Eddie and his mates suddenly decided to fry burgers at midnight, when the house would reek of burning fat. Eddie didn't often put things away or close a cupboard door. But if he did, it would be with a colossal BANG as if he was trying to smash up the kitchen.

My father might be trying sometimes but he doesn't do that.

And so at night, Kilmory Cottage settles into stillness, broken only by the gentle sounds of wind and sea. And tonight, as I edge closer to Frank, who I think is asleep already, I have thoughts.

Perhaps he's not *fully* asleep. Maybe, if I go very gently and don't scare him, then he might be up for it. Because it's been a very long time since we've had sex. At first, when Eddie's news broke, it was the last thing on my mind. We were so upset and, gallingly, Frank seemed to be blaming me.

I thought you gave him the contraception talk!

Then things settled a little, but it still didn't happen because Frank was spending an awful lot of time in the shed. Still is actually. No change there. And now Dad's here, but unlike our kids, he heads up to bed early, always by ten p.m.

So there's no reason why we can't do it, I decide, edging closer to Frank. I kiss his shoulder, his neck, the particularly sensitive bit by his ear. He is naked as usual – Frank can't stand wearing pyjamas – and instead of my usual fleecy PJs I've pulled on a silky slip.

Already, I'm feeling a bit *stirred up*. Frank is still an extremely good-looking man. I don't quite get the vibe of, 'Oh my God, what's he doing with that *crone?*' when we're out together. But it's a fact that he's more attractive than I am. He's been mistaken, variously, for Dennis Quaid, Richard Gere and Al Pacino – not that these men look like each other especially. But you might expect him to be in movies rather than toiling away at Dev's garage.

I slide an arm across his chest. Frank is lying, rigid, on his back. I don't mean rigid in an *exciting* way. I mean his entire body is as rigid as a door, arms clamped at his sides.

I try kissing him ever so gently again, wondering why he's still not responding. Is he dead? He still feels warm, and I think there's a pulse. As I snuggle closer, resting my head against his chest, I can feel his heart beating.

Thud-thud-thud it goes. So yes, there is life. But perhaps he used up all his libido in Paris? Can it wear out like a fan belt on an ancient car?

Undeterred, I gently tease the soft hair on his broad chest and kiss him there. He smells so delicious. I've always loved the natural scent of him. Daringly, I start to slide a leg over his, interpreting the fact that he doesn't flinch as encouragement. I edge the leg further. Then a bit further still, my body following the leg – as if the leg is the advance party making sure it's okay to proceed. While he's still not responding, I'm encouraged by the fact that he hasn't wrestled me off him or called the police. So I lower my hand from his chest, moving gently over the fuzzy warmth of his belly. Then lower still, down between his legs and around his—

'What're you doing?' he barks.

My hand and leg fly off him. 'I was just, I thought—'

'Pulling it, like it's an emergency cord—'

I sit bolt upright in bed. 'I did *not* pull it! I just touched you. Am I not allowed to do that anymore?'

'Sorry,' he mutters, exhaling forcefully. 'Made me jump, that's all.'

'So I gathered,' I snap. *And actually, it was an emergency just then! I needed you to make me feel loved and wanted, and that you still fancy me. Because you might not realise it but we haven't had sex since Paris!*

'It's your dad,' Frank mutters, staring up at the ceiling. 'I can't do it with your dad here.'

I blink at him in the darkened room. 'He's not right *here*, is he? Not watching—'

'You know what I'm talking about—'

'—He's not looming over us with a clipboard, taking notes—'

'Fucking hell, Carly. Thanks for putting that in my brain.'

Huffily, I edge away from him so no parts of our bodies are touching. 'He wouldn't hear anything,' I murmur. 'You know he refuses to wear those new hearing aids. The Bluetooth ones. Says the batteries only last a day, which I find hard to believe—'

'Talking about hearing aids is hardly doing it for me,' Frank announces. Then he rolls over abruptly so his broad back is facing me. And within seconds he seems to be sleeping, apparently unbothered by the fact that I might feel rejected or upset. There's certainly been no kiss or cuddle or even a touch, just to reassure me that everything's okay.

I lie there, watching our gauzy curtains moving slightly in the draught from our creaky old window. Somewhere in the distance, a boat sounds a horn and slowly, I start to feel my blood bubbling up to a rolling boil.

There's no way I can sleep now as Frank snores softly – blissfully! – beside me. So I swivel out of bed, tug on my dressing gown and pad through to the bathroom. Here I inspect my face in the mirror, to check whether I'm actually hideous and that's why Frank won't have sex with me.

My light brown hair is fading, like the board games displayed for years, and now sun-bleached in our local newsagent's window. My cheekbones have vanished along with my favourite pink china cup. On top of that, something I can only describe as jowliness seems to be happening around my jawline and chin. My eyes – my best feature, Frank always said – have dulled from green to a dirty puddle hue. I didn't even know eye colour could change! How is this possible? And as I peer closely, I can see that, while my left eye is normal-sized, the right one is now smaller, like a little raisin peering back at me. Midlife Shrinking Eye Syndrome, I think you'd call it. When did *that* happen?

Oh, I'm not hideous, I do realise that. As one of our library regulars announced to me last week: 'Good to see you, Carly. I love seeing your homely face.' Not ravishing like Cate Blanchett – but homely like a slab of pie. I caught Jamie laughing hysterically in the cookbook section.

'Well, you *are* nearly fifty,' I tell myself out loud. 'What d'you expect?'

Actually, thirty minutes ago I was expecting Frank to throw me up against the headboard but never mind! I creep quietly downstairs and put the kettle on, opening a cupboard to extract a packet of biscuits from among the selection of party goodies I've bought for Dad's birthday.

He'll be eighty-five on Saturday, and although I know he won't want any fuss, I'm planning to force a tiny celebration on him. Ana is arriving on Friday evening and the next day we'll have a little party. Which reminds me, Eddie never replied to my message asking him to send his Granddad a card. *He's an adult man*, I remind myself, *soon to be a dad. He doesn't need you reminding him to send birthday cards!*

Now my gaze is pulled by the assortment of photos pinned haphazardly to the corkboard by the cooker. There's Eddie, aged seven, delighted with his dad's childhood train set that we'd brought back on one of our Portuguese trips. He'd played with it obsessively until everything fell apart. There are also pictures of me and Frank, in our twenties, thirties and early forties, in my pre-jowly times. And here's Bella about to set off Interrailing, all tousled dark hair with a huge rucksack on her back. And here's Ana standing proudly next to a portrait she'd painted, as part of her portfolio for her art school application. Then Bella again, laughingly cutting up an L-plate with garden shears, on the day she passed her driving test. I hate to compare them but I look back at Eddie, who's heading for nappies and night feeds and car seats – he can't even drive! We funnelled enormous amounts of cash into lessons until his instructor, grumpy old Tony Devlin, declared that he 'didn't have the aptitude'. Couldn't he have told us this before we'd paid him eight million pounds?

'Hey,' comes the sudden voice.

'Frank!' With a jolt, I swing around to face him. 'Didn't hear you coming down.'

He is standing in the doorway in his dressing gown, rubbing at an eye. 'Just wondered where you were,' he says.

'I couldn't sleep. Want some tea?'

'Not for me.' A pause hovers. 'Carly, I don't mind your dad being here. You know that, don't you?'

'Yes, I know that,' I say, filling a mug from the kettle. I'm really not keen on discussing this now. 'You haven't seen my cup, have you? The china one Prish bought me? It's been missing since Eddie moved out. He must've taken it—'

'It's just, *you know*,' Frank interrupts, with clearly more pressing matters to discuss. 'About your dad being here. It's just . . .'

'I do know.' I nod.

Frank exhales. 'I mean, dinner on the dot of six, never mind that I'm barely in through the door—'

'I *know*, Frank—'

'And earlier tonight, I'd literally just gone into the bathroom and he was banging on the—'

'He's old!' I exclaim. 'If he needs to go, he needs to go, Frank. He can't help it . . .'

'Okay, but what about the way he commandeers the TV? When's the last time we watched something we wanted?'

I'm about to protest, but of course he's right. '*Cash or Crash* drives me mad too, you know.'

'But it's not just the watching, is it?' he goes on. 'It's the shouting at the telly. The ridiculing those poor people who get the questions wrong. *I'd* get them wrong! Did you know the name of the stately home owned by the Marquis of Bath?'

'Um, it's Longleat—'

'But you know what the worst thing is?' He raps his knuckles on the table. 'We don't eat here anymore, like we used to, all of us sitting around together like a proper family. Now we have to eat through there, off trays on our laps, with the TV on at full volume. We can't even *talk*—'

'—I know, Frank, I hate it too!' I turn away from him, pull open the washing machine door and yank out a clump of damp washing that falls onto the floor. 'D'you think I don't mind those things?' I straighten up and glare at him.

'The trays, the blaring TV,' he rants on. 'It's like living in an old people's home! And it's fine, we can deal with it, but don't be all huffy and storm out of bed because I didn't feel like—'

'Frank, I didn't storm!' I cry out. 'And it won't be for much longer—'

'I'm sorry but he's being unreasonable,' he announces.

'I know he is, Frank. I know. He always has been.'

'But he hasn't always been *here*.'

'No, but I've always had to deal with him, don't you see? Can't you imagine what it's been like all my life? I feel sorry for him now and I want to help him. But just because he's had botulism doesn't change who he is as a man, how unreasonable he is—'

I stop dead. Dad has appeared, with silvery hair askew, in the kitchen doorway.

'Oh, Dad.' My heart is banging hard.

He purses his lips and blinks slowly. 'Unreasonable, am I?'

'I'm sorry, I didn't mean—'

'Unreasonable by *not dying*?'

'Dad! I didn't mean *that*,' I start. 'Please. We were only talking. Things just get a bit much sometimes. And why are you up? Are you feeling okay?'

'Just came down for a drink,' he growls, stomping to the cupboard and snatching a glass and filling it to the brim from the tap. 'Aren't you always saying I should drink more water?' He takes a noisy slurp then bangs it onto the worktop and leaves the room.

'Dad, please come back! I'll make you some tea . . .' I scuttle after him, but he is already heading upstairs.

I follow him and we stop, facing each other on the landing. 'Please, Dad.' I touch his arm. The sight of him standing there, a little stooped in his faded old tartan pyjamas, crushes my heart.

'It's all right,' he snaps, looking away.

'It's *not* all right. I don't want to see you upset. Look, Ana's coming over at the weekend especially for your birthday—'

'You know I don't bother with birthdays. And I don't want any fuss.'

'Well, this year you are,' I say firmly. 'We're having a party on Saturday for you—'

'A party?' He looks aghast. 'No way!'

'Please, Dad. It's not a *party*-party, it's just a little—'

'I think I should move back to my own place,' he retorts.

'Oh, no. Don't react like this,' I start, welling up now. 'You're welcome to stay with us, you know that. And Ana will be upset if you're not here.'

'Well, I'm sorry about that,' he says tersely, shaking my hand from his arm and storming off into his room. 'I'm going to pack up my things. I've been under your feet for quite long enough.'

CHAPTER THIRTY-TWO

Eddie

All's quiet when Eddie comes home after his shift on Thursday night. He assumes Raj and Calum must be asleep. They're like that these days, off to bed early like a couple of monks.

Although he doesn't have his phone he reckons it must be nearly midnight. He is absolutely shattered, not only from his shift, but also from running on adrenalin all day following his thrilling morning with Lyla. Marius commented that he seemed a bit 'giddy' today: 'Great to see you buzzing, Eddie. But can you dial it down a bit tomorrow when Jill Gilbert's in?'

Eddie laughed it off. But really, it's a wonder he's managed to keep his mind on the job at all today. What he'd dearly love to do now is fall into bed. But he can't do that yet, because tonight he has important stuff to do.

On his way to the bathroom he notices that Raj's bedroom door is open, and there's no one there. Calum's is open too. He wonders where they've gone, now they're such boring old men? Late night bingo, perhaps?

This is great, he decides, heading into the living room where he surveys the usual chaos. Despite being clean-living professionals, Raj and Calum don't half leave a mess sometimes. Sweaters and T-shirts are flung everywhere, and dirty plates are cluttering the woodworm-ridden old crate they use for a table. It's no place for a baby, Eddie reflects. But of more immediate concern is that it's no place for a girl like Lyla. He sets about gathering everything up, and then washes up the pile of dirty mugs and glasses with an enthusiasm he's never experienced before, when engaged in a domestic task.

Now he notices that the living room rug has acquired a gravelly layer of crumbs. Eddie can imagine that Lyla's the type to pad around barefoot. He can't have her resting her dainty little pregnant feet on *that* when she comes over tomorrow after his shift. So he starts looking for the hoover, hoping now that neither Calum nor Raj are planning to work from home tomorrow, as they do occasionally. With a shudder he remembers Lyla describing Raj as 'handsome'. Eddie would far prefer to have the place to himself.

Having checked the hall cupboard, and found only a headless shop dummy and a mangled bicycle wheel, he has no idea where the hoover might be. Or if they have one, even (no one's used it since he's lived here). Finally he locates a dustpan and brush buried under the sink, and makes do with that. Then he turns his attention to his bedroom and realises, with a jolt of horror, that this will not do at all.

It's dingy and depressing and, he realises now, a bit smelly. He can't possibly invite Lyla into his sleeping quarters when they're in this state. At the bottom of his wardrobe he finds the new bed linen set, still in its clear plastic packaging, that his mum ordered for him. He'd flung it in there without much thought – irritated, actually, at her 'interference' – but now he decides that these items are in fact extremely useful. They're a stripy design, grey and blue; perfectly acceptable for a young man to have. Not that his mum would have picked a SpongeBob set, but still. Eddie is conscious that everything has to be just right for Lyla.

Spirits rising now, he strips off his grubby bedclothes and stuffs them into the wardrobe to be dealt with at a later date. Then he rips the packaging from the new set and pulls it all out.

Eddie frowns. A vital component seems to be missing.

There's no sheet! Where's the *sheet*? He checks the label on the packaging: *Pure Cotton Duvet and Pillowcase Set*. What's the use of that? Is he supposed to sleep on a bare mattress, like it's a crack den? Eddie can't imagine Lyla would be crazy about that. What can he use instead? A tablecloth? Of course there isn't a tablecloth here; there isn't even a *table*.

There's the option of putting the same sheet back on. But on further inspection Eddie discovers that it has a huge greyish patch in the middle. And by 'middle' it's more like the whole sheet, apart from the edges, from where he's been lying on it. So the greyness must be his skin cells that have fallen off in the night. Is this the colour he is now, from these long, hard shifts in the kitchen?

Tentatively, he sniffs the sheet. Ew, no, this definitely can't go back on the bed. Five months is too long to sleep on the same sheet, he realises now. But Eddie can rectify that. He bundles it up and carries it through to the kitchen, locates some washing powder under the sink and stuffs it into the washing machine on the quickest cycle.

With it churning already he bounds back to his room to tidy and even *dust*, wincing at the filth that comes off onto the pair of boxers he uses as a duster.

Now for the most challenging task – the one he's put off until last.

Eddie rotates his clicky shoulders, takes a big suck of water from Raj's spout bottle and pops a handful of vitamin pills he swiped from the tub in the kitchen. Thus fortified, he eyes the blind, still propped up in the corner in its cardboard tube. He steps closer, squaring up to it as if it might fight him.

Eddie Silva is a hard-working man now and a father-to-be. Surely he can put up a simple window covering?

He knows there's zero chance of there being any tools in the flat. (Where is Eddie's dad when he needs him?) But he can improvise, can't he? He has a good brain, Marius reckons. He's *resourceful*. So Eddie tips out the components out of the tube, tossing aside the sheet of instructions as obviously he won't need those. Now he picks up the little packet of screws and two white plastic thingies. Brackets, he surmises, to hold the thing up. How can he fix them in place without a drill, a screwdriver or a ladder to stand on? Even at six foot tall, Eddie can't reach the top of the window.

Filled with determination now, he fetches a wooden

chair from the living room, plus the only frying pan in the flat. With the washing machine whirring reassuringly, Eddie tries to measure the blind's width 'by eye'. Then he climbs onto the chair and, wobbling a little, he places a bracket above the top left corner of the window. He fits a screw through the hole and whacks it hard with the frying pan.

Shards of wood and plaster fly out at him. But amazingly, it stays up!

Somehow Eddie needs to know *exactly* where to place the second. He clambers off the chair and checks the blind's width from the instruction sheet he'd tossed aside. Then he stares up at the top of the window, wondering how wide fifty-two centimetres might be.

The presenter of *Cash or Crash* pops into his mind. With his neat little teeth and a caramel tan, he always looks a bit too pleased with himself. 'Okay, Eddie. For a chance of the jackpot of ten thousand pounds . . .' expectant pause . . . '. . . how wide is fifty-two centimetres?'

Eddie's brain seems to freeze. Now he's cursing himself for not searching Lyla's flat for his phone. In his panic he'd been more concerned about rushing off to work. However, not having it about his person is making him feel all out of kilter, because googling everything is Eddie's way of navigating life. For instance, Jill Gilbert's restaurant reviews. Eddie has pored over them as if prepping for an exam.

Suddenly, it's as if his brain switches on. Fifty-two centimetres is *fifty-two centimetres you idiot!!!* – i.e. the width of the blind! All he needs to do it hold it in place and make a pencil mark at its end. He peers up at the top of the window again, trying to dredge up the energy to get this thing done. His mum would announce sometimes that she was tired after cooking dinner – but she never cooked for ten hours straight. If only his dad were here. Then the blind would be up already, and everything would be all set for tomorrow and Eddie could go to bed.

He hears the washing machine bleep in the kitchen, signalling that the cycle is done. He runs through to pull out the sheet. In the absence of a tumble dryer he'll have to dry it somehow. There's only one answer to that, Eddie decides. He's not going to blast it with Raj's hairdryer for hours on end. Instead, in a burst of rebellion, he does something he has been warned, very firmly by his prematurely aged flatmates, to never do.

Eddie marches into the hallway to the little gizmo stuck on the wall and he *puts the heating on.*

Yes, in June. It's expressively not allowed 'until at least November', Raj declared. But Eddie is sick of house rules and, with the sheet now bunched over the living room radiator, he heads back into his bedroom.

And this is where he's hit by a tidal wave of exhaustion. Tottering on the wobbly chair with the blind, the bracket and the frying pan, Eddie is painfully aware that today's shift was especially hectic and he really should be lying down. Instead, he is holding up the blind horizontally and, quivering with the effort, trying to position the bracket at the same time. He's young and healthy and he should be able to do this when his dad can build a truck with his bare hands, from bits of crap lying around in Dev's garage. But Eddie is shaking, and he drops the blind, then the bracket. Then the spindly chair tips, propelling Eddie forward towards the window where his head and forearm and the frying pan smash into the glass.

Eddie screams as the window shatters and somehow he ends up on his bedroom floor with bits of glass and some kind of dark liquid splattered all over. His vision is swimming but he manages to raise his arm and look at it. The sight of it – all that blood pouring out of him – triggers a surge of nausea. Briefly, he thinks: *Jill Gilbert's booking at one o'clock!*

And then Eddie isn't worrying about restaurant critics or what Marius will do to him if he doesn't show up for work, because he promptly passes out. At least, he thinks that's what happened because now Raj is here, Raj and Calum, and they're crouching over him in the harsh glare of his bedroom's centre light.

'Mate . . . what happened?' Calum cries out.

'I . . . I was just trying . . .' Eddie starts. 'I fell. Cut myself . . .'

'Yeah, I can see that.'

'Blind,' Eddie croaks.

'You can't see? Fucking hell,' Raj gasps.

'No, the *blind*.' Eddie manages to indicate the broken window. 'I was trying to put it up. I just, uh . . .'

'Why didn't you ask us to help you?' Calum exclaims.

Slowly, painfully, Eddie manages to sit up. 'You weren't here.'

'Yeah, we were at a spoken word night,' Raj murmurs.

'A what?'

'Y'know. Poetry. Kind of free-form stuff.' Raj pauses

and then, trying for a joke, he adds, 'If we'd known you were gonna throw yourself through the window, we would've asked you along.'

'Uh.' Eddie grunts. 'Not really my thing—'

'Yeah, well, we're getting you to hospital, mate,' Calum says now, wincing at the gash on Eddie's forearm that's possibly still bleeding; Eddie doesn't know, he can't bear to look at it.

'I don't need hospital. I just need to sleep—'

'Nope, you're going,' Raj announces, jumping up, already gripping his phone. 'I'm getting an Uber. No arguments. We're coming with you, all right?'

So that's what they do. The three of them go to hospital in a car that smells strongly of synthetic cherry air freshener. Eddie is jammed miserably between his friends on the back seat, his bad arm rather messily bandaged in a greying towel with a Lidl carrier bag taped over it.

To give them credit, Calum and Raj aren't such arseholes after all. In fact Eddie can't help feeling touched when they sit with him the entire night, in this grim waiting room with damaged people arriving, limping and bleeding and off their faces, some of them – arguing and punching the vending machine.

Numerous people are seen before Eddie. Fair enough, he thinks, that guy looked like his ear was hanging off – but is he ever going to get out of here? Meanwhile Calum and Raj have work to go to, yet they're still making no move to leave. Eddie does too – or *did*. His shift was meant to start at seven-thirty a.m. An early today, which he was pleased about, as it meant he'd be free to see Lyla later. But seven-thirty has passed and by eight o'clock Eddie still hasn't been seen, and nor has he figured what to do about contacting Marius.

Finally, as Calum reluctantly heads off to the office, Eddie asks to borrow Raj's phone. Of course he doesn't know Marius's number, and nor can he access the Bracken kitchen's WhatsApp group. So he googles the restaurant and calls the main number. It's the booking line – an answerphone. He leaves a garbled message, actually forgetting to say his name, and hangs up.

'Think he'll be okay with that?' Raj asks, looking doubtful as Eddie hands him his phone.

'Yeah, be fine,' he replies, feigning confidence. Later still, at ten-thirty a.m., Eddie looks at Raj. 'You should go now. No point in waiting with me anymore.'

'I'm not going anywhere,' Raj says firmly. 'I've texted my manager, he's cool.' How amazing to have a 'cool' boss, Eddie reflects as finally a nurse calls his name, and he is taken through to a small curtained cubicle where he is examined and then left interminably, to the point at which he worries that he's been forgotten about.

Finally, Eddie is treated. While the small cut on his forehead is merely given a clean, the wound on his arm requires stitches. Forty minutes later he is released back into the bright and breezy Edinburgh day, with Raj having waited patiently to take him home. No point in going to the restaurant now, not in the midst of lunchtime service. He simply can't face the wrath of Marius, and what use would he be anyway with his right arm out of action?

Two hours later, as Jill Gilbert tucks into her mussels in a smoky red pepper sauce, Marius leans against the huge industrial fridge in the kitchen and taps out a message on his phone.

What happened Eddie? Where are you today? You'll be paid up to yesterday. Don't you dare bother coming back.

CHAPTER THIRTY-THREE

Carly

It took intensive negotiations for the Natural History Society to agree that their table could remain in its new position. I managed to handle Thelma Campbell with extreme delicacy, when the others were too scared to deal with her.

And this is what it took to persuade Dad not to pack up and leave on Thursday night. Admittedly, I milked the Ana card. *She's been so looking forward to seeing you, Dad. I told you she has a summer job in the V&A in Dundee? Something about design principles linked to Dundee's industrial past. She's dying to tell you all about it . . .*

As he was an engineer, I hoped that would hook him. Plus, despite Dad pretending that he's not remotely interested in anyone, I know he loves his grandkids. So he agreed to stay: 'Just to get this birthday over and done with.'

Ana arrived on Friday evening, a whirl of chatter and

energy, and even Frank seemed more like his old self as the three of us sat up late, discussing her granddad's party.

'Obviously, we'll put *Cash or Crash* on,' she announced.

'At a birthday party?' Frank exclaimed.

'Yeah, it'll be fun,' she insisted. 'We can do teams. I can't believe Eddie can't make it!'

'Oh, it's fine, love,' I said. 'You know what restaurant work's like. He couldn't get out of his shift.'

'Shame. Honestly, I can't believe he's cooking for a living now.' She turned to her dad. 'Remember how you tried to get him involved in the food truck? Thought you could be a team?'

He laughed, shaking his head. 'Yeah, that worked, didn't it?'

'But Eddie says this is "proper cooking",' I added.

'Oh, of course.' Ana smirked. 'So how many are coming tomorrow?'

I counted them up. 'Us three and Granddad. And Ian and Sandra—'

'Oh, that couple he and Maggie used to go out with? I thought he'd dropped them after Maggie left?'

'He did, darling.' We exchanged an eye-roll. For years the two couples went out together at least once a week. They even went on holiday together once, to Menorca, under Maggie's instigation (Dad doesn't believe in holidays). 'Sandra came into the library,' I explained. 'Said she's tried to call him but he never answers. She didn't even know he'd been in hospital . . .'

'Oh, Mum. What's he like?'

'And I've invited Prish and Myra, his neighbour. She's been kind to him . . .'

'So, eight of us?' Ana said. I caught something then: a flicker in her brown eyes.

'Yes, love. D'you think that's enough?'

'Definitely.' She grinned. 'I just think you have enough food in for fifty. That's all.'

*

And now, on this bright Saturday morning, Frank and Ana and I greet Dad with birthday cards and gifts. Bella's arrived in the post but, notably, there's nothing from Eddie. He has enough on his mind, I tell myself, deciding to let it go.

As well as Dad's requisite six-minute boiled egg, I dish up piles of grilled bacon and pancakes. 'This is way too much,' Dad keeps insisting, but I can tell he is enjoying the attention. It's Ana who suggests a stroll along the beach after breakfast, and I suspect that's why Dad agrees. So we all set off, and we meet Marilyn from the library and throw sticks for her dog, and Raj's mum waves as she jogs along the seafront. And then, as we're turning back towards home, my heart seems to burst at the sight of the figure coming towards us.

She waves with both hands, long hair blowing across her finely boned face. 'Bella!' I cry out, running towards her. 'My God, you're here! Why didn't you say?'

We hug tightly and her dark eyes well up. 'Just had the urge to see you, you know? With it being Granddad's birthday. Thought I'd surprise you.'

'This is wonderful, love. But I still don't understand how—'

'I got the five o'clock train this morning.' She grins as I wrap my arm around her shoulders. I can't help wondering if that's the real reason, or if London is still feeling a bit too much.

'Up here again, Bella?' Dad says with a wry smile. 'You can't stay away!'

'Yes, Granddad, because it's your birthday. Don't mind, do you?' she teases.

''Course not. Lovely to see you, Bel. But I don't want any fuss, mind.'

'Don't worry, Granddad.' She links her arm in his as we start to head back to the house. 'There'll be absolutely *no* fuss.'

It's a lie of course because the party is happening later. And rather than having Dad hovering around, protesting that it's all far too much, I enlist Frank and the girls to whisk him off on another walk, this time to town, on the pretence of Bella wanting to check out the new tea room. 'Come on, Granddad,' she says. 'We'll get ice creams.'

As soon as they've gone I start setting out Dad's birthday tea, and Prish arrives, armed with home-made cakes and brownies. 'This looks lovely,' she announces. 'He'll be so pleased, won't he?'

'I hope so.' I smile, relieved now that Dad seems to be enjoying his day so far. 'Thanks for doing all that baking,' I add. 'You know it's not my forte . . .'

'It's fun for me. And your dad deserves a party after everything that's happened to him.'

I nod as we set out plates and glasses. 'Yes, he does. He's not the easiest but, after the other night—'

'Oh, that sounded awful.' She knows about Dad storming up to his room, threatening to move out. 'It can't be easy at the moment,' she adds.

'No, it's not. I know Dad's difficult, but when Frank starts on about him I just feel stuck in the middle. And what can I do anyway? If it'd been his mum or dad who'd needed to move in, we'd have dealt with it.'

'But they had Frank's brothers,' she says. 'And your dad only has you.'

'The perils of being an only child.' I smile.

'Well, I think you're brilliant with him,' she says as we carry on setting everything out. Prish brought up her four kids with little help from her unfaithful husband. Her three sons and daughter all adore her. They never accuse her of *trundling*.

Through the window now I see my family crossing the street towards our house. 'I don't blame Frank for getting grumpy,' I add. 'We thought we were all sorted when Eddie moved out. Remember how desperate I'd been, for me and Frank to have the place to ourselves?'

Prish chuckles and then the door opens and everyone tumbles in, greeting Prish fondly. Then Ian and Sandra arrive, hugging Dad as if there hasn't been a blip in their friendship. 'Looking well, Kenny!' Sandra announces. 'Getting the star treatment here?' And then Myra arrives, laden with yet more home baking, and Frank goes off to do drinks.

And it's lovely, considering that Dad didn't want a fuss. There are fancy crackers and the posh cheeses he secretly loves, rather than a big block of cheap Cheddar with a reduced sticker on it. There are Prish's cakes and brownies and Myra's muffins, plus Dad's favourite Battenburg, and plump strawberries and sparkling wine. He acts as if it's a wild extravagance, as if we're feasting on lobster and caviar. But he also loves it, and seeing him surrounded by friends and family lifts my heart.

We divide into two quiz teams with Dad pointing out that they are unevenly numbered, yet unwilling for anyone to opt out. Then *Cash or Crash* is switched on at a suitably eardrum-shattering volume and we all yell out the answers. When I go through to the kitchen during the ad break, Frank appears at my side. 'This is nice, isn't it?' he says.

'Yeah. I think Dad's having a lovely time.'

He smiles then, and places his hands on my shoulders. 'Well done, you.'

'Oh, it's not just me, is it?' In fact I'm surprised and delighted by the compliment.

'It pretty much is. Like everything around here.' His gaze meets mine, and he kisses me gently on the lips.

I smile up at him, lost for words for a moment. 'I think the two of us have done pretty well, Frank. If we're allowed to say that—'

'I think we are,' he starts, and then Bella yells, 'Mum!'

'What is it, love?' I call back.

'It's starting again. C'mon, we need you on our team!'

'Hey, what about me?' Frank says, following me back to the living room where everyone is squashed onto the sofa and chairs, and our daughters are installed on floor cushions. The house is feeling very full again, with the girls sharing what used to be Eddie's childhood room.

'Aren't I needed on the team?' Frank asks, feigning dismay.

Dad snorts. 'Haven't heard *you* getting many questions right, Frank.'

'No, well, my talents lie in other areas,' he says, catching my eye with a smile.

'That's right.' Dad swivels to him, holding out a crystal glass. 'Put another dram in that for me, would you, Frank?'

'Right, so my talents are bartending,' Frank says, with a good-natured eye-roll. 'So what's it to be, Kenny? The Laphroaig or the Balmoral?'

'Let me try the royal stuff,' he says, nodding towards Ian and Sandra. 'Nice present, that.'

'We didn't know what else to get you,' Ian says.

'You *are* the man who has everything, Kenny,' Sandra jokes.

A reluctant smile crosses his lips. 'I s'pose I do,' he says with a note of surprise. Perhaps it takes a day like this to remind Dad how much we love him.

Drinks are replenished for the show's second round, and we're all poised for the quick-fire segment.

'*Macbeth*!'

'Tower of London!'

'Anne Boleyn!'

'It's Catherine of Aragon,' Dad retorts, rounding on Ana.

'Is it?' she mouths, looking at me.

'Anne Boleyn is the correct answer,' the presenter announces and Ana's face breaks into a triumphant smile. She laughs and Dad knocks back his scotch. Then we're all poised again, and I can virtually *see* the waves of intense concentration coming from my father; the man who apparently doesn't need me, or anyone at all.

When the front door bangs, I assume Ian and Sandra must have contacted another friend of Dad's. A surprise guest? How lovely!

Still clutching my glass of wine, I make my way past everyone to the living room door.

'Hurry up, Mum,' says Bella. 'It's literature, your subject—'

'Yes, one minute, love . . .' I push open the door and there, in the hallway, is Eddie. Eddie with a tear-stained face, a cut on his forehead and his arm thickly encased in a white bandage.

'Eddie! Oh my God, darling. What happened to you?'

I go to hug him and he winces, pulling back.

'Hi, Mum.' A small rucksack thuds to the floor.

'Oh, love.' My eyes fill with tears. 'What's happened? Please tell me.'

'Just an accident. Nothing serious. I'm okay.'

'Why didn't you call? I could've come to get you—'

'No phone. I left it at Lyla's and—' He breaks off and rubs at his eyes.

We stand there in silence for a moment. 'Copenhagen, you fool!' Dad yells at the TV.

Eddie's mouth twitches and he lowers his gaze. 'Come through, love,' I say gently. 'Everyone's here. Remember it's Granddad's birthday?'

'Oh God, yeah.' I try to lead him through by the hand but he stops in the hall. 'Mum, if it's all right,' he says in a small choked voice, 'I need to be here with you and Dad, okay? I want to move back home.'

CHAPTER THIRTY-FOUR

July

Living at Kilmory Cottage: Carly, Frank, Kenny, Eddie

Bella and Ana both offer Eddie their beds that night. No, he'll be fine, he insists. 'You've had a rough time, Ed,' Bella reminds him. 'Honestly, I don't mind. I'll sleep downstairs on the sofa.'

'I'll be *fine*,' he says, a little more forcefully now that Prish, Myra, Sandra and Ian have left. The sofa will be FINE, seeing as Granddad seems to have moved into his room now!

Eddie observes me, pointedly, as I spread a sheet over the sofa, and then bring down the spare duvet we'd always kept for sleepovers, and which Dad rejected in favour of blankets. 'I hope you're comfy here,' I say, feeling helpless as to how to make him feel better. He's already spilled out what happened: the blind fiasco. *The blind you ordered, Mum.* As if that, like the pregnancy, was somehow also my fault. Imagine, buying him an item that would result in injury and unemployment! And hadn't he told me that he'd put it up months ago? Why had he lied about that?

'What happened exactly?' Frank asked. Eddie muttered that the stepladder he'd used, in order to position the blind accurately – *according to the instructions* – had suddenly collapsed. And then his boss had been totally unsupportive – sacking him with no notice, for having an accident! Eddie had only found out when he'd borrowed Raj's phone again and finally managed to get hold of Marius at the restaurant. As he doesn't know Lyla's number, he's been unable to contact her – and instead of being at home when she was due to visit, he'd opted for drowning his sorrows in the pub. When he'd woken this morning, depressed, hungover and still phoneless, all he could think of was to grab a bag of essentials and catch the next train home.

We'd all gathered around him, dispensing sympathy and careful hugs, so as not to knock his bad arm. 'It's *fine*,' he said sharply as I fussed over him, asking if it hurt, or whether he needed painkillers.

I glance at him now, all pale and exhausted and looking as if he's been in a fight. I've already texted Suki, explaining briefly what's happened and asking for Lyla's number. As she has yet to reply, I assume she's up at the cabin. 'I'll just fetch you a pillow,' I say.

'Yeah, if you've got one,' he mutters.

I frown, suddenly reminded of my petulant, pre-Edinburgh son. *Now you're deciding which Quality Street I like?* 'Eddie, of course there's a pillow—'

'—Or I could make do with a cushion.'

Don't rise to it, I tell myself. He's been through an

awful lot. 'Sure you'll be okay down here?' I ask later, when he's tucked up.

'Yeah.' *Please go away now,* is the strong signal he's sending out. The fact that he has Lyla's number now – Suki got back to me, full of concern – hasn't seemed to lift his mood.

'You know the girls are heading off tomorrow, so you'll have a bed then,' I add. Eddie nods, duvet pulled up tightly to his chin. 'You're not really fed up that Granddad's in your room, are you?'

A shrug. 'Not really.'

I peer at him, trying to make sense of this. 'Eddie, you'd moved out. I didn't think you'd be back. And you knew Granddad had moved in with us—'

'I didn't know he'd have my room!'

I open my mouth, stunned by his outburst. 'Should we have asked permission?'

'It would've been nice to know it was still there,' he mutters, looking a little shamefaced now.

'It *is* there,' I say, patience fraying now. 'And it's only temporary, Granddad being here—'

'Yeah,' Eddie says. 'It's just that some parents keep their kids' rooms *exactly* as they are.'

*

As a *shrine*, he meant, which kills Prish, Jamie and Marilyn when I tell them at the library on Monday morning. 'Like you did, Prish,' Jamie teases. 'Didn't you have Joe's room up on Airbnb before he'd unpacked his stuff in uni halls?'

We laugh, and as the days go on, I take to offloading about my home situation on a daily basis. Since the weekend at the cabin, Suki and I have also been messaging occasionally. Oliver was concerned about my dad, she's told me, and she's reassured him that everything's okay. I'm enjoying the connection with her, mainly because we're sharing a huge thing here; the arrival of our first grandchild. Happily, the focus is more on the birth, and the baby, than the parents' relationship. What names do we think they'll choose? Does Lyla have a birth plan? We share our own birth stories and admit how nerve-shredding it'll be for us, when the day finally arrives.

Also, surprisingly to me, Suki seems to enjoy my updates on home life. *Carly, you're a saint,* she's said on more than one occasion. Of course it's not true because often my thoughts are far from saintly. But all of this helps to keep me sane while I'm living with Frank, Eddie and Dad. A lone female now, missing my daughters and concerned about Bella, even though she insists she's okay.

Meanwhile Dad keeps insisting that I'm trying to overfeed him. And Eddie's lengthy soaks in the bath trigger much door banging from Dad. In turn, Eddie is appalled by our new dinner-on-laps regime with the endless quiz shows, and the way his granddad leaves his pill packets scattered all over the bathroom.

'Everything's gone so *weird* here,' he's complained. As if, during his absence, Kilmory Cottage was taken over by an invading force, who have instilled a harsh and unsettling new regime, and no one thought to warn him. Plus, since his spell in Edinburgh his already tenuous ties with his remaining Sandybanks friends seem to have weakened even more. Without a phone, it seems, you just can't communicate with anyone (when I suggested he popped round to see a couple of old mates in person, he looked aghast). Quite reasonably, Frank says we're not buying him another phone, not when there's a perfectly good one sitting in an Edinburgh flat. Why can't Lyla post it to him? I have no idea, and am loath to broach the subject. Perhaps she, like Eddie, is allergic to anything to do with the postal system.

Meanwhile I might have expected that, as a professional chef, Eddie might offer to cook now and again. But instead, he has taken to patronising me in the kitchen. 'Your knife skills are terrible,' he hectors, looming over me in his hooded brown robe as I dice an onion. Yep, now they're reunited – the disgusting article was given a boil-wash in his absence – and he's taken to wearing it again like a second skin. 'You should *never* stir a paella, Mum,' he scolds. 'You're breaking down the starch in the rice and that's what's making it sludgy.'

This from the boy who incinerated my best pan and grated his thumb!

Another night, as I prepare a quick dinner: 'When you're making a vegetable base like that, you need to chop the shallots and carrots really finely, to make a *mirepoix*—'

'Eddie, it's just a pasta sauce.'

'—and you should braise it gently for a very, very long time, in butter.'

I form a rictus smile. 'Thanks, love. I'll do that.' He'll settle down, I tell myself. It's just that he has no job to go to and nothing much to do. Meanwhile Frank has returned to the shed.

'I could burn it down when he's out at work,' I suggest, during a Monday lunchtime walk with Prish. '*And* Eddie's robe—'

'Oh, is that back in action?' she asks, trying to stop a laugh. I suppose it *is* funny, in a demented sort of way. And I can't help smirking when I glimpse *The Empty-Nester's Handbook* sitting there on the bookshelf.

However, one morning I'm not laughing at all as Frank and I stroll along the seafront together. 'Fancy walking to work with me this morning?' I'd asked. 'We never get the chance to talk properly anymore.'

Although a little nonplussed, he'd agreed. Three weeks since Eddie came home, and I was desperate to have some time alone together.

'Can you believe this has happened to us?' I ask now, glancing out over the choppy sea. The ferry is making its way towards Arran, and the island is shrouded in mist.

'Not really, no,' Frank replies.

'D'you think Eddie's all right? I mean, I worry about his mental health—'

'He'll be fine when he gets his phone back,' he says sharply.

I bite my lip. 'Maybe. I hope so. Why won't Lyla post it?'

Frank merely shrugs and grunts.

'We could pick it up when we go over to collect his stuff,' I add. 'When d'you think we should do that?'

'I don't know—'

'D'you think he's going to give up the flat? I've tried to ask but he just shuts me down. I guess the guys will want to find another flatmate—'

'Can we stop obsessing over what Eddie's doing or not doing?' Frank blasts out.

I stop and stare at him. 'I'm not! I'm just . . . *wondering*. That's all.'

We start walking again in silence. My heart is thudding, and my chest feels tight. 'The thing is,' he announces with startling force, 'it's not really our job to be in charge of his life, is it?'

I take a breath, trying to stay calm. I can't face an argument now, not right before I head off to work. 'I know it's not,' I reply. 'But it's the way things have turned out.' I turn away from Frank, barely able to look at him now. Instead, I glance down at the beach where several dog walkers are walking together in a group. Their dogs are running and playing, delighted to be in a pack. And then I see a familiar woman in a tracksuit striding along the seafront. It's Janine, Calum's mum, who has a stream-of-consciousness way of speaking, and who of course knows all about Eddie's baby.

'Who'd have thought it?' she announces, catching her breath.

'I know!' I force a smile.

'Remember that time at your barbecue, you were saying he had quite some growing up to do? But boys are like that, aren't they? Late developers, lagging behind . . .' By 'growing up' I'd meant helping in the house, and perhaps ingesting some fruit now and again. Not making a baby. 'You do your best to help them along their way,' she goes on. 'But they have to get there by themselves, don't they? It has to come from *them*, not us. Look at Calum, nearly dropping out of uni. Couldn't take the pace. And now he's flying, loving his life . . .'

'I'm glad he's doing so well,' I say, glancing at Frank. He's been standing there, as mute and unmoving as the sea wall.

We part ways and finally, the man speaketh. 'What was all that about?'

'You know Janine. She just goes on a bit.'

'Maybe she's right though,' he adds. 'Maybe we should've kept out of things with Eddie.'

I stare at him. 'What're you talking about?'

'Oh, I don't know,' he blusters. 'The stuff we get involved with—'

'Like what, Frank? Like helping him move, and trying to be supportive when he needs us—'

'Didn't we say this was our time now, when we were in Paris?'

'Yes, but quite a lot's happened since then—'

'Tell me about it!'

'What're you angry about now?' I exclaim. 'Eddie coming back home? He had an *accident*—'

'Yeah, trying to put up the blind! Did you honestly think he'd be capable?'

'What? You mean you're actually blaming me for this? Like not giving him the proper facts-of-life talk, remember you blamed me for that too—'

'I did not!'

'Frank, I had to beg you to tell him anything,' I protest. 'Like how to wash his willy properly. How to take proper care of it—'

'I told you at the time it's pretty basic,' he snaps. 'It's not a pet. It doesn't need training or taking out for walks—'

'Okay, fine! But he still needed to know stuff and that was *your* job. To explain it all to him. Because, in case you haven't noticed, I don't have a penis—' I break off abruptly as Thelma Campbell from the National History Society approaches with her bichon frise. A stately six-footer with tightly-set pewter curls, Thelma arranges her expression into a pert smile.

'Morning, Carly.'

'Morning, Thelma.'

Dammit, now she too is stopping to chat. This is small-town life. Everyone knows – and observes – everything. 'Has that book I ordered come in yet?' she asks. 'The one about migratory birds, with the QR codes so we can listen—'

'Er, I think so, I'll check—'

'It has the sound of every native bird of Britain,' she announces to Frank, who manages to form an expression of wonder.

'Wow,' he murmurs.

She nods proudly, as if she had compiled all the bird sounds herself. Then she's off and, without saying goodbye to Frank, I turn away from the seafront and storm off to work.

CHAPTER THIRTY-FIVE

I'm not the only one having a bad day. Prish's date in Glasgow last night – with a man she's been talking to for several weeks – was a let-down. 'He suggested we book into this budget hotel by Central Station,' she tells us.

'The kind of place where an eighteen-year-old loses his virginity to an escort?' Jamie splutters.

'Oh, God. Stop it,' she exclaims, laughing now.

Then later, Jamie announces: 'Well, the outlaws are coming up again. Interested in buying a cottage on Arran!'

'Why are they doing that?' I ask. I know they live down in Wiltshire. So it's not exactly handy for them.

'You know when people have too much money, and don't know what to do with it?' he says. 'They love their visits up here, and want a place close to their precious boy.'

'So it'll still be the spare-room situation, whenever they come up to house-hunt?' I ask.

'Yep. But I thought next time, I could move out while

they're staying. Maybe pop round occasionally, pretend to be the Deliveroo guy.'

'Oh, Jamie. This is unbearable, isn't it?'

He exhales. 'What d'you do when the person you love turns out *not* to be who you thought they were?'

Briefly, I think of how Frank was this morning. 'I wish I had the answer to that.' Then, as the last lenders leave, I check the wall clock. The thought of going home causes a sinking feeling in my stomach and, clearly Jamie's feeling the same. 'Don't suppose you fancy a quick drink?' I suggest.

'Love one,' he enthuses.

'Don't tempt me,' Marilyn says, regretfully. The only one among us with young children, she's always off on the dot for the childminder dash.

'Prish?' I say hopefully. 'C'mon. I think we all need it tonight.'

We're not really a drinks-after-work group. The pubs around here, once bustling with locals and tourists alike, are now pretty faded, frequented mainly by old men and dogs. But right now the Harbour Bar seems like an appealing prospect. So I message Frank, saying I'll be a bit late back, and can he sort out dinner please?

Sure, comes the one-word reply.

Don't worry about me, I add. No response to that as, clearly, he doesn't. So we all leave the library, and on this warm July evening it feels right not to be going home just yet. We head for the Harbour Bar where, as expected, several elderly men and a couple of dogs are gathered. Even on this summer's evening, a small fire is flickering.

As we settle around a corner table, my heart lifts as I look around at my friends.

'Oh, I needed this,' Jamie announces.

'Me too,' I say.

He takes a big sip of beer. 'I'm sick of pretending to be a fucking housemate!'

'Tell Lewis he *has* to tell them,' Prish says, leaning forward.

He looks at us, running a hand across his stubbled jaw. 'What would you do if it was one of your kids?'

'Who said they were gay? You think I'd mind?' I look at him incredulously.

''Course not,' he says.

'Ana's had girlfriends and boyfriends,' I add. 'Jamie, I don't care. It sounds trite, I know, but I just want them to be happy—'

'Carly's right,' Prish cuts in. 'Tell him, Jamie. Sometimes you've got to grab the bull by the balls.'

'Erm, I think that's horns?' He laughs.

'Horns, balls, whatever,' she retorts. We finish our drinks and, rashly, decide to have another, all of us feeling a whole lot better just being together as we take it in turns to talk and listen. More drinks follow, because this is such a treat and the pub offers the perfect view of tonight's pink and orange sunset. Then the sun slips like a ball of gold over the horizon, and by the time we step outside, it's a quarter to ten and the light has finally dimmed. Summer days are long here, and tonight has been a special one.

'I should call a taxi,' Jamie says reluctantly, checking his phone. 'Reckon Brian'll take me out to the sticks?'

To his village, he means. Sandybanks has only two taxi companies, both one-man operations, and Brian is everyone's default option.

'Try him,' I say. 'If he can't, you can stay at mine.'

'*You* don't have room,' he teases. 'You're full to the rafters! Wish we could go on somewhere else, though . . .'

'Me too,' I say, shocked by how very strongly I do *not* want to go home. 'We could have another drink at my place. But . . . y'know. With Frank and Dad and Eddie there . . .'

'They wouldn't approve of three pisshead librarians bowling up?' Jamie sniggers.

'We could pretend to be sober,' Prish giggles. 'Like teenagers.'

'How about we all go to yours, Prish?' Jamie asks her hopefully.

She smiles. 'You're welcome but I don't have anything in. Kids cleaned me out last time they were over. So it'd be cups of tea, I'm afraid . . .'

Jamie checks the time on his phone. 'If we hurry up we'll just make the offy.'

'We could drink beer on the beach,' Prish announces, eyes shining in the blue-white light of the streetlamps. 'Like proper teenagers!'

'We could.' I nod. 'But we'd be freezing our arses off. And actually, I have a better idea.' I beam at their eager faces. 'How d'you fancy wine and a load of leftover party food?

*

Eddie did this once. At least, there was one incident I was aware of; there were probably other occasions too. But the time I'm thinking of, he stole two bottles of wine from the house to drink somewhere – probably at the bandstand – then denied it strenuously. *You and Dad must've drunk it all!*

Tonight, like accomplices in a robbery, Prish and Jamie hover on the pavement as I creep into my house. It's not Eddie nicking booze this time. It's me. As expected, Frank is out in the shed and Dad is already upstairs in his room. Or rather, the room that should rightly be Eddie's, apparently. My son is upstairs too, presumably with headphones on. So I sneak through to the kitchen and lift out a bottle of sauvignon from the fridge. Then I open a cupboard and take all the leftover food from Dad's party: the unopened crackers and crisps and biscuits. Sleepover food really. The kind of stuff I always got in for the kids.

How to let Frank know I won't be back until morning without telling an outright lie? My eye is caught by the magnetic notepad that's stuck to the fridge. CANCEL CITROLAX!! is written in huge capital letters on the front sheet. I peel it off, and then take off a fresh sheet and write:

Having a night with Prish and Jamie. Will be back early morning. Don't worry! Will explain tomorrow. Love C xx.

Frank will think I've gone mad because I never stay out overnight. But he'll assume we're all staying at Prish's. Where else would we be? Shrugging off a twang of unease, I leave the note on the worktop, and pack our night picnic into a carrier bag. After padding through the hallway, I close the front door quietly behind me.

The three of us march along quickly, giddy with the realisation that what we're doing is crazy, but we're going to do it anyway. 'There's no CCTV, is there?' Jamie asks as the library comes into view.

'It hasn't worked for years,' I tell him. At the library's main door now, I fish out my big bunch of keys. Heavy rain starts to fall suddenly.

'Quick!' Prish commands as I open the heavy door. We step in, pausing to register the still darkness, the orderliness of our workplace. *Drip-drip-drip.* The only sound is rain plopping into a bucket. Then Jamie clicks on a light and we spring into life, fetching mugs and utilising the meagre selection of mismatched plates in the kitchen for our snacks.

The children's section is rearranged swiftly as we pull three primary-coloured beanbags close together, and place a low plastic table in the middle. Wine is sloshed into mugs, and on this summer's night, the three of us have a little party. We drink and eat, and then put on music through the tinny speaker that the toddlers' singing group uses. We even get up and dance, revelling in the naughtiness of our library lock-in. And we talk about *everything:* how Prish – a fifty-eight-year-old mother and grandmother – has decided to forget about meeting 'the one', and will instead enjoy meeting 'the many!' as she puts it. Jamie tells us how he plans to invite himself on a trip to Arran, next time Lewis's parents are staying. 'I'll out Lewis to his mum and dad on the ferry,' he announces.

'Yes! What's the worst that could happen?' I ask, swigging from my mug.

He pulls a mock-horrified face. 'He might throw himself overboard.'

'Or *they* might?' I suggest.

'That'd be a result!' He grins, then turns serious. 'I think he'd dump me,' Jamie adds. 'But, y'know. Maybe that's not the worst thing . . .' He turns to me. 'What d'you think?'

'I think the worst thing we imagine often turns out to not be so bad after all.'

'Oh, profound,' he announces, and we laugh. But right now I believe it, because even though I'm going to be a granny soon, and have no idea what to do, or how to help – should I be knitting? I can't even knit! – I'm with my friends and I'm *here*.

When Mum was dying I sat at her bedside in the hospice and held her hand. Mostly she'd been sleeping. Her soft fair hair was neatly combed, her thin body very still in a cotton nightie patterned with forget-me-nots. Everything was closing down, yet there was a sense of peace and calm in her little room.

'Carly?' she said suddenly. Her voice was soft but still gave me a jolt.

'Yes, Mum?'

'You know where I'd like to be?'

Oh God, I thought – this is it. I thought I'd been coping, with Frank's help. He was living with me, having left his life in Portugal, because I'd needed him. And Mum had been so terribly ill, fading away before my eyes. It would be kinder, I'd thought sometimes. Kinder for her to slip away. But I didn't think that now. She was my mum! She couldn't die! How would I ever manage without her?

'Where, Mum?' I whispered.

Now I look at Prish and Jamie. 'You know just before my mum died?' I start, and Prish grabs my hand.

'Oh, darling. Don't be sad tonight!'

I shake my head quickly and smile. 'I'm not. Really. But she said this thing, about where she'd like to be right at the end . . .' My voice cracks and I take another sip of wine, tepid now in the mug.

'Oh, Carly.' Jamie squeezes my hand.

'. . . I thought she'd say Heaven or something,' I continue. 'She wasn't religious, but what else was she going to say?' I pause and look at my friends.

'What *did* she say?' Jamie prompts me.

I smile. 'She said John Lewis.'

'John Lewis?' Prish exclaims. 'Why?'

'Because she always reckoned nothing bad could ever happen in there.'

'And she was right,' Jamie asserts. He looks around at our neatly ordered library shelves, the empty tables. 'Like here.'

'Yes, nothing bad could *ever* happen here,' Prish agrees.

'Unless we mess with the Natural History Society's table again,' Jamie remarks with a shudder.

'If we can handle Thelma Campbell,' I say firmly, 'we can handle anything, can't we?'

''Course we can,' Jamie says, and then we hug and finish our wine and doze a little on the beanbags. And when we wake just after six a.m., dawn is creeping in through the stained-glass windows.

We're bleary and a little shellshocked at what we've just done. Jamie stretches like a cat, and Prish jumps up. 'We'd better clear up,' I suggest, surveying the cluttered table. So we quickly bag up the leftovers and wash up and put the beanbags back just so.

'Like teenagers getting rid of the evidence before the parents come home,' Jamie suggests.

I check my phone, seeing that at some point during the night, it ran out of charge. No one has a charger but it'll be fine, I reassure myself. I left Frank that note, so he won't be worried. We do a final check, and then leave the library, locking up and heading off for a quick change and freshen up before our working day begins.

'See you at nine then,' Prish says, grinning, as she and Jamie stride away together. She's persuaded him that, with three adult sons, she's bound to have a clean pair of boxers kicking around somewhere. I watch them cross the street, my heart skipping with sudden alarm as it sinks in properly, what I did last night.

The bright morning sun beams down onto our seaside town. I inhale deeply, and try to fully engage my core, as I ready myself to face the music.

CHAPTER THIRTY-SIX

Eddie greets me, wild-eyed, as I step into the house. 'Where've you *been*?'

'Uh, I was out, love. I was with Prish and Jamie.'

'What, all night?' It occurs to me that Eddie being up at this time is a monumental occasion, worthy of a future public holiday: *the first time Eddie Silva ever saw the dawn.*

'Yes,' I reply, shamefaced now. 'Sorry if you were worried. I did leave a note—'

'I wasn't *worried*,' he says quickly. 'Just couldn't sleep. Not used to a single bed.' Is he forgetting he had one in Edinburgh? He jabs a hand into a pocket of his tracksuit bottoms and thrusts my father's antique phone into my face. 'And I *can't* use this, Mum. I'm sorry.'

I glare down at it. 'Never mind that now. Where's your dad? Has he left for work yet?'

'It's like walking about in 1996—'

'You weren't *born* in 1996. How d'you know what it was—' I cut off as Frank appears on the landing, in jeans and the rumpled yellow bear T-shirt, apparently pulled on in haste.

'Carly!'

'Hi, love.' I look up, determined to try to breeze this out, despite my dully throbbing head.

'You've been out all night!'

'Yes, I, um . . . I left you a note.'

'Did you? I never saw anything.' He frowns as he comes downstairs.

'I definitely did.' I hurry to the kitchen and look around for it, but it's gone. Now Eddie and his dad follow me into the kitchen.

'Dad,' Eddie starts, 'it was really kind of you and Mum to get Granddad a new phone and give me his old one. But maybe you could've done it the other way round?'

'That was Granddad's birthday present,' I remind him. 'And it's not even a smartphone, Eddie. You know he can't abide them. Anyway, could you *please* stop going on about your—'

'Also, my robe's gone,' Eddie announces. 'Like, just disappeared. Did you wash it?'

'No!' I exclaim.

'Have *you* seen it, Dad?'

'Eddie, could you give us a minute please?' Frank snaps and reluctantly, Eddie slopes out of the kitchen.

'Frank,' I start as we face each other, 'I'm sorry. It was a completely spontaneous thing last night.'

'I've been trying to call you!'

'Have you? I'm sorry, my phone ran out of charge. We just had a few drinks after work. And it went on a bit late, and we were having such a lovely time . . .' I stop, catching myself babbling excuses. 'I needed time with my friends,' I add firmly.

'Why?' He blinks at me.

'Has *anyone* seen my gown?' Eddie cries out from the hallway, which must have alerted my father, as now he's coming downstairs to join the jolly gathering. He appears in the kitchen in pyjamas and slippers, looking rumpled and pale.

'What were you doing in the garden last night?' he asks Frank.

'Nothing.' Frank removes a loaf from the bread bin and drops two slices into the toaster. Weird behaviour, I decide – to suddenly busy himself by making breakfast.

Dad looks at me, as if awaiting an explanation. 'I don't know, Dad. I wasn't here—'

'She *wasn't here*,' Frank crows. 'She was out all night—'

'Can you stop calling me "she"?' As Frank's toast pops up, I grab his arm and lead him out into the back garden. But Dad follows us, and Eddie reappears a moment later.

'It's the ringtone,' he insists, still brandishing my father's old phone.

I glare at my son. 'What's wrong with it?'

'Listen!' He makes it ring, shrill and tinny like a child's toy phone. 'I can't handle that—'

'Those powders came again,' Dad announces, 'with my medications. The ones that are meant to help my *movements*. I thought you were going to stop them?'

'I tried to, Dad. I left a message—'

'The ringtone,' Eddie starts again.

'You can't handle a ringtone?' I snap. 'How are you going to handle a screaming baby at four a.m.?'

'Why don't you *change* the ringtone?' Frank thunders.

'I've tried! It won't change! It must've been made when they only had one ringtone. Like when they only had one channel on TV—' Eddie breaks off suddenly and peers at some unidentifiable object at the bottom of the garden, close to the shed. I follow his gaze. A small pile of something has been dumped on the grass. It's smouldering a little, I realise now.

'What's that?' I ask.

'Nothing.' Frank looks down at his feet.

'I told you,' Dad announces. 'Frank was out here last night. I saw him—'

'Were you having a camp fire?' I blink at him.

'Are you *all right*, Dad?' For once, Eddie looks concerned.

'I burnt your robe,' Frank mutters.

We all stare at him. 'You . . . *burnt my robe*?' Eddie pales in the weak morning sunlight. 'Have you gone completely mad?'

Frank shrugs. 'Maybe. Yeah, maybe I have.'

'Frank!' I splutter.

'Well, you know,' he says in an eerily measured tone. 'You weren't here and I was worried and couldn't sleep. And I'm sick of the sight of it, y'know? That fucking robe? So I thought, what can I do, while I'm pacing about, worrying about where Carly is?'

'I left a note!' I cry.

'There was scrappy bit of paper in the kitchen,' Dad murmurs. 'I came down for a drink. I was just tidying up—'

I turn to him. 'You threw my note away, Dad?' Then, to Frank: 'I'm sorry you were worried. I really am. We just . . .' I clear my throat. 'We actually spent the night in the library.'

'What?' Frank shakes his head in disbelief. 'For a moment there I thought you said you spent the night in the library.'

'Is that allowed?' Eddie gasps, suddenly a bastion of law and order.

'No, it's not,' I reply. 'But we did it anyway. We had a library lock-in and you can report me if you like—'

'Who to? The council?' Dad looks as if he's actually considering this.

'Whoever you like,' I say, already turning back to the house. 'I'm going to get showered and changed. I have to go to work . . .' I march back inside and pour myself a huge glass of water and guzzle it down.

'Bit hungover, are you?' Frank has appeared in the doorway.

'Just a little. Can we talk later?' I head upstairs, hoping to shake him off, but he catches up with me on the landing.

'I can't believe this,' he mutters.

'Well, I'm sorry. But that's what we did.'

'It's mental,' he announces.

'It is, yes.' I make for the bathroom and lock the door. *Sod him*, I think, closing my scratchy eyes as the shower rains on me. Robe-burning maniac. And he thinks *I'm* mad?

Frank is still lurking when I emerge from the bathroom. In our bedroom he sits on the edge of our bed, brooding, as I dress in silence. As I head downstairs, he follows me. I snatch a slice of cold toast from the toaster and eat it dry, washed down with more tap water. Dad is sitting at the kitchen table, observing us all, and Eddie is squinting at the substandard phone.

'Oh,' he announces. 'Lyla's messaged. She says she'll bring my phone! Her uncle's driving her over. Can she stay here? Is that all right?'

'Jesus Christ,' Frank breathes.

'Yes, of course,' I say distractedly.

'Can we have my old room? It's just, the bed's bigger—'

'Oh, are you throwing me out of my room now?' Dad's eyes widen.

'Of course not, Dad. Eddie, you and Lyla can stay in the girls' room, where you're *currently sleeping*—'

'But it's single beds!'

'Well, that's all right, isn't it? It's still a bedroom—'

'What's wrong with single beds?' Dad asks. 'Plenty of people would be grateful—'

'Please don't start on about how *grateful* I should be, Granddad,' Eddie wails.

'I can't handle this.' Frank glares round at all of us. 'I'm sorry but I can't deal with this anymore.' He marches out of the kitchen and stomps up to our bedroom. This time it's me who's following him.

'I'm sorry, Frank,' I start. 'This isn't huge fun for me either, you know.'

There's a strange look in his dark eyes. It's not anger. It's more like desperation. 'D'you realise how worried I was last night?'

A wave of shame surges over me, and my cheeks flame. 'I'm really sorry. I should've come home after the pub, or at least called you then. Honestly, I had no idea my phone was dead. I just needed a little bit of time away from—'

'From *me*?' he snaps. 'Is that it?'

'No, of course not! Just time away from . . . all this. *You* know. This house. That's all.'

'Yeah, and I think I do too,' he announces, marching over to the chest of drawers. He yanks open a drawer with such force, the chest wobbles and Mum's green glass vase topples over, landing sharply on its side.

'Frank!' I charge over and pick it up, examining the small fracture in the glass. 'It's broken.' But when I see what he's doing, the vase no longer matters. Because now Frank is tugging things out of drawers, seemingly at random: jeans, boxers, T-shirts. He reaches up to the top of the wardrobe and tugs down the battered old leather holdall he took to Paris.

Something seems to crumble inside me as he throws it onto the bed and starts to stuff his clothes into it.

'Sorry about your vase,' he mutters.

'It doesn't matter! What are you doing, Frank?'

'Going away for a bit.'

'Away? What d'you mean? Where are you going?'

'I don't know yet.' He throws in more clothes and then zips it up forcefully. 'Somewhere. Anywhere away from here.' He looks at me, brown eyes wet and filled with anguish.

'How long for? When will you be back?'

He doesn't answer. Instead, he flings the bag over a broad shoulder and storms downstairs, and then out of our house, banging the door behind him.

I stand there in our silent room, unable to go after him

or do anything at all. Instead, I just hold Mum's green glass vase and stare down at it. It's cracked, irreparable. Like our marriage, it seems. And it feels as if my heart is broken too.

CHAPTER THIRTY-SEVEN

Somehow I manage to stagger through the working day. Apart from Marilyn, who was thrilled to hear about the night's escapade, we're all a little hungover. Prish and Jamie reassure me that Frank's overreacted because pressures have been running high. He needs a little cooling-off time, that's all. Meanwhile books are returned and borrowed. Thelma Campbell comes in to order a reference book about Victorian ferneries. A confused-looking young man, who appears from time to time, installs himself in the comfiest chair and has a doze. I wake him gently and hand him a coffee. 'Thanks,' he murmurs with a smile.

Later, my heart is filled with hope as I march home along the blustery seafront. It'll be okay, I tell myself. Frank just had to let off some steam, and why not? We all have to do that sometimes. But by seven o'clock, when he's usually home from the garage, he still hasn't shown up. By eight, I'm frantic. I call and call and call. Frank doesn't pick up. Dad is clearly unbothered and Eddie seems to have barely noticed; too busy anticipating the return of his phone. 'I literally can't take this one out in public,' he announces over dinner, and I manage not to point out that he never goes out anyway.

'Diddums,' Dad says.

Eddie stares at him. '*Diddums*? What does that mean?'

'No need to be rude,' I exclaim, clearing the plates.

'I'm not!' He shrugs dramatically. 'Oh, and you do remember Lyla's coming to stay tonight—'

'Is she?' I stare at him.

'Yeah, I told you, didn't I?'

Oh, sorry! I've just been a little preoccupied with your dressing-gown-burning father who seems to have left me. 'I think you did,' I murmur.

'Another person moving in? Getting a bit crowded around here, isn't it?' Dad asks, forkful of spaghetti halfway to his mouth. I look at him, wondering how I'll ever manage to raise the issue of him moving back to his own place. Because really, there is absolutely no reason why he shouldn't. However, I suspect he's enjoying being a spectator here, with all the activity and bizarre events: the burning of clothing, the breakdown of my marriage. Makes a change from *Cash or Crash*.

'Lyla's not moving in,' I say, more forcefully than I intended. 'Just visiting.' I glare at Eddie. 'That's right, isn't it?'

'*Yeh*-ah,' he says, still eye-rolling me at twenty-two years old. Imagine, assuming that someone might move into Kilmory Cottage without clearing it with me first!

In the sanctuary of the kitchen, I replay recent events, making a mental list of what I should have done.

Not gone for a drink after work.

Not had any fun whatsoever.

Definitely not had the library lock-in.

Or at least called Frank to tell him, and not expected a perfectly clear note to remain where I'd left it. Because nothing is where it's supposed to be around here anymore. Dad puts kitchen things in weird places and, although Eddie's made a perfunctory attempt to tidy his room in preparation for Lyla's arrival, he still hoards mugs and glasses and suddenly we'll have no bread, and the cheese I'd planned to use for a lasagne has all been guzzled. My expensive shower gel – a gift from Jamie – was all used up during a *single* shower, the empty bottle tossed close to (but crucially not into) the bathroom bin.

And Frank. Frank is not where he's supposed to be either. I go out to look for him, expecting to see him walking down the street towards me. He's sulking, I reason. He's staying late at the garage to pay me back.

I walk, miserably, to the end of the street, tempted to keep walking and walking, right along the seafront until Sandybanks peters out. I could do that. I could just keep walking. There's a mile or so of countryside and then the next town, posher than ours, where the chip shop does scallops and lobster, and people flock to it from miles around.

However, at the end our street I stop as a battered old Land Rover turns into our road. I blink at it. A young woman waves from the passenger window, and I turn and watch as it slows down, and then stops, outside our house.

I hurry back towards it as Lyla, and then her uncle Oliver climb out. 'Hi!' she says brightly. She is roundly, *splendidly* pregnant. The sight of her causes my eyes to well up instantly.

'Lyla, hi! Oliver! Nice to see you!' So it's real. Of course I knew it; but now her bump is high and round beneath a lightweight sweater.

'You too,' Oliver says with a wide smile. 'This is really lovely.' He looks up and down the street. 'What a view you have.'

'I know, we're ever so lucky,' I gush. 'Anyway, do come in!'

As I lead them into the house, I'm aware of seeing the place through newcomers' eyes. The scuffs on the walls, the worn stair carpet, the dated lamps. What must they think? 'Eddie?' I call out. 'Lyla and her uncle Oliver are here!'

He emerges from the kitchen and smiles unsteadily. 'Hi, hi . . .'

Then Dad appears, making his way downstairs. 'Hello?' He looks quizzical.

'This is Kenny, my dad,' I start. 'Dad, this is Lyla, Eddie's, um . . . and this is her uncle Oliver. We met that time I went up to Suki's place in Perthshire—'

'Oh yes, when I ended up in hospital,' he announces.

Oliver seems to flinch. 'So sorry about that. I hope you've recovered?'

'Never been better,' Dad says firmly.

A pause hovers. 'So, Eddie, d'you want to show Lyla your room?' I suggest. 'I assume you're staying, Lyla?'

'Just tonight, yes. If that's okay?' She smiles brightly.

'Of course it is,' I say.

'Great.' She fishes into the pocket of her loose, silky

trousers and hands Eddie his phone. 'It was down the side of the sofa. Sorry I didn't get it to you before now . . .'

'Thank you so, so much,' he exclaims, like a man being thrown a lifebelt in stormy seas. He takes it from her and presses it to his heart. Then up they go upstairs together, and Dad, Oliver and I settle in the living room, where no one wants a drink of any kind, and Dad is literally twitching, wanting to put the TV on.

'Have you lived here long?' Oliver leans forward, hands pressed together, and glances out at the view.

'Erm, yes. Twenty-two years,' I reply.

'Wow. A long time.' He nods.

'It is. We thought it'd be a good place to raise a family.'

'Yeah, I can imagine. It really is *great*.' I can sense a hormonal flush coming over me as the conversation limps on.

'So, you live close by?' Oliver asks my dad. No, he lives here! He rules this house!

'Few miles up the coast,' Dad replies. He doesn't ask Oliver anything about his life, and seems to be observing him archly as I turn to grilling him about his latest beaver reintroduction project which, as it turns out, is why he's in the area.

'Just doing an exploratory visit,' Oliver explains. 'And Lyla wanted to see Eddie, so . . .' He tails off and smiles. 'I'd better get going. Nice to meet you, Kenny . . .'

'So, it's all right to bring beavers to an area so they destroy the forestry and remodel the waterways, is it?' Dad blasts out.

'Dad!' I exclaim in shock, but he only shrugs, self-satisfyingly.

Now standing, Oliver takes a beat to reply. 'It is a controversial issue,' he concedes, levelly. 'We always do a really thorough survey, though. And of course everyone has to be in agreement that it's the best thing for the location. Because you're right, they do change things dramatically. They're little engineers really, as I'm sure you know—'

'Dad's an engineer,' I chip in, inanely, as if this might persuade my father to approve of Oliver's work.

'Really?' Oliver looks suitably impressed. 'Well, anyway—'

'Yes, we shouldn't keep you,' I babble, and then Oliver calls up to Lyla and she appears, descending the stairs carefully, all smiles and long, loose golden hair and that magnificent bump.

She hugs Oliver. 'Bye, Uncle Olly. You're coming to pick me up tomorrow?'

'Yeah, of course, love.'

'Where are you staying?' I ask him.

'Premier Inn. Only the best.' He grins. Then he heads out and climbs into the Land Rover.

We've all come out, and I'm gripped by an urge to run over before he drives away and say, *Sorry about that – and how awkward it was. It's just the way Dad is – but it's not only that. Frank isn't home and I'm starting to think he might never come back. So, you know. Timing . . .*

Obviously, I don't say any of that. I don't say anything at all. As Lyla and Eddie head back inside, I raise a hand. Oliver looks back and something catches between us. He smiles, in a *what-was-all-that?* kind of way.

'Sorry about the beaver thing,' I call out, and quickly shut the door.

In the hallway now, aware of Eddie and Lyla chatting upstairs, I check my phone for messages or missed calls. I'm itching to call Frank again, but is it better to let him call when he's ready? Jamie was right; he probably just needs a cooling-off period. He'll be at a friend's, I decide. Frank has plenty of mates locally; they go hiking sometimes, and for the occasional drink. But he's not an out-every-night kind of man. Far from it. It's home that Frank loves – or at least, he *did*.

Later still, at just gone eleven when I'm getting ready for bed, my phone rings. 'Frank!' I say. Thank God he's okay.

'Hi,' he says dully. Then nothing.

'Where are you?'

'Never mind. I just can't be there at the moment.'

'What, here with us? With me?' My voice fractures as I glimpse Mum's cracked vase on the chest of drawers.

'I just can't be at home right now,' he says quickly, 'so I've got somewhere to stay—'

'Are you with a friend? With Dev or Mick or—'

'I've just found somewhere. And I wanted you to know I'm all right . . .'

'Frank, tell me where you are!' I plead. 'Are you in a hotel? This is crazy! You don't need to stay away from me. I told you I'm so sorry about last night. And I really am. It was mad and selfish and—'

'I'd never do that to you,' he announces. 'Never.'

My stomach seems to clench and a tear rolls down my face. 'No. I know that.'

The pause seems to hang. Lyla's bright laughter filters through from Eddie's room. I should be happy that she's here, and that she and Eddie seem so much more at ease together now. Surely that should tell me that everything's going to be okay?

However, I'm not sure it is now as Frank says, 'I'm going now. I'll call you.' And then he's gone.

CHAPTER THIRTY-EIGHT

August

Frank

It had just reached the point where it had become *too much*. Kilmory Cottage had always felt a bit on the poky side when there were five of them there, but it was different back then. They'd all fitted together, like jigsaw pieces, even if it felt sometimes as if those pieces had to be jammed together – because they were a family.

Lately, though, it's felt like the pieces are all from different jigsaws, like the time Ana tipped out all the boxes onto the living room floor. That evening, Frank had come home from work to find Carly staring down at literally thousands of pieces, from all the puzzles they owned.

'I don't think I can sort these,' she admitted. And she'd started laughing and Frank had teased her that of course she could separate out all the pieces. Because if anything could be sorted, Carly could do it.

When Frank met Carly in the bar he was working in, it was like the world suddenly turned brighter. She dazzled him. She was gorgeous, for one thing, with those intense green eyes, long, tumbling light brown hair and a sensuous mouth.

My God, he loved her. He still does. And he loves their children – he's never wavered on that, even through the difficult teenage years, which Eddie doesn't seem to have grown out of, even now. How he tried their patience and shredded their nerves with his under-age drinking and dope smoking and then party drugs – dilated pupils and tremors at breakfast.

Throughout it all, Carly was – is – an amazing mum and their children are brilliant. The girls anyway, although privately he thinks Bella was a bit rash, rushing off to London, and he wishes she was closer. Of course, Eddie has consumed the lion's share of Carly's attentions. Frank believes that he too could be brilliant, and have an amazing life, if only he could get himself together. But since the Paris holiday Frank has felt as if things have spiralled out of control.

There's the pregnancy, obviously. And there was that terrible lunch in that stuffy Edinburgh club. And he and Carly bickering so much lately. No wonder really, living with their depressed son and his belligerent granddad.

Frank hasn't known what to do or say in his own home. So he took the mature and sensible step of hiding away from everything in the shed. What could he do to make things better?

He'd started a project out there, working away through all those bitterly cold nights, with the smelly fan heater whirring. But it was a stupid project, more for himself than to benefit anyone else. Because was it really any good, what he was making? Eventually, with confidence waning, he'd given up on it, hiding away the various components before anyone saw it.

Frank isn't in the shed now. A week has passed since he stormed out of Kilmory Cottage and found himself at Dev's garage, all locked up for the night. Frank knows he's made some bad decisions in the past, with the ice cream shop and the pastéis de nata bakery and finally the food truck. Thank God for Carly and her steady job at the library. Landing a job here at the garage, with his good mate, had been one of Frank's better moves, and he loves the work.

The night he left home, Frank unlocked the garage's side door and came in and made a cup of tea. He thought he'd bed down there for the night, in the little office area in a corner of the main garage space. Dev is the only one who uses it, perched on the grubby swivel chair while on the phone.

Frank sat on the chair, swivelling, wondering if he could sleep on it. And he tried, closing his eyes momentarily, even nodding forward in sheer exhaustion. But the chair wouldn't stop moving, even when his body was still. And it was cold in there; colder than outside, bizarrely. Frank had his jacket on, but he needed another insulating layer – like Eddie's hooded robe. That would've done, but in a fit of frustration he'd set the thing alight in the garden. And then he'd walked out on his family because he couldn't handle them anymore.

Frank got up and wondered what to do. Yes, there were friends he could go to – Dev, for instance. But he couldn't face just showing up, and having to explain that he'd lost it over an eighty-five-year-old man and his son who he loves with every cell of his being.

What kind of example has Frank set him? What kind of role model has he been? A shit one! He jeopardised their futures with his crazy business ventures and has tortured himself for it. For a few years it felt like things were settled, and he'd dared to hope that Eddie would get his act together and he and Carly could enjoy more freedom to do their own thing. Even to have a proper conversation without Eddie listening in. That would've been nice! Then the pregnancy happened and somehow, Frank felt that this, too, was his fault. The bad example he'd set, with his fecklessness.

All those years ago Carly had gone on at him to do 'The Talk'. The 'birds and the bees' as British people say in their coy and confusing way. But it's not just the British who are buttoned up about sex. Frank's parents – much loved and missed – were devout Catholics, never entirely happy that he and Carly hadn't married, although they didn't say as much. And Frank's father would no more have walked naked around their farmhouse than discussed the facts of life with Frank or his brothers.

Frank simply hadn't known how to open up the conversation. And the more Carly had urged him to do it, the more he'd been determined to duck out of the responsibility and leave it to her.

And now look what's happened. It could all have been avoided if Frank had stood up to his responsibilities and been a proper dad!

Away from home that first night, seeped in shame, Frank had hunted around in the various cupboards in the garage. Finally he located a sleeping bag with a rusting zip. It was musty and lightly daubed with engine oil. But it would have to do. And there was a very flat, faded cushion that a local black-and-white stray cat, who the garage team had named Badger, wandered in to doze on sometimes. Frank locked up the garage again and carried his bedding round to the scrubby waste ground round the back, where his old food truck has been parked for the past couple of years, slowly decaying. Clapped out and redundant, like Frank felt now.

Would things have been different if Frank had managed to get Eddie to focus on something? Like football, for instance? Frank adores football; FC Porto is his team. He'd tried to enthuse his son, even training as a coach with the Sandybanks junior team. But Eddie had roamed around on the fringes, more interested in watching a ladybird crawling on a leaf than anything that was happening on the pitch.

Feeling a sharp pang of regret and of missing his family, Frank had opened up the van. Inhaling the cold metallic air, he'd dumped the grotty sleeping bag and Badger's cushion on the floor where he'd once stood, frying steaks and serving customers through the hatch at the sole festival he'd taken it to.

A keen fan of rock music, Frank had tried to enthuse Eddie in that direction too. But the guitar he bought him went the way of the FC Porto strip and the football boots: dumped in the corner of his son's bedroom, before migrating eventually to the loft.

Frank climbed into the driver's seat, fumbled for the ignition key on the unwieldy bunch and jabbed it in. After a few false starts the engine puttered into life. Luckily, he'd been running it from time to time, just to turn it over. Now he adjusted the settings and a meagre heat started to permeate the truck. There was a dim light, which he could use sparingly so as not to run down the battery. Frank knew there were a couple of battery-operated lamps, too, in the garage.

Frank let the engine run for a while, his gaze skimming the crumbly brick walls at the backs of various businesses some distance away. A sign painters, a tyre fitters and a theatre, a remnant from Sandybanks' heyday as a holiday destination, long shut down. No one would bother or even notice him here, he decided. So, when the chill had lifted, Frank turned off the engine and crawled into the sleeping bag, resting his head on the not especially fragrant cushion as he tried to go to sleep.

Since that first night he's had one brief conversation with Carly. He didn't want her to worry. The next night he texted her, and he's done so every night since then. But he won't tell her where he is, no matter how much she pleads with him or how frustrated she becomes. And now Frank has been living here for a week, and no one knows he's doing this – not even Dev. Because by the time his friend and the other lads arrive for work in the morning, Frank is already working, wearing the spare overalls that are always hanging around in the garage. Sunday was easier as the garage is closed then, and Frank was alone.

'You're doing long hours, Frank,' Dev remarked this evening.

'Yeah. Just feel like it at the moment,' he replied, not meeting his friend's eye.

'Is everything all right with you, mate?' Dev peered down at him in concern.

'Yeah, all good.' Frank was crouched on the ground, about to change the spark plugs in a twenty-year-old tractor.

When he glanced round, Dev was still looking intently at him. 'Forgotten you have a home to go to?'

Frank forced a laugh. 'No. 'Course not.'

'It's just you're always here, mate! Fancy a pint?'

'Uh, not tonight. Maybe another time.' He couldn't face Dev gently probing him about what was going on at home.

Dev shuffled a bit, as if reluctant to leave his friend alone, but unsure of what to say. 'See you in the morning, then? And don't stay too late. Carly's going to be worried about you!'

Frank sat up, pushing back his hair and trying to look normal. 'Yeah. Don't worry, I'm nearly finished up.' He feigned a jovial tone and sensed his body relaxing as his friend left the building.

And now his body feels as if it's been run over by said tractor as he wakes in the musty sleeping bag on the floor of the truck. With some difficulty, as if he is ninety years old rather than a mere fifty, he gets up and heads to the garage where he lets himself in and has a thorough strip-wash in the cramped bathroom.

He pulls on clean boxers, then one of the two pairs of joggers and a T-shirt he bought from the supermarket, having crept in there at ten to ten – just before closing – to stock up on essentials. Shaving foam, disposable razors, deodorant, liquid soap, a big bottle of water and basic food supplies. Like preparing for the camping trip they went on to Arran, when the kids were little.

Frank shaves now, wondering how much longer he can get away without washing his hair. Didn't Ana go through a phase of not washing hers, when she first went to art school? 'It self-cleanses!' she'd announced, tossing back lank, greasy locks on a visit home. 'No chemicals, no plastic waste. Much better for the environment!' Carly had joked that, when she'd finally washed it, she'd have gunked up the entire plumbing system of Dundee.

And now Frank watches the water swill away down the plughole in the tiny grubby sink, used only by men in oily overalls. He thinks of Carly at home, having her shower, calling out goodbye to Kenny and Eddie and heading off to the library.

Frank, please. Where are you? Come home.

Okay I accept you need space or whatever but I need to know where you are!

So worried, Frank. Are you at a hotel?

As he fills the kettle he rereads all the messages that have pinged in over the past seven days. He's replied to most of them. *I'm fine. Please don't worry.*

Are you at work? Can I come to the garage? she asked a few days ago.

Please don't, he replied.

Why not?

I can't talk about things with the guys here.

Meet me somewhere then?

He couldn't do that, and he still can't. Because Frank has gone from losing it, in a fit of temper, to feeling stupid and ashamed.

At least there have been no messages from Bella and Ana. This means Carly hasn't told them yet, which he's relieved about. Nothing from Eddie either, who *does* know – and this hurts him.

It just shows, he decides, making his mug of tea, that he made the right decision in getting out of their hair.

So Frank gets stuck into his work, feigning jollity when Peter Crow comes to pick up his tractor and even sitting outside, on folding chairs, having a sandwich with Dev in the warm August sun. The afternoon goes quickly. Dev is out, servicing a farm vehicle in situ and, taking advantage of the boss's absence, the other guys have snuck off early to enjoy the late afternoon sun.

Exhausted now, Frank can't face retreating to the truck on such a beautiful afternoon. So he pulls off his overalls and heads to the beach himself. And there, in the distance, he spots Carly and Kenny, walking side by side. They seem to be watching a dog running in and out of the sea.

Frank observes them at a distance, sensing an ease between them that he doesn't remember being aware of before. Carly even links her arm in his. A father and daughter, looking out over the peaks of Goat Fell on Arran. The ferry with its red and black funnel, edging closer as it comes into the port.

It's me, Frank decides, walking away from them now. *I must be the problem. They're getting along so much better now I'm not there.*

He walks away, and keeps on walking and walking until he's left Sandybanks behind, and the sky gradually darkens until it's properly dark. Then finally he heads back, the sea glittering beneath a full, bright moon.

Frank lets himself back into the truck where he crawls into the rank old sleeping bag, and rests his head on Badger's cushion and tries to sleep. However, he can't sleep tonight. Not when he doesn't know how long he can stay there, or whether he's ruined his marriage forever.

Somehow, he's got himself into this awful situation, and he has no idea what to do next.

CHAPTER THIRTY-NINE

Living at Kilmory Cottage: Carly, Eddie, Kenny

Carly

On day ten, I crack.

It's Dad's egg that does it. Dad's egg that's so over-boiled the yolk resembles yellow wall cavity filling, encased in a white rubber jacket. 'Carly!' He calls me over to examine it.

'I'll do you another one,' I say.

'No, this'll do.'

I glance at him, hating the way my mind is spiralling now – to thoughts of when Dad might consider moving back to his own flat. It sounds terrible because there *is* room here; we have a bedroom each. In fact, the household feels eerily depleted. Not because Frank is a big, tall man who'd always occupied a lot of space with his chatter and interfering pan-poking and the way he pottered about, always doing stuff. I mean, it's not *just* that.

The void he's left feels even bigger. Because it's not just the physical Frank who's gone – but *us*. The way we've always been together. That's gone too, and now I rattle around at home not quite knowing what to do with myself.

Guilt niggles at me as I watch Dad, biting into his toast. 'Here, let me make you another one.' I open the fridge and scan the contents. 'Oh, Dad. That was the last egg . . .' I look at him, expecting him to say, *Don't worry, toast is fine*.

He just sits there, looking at me expectantly, saying nothing.

I blink at him. It's a cool, breezy Sunday morning, and I've tried to rally myself with the promise of a day in the garden. It's looking neglected, the roses growing straggly and weeds sprouting between my hollyhocks. 'We're out of eggs, Dad,' I clarify.

'Are you?' he asks.

What d'you want me to do? Run to the shops to get more? Expel one out of my arse? The fridge starts bleeping. I've been standing there with my hand on the open door. I close it and push back my hair. No sounds from Eddie yet; at nine-forty he'll still be asleep. 'I'm going out for a walk,' I announce.

I make for the kitchen doorway. 'Will you get eggs?' Dad calls after me.

'Yes,' I say, obediently, already shrugging on my jacket and heading out of the house.

I don't know where I'm going. I just need to get out of this house, like Frank did ten days ago. Where *is* Frank? He's replied to some of my messages, just to say he's okay, and expressly asked me not to show up at the garage. I haven't wanted to anyway. I've been desperate to see *him* – of course I have – but not at his workplace, not with

Dev and the others around. And he's refused to meet me on the beach, or anywhere else.

What is he doing? How is he spending his evenings and weekend days without me? Tears sting my eyes as the sharp wind hits my face. Then I realise. Frank is a doer, always making or building or fixing something. He's not a sitter-rounder kind of man. So of course he'll be working, even on a Sunday. He'll be putting in extra hours to help Dev, and keep himself occupied – and there'll be no one else there.

I pass the redundant roundabout and the overgrown crazy golf course, then take the road away from the sea. Heading for the edge of town now, I pass a few dilapidated buildings with faded signs, until I come to Dev's garage.

The main door for vehicles is shut with a hefty padlock. I go round to the side, where the flaking wooden door is ajar. Heart fluttering, I step in and look around. The main fluorescent light is on, and under its blue-white glare various tools are lying around. It looks like someone's working in here today. 'Frank?' I call out tentatively.

Nothing. I prowl around, crouching to check under a truck with a missing wheel. 'Frank? Are you here?'

I step back outside and go round the back of the building. Parked a little distance away, on scrubby ground, is Frank's old food truck. The truck he insisted was such a bargain, and he'd be off to festivals, selling steaks in ciabattas. The girls were far too busy with their numerous extra-curricular activities to get involved. But maybe Eddie could help him? Father and son, food and music – what could be better than that? Maybe this was something they could do together, that would bond them!

For a moment I just stand there. The truck is dark burgundy, rusting and faded now. The lettering – *Silva's Steakout* – is painted in yellow on its side. Ana did it for him, sketching numerous designs on paper before she felt confident enough to paint it onto the van.

It's not the van, or Ana's lettering, that I'm looking at now. It's Frank, who's sitting there, facing me from the open door of the truck.

'Frank. You're here.'

I go to him, and then stop.

'Yep, I'm here.'

I open my mouth to speak but realise I don't know what to say. 'I've been so worried,' is all I can manage.

'Sorry about that.' He looks tired, and a little unkempt in black sweatpants and an old sweater, but otherwise okay.

'I don't understand why you're here,' I say. 'It's been ten days—'

'Yeah, I know.'

'Have you been sleeping here?'

Frank nods, his attention caught briefly by a black and white cat that pads towards him.

'It must've been awful,' I murmur.

'It's been all right,' he says with a shrug. He leans forward to pat the cat, who's rubbing at his ankles. 'This is Badger.'

'Oh, yes. You've mentioned him . . .' I'm trying not to cry.

Frank looks up from the cat, meeting my gaze. 'I just had to get away, Carly.'

I nod, sort of understanding. And now I'm here, in front of the truck that caused so much grief between us, I remember the hopes he had for his thrilling new venture. First stop, a little festival in Cumbria. Next, Reading, Glastonbury, the Isle of Wight. There'd be festivals further afield, in France, Spain and Portugal. Silva's Steakout would take over the world!

When Eddie clearly hadn't been interested, Frank had asked me to go to that Cumbrian festival with him, to help. And I'd been so mad, because we were in such debt after he'd bought that damn truck, I'd said no.

'Frank.' I walk towards him, my eyes filling with tears as he gets up, and we hug. 'Please don't stay here, honey. This is awful, you being away from us. It was all so silly. If you're trying to punish me for the library night—'

'Of course I'm not.' He pulls away, shaking his head. He still looks so handsome, even with his hair unwashed and all mussed up, in the weak morning sun. 'I'd never punish you—'

'Please come back then!'

'No. Not now. I just need to be here—'

'All by yourself?' I exclaim.

His gaze drops. Badger has stretched out on the ground now, and stretches luxuriantly. Frank crouches down to stroke him.

Okay, then! I hope you and Badger will be very happy together! I want to shout it out, like a child. But instead, I manage to muster any semblance of calm and logic I have left in me. And I say, 'All right, Frank. You do whatever you need to do.'

And then I turn, breathing deeply as if that will stop the tears, and I walk all the way home.

CHAPTER FORTY

When Eddie dropped his trousers on the way back from Scout camp, pressing his bare bum up against the coach window, *of course* it wasn't Frank who was summoned into the meeting hall for a discussion. It was me – shabby mother, hanging her head in shame on a stackable plastic chair.

We can't have that kind of behaviour, Carly. It brings the whole troop into disrepute. As if I'd been the one flashing my bare arse at drivers on the M8!

I'm beyond accepting responsibility for anything now. Eddie's situation with Lyla? In a few short weeks the baby will be here. Since her overnight stay, a couple of weeks ago now, I feel that at least we had a few perfectly pleasant – albeit superficial – conversations. Chatting as we waited for the kettle to boil, kind of thing. Updates on her mum and Uncle Oliver. But I didn't want to grill her about how she's feeling emotionally, and I still barely know her really.

At least she and Eddie seem to be in contact. Are they a couple? Or just 'talking'? Who knows how they plan to look after a baby together and bring up their child. But really, that's for them to figure out. I truly believe that now because, since that day when I found Frank sitting in the door of the food truck, something has switched in me. At nearly fifty years old I have realised that I'm not responsible for everything that other people choose to do.

Whatever's going on between Eddie and Lyla, the baby's going to be born. That's just nature. It's not going to wait patiently inside the amniotic sac until a time at which my son has properly grown up, and started flossing and eating vegetables. It's coming, ready or not.

As for Frank, I've been over to see him several more times at the truck, taking provisions as if he's a kid, camping out at the bottom of the garden. I unearthed our spare duvet which, having been rejected by Dad – and used only briefly by Eddie – I'd assumed was as redundant as the high chair that's still stashed in the attic. Frank seemed grateful for that, at least – and the pillow and fresh clothes I'd also brought him. But still he wouldn't even talk about coming home.

It was Prish who suggested that perhaps I should leave him be. 'I know it's not easy,' she said, 'but for whatever reason, he's made this choice for now. And going there and pleading for him to come home is only making it worse for you.'

Of course she was right. So I go to work, and I look after Dad, and in some ways it's easier to manage him without Frank being around. I no longer feel torn between catering to my father's needs, while trying to appease Frank. I still worry about Frank – of course I do – but I've accepted now that I can't force him to do anything he doesn't want to do.

I never have been able to really. He's a stubborn man, as is Eddie. However, recently, I have noticed a slight change in my son. In the kitchen, for instance. 'You should never stir a paella' has morphed into Eddie *making* the paella. 'Easier to do it myself,' he announced. Perhaps he can't bear to witness my 'terrible knife skills' any longer. Or maybe it's an act of compassion on his part, since his father left us.

'So, you and Dad,' he ventures one evening, as we clear up together after dinner. 'D'you know what his plans are at all? I mean . . .' His brow furrows. 'Is this *it*?'

'Honey, I really don't know,' I tell him.

He sighs. 'This can't be easy for you. Are you all right?'

I look at him, surprised by his concern. 'D'you know what, Eddie? It's awful. Of course it is. But you know what your dad's like. I've never been able to change his mind about anything. So I'm just having to get on with things.'

He nods, drying our new pan with a tea towel. Apparently, our existing frying pans were all substandard – as is all of our kitchen equipment! So he made me upgrade to a 'proper' paella one; cast iron, eye-wateringly expensive. 'You're good at that,' he murmurs, and I smile. Coming from Eddie, I take that as a glowing compliment.

'I was thinking of going over to Edinburgh at the weekend,' he adds.

'To see Lyla?'

'Uh-huh.' A pause as he polishes the knob on the pan's lid. 'Don't fancy driving me over, do you?'

'Oh, right.' I laugh. 'You want a lift—'

'No, I could get the train,' he says quickly. 'I just thought it'd be nice for you to come.' He's *definitely* worried about how I'm doing without his dad.

'Where are you going now?' my father asks, appearing in the doorway. As if I'm forever nipping off to places.

'We're just talking about a day in Edinburgh,' I reply. 'Would you like to come, Dad? We could do the castle, museum, all that?' I turn to Eddie. 'I'd like to see Suki. We could take her to lunch maybe? Not at that club—'

'God, no. We'll think of somewhere else. I'll see what Lyla says.' So I text Suki and we arrange a date, and when the day comes Dad announces that he'd rather stay home, 'if that's all right with everyone,' he says. I look at him. It's unlike him to be concerned about what anyone else might think.

'Of course, Dad,' I say. 'Is everything okay? Are you feeling—'

'I'm fine,' he says quickly. 'It's just . . .' We're alone together in the kitchen. His gaze falls to his slippered feet. 'I'm not really on my own very much these days,' he adds. 'I thought . . . you know. I actually wouldn't mind staying here in an empty house.'

'An *empty house*.' I make a mock-confused face, as if struggling with the concept.

He nods, and a glimmer of amusement crosses his mouth. Of course, Dad's flat, a mere few miles along the coast, is empty. Back there, he could enjoy as much solitude as his heart desires. But perhaps there's a certain pleasure that can be found only in a home that's temporarily empty. 'Okay, Dad,' I say. 'If you're certain.'

He assures me that he is, and then he adds, 'So Frank's not coming?'

I shake my head. 'No, Dad.'

'Hmm.' I sense him scrutinising me. 'How long's he been gone now?' I glance out at the back garden. On this glorious blue-skied Saturday the border is ablaze with colour.

'Just over three weeks,' I reply. In fact I know exactly, to the day. I could call him now. We're still texting; it's not as if we're not in contact. He knows I don't get every Saturday off, and that we have a rota. So a full weekend together always felt pretty special. And normally, there's no way Frank wouldn't join us on a family day out.

I look at Dad, realising that he wants to ask about Frank – and whether I'm okay. 'And . . . are you all right?' is the best he can do. But I appreciate his effort, because I know that concern doesn't come easily to him.

First Eddie, and now my father, wondering how I'm feeling! It's all very new and unexpected. Somehow, it's taken Frank leaving for this to happen.

'It's really hard, Dad.' I shrug.

He nods, seeming to process this. 'You could ask him along today?'

I hesitate, wondering how to couch it, and deciding to just say it as it is. 'D'you know what, Dad?' He looks at me expectantly, and there's a glimmer there in his sharp blue eyes that might – incredibly – be sympathy. 'I don't want to,' I say, turning away so he can't see my face. 'I'm pretty sure he'd say no, and I don't think I can stand the hurt.'

CHAPTER FORTY-ONE

This time it's not Suki who's taken care of everything. It's Lyla. As we near Edinburgh, she texts Eddie directions to our meeting point. And there she is, waving in the distance, just as she had in Suki's private members' club. Only now, under a brilliant blue sky in Princes Street Gardens, I'm not rigid with shock. I haven't been led here under false pretences. My heart lifts at the sight of her; all smiles, pink cheeks and prominent bump.

'Hey!' She greets us with hugs, and then Suki approaches, and to my surprise, I realise her brother is here too. Oliver smiles a little awkwardly, perhaps feeling as if he's a bit of an add-on to our day.

'Hope you don't mind me joining you,' he starts.

'Of course not.' I smile, surprised by how happy I am to see him. There's something about his calming presence that seems to balance Suki's perpetual effervescence.

'We've brought a picnic lunch,' she announces as Oliver unpacks a blanket from his small rucksack.

'Oh, thank you,' I say. 'What a lovely idea.'

'Seemed too nice a day to be indoors,' Oliver says.

'We brought Portuguese custard tarts!' Suki produces a white box from one of the numerous bags. She looks around quizzically. 'No Frank today?'

'Mum, I *told* you,' Lyla says quickly, frowning.

Suki looks crestfallen. 'Oh, I *am* sorry.' Her blue eyes widen with concern as she turns to me. 'I'm sorry, Carly. I didn't want to mention it. From what Lyla said, I thought it was just a temporary wobble—'

'Well, I'm not really sure.' I've deliberately avoided mentioning it to her in my messages. It seemed selfish, somehow, to take the attention away from the baby.

'I didn't mean to put my foot in it,' she murmurs.

'Honestly, it's okay—'

'What was I thinking, going to the Portuguese bakery!' She exhales at her own stupidity.

'Suki.' I touch her arm, glad the others are busily setting out our lunch – a seemingly endless array of deli treats – on the tartan rug. 'You brought all this food. It's really thoughtful, and don't worry, I can eat a pastéis de nata without crying . . .'

She hugs me again. 'It'll all be okay. I'm sure of it.'

'Well, I hope so.' I muster a bright smile. 'It's good to see you all,' I add. And it's true; I'm grateful for her warmth and caring, and relieved to be away from Kilmory Cottage for the day.

We sit in the sunshine, tucking into the picnic and insisting, eventually, that Lyla relocate to a bench. 'Mum, you fuss so much,' she chides her as she gathers herself up from the blanket. Each of my pregnancies turned me almost spherical, my head and limbs stuck-on appendages to the colossal bump. I existed in vast dungarees, bought for me by Frank from an army surplus store in Glasgow. There's nothing army surplus about Lyla now, in her black leggings and a floaty turquoise cotton top, blonde hair scooped up artfully. She really is *glowing*. I always thought that was a myth. And as she and Eddie fall into quiet conversation, I wonder if she'd have preferred for them to spend time together alone.

I glance at Oliver. His hair is cropped short, his face and arms lightly tanned. He looks fit and well, at ease with himself in the bright afternoon sun. 'Are you staying in Edinburgh at the moment?' I ask.

'Yeah,' he replies. 'Just spending a bit of time at Suki's.'

Suki casts him a fond smile. 'He's been a darling, Carly. Like you wouldn't believe.' She pauses, as if unsure whether to go on. 'Me and Tom have split,' she adds.

'Oh, I *am* sorry!'

'Hmm. Yes. Turned out he wasn't as great a builder-stroke-plumber as he made out.' She emits a wry chuckle, as if it had all been about U-bends and differing opinions over mixer taps.

'There's been a bit of an issue with leaks, flooding the flat downstairs,' Oliver explains.

'Yep. Bit of a cowboy as it turned out.' She glances around as a group of tourists stop to photograph the castle.

'Sounds like a nightmare,' I say.

'You can't imagine.' Suki shudders and quickly gathers herself. 'But anyway. We're getting things sorted together, aren't we, Ols?'

'It'll be okay, sis.' I glance at him, wondering if he's always assumed this capable older brother role. It's clear that he cares about her, and as Eddie and Lyla wander off for a stroll together, I learn that he's 'project-managing the rescue operation', as Suki puts it.

'Oh, I'm just helping out.' He smiles, shrugging off her praise.

'But once we have tradesmen in, I'm decamping to Lyla's for a bit,' Suki adds.

'Right,' I say, remembering how she'd described following her daughter to Edinburgh. 'She'd have enrolled on my uni course if she could!' Lyla had told us, and I wonder how she really feels about her mother moving in.

We're packing away the picnic remains as Suki checks the time. 'Oh, God. It's nearly two already. I said I'd pop over to see Dinah's thing in a gallery in the New Town. She's part of a group exhibition and all the artists are doing a talk . . .' My body tenses, and as I catch Oliver's eye I know he's thinking the same thing. *Please don't ask me to come along.* 'With everything going on at home, I'd forgotten to mention it.' She looks apologetic. 'Don't suppose you two fancy coming? Everyone's welcome . . .'

'D'you know, I think I'd rather enjoy the sunshine,' I say, surprised by my honesty.

Suki smiles, smoothing her hair as she gets up from the blanket. 'Sounds like a sensible option.'

'How about we get a coffee?' Oliver suggests. 'And maybe have a wander round the museum?'

'That sounds great,' I say, relieved. 'Suki, you don't mind, do you?'

'Of course not. But I'd better dash because I did promise.' She hugs us goodbye. 'She'll probably have me handing out canapés,' she adds with a small laugh. 'So I'll say bye now. See you next time?'

'Definitely,' I say, thinking, *Next time will probably be when the baby's born. When we are grandmothers.* It hardly seems possible as I watch her, looking barely old enough to be Lyla's mother as she hurries away.

Oliver rolls up the blanket, stashing it into his rucksack, and we find Eddie and Lyla perched on the edge of the fountain, deep in conversation. Plans are made to reconvene later, and Oliver and I stroll across the park. It's one of those picture-perfect days with a bright, high sun, and a wisp of cloud in the clear blue sky.

'Shall we grab some coffees and find a bench?' Oliver suggests.

'Good idea.' I smile, and despite everything, I sense a lightness at being here, away from home. It's Frank's choice, I remind myself, to do what he's doing. My emotions veer from devastation that he's embarked on his bizarre truck life, with only a stray cat for company, to disappointment, and even anger, that he's doing this to us. Of course I've had to tell the girls what's going on, but I've played it down, saying their dad 'just needs a bit of space. It's only temporary,' I've assured them. 'Just a blip.'

'But he's staying in the *truck*?' Bella exclaimed.

'Things got a bit intense with your granddad around,' I said lightly. 'There was only so much *Cash or Crash* he could handle.' As if the only issue was a maddening quiz show presented by a man with an orangey tan.

'Eddie pretends he's barely noticed that his dad's not around,' I tell Oliver now, when he asks how things are at home. 'But I know he needs him. This enormous thing's about to happen in his life and Frank isn't there.'

'And Eddie won't go and see him?'

I shake my head. 'No, he flatly refuses. Says his dad should be coming to see *him*.'

'D'you think Frank just can't cope with it all?' Oliver suggests. We are side by side on a bench now, clutching coffees in the shade of a sycamore tree. It felt entirely natural to spill it all out.

'I don't know what he's thinking,' I reply.

Oliver nods. 'And this stage is meant to be easier?' he says lightly.

'When the kids are all grown, you mean?' Despite everything, I smile. He has a way of lightening things.

'Yeah. You know – when we're supposed to have it all figured out?'

I chuckle. 'That's what it says in the book.'

'Oh, what book's that?'

'A kind of self-help guide I found in the library. *The Empty-Nester's Handbook*. Apparently we're meant to be embarking on a thrilling new chapter right now.'

'Oh, right.' He laughs wryly, then looks at me. 'There's a baby coming, though.'

'Yes.' I nod. 'That is pretty thrilling, isn't it?'

'It is,' Oliver agrees.

'You're going to be a great-uncle!'

'Jesus,' he manages, and as we stroll back through the park I reflect that life really is thrilling; at least, this little part of it. And even though Frank is living in a derelict food truck, and I've found myself living with my father and son and every damn day I have to pick up wet towels from the bathroom floor, today feels pretty special. Because I sense that I've found a new friend and that, somehow, he seems to get it.

'I don't think we'll make it to the museum now,' Oliver remarks.

I smile at him. 'I don't know where the time's gone. Sorry I've gone on about Frank . . .'

'Not at all,' he says emphatically. 'What were you going to do? Say everything's fine?'

'You'd have known it wasn't.'

'Yes, I would.' Oliver seems to hesitate, then adds, 'I'll be over your way again in the next couple of weeks. We're doing a full survey on the site . . .'

'For the beavers?'

'Yeah. I was going to suggest meeting up, if you'd like to? Maybe I could pop into your library, explore this natural history collection of yours?'

'Oh, yes! Please do. It'd be great to see you.'

He seems to study my face. 'Are you sure? It sounds as if you have an awful lot on your plate right now.'

'No, that'd be lovely,' I say firmly. 'And y'know, me and Frank will probably have things sorted by then.'

'I do hope so.'

'Thanks, Oliver. I mean it,' I add firmly. 'It's been good to chat today. I can't really talk to Eddie about anything personal, and me and Dad . . . well, we get along fine. But it's not really his thing. Listening, I mean. Or feelings . . .'

Oliver chuckles. 'Sometimes it's just good to be out of the situation for a little while.'

'Yes, exactly. Do let me know when you're over, though, won't you?'

'I will, definitely.'

We're heading towards Eddie and Lyla now. Waiting there in the warm afternoon sunshine, they look – well, *together*, is the only way I can interpret it. But who knows? God forbid I make any assumptions.

I glance at Oliver, realising I don't really want to go home yet. I'd like to talk for longer. But now Eddie is striding towards us with an undecipherable look on his face. 'Hey, love,' I start. 'Everything all right? We should probably head off soon—'

'Yeah, okay.' Eddie tilts his head, indicating that he wants a private word, and we step away from Lyla and Oliver.

'Everything okay?' I ask again.

'Yeah, fine. Sort of.' He glances around the park.

'What is it?'

'It's, uh . . .' He pulls a face, and my heart seems to freeze. Please, no. Not, *I have something to tell you, Mum* again. 'It's Lyla,' he starts.

'Is she all right?' I ask, alarmed.

'Yeah. Yeah, she's fine. But not really,' he adds quickly. 'This stuff with her mum and the boyfriend, all the drama and the flooding and . . .' His cheeks redden. 'It's all been a bit much for her, to be honest.'

I touch his arm, tanned golden brown below the T-shirt sleeve. 'I bet it has. It's not exactly what she needs right now, is it?'

'Nope.' He looks down and shakes his head. 'And now Suki wants to move in with her!'

'Yes, she told me. Isn't . . . that okay?' I ask hesitantly.

'No! The thing is, it's Suki's place Lyla's living in. I mean, Suki owns the flat. So what can she do?'

'But it's actually Lyla's home,' I remind him.

'That doesn't seem to matter.' He grimaces, meeting my gaze directly now. 'She just needs a bit of space, Mum.' He glances over to where Lyla and her uncle are watching, bemused, as a group of children roll sideways down the nearby grassy slope. 'Can she come home with us?'

'What, Lyla?' I exclaim, then quickly assemble the correct reaction. 'I mean, yes, if she'd like to. Of course she can.'

'But . . . do we have space, Mum? Honestly?' He blinks in the sunshine.

I smile. '*Yes*, we have space, Eddie. Of course we do. But isn't she a bit close to her due date to be away from home? It's only—'

'Mum, it'll be fine,' Eddie says firmly, seeming to relax now.

'Well, shouldn't she okay it with her mum?'

He splutters. 'She's an adult! She can do whatever she likes.'

'Yes, of course,' I say quickly, trying to suppress a laugh.

Eddie grins. 'Can I tell her it's okay then? And yes, she'll call her mum to tell her. And then we'll nip over to her place and get her stuff . . . Is that all right?'

I glance at Oliver, who's clearly gathered from Lyla what's going on. He smiles, raising a brow, and I smile back. 'That's fine, Eddie,' I say as we make our way towards the bustling throngs on Princes Street. 'Of course Lyla can come home with us.'

CHAPTER FORTY-TWO

Frank

It's the photos that do it. The sunny, happy pictures of his family, apparently taken yesterday when they were picnicking in Princes Street Gardens without him.

Carly and Eddie, with Lyla and her mother and some good-looking man who he doesn't know.

Something seems to clench in Frank's chest as he sits in the truck's doorway, glaring forensically at the photos. He doesn't bother with social media normally, but recently he's been sucked right in. He pores over pictures of Ana and Bella out and about in Dundee and London, hoping to feel closer to his family – or at least have a vague idea of what's going on. Carly posts rarely, and Eddie never does, he's discovered now. He's also started watching Suki's account (not Lyla's – that would feel a bit wrong. There's a law, Frank believes, against following the account of a younger person you're not biologically related to).

It's one of Suki's pictures he's examining now as Badger nuzzles his bare ankle. Frank zooms in, not to study the faces; he's done that already, wondering why Carly was at a picnic with a man he's never seen in his life. Trying to quell a rush of insecurity, he homes in on the inanimate objects in the photo, thinking that'll be less painful.

He's wrong. Because sitting there in a white box are several pastéis de nata. The Portuguese custard tarts that nearly ruined his family. Not these *actual* tarts, being enjoyed in an Edinburgh park on a beautiful summer's day with a handsome bastard in a grey T-shirt. No, the almost life-ruining pastries are the ones Frank produced, or *tried* to produce – having hired a dopey guy who claimed to have 'loads of baking experience', yet spent most of his shift smoking weed in the alleyway and turned up with suspicious white powder caked around a nostril. It wasn't icing sugar, Frank knew that much.

What had he been thinking, taking on the lease of the bakery in a faded seaside town? Frank wonders if his brain had turned into actual custard at that time. In fact, maybe it has now. Ana and Bella seem to think so, judging by the barrage of messages he's received, since they first found out he was living here. Frank's only consolation is that neither daughter has rushed back to Sandybanks to try and force him to go home. But perhaps that's *not* such a good thing. Maybe his beautiful girls are scared of what he's turned into here in his weird little lair.

Frank won't be here much longer. Already, Dev has deduced that he's been living in the truck, and nags him constantly to move into his place temporarily. That is, if he really can't go home. But he doesn't want to impinge on his friend, even though Dev is single and has plenty of room. Frank has another idea instead. So on this cool, breezy

Sunday morning, he heads for the beach where he strolls along, keeping an eye out for Carly in the distance and torturing himself over possible identities for Picnic Man. Is something going on? 'Fast work,' he and Carly agreed, when it became apparent that a baby had been conceived before Eddie had so much as unpacked his toothbrush. Frank might say the same about Carly, creating a new life of friends and picnics and unfamiliar men, without him.

There must be something, he reflects, brow set in a frown as he climbs the steps back up to the seafront. Otherwise, why wouldn't Carly have asked him to go to Edinburgh too?

Frank winces as his gut aches, although that might be from the rank supermarket steak pasty he chomped down for breakfast. But there's another duller, deeper pain that never leaves him now. He adores Carly. He always has. He is in awe of her beauty, her intelligence, her compassion and infinite kindness. And, he decides now, he is no good for her. On this bright August morning, Frank feels as if his heart has broken.

He strides into town, momentarily grateful that the library is closed, as is pretty much everywhere on a Sunday around here. The town is sleepy with just a small cluster of people waiting at the bus stop. When he sees Thelma Campbell approaching with her little white dog, Frank steps quickly into a side street. Carly accuses him of never remembering the names of anyone he's not biologically connected to – but he knows her, and she seems to be everywhere. The other day she loomed at him like a store detective as he bought shaving foam in the supermarket.

The diversion has sent Frank in the direction of home.

He keeps walking, as if he is powerless to stop. It's as if Kilmory Cottage is emitting a powerful magnetic force. But when he sees the house in the distance, and his old banger parked outside it, he knows he can't just walk in as if nothing has happened. With a deep sadness in his gut, he decides he'll fetch his car tomorrow when he knows Carly will be at work. In the meantime he has something else to attend to. So he turns around and heads back to the town's main street, where he stops outside the letting agent's. Affecting an overly casual stance, he skims the selection of flats to let in other nearby towns. Then, glancing up and down the street to check that no one he knows is in the vicinity, he quickly takes photos of any place he could possibly bear to live in, and afford.

Then he strides back through town and along the seafront, past the birthday cake roundabout that's as redundant as he is – at least as a partner and dad. What a fuck-up he's made of everything, storming out after a stupid squabble over Kenny living with them. Okay, it wasn't just that. It was a build-up of things that finally burst out of him, and this normally gentle and mild-mannered man just lost it. And then the days went on, with his family seemingly managing perfectly well without him. And Frank was too ashamed, too wrapped up in dogged stubbornness, to go home.

At least he still has a job – and a plan now. First thing tomorrow, he'll call the letting agency and find himself a proper building to live in, rather than a truck. And then, Frank decides, he can start to live something vaguely resembling a normal life.

CHAPTER FORTY-THREE

Living at Kilmory Cottage: Carly, Eddie, Kenny, Lyla

Carly

Of course I want to look after my elderly dad and a pregnant young woman. Of course I meant it when I said to Lyla last night, 'I'll pick up some shopping on the way home from work tomorrow. Is there anything you'd like?'

She scrunched up her face as she considered this. 'There's a few bits and pieces. But I can get them. Or we can go out, can't we, Eddie—'

'Honestly, it's no trouble,' I said. 'Just leave me a list. I'll probably be out before you're up and about in the morning.'

She smiled her thanks. A week, Lyla's been here. Sharing Eddie's room, of course. It's fine, her being here, but she's also only a month away from her due date and I'm trying to look after her without fussing overly. It's a delicate balance. She seems so young, and while I'm not likening her to a small domestic animal, it feels a little like looking after someone else's pet.

Is she comfortable? Too hot, too cold or hungry? Meanwhile my Dad keeps interactions to a minimum, as if frightened of her condition. As if the baby might be born right there on the rug, in front of him, and thrust at him all pink and screaming for him to *do* something with.

He's actually afraid of Lyla, I realise. So, although it's not exactly convenient, we now do our evening meals in two shifts. Together, Eddie and Lyla cook their light and colourful East Asian–inspired dishes. Then, as Dad would no more consume one of his slippers than a poke bowl, I make the hefty beige meals that meet with his approval. Meanwhile Bella's old smoothie maker has been rinsed thoroughly of its spiders and is now in constant use. Eddie and Lyla chatter and giggle as the house trembles under its high-pitched whirr. They're like kids let loose for the first time in the kitchen. Lyla also enjoys baking gritty little cakes with seeds in them, which Eddie and I pronounce 'delicious'. Dad eyes them suspiciously, as if they might contain drugs.

Shame they don't, I figure, as I pick up the shopping list Lyla left out last night.

Seeds: omega mix, golden flaxseeds, chia (finely milled).
Powders: maca, spirulina, mushroom.
Jar of ghee (organic grass-fed) if you can get it!
Please let me know cost. Thanks so much!
L xx

It's like a test, I decide as I set off to work. A test to track down powdered mushrooms in a town where you can't buy a flat white.

I unlock the main door and step into the library. Cool sunlight filters in through the arched windows. I make my customary instant coffee and drink it slowly, revelling in the calm and stillness of the place. As it's a Saturday we'll soon be busy with lenders, plus the various groups that meet here. But for now the gleaming tables are bare, the building silent.

Then the library wakes up like a sleepy old giant as Prish arrives. Jamie, I gather, is planning to confront Lewis this weekend, having reached the end of his tether about being a guilty secret at thirty-eight years old.

Now our lenders start to wander in. There's Bill, who's researching his family tree, and Jemma with her toddler, who always comes in for Story Corner. There's Laura who likes to read, quietly, on the sofa in the sci-fi section. Then more parents and children arrive for the story, read by Prish, who's fantastic with the kids.

As soon as that's over the Natural History Society arrives. Thelma breezes in now, a buff cardboard folder tucked under her arm.

'Carly?' Her voice cuts though the stillness.

'Thelma, hi!'

'That bird-calls directory hasn't come in, has it?'

She's been asking this for weeks. 'I'm sorry, no. It looked like it was available on the system but it hasn't turned up. I have chased it,' I add.

She frowns. 'Disappointing.'

'It is, yes,' I say. 'I'm sorry.' In fact today I'm more concerned with tracking down at least some of the items on Lyla's shopping list. Which seems ridiculous as they're hardly essential to life.

I head out anyway, skipping the lunchtime beach walk for scouring the supermarket alone, and coming up with precisely nothing. By the time I'm back at the library, Prish is sorting through a pile of new acquisitions on a table by the kitchen hatch. 'No luck?' she says.

'Nope, nothing. I'll have to order the stuff online, I think.'

She raises a brow. 'Couldn't Lyla do that?'

I shrug. 'I guess so.' I pause. 'You know, I have no idea what Lyla does for an income. I'm starting to think the copywriting business isn't the runaway success she's led her mum to believe.'

'Well, she'll have plenty of other stuff to think about in a few weeks,' Prish reminds me. 'How long is it now?'

'Only a month,' I reply.

She pulls a wry expression. 'And how long is she planning to stay with you?'

I can't help laughing, because I know what she's implying. Who else is going to end up living at Kilmory Cottage? I keep expecting Bella to announce that she's moving back home too. She'd be welcome of course. But how would I fit everyone in? 'Who knows?' I say now. 'No one tells me anything—' I stop as a figure catches my eye, strolling into the library. 'Oliver, hi!'

'Hi.' He beams. 'I was hoping you'd be in today.'

I catch Prish looking at us expectantly. 'Oliver, this is Prish. Prish, Oliver is Lyla's uncle . . .'

'Hi, Oliver.' She smiles brightly, and then I beckon him away and indicate the group installed around the big table.

'Natural History Society,' I whisper. I pull a fearful expression and he grins.

'They do look intimidating.' We watch as Thelma addresses the group, her strident tones cutting through the building. *I want to stress that submissions for the newsletter must be on topic . . .*

'Would you like to see our natural history section?' I ask.

Oliver hesitates then says, 'I really just wanted to say hi. I'm taking Lyla out for a coffee later. Eddie too, if he wants to come. You're welcome too, but I assume you're busy—'

'Yes, I'm here till five-thirty. But how long are you in the area for?'

'A few days,' he replies. 'Thought I'd take a trip over to Arran sometime. Seems crazy not to when the ferry's so close . . .'

'If you'd like to do that tomorrow, I'm free,' I say without thinking. Perhaps he'd rather explore the island with Lyla, or alone?

'That'd be great.' He looks genuinely pleased. 'If you're sure I wouldn't be taking up your weekend?'

'Not at all,' I say, briefly thinking: is this actually okay? What if Frank comes back and thinks it's weird? But then he won't, will he? All this time I've been waiting and hoping and he still hasn't come home. 'Arran's so beautiful,' I add. 'I'm sure you'll love it.'

Oliver grins. 'I'm looking forward to it already,' he says.

CHAPTER FORTY-FOUR

And so next day, while Dad is eating his egg and toast, Oliver arrives and off we go. As the ferry leaves the mainland, he tells me how he spent his fiftieth birthday last week, taking up the floor of Suki's bathroom. 'That doesn't sound like the right way to mark your half-decade,' I suggest.

'Well, I didn't want any fuss.' He chuckles.

I look at him and smile. We're standing on the deck, the wind whipping across our faces, the sky a wash of sheer blue. 'You sounded exactly like my dad there!'

'It's true though. But actually, I did have a nice day. I FaceTimed the boys. The three of us are having a week together in October, so . . .'

'And d'you know where you're going to settle?' I ask. 'You seem to be moving around a lot . . .'

'It's the nature of the job,' he replies. 'And if there's no accommodation on site, then it's usually a budget hotel. But yeah, I do need to find a permanent place. I'm thinking somewhere up north, but not too far. Somewhere close to Suki's cabin, maybe. A little cottage.'

I nod, taking this in. 'You wouldn't mind being so remote?' On your own, is what I mean.

'I know people in the area,' he says, 'involved with the squirrel watch and the red kite feeding programme. There's a lot going on out in the wilds, you know,' he adds with a wry smile, and I smile back.

'Sounds like it.' An easy silence settles as the ferry approaches the island. Although the day is clear and bright, a wispy low cloud has now shrouded the jagged peaks. We've brought my car rather than Oliver's Land Rover. It seems important to be the guide today, rather than a passenger. From our numerous family day trips I know the island well. So we start by driving to the village of Lochranza, with its ruined castle and sparkling bay, where we watch seals, speckled grey and almost indistinguishable from the rocks they're basking on. Then we head inland, following winding lanes bordered by lush green fields.

We stop off at Brodick Castle, and as we stroll around the manicured grounds, I tell Oliver that my fiftieth birthday is approaching too. 'So, are you planning anything?' he asks.

I shake my head. 'I'd thought about a little party at the house. But I don't know. With Frank gone . . .'

'I'm sorry,' he says. 'This must be really hard for you.'

I blow out air and look at him. 'There are more important things coming up than my birthday,' I say, although I know that's not what he meant. 'What d'you fancy doing next?' I'm keen to veer away from the subject.

'I'm up for anything. Any ideas?'

'We could do a hike?' I suggest. 'If you're feeling energetic?'

'You don't mean climbing Goat Fell, do you?' He smiles and his eyes widen; clear and blue, catching the sun.

'No, nothing as ambitious as that. But there's a walk I know, and the perfect little pub halfway round.'

'Sounds great,' he says. And so we park close to the start of the footpath, and as we walk I feel it again: how easy he is to be with. And how, separated now from the mainland by water, I can almost pretend that my life is normal, and that nothing sad or worrying has happened at all. I'm just exploring Arran with a friend. Because Oliver *is* a friend now; something separate from my family, from the rest of my life.

We stop to admire the glorious sweep down to the shore. 'You know this island really well, don't you?' he remarks.

'Pretty well, yes. We brought the kids here all the time.'

His gaze skims the incredible view: sparkling blue water, dotted with a few sailing boats, and the ferry making its way to the mainland. With Kilmory Cottage so full of people and noise, the sense of calm openness here is blissful.

'You mentioned your childhood was unconventional,' I say. 'That time at Suki's cabin, remember?'

'Oh, yes.' Oliver nods.

'I hope I'm not prying,' I add. 'I'm just curious—'

'It's more that Suki and I were pretty much free range,' he says.

'You mean your parents didn't take care of you?'

'Oh, they loved us,' Oliver says. 'But they were busy doing their own stuff. Away a lot on their travels, having adventures. We had horses and land and everything we wanted really, apart from anyone caring about what we got up to.'

'That sounds . . .' I hesitate. 'Kind of sad.'

Oliver shrugs. 'It was all we knew really. But yes, we did compare ourselves to our friends and it was obvious that in our family, things were different.' That might explain why Suki wants everything picture-perfect, I reflect. The cabin covered in fairy lights. Lyla's pregnancy being a wonderful thing, right from the start.

'D'you think it affected you?' I ask.

Oliver looks at me, seeming to turn this over in his mind. 'I'd say me and Suki did everything we could to have incredibly settled and conventional family lives. I mean, we both wanted to keep our marriages together. But our partners had other ideas.'

'I'm probing way too much. I'm sorry . . .'

'It's okay, honestly.' He looks at me then, and something seems to turn inside me. We are sitting in perfect silence. There's not a sound; not a bird's call or the whisper of wind through the trees. I take a breath, about to speak, when I realise how closely we're sitting, shoulders touching.

And I start to tell him that I haven't known how to be, with Frank, or Eddie. I haven't been able to ask my son about the baby, or how he feels about impending fatherhood or *anything* that really matters. 'My grandchild's growing every second and I haven't been able to talk about it.' It comes out in a rush. 'Oh, I have my friends of course. But I don't want to go on about it, you know? And what is there to say really?' *And the person I really want to talk to has gone,* I reflect.

'It's natural to want to help and be involved,' Oliver says. 'Y'know, Suki feels pushed away by Lyla sometimes. But she keeps clinging on. My sister's not one to let go, as you might've gathered . . .' He smiles knowingly and I laugh, feeling better already.

'I'm not expecting to decorate the nursery or buy mobiles or be involved in discussions about names,' I add.

'Well, I think it'd be a very nice thing, to buy a mobile.'

I look around at his handsome face, lightly weathered and tanned, his blue eyes bright. 'I will then,' I announce. 'I'm going to buy a mobile, before the baby's even born!' I stop then. 'Is that bad luck? To buy a present before the baby's arrived?'

'Honestly, I have no idea . . .' Oliver smiles. 'I don't think so—' And then he stops, and I don't know what happens – how things change or how it starts. Only that it does.

We look at each other and then we kiss, Oliver and I. My head spins and everything else fades from my mind: Frank, my family, my life at home. Dad and his quiz show. Worrying about my son or his future or any of that. We are just here, perched on a rock on the hillside, the mountains' jagged peaks behind us and the iridescent blue of the sea below. I feel giddy and reckless as the kiss goes on and on. Then we stop and Oliver looks a little taken aback, as if he hadn't expected that either.

'Oh,' is all I can say.

'Oh,' he repeats, smiling now. His is gaze is on mine and he pulls me in for a hug. I don't feel guilty about the kiss, or even guilty about my lack of guilt. We just sit together in comfortable silence, gazing down to where the lush green of the island meets the glittering sea. And then, still without saying anything – because there's no need – we get up and stroll, hand in hand, back along the winding path, down the hillside. The plan to stop off at the pub has been forgotten. Hours have spun by without us noticing.

As we climb into my car, I'm still a little stunned. What have I just done? I've kissed Oliver! We drive onto the ferry in silence and stand on deck as it carries us back to the mainland, and my home. And we talk about ordinary things as if nothing has happened. Oliver's environmental projects and plan to settle in Perthshire, and my life as a librarian in a sleepy seaside town. It's as if we are simply heading home after a day out.

As I pull up outside Kilmory Cottage, I ask Oliver if he'd like a coffee, or something to eat, before he heads to his hotel. I realise how much I want him to say yes.

'That'd be nice,' he says. 'If you're sure that's okay?'

'Of course it is,' I say.

We step into the house. 'Eddie? Lyla?' I call out. They're not downstairs, and Dad isn't either. 'Dad? Are you home?' I check the back garden, then come back inside. I look at Oliver and frown. There's a noise at the top of the stairs, and I go through to the hallway and see Eddie standing there.

'Eddie, hi!' His eyes are wide, his face gaunt. Can he possibly know what's happened today? Do I look different somehow?

'Mum—' he starts.

'Have you seen Granddad, love?' I ask.

'Gone out. Something about powders?' he says distractedly. 'At the chemist? Said he's gone to have it out with them . . .'

'Oh, God,' I groan and turn to Oliver. 'They keep including this laxative stuff with his prescription. It *enrages* him. He acts like it's a personal affront—'

'Mum!' Eddie says, more forcefully this time.

'What is it, love?' I ask as Lyla appears beside him, looking shaken. And now I realise that something is wrong. Something is happening.

'Carly?' Lyla looks down at me, chalk pale. 'I've had this thing. I'm sorry. It's all on the bed, it's a mess . . .'

'What?' I cry out.

'This sort of . . . *flood*. I think my waters—'

'We think Lyla's waters have broken,' Eddie announces.

Oliver and our kiss; it all disappears from my mind in a blink as I hurry upstairs towards them. 'When did this happen?'

'Just now.' Eddie's eyes are round with fear. '*Literally* just now, before you came in . . .'

'Okay,' I say, telling myself to stay calm. 'Lyla, we need to get you to—'

'We know that, Mum. We know,' Eddie says firmly. Then my boy who flung Quality Street around the living room takes his girlfriend's hand and says, 'C'mon, Lyles. Come downstairs, darling. Don't be scared. Everything's going to be okay – but we need to get you to hospital right now.'

CHAPTER FORTY-FIVE

Eddie

Despite all the meat cuts and offal at the restaurant, Eddie is still terrified of blood. At least, *human* blood. That time with the blind, when his arm crashed through the window, he passed out. He remembers Raj's face looming over him, not quite in focus, like something out of a bad TV show.

Now Eddie is clutching Lyla's hand in the back of his mum's car. Although he's trying to appear calm, he's terrified that he won't be able to cope with the whole birth thing, the sight of the baby coming out and – oh God, he can barely even think about it.

Lyla didn't want to sit up front. She wanted to be next to him because she's freaking out a little. Lyla had just wanted a bit of time with him at the seaside, a sort of holiday away from her fussing mum before the baby came. Just a little breathing space – a babymoon, she called it – before her life changed forever. But this wasn't supposed to happen here.

In the few minutes since they left home, Eddie's been

googling like his life depends on it. 'I think you might be inducted,' he says.

'*Induced*, love,' his mum corrects him from the driver's seat. He hates it when she's right. 'But yes, I think they'll want to get things going,' she adds. 'Contractions should start, and then you'll be on your way, Lyla. Don't worry. Everything will be fine.'

'Okay,' she says quietly.

Eddie stares at the back of his mum's head. His own mother, acting like she knows stuff? And can remain calm in a crisis? If his brain wasn't buzzing with what lies ahead, Eddie might be impressed.

They've left the town now. Oliver has stayed at the house – something to do with being there to let Granddad in, because he mightn't have his keys? Eddie wasn't paying much attention to what was going on.

Already, they're out into green and undulating open countryside, a little way inland. There isn't time to deliver Lyla safely to the Edinburgh hospital where she's supposed to have the baby. Instead, they're going to the hospital closest to Sandybanks. No one has managed to get hold of Lyla's mum. She's away for the weekend, apparently – seemingly with no phone signal.

Now Eddie is hanging on to the hope that this baby will emerge into the world in an entirely new, never-seen-before way – a medical first. That is, perfectly clean with not a speck of blood or that white mucusy stuff to be seen. What he'd *really* love is for the baby to come out dressed in a little outfit, as if handed to them in a shop. Eddie knows it's mad, to expect this. But it's the only way he can cope with what's ahead.

His mum parks up and the three of them climb out of the car. Oliver had wanted to bring them in his Land Rover, but Lyla had insisted on Eddie's mum driving them instead. 'I'll just feel better,' she announced, 'if there's a woman there. Sorry, Uncle Olly.'

As they make their way towards the hospital entrance, Eddie realises why this is. Lyla expects him to duck out and be unable to stay with her, and then his mum can step in instead. Lyla knows all about Eddie's blood phobia. She doesn't think he's up to this.

Outside the hospital, next to a huge no smoking sign, a man in a wheelchair is connected to some kind of machine by tubes and is smoking a cigarette. Eddie's stomach turns. They step through automatic doors into reception and Eddie looks at his mum.

He could do it now. He could tell her he's sorry but he can't go in. That there's no way he can watch a tiny person being hauled out of Lyla's vagina. He's not a medical person; he's a chef. At least, he *was*. And he's not built for this kind of stuff.

His mum is talking to the receptionist but Eddie can barely decipher her words. 'We've called . . . yes, her waters have broken,' she explains calmly. That's all he can hear because something is pounding dully in his ears.

She's going to be induced. Eddie doesn't know how this will happen, and there wasn't time to google it. He thinks about the box of scented oils Suki bought Lyla to use during labour. It's sitting in Lyla's flat in Edinburgh – no use at all. And she'd wanted a home birth but obviously that's not going to happen. What's the point of making a 'birth plan' where human bodies are concerned? Bodies that vomit and crash into windows and have to be sewn back up? *Nothing* can be planned, Eddie reckons. Everything is completely out of control.

'Eddie!' His mum's voice snaps him back to the antiseptic-smelling reception area. 'Lyla needs to go through now. Are you are okay to go with her?' He looks at his mum, who somehow managed to go through this three times – first with him and then his sisters. Why would anyone do this to themselves more than once?

He hears himself saying, 'Yes.'

'D'you want me to come too? I can, you know, if you'd like . . .'

For a moment Lyla looks at him as if to say, *That's a good idea, isn't it?* 'No, no. It's fine, Mum. Thanks.' Then his mum hugs him, and Lyla too, and she looks as if she'll cry as she turns away. Eddie is suddenly reminded of his mum dropping him off at Kyle McShannon's birthday party and being horrified when he realised she wouldn't be staying too. All those people and noise and balloons everywhere that might burst in his face! How was he going to cope?

He stares after his mother, heart banging. He has to muster his every smidgeon of willpower not to shout, *Mum, wait! I can't go in with her. I'm coming with you!*

Eddie and Lyla are taken along a corridor by a nurse who looks around the same age as they are. There's a whiff of school dinners and somewhere, people are laughing loudly. Lyla's waters have broken a month early and now the baby's going to have to come out. How can anyone laugh at a time like this?

The nurse ushers them into a tiny room. 'We'll take

your blood pressure, Lyla,' she explains. 'And then the doctor's coming to talk to you. We're going to induce labour today. It's important we do that, as your waters have broken and we don't want to risk infection.'

We know her waters have broken! Eddie wants to yell. *Why are you stating the obvious?* But he's relieved to hear that this induction/inducing thing isn't done by putting Lyla into some kind of space capsule, as he's feared – but with pessaries. 'It can take a few hours,' the nurse explains, 'for things to get started.' They're taken to another room then, and for a brief moment Eddie thinks: *it's not too late. I could tell Lyla I can't do this. There are plenty of proper medical people here, and what can I do anyway? Sit here, freaking out?*

Instead, Eddie holds Lyla's hand, and they wait, until finally things start happening.

Lyla has talked about how she'd like the birth to be, with perfumed oils and gentle music playing. She's even made up playlists, but neither of them are thinking about playlists now. Because the contractions seem to rack her body, and she's groaning in pain each time one comes. Yet she doesn't want drugs. Where's the logic in that? Eddie thinks wildly. What sane person would turn down mind-altering substances, offered for free – and legally! – on the NHS? Then she wants – no, *needs* – whatever drugs they can give her because the pain is unbearable.

There's a plastic mask on her face now as she inhales some concoction called gas and air. That doesn't sound like much. Is it strong enough? The contractions keep coming, and Eddie feels helpless parked there on a blue plastic chair, as if at a school assembly with the head teacher droning on and on. He wants to help somehow – to *do* something. Should he have brought some of those seedy cakes she made, or the acoustic guitar his dad bought him years ago? No, he only knows two chords. That would probably just annoy her. Now he badly wants some of that gas and air. But the nurse with her silvery hair pulled into a ponytail is – rightly – focused on Lyla, telling her to push. He can't imagine it'd go down well if he asked if he could possibly get bombed out of his skull?

They're talking about Lyla dilating now, and he doesn't think they mean her pupils. There's the ponytail nurse, and another nurse with a tiny flower tattoo on her wrist. Lyla is bellowing now, like a farm animal – is bovine the right word? Calum grew up on a farm and Eddie was always afraid of the cattle; the weight and heft of them, their huge damp nostrils and flies buzzing around their eyes.

'I can't do it!' Lyla shrieks.

'What?' Eddie exclaims, grabbing at her hand.

'I can't get the baby out of me—'

'You're doing fine, Lyla,' says ponytail nurse. 'Push—'

'I can't push! I've been pushing all night!' Lyla announces – and Eddie realises that hours have spun by and he has to agree that Lyla can't do this. So that's that sorted. Quite simply, she can't get the baby out. So what happens now? he thinks in panic. Will it stay inside? Be *reabsorbed* somehow? It's not as if she can send it back like a badly fitting jumper. There's no returns form. Just a terrifying blur of shouting and pushing and Lyla is crying now, and the flower tattoo nurse looks around at him as if only just noticing that he's there.

'We're going to call someone in,' she tells him.

'What does that mean?' Eddie cries out. A doctor, he supposes. Or someone higher up the management chain? He assumes they don't mean a plumber.

'We're getting the registrar,' the ponytail nurse explains, and time seems to swirl in an almighty soup of pushing and crying while Eddie thinks: *registrar?* Aren't they for weddings? And a terrible thought hits him: they're going to get married because Lyla is about to die in childbirth, like in the olden days when women gave birth in huts on piles of straw. And now he's gripping her hand, as if holding on to her is the only way he can stop her from slipping away.

A woman arrives. An impossibly glamorous woman in a red dress and full make-up, looking utterly out of place in the bleak hospital setting, as if she has breezed in by mistake, expecting a party. Eddie almost expects her to be carrying a bottle of wine.

Immediately, the chaos subsides as the woman assumes control. She speaks sternly to Lyla: 'Push, Lyla. Push, as if you're doing a great big shit.'

Eddie blinks in shock that this posh-looking woman in red lipstick can speak like that. Then there's some terrible object being wielded about. A shiny thing like the tongs his dad uses when he's barbecuing his special Portuguese beef, only they're not for a barbecue, they're being inserted— Oh God, he can't look. There are yelled commands to PUSH PUSH PUSH, and Lyla is wailing but she's also magnificent, Eddie realises – this girl he met at a party in a smelly flat. Then everything seems to stop: the cries, the mayhem, Eddie's life as a carefree young man. And the red-dress woman hands a small thing to the ponytail nurse, and Eddie thinks they're wrapping it; he can't take in what's going on because he is crying in great, racking gulps.

The thing is handed to Lyla like a parcel. Eddie watches as Lyla blinks through sweat-drenched hair, and holds their baby daughter and puts her to her breast.

And her tiny mouth purses, and tears pour down Eddie's face as he stares at his daughter, the most beautiful thing he has ever seen in his life.

CHAPTER FORTY-SIX

September

Living at Kilmory Cottage: Carly, Kenny, Eddie, Lyla, Grace

Carly

We couldn't believe how small she was, and how perfect. Baby Grace, already forming expressions, her eyes big and round and shiny blue, assessing the world.

'Oh, Frank,' I murmured. 'I can't believe it. Our granddaughter.'

'Yeah.' His voice cracked, and we sat together, and came back day after day as Grace seemed to gather strength with every minute of her new life.

We didn't talk about *us*. All that mattered was coming to see Lyla and Grace. It was about them, not Frank and me. And that's what Suki said too, when we had the chance to talk. As soon as the news had reached her, she'd driven straight from her cabin, gaining a speeding ticket en route.

'I just wanted to say,' she told me, as we did a coffee run to the hospital canteen, 'I did figure out that Lyla and Eddie weren't really together all that time.'

'Oh.' I exhaled, not knowing what to say to her. 'I'm so sorry . . .'

'Carly, it's not your fault!' she exclaimed. 'You just went along with it. I realise that. You didn't want to make things difficult for them.'

'It was just sprung on us,' I started. 'That first time we met you for lunch.'

She smiled. 'I had my suspicions then. You can tell, can't you, if people have a genuine connection?'

I nodded. 'So . . . why did you go along with it?'

'Oh, the story she concocted was so cute, I wanted to believe it had happened that way . . .'

'What *was* the story?' I asked hesitantly.

Suki linked her arm in mine, and, instead of us taking the coffees straight back to the ward, she motioned for us to sit at a window table. Here she told me how, apparently, Lyla had been sitting alone, engrossed in a novel on a bench in Princes Street Gardens, and along had come Eddie and asked what she was reading . . . She broke off and we laughed.

'Oh, Suki. Not that old one.'

'I thought it was so cute!' She shook her head. I didn't want to tell her that Eddie would never ask *anyone* about a book they were reading.

'I still can't understand it,' I added. 'Why Lyla concocted all that . . .'

'Oh, it's probably my fault,' she said quickly. 'I'm far too controlling. Her dad was always telling me that. Following poor Lyla to Edinburgh, when all she wanted was to enjoy her student life . . . I mean, who wants their mum living down the road? I'm sure she'd chosen Edinburgh to get away from me!' She shuddered.

'I can't imagine that,' I said. Although, in truth, I could.

'And she knows I like a romantic story with a happy ending,' Suki added. 'But I realise that real life . . .'

'It's a bit more messy than that,' I remarked, and she nodded.

'It is.'

'But it's also wonderful,' I added, as we got up and carried the coffees back to the ward. Ana was there, chatting to Lyla, having come over from Dundee. And next day my dad came in with us, admiring Grace from a distance, although he didn't seem to know what to say, other than a gruff, 'Well done.' And when Lyla started breastfeeding – well, that nearly ended my father. I had to whisk him off for a cup of tea. Then Lyla's dad, a loud man in corduroys and a cream linen shirt, arrived from Gloucestershire. And on another visit, by coincidence Frank and Oliver arrived together.

If a certain static charge fizzled in the air – a sense of something off-kilter – then I quickly dampened it down. And when Oliver caught my eye, we exchanged a look that seemed to say everything we needed to say. That our day together on Arran had been special, and perhaps something both of us had needed. But that was that. It was a lovely memory that could be put away now, as there were more pressing matters to think about.

And now Lyla and Grace are home, staying at Kilmory Cottage for the time being. 'I like it here,' she announces one morning, installed on our worn-out brown sofa with Grace latched on to her breast. 'It's so peaceful and I love the thought of the first part of her life being by the sea. Is that all right, Carly? I don't really want to take her all the way across the country just yet.'

It's only Edinburgh, I reflect; ninety minutes away. But I understand how she feels, because when Eddie, Bella and Ana were born I just wanted to hunker down in our own little world.

'Yeah, I hope you don't mind,' Eddie offers.

'Of course I don't,' I say truthfully. 'I love you being here.'

'Thanks so much, Mum,' he says. I look at my son, realising how different he seems already. No longer the boy who'd shudder at the sight of lettuce on his plate, or leave a loo roll unravelled on the bathroom floor. In fact, he and Lyla have taken to parenthood as if this is what they were designed to do. They feed, soothe, change and bathe their daughter, seemingly without needing to refer to any instruction manual. I remember the battered old book – *Your Essential Guide to New Motherhood* – I'd pored over endlessly, as if that would save us. I'd always believed that the answers to everything could be found in books.

Meanwhile, I'm on hand to do whatever they need me to do. Mostly, it's support worker duties: laundry and cleaning and making sure we have food to eat. I try to stay in the background, reminding myself that I must not interfere. Having managed to take leave from work, I keep the kettle at a rolling boil, and the washing machine perpetually churning.

We have simple meals, with Lyla's requested exotic ingredients remaining unused. The powdered mushroom has been shoved to the back of the cupboard. There are no dual mealtimes now. Dad has to eat with us – it's the only option because I'm not a short-order cook! – and

I've banned blaring teatime TV. Our home is strewn with muslins and babygrows and the array of toys Suki brought over, which Grace can't play with yet.

So there's no *Cash or Crash* at this present time. We don't even know who's gone through to the final. Dad is put out, of course he is. And although he's admitted that Grace really is the most perfect little thing, he reels back whenever she's brought near him, as if she is a bomb about to blow up in his face. Whenever Lyla starts to feed her, he scuttles out of the room.

'So are the new parents managing okay?' Jamie asks, one crisp Sunday morning as we step around seaweed on the beach.

'They're doing amazingly well,' I reply. 'It just seems natural. Honestly I don't know why I'm surprised!'

'See, he's more grown up than you gave him credit for,' Jamie teases, and I smile. He is staying at Prish's temporarily, having had enough of the pretence whenever Lewis's parents were around. 'I'm thirty-eight,' he reminded us. 'I'm not living like this anymore.' He likened their situation to dating a married man 'who keeps promising to leave his wife and never does. It goes on and on, and the years slip away and if Lewis wants to change things, he knows where I am.' I'd expected him to be heartbroken but in fact there's a lightness about him now. A sense of relief, perhaps, that at least he's taken control.

Today Jamie, Prish and I have brought Grace out to see the sea. However, full of milk from her morning feed, she's been dozing peacefully in the baby carrier on my chest.

'I'm so glad they've taken to all of this,' Prish remarks, meaning Eddie and Lyla.

'Me too,' I say truthfully. 'Y'know, less than a year ago Eddie was lying around in that hooded robe, horrified when I found a job he might apply for. It seems like worlds ago now,' I add. Paris, too, I reflect – when Frank and I were celebrating finally being empty-nesters.

My phone rings, causing Grace to stir against my chest. I step away from my friends and take the call. 'Carly? It's Thelma. Is your dad still keen, do you think?'

We hatched a plan last time the Natural History Society convened in the library. Bravely, I strode over and broke my way into the group. I explained that, after Dad went storming into Sandybanks' sole pharmacy – from which he is now barred – I needed to find him something to focus on. Something other than unsolicited orange-flavoured powders, to be mixed up with water.

'He's looking forward to it,' I tell her now. 'He loves nature – birds especially. And he'll be glad to be out of the house. We have a new baby at home at the moment—'

'Oh, goodness!' she gasps. 'You're a grandmother?'

'Yes, I am,' I say proudly. 'So it didn't take much persuading for Dad to agree to try something new.' I hesitate, aware of treading carefully. 'I have to tell you, Thelma. Dad isn't exactly the society-joiner type . . .'

'We'll make him very welcome,' she assures me in her clipped manner. 'So, our field trips are usually half a day. Nothing too strenuous because none of us are getting any younger.' A small chuckle. It's the first time I've heard Thelma Campbell laugh.

'So it's a fossil-hunting trip?' I say.

'That's the idea. It involves a *little* bit of clambering over rough ground—'

'Really?' I ask, alarmed.

'But don't worry about that,' she adds, and I can tell she's smiling. 'There's a very nice tearoom nearby. Tell your dad the minibus will pick him up on Tuesday morning at ten.'

We finish the call and I catch up with Prish and Jamie, who have strolled on ahead. 'All sorted?' Prish grins.

'I think so, yes.'

'Maybe this'll encourage him to be more independent again,' Jamie offers. 'Going on this trip, I mean—'

'He's actually talking about moving back home,' I cut in.

My friends stop and look at me. 'But he seemed to be loving it at your place,' Prish says in surprise. 'What's brought this on?'

I smile, and glance down at Grace. 'There's been a few things. His routine, for one. It's all gone to pot . . .'

'Well, that's to be expected,' she says with a wry smile.

'And he says he can never get into the bathroom, and when he finally does, he looks at the pot of toothbrushes and there's about eighty-five of them and he can't figure out which one's his.'

Jamie laughs. 'How many people are you actually living with, Carly?'

'Just four,' I reply. 'Well, five of us of course,' I add quickly. 'But Grace doesn't have a toothbrush yet.' I touch the blonde hair on her head, soft as my mother's powder puff. 'But this one takes up quite a lot of space, and Dad says the house is feeling a bit overcrowded for him now.'

CHAPTER FORTY-SEVEN

Eddie

Eddie knows it's not unusual for parents to split up. Calum's mum and dad are divorced and Raj's parents went through a rough patch. His own parents have too. Years ago, he'd hear them arguing in the kitchen late at night – about money usually. His dad doing something stupid like taking out a massive loan to buy a food truck or whatever.

However, no matter how bad things were, he always knew they loved each other. And that everything would be okay.

And now, he's not so sure because everything has changed. He knows his dad was upset about the whole baby thing. That was understandable. And maybe it wasn't easy for him either, when Eddie's granddad moved in. But then everything escalated and, next thing Eddie knew, his dad had moved out! Like, left his mum, who he's always been devoted to. Even with the baby here – and of course she's his main focus – Eddie is still reeling with the shock of it all. And the *really* crazy thing is, his dad isn't staying with a friend, like Dev or any of his other mates who he goes to football with occasionally. No, he's living in the truck.

One cool, autumnal Sunday morning Eddie tells Lyla and his mum that he's going out for a walk. His mum looks surprised because normally, Eddie doesn't walk anywhere just for the sake of it. But he slips out before she can fire any questions at him.

He strides along the seafront, past the abandoned birthday cake roundabout and the overgrown crazy golf course, wishing Calum and Raj were still here. They've been over to visit, and to meet Lyla and Grace, which went fine – although they did seem pretty terrified of the baby. ('Want to hold her?' Eddie asked. 'No thanks!' they chimed.) But now they're in Edinburgh, leading their whizzy and wholesome lives with their vitamins and massive water bottles. The few friends he has left in Sandybanks, Eddie doesn't really want to see. Because they'll be getting stoned and playing video games and eating takeaways. And Eddie's worried that, if he sees them, he'll see his old self reflected back. That's all teenage stuff, and he's not a teenager anymore. He is nearly twenty-three and a father now.

He marches onwards, passing dog walkers and old couples and parents with buggies, hoping he won't be spotted by anyone he knows. That's the thing about small-town life, Eddie reflects. Everything you do gets commented on. He's been grateful to settle into Kilmory Cottage for this first little while, as he and Lyla have grown used to the way things are now. It's been brilliant, too, having his mum there to help. She doesn't annoy him like she used to. She's different, he thinks. Or maybe it's him? But tomorrow Suki is coming over to collect him and Lyla and Grace, and they'll drive over to Edinburgh to start their new lives in Lyla's flat.

Eddie will have to find a job pronto. He's prepared to do anything, to show Lyla that he isn't some idiot who can't stick at anything. But right now, the prospect of job hunting has been shunted to the furthest corner of Eddie's mind, as now he has arrived at Dev's garage.

Of course he's been in touch with his dad, and he visited Lyla and Grace in hospital. Perhaps naively, Eddie had thought that as soon as they were home, then his dad would knock this crazy truck thing on the head and come home too. But he hasn't. And with everything that's happened, Eddie hasn't been able to face him here. Too depressing and difficult, he'd decided. He's tried to focus on Grace and push away images of his dad's terrible living conditions to the back of his mind.

It was a conversation with Bella that prompted him to finally come here to see him. She called the other night, out of the blue. They rarely speak on the phone. 'Eddie, I feel terrible that I've not been up to see Grace yet,' she said.

'That's all right.' He genuinely hasn't minded. He isn't wired that way, to crave attention and fuss.

'It's just, I've had loads of work to do for a job interview,' she added, 'and I haven't been able to take time off. I'm sorry. I'll be up as soon as I can . . .'

'Don't worry about it. Honestly. So, what's the job?'

'Um, just another marketing role.' She sounded surprised by his interest. 'Different company. They're smaller but the job's a lot more varied and I'll have loads more responsibility when I start—'

'When you start? So you got it then?'

'I did, yeah!'

It's hardly a new thing, for either of his sisters to succeed at something. It's often felt to Eddie that opportunities simply land in their laps. But it feels different this time because he's heard his mum talking to her friends about Bella, and that she wondered if she might move back home. *How will we fit her in?* had been his first – panicked – thought. But he was shocked too because he'd thought Bella had the perfect life in London.

'I'm really happy for you,' he told her. 'You are amazing, you know that?'

'Oh, stop it,' she chided him.

Eddie sniggered. 'So, are you pleased, then?'

'Yeah, of course I am! I'm *so* pleased. So I'll be up to see you soon, okay?'

'Great.'

Bella paused. 'And you will do that thing you promised to do, won't you? Please, Ed, before I come up?'

He assured her that he would. Because as usual Bella was right. He had to muster the mental strength to go and see their dad at the garage. It was his duty – as the only one at home now – to get to the bottom of what was going on.

Now Eddie turns away from the seafront, following the road that takes him past a new tea room – unusually stylish for Sandybanks – and the little pottery place that only opened last week. And now he has reached the garage where his dad works, and he's feeling a little shaky and nervous. He heads round the back of the building, stepping around pieces of rusty old engine, and spots a black and white cat who's watching him intently. Then he sees his dad sitting in the doorway of the truck. Something seems to set hard in Eddie's chest.

'Hi, Dad.'

His father looks up and blinks in surprise. He's eating what looks like Weetabix from a chipped bowl. 'Eddie. Hi!'

He's lost it, Eddie realises. How can he possibly be living here? His dad's always been there, strong and solid, whenever he's needed someone to talk to. Even when he'd thrown himself into those mad business schemes, he'd always been *Dad*. Dad in his old worn-out jeans and that awful yellow T-shirt with the cartoon bear on the front. And Eddie always believed that, whatever stupid stuff he got up to, his father would always be there for him and that would never change.

'Dad . . .' Not knowing how to start, Eddie looks around and perches on a small stack of wooden crates. 'What are you doing here?'

His father exhales and sets the bowl on the ground. 'It's hard to explain,' he says.

'Try then,' Eddie says, more forcefully than he intended.

His dad rubs at his unshaven jaw and pushes back his hair. Eddie thinks it's gone a bit greyer these past few months, though that might just be dust and dirt from living here. He's almost ashamed to see his own father in a vile old sweater and grubby black sweatpants, his brown feet bare and looking like they need a good scrub. But he won't get upset. He's not here to beg or plead, and he certainly isn't going to cry in front of him.

'I just . . .' his father starts, and Eddie sees with horror that his eyes are wet. He has never seen his dad cry. *Please don't cry!* he wills him. *Because then I won't know what to do!* 'I know it's my fault,' he adds.

'What is?' Eddie stares at him.

'All of it.' There's more face rubbing and Eddie notices that the cat is still watching him. 'The way I've been,' his dad goes on. 'The impetuous decisions. All the stuff I've put your mum through over the years. And then the pregnancy—'

'You think that was *your* fault?' Eddie asks incredulously.

'Well, yeah. Kind of—'

'So you think it's all about you, do you?'

His dad looks at him, clearly shocked. 'No. Not exactly. But I haven't set you a good example, have I? I've—'

'Dad, for a start,' Eddie lurches in, surprised by the firmness in his voice, 'it's not your fault. Nothing is. And we're happy about Grace. Can't you see that? We're *so* happy. We love her so much!'

'Yes, but—'

'—And you've been an amazing dad. You always have. But you're not so amazing now, are you?' Fury surges up in him as his dad's mouth falls open, and he jumps up from the crates. 'Look at you, sitting here, living like . . .' He checks himself, shaking his head. 'You shouldn't be here. That's all.'

'It felt like the best thing,' his father mutters, 'for everyone. I've been to look at some flats to rent—'

'This is sounding like self-pity now,' Eddie snaps. 'I'm sorry, Dad, but it's just not good enough.' He's about to say, 'man up', but stops himself. 'We need you,' he adds.

'Who does?' his dad exclaims, and Eddie is about to reply when something splatters onto the back of his neck. He cringes and puts a hand there, tentatively.

'Oh, *shit*.' He takes his hand away and glares at it. 'A seagull just crapped on me.'

His father's expression softens and he gets up from the truck's doorway and examines the back of Eddie's neck. 'Oh, Christ. That's quite a splat there, son. God knows what it had for breakfast. We'd better get you cleaned up . . .'

Together, they head into the rank little bathroom in the garage where Eddie's dad wipes away as much of the mess as he can with the few paper towels left in the dispenser. It reminds Eddie of his dad washing his hair when he was a little boy. Eddie hated hair washing time. He'd make a terrible fuss, pushing away his mum and wailing that the shampoo stung his eyes. He'd only let his dad do it. His kind and patient dad.

And now his father is trying to blot the water splashes from the back of Eddie's sweatshirt with a grubby towel. He hangs it back on the hook, and they step back outside into the chilly morning. Eddie looks at his dad, wanting to hug him, but they're not really the hugging types.

'Thanks, Dad,' is all he can say.

His father smiles. 'That's all right.'

They walk in silence across the rough, weedy ground

towards the truck, and then Eddie grabs at his father's arm. And they do hug then, in a close, tight way that Eddie can never remember them doing before.

They stand there, holding each other in the weak September sunshine until Eddie pulls away and looks his father directly in the eye. 'C'mon then,' he says firmly. 'Pack up your things, Dad. It's time to come home.'

CHAPTER FORTY-EIGHT

Currently living in Lyla's flat: Lyla, Eddie, Grace

Three days later and Eddie and Lyla and Grace are living in Lyla's smart and spacious Edinburgh flat. The pale sofa was pristine, last time Eddie was here. Now it's splattered in baby sick and God knows what else. And the flat smells kind of funny: of sour milk with an undertone of nappies and baby wipes. But neither of them care because this feels like home now, for their little family.

Eddie has gone out for provisions when he decides to detour along the bustling thoroughfare of Princes Street. He just wants to see a bit of life, to remind himself that a world exists outside of the flat. Briefly, a display of skateboards and skate wear catches his eye in a shop window. But that's the last thing he's going to spend his money on, because funds are critically low. When he bought his mum that replacement china cup at the new pottery place in Sandybanks, he baulked at the cost. But it was worth it to see her reaction.

'Oh, Eddie, you needn't have!' she announced. But

he could tell she was pleased, and although he has never confessed to the crime, it was his way of saying sorry, as well as thanks. Eddie reckoned his mum knew that too.

Now he walks on, figuring that he should get back to the flat soon. It doesn't quite feel like home yet – not in the way that Kilmory Cottage always felt like home, even when he was desperate to leave the place. But he's sure it will, once they're properly settled.

Eddie is figuring out what he needs to pick up from the shops when he spots a tall, powerfully built figure with a swathe of dark hair striding towards him. It's Marius from the restaurant. In shock and shame, Eddie swings around the corner and hurries up the street.

'Eddie!' comes the deep voice behind him. 'Hey, Eddie!'

Pretending not to have heard, Eddie hurries on, then swerves into the nearest shop. It's a perfume place, heady with scents that make his head swim. He freezes, afraid that any sudden movement will cause him to knock over one of these priceless bottles with what looks like real gold on their labels. In a terrible flashback, he remembers knocking over a full glass of wine in Suki's club.

'Can I help you?' A smart young man has approached him.

'No, no, I'm just looking . . .' Eddie is sweating now, not knowing what to do next. The shop door opens and to his horror, Marius strides in. What is he going to do to him?

'Young Eddie.' Marius smirks, and glances around the shop with gleaming brown eyes. 'Buying the girlfriend a present?'

'Er, yeah. I just thought—'

'Listen.' Marius raises an arm, and for one bonkers moment Eddie thinks he's going to slap him. But instead, a large, meaty hand rests heavily on his shoulder as he says, 'Look, Eddie. I know things didn't turn out too well but you had a lot on your mind back then. And I was probably a bit hasty . . .'

Eddie clears his sandpaper throat. 'Were you?'

'Yeah.' Marius removes the hand and steps back and looks at him. 'If you're still interested, come over and see me tomorrow. We took on someone new but he's been a bloody disaster. We need someone keen and hard-working who actually listens and wants to learn.' He pauses. 'D'you know what I'm saying?'

Eddie nods mutely, sensing his cheeks glowing hot.

'See you then, Eddie.' Marius raises his bushy dark brows, then he saunters out of the shop.

CHAPTER FORTY-NINE

Currently living at Kilmory Cottage: Carly, Frank, Badger

Carly

What fools we were, to think we could relax and think everything's sorted. Because it's never sorted, I realise, as Frank and I sit on the rock together, looking out to sea. Something always rises up at you when you least expect it.

'So, Jamie's left Lewis,' I tell him.

'Jamie?' Frank looks quizzical.

'Jamie, my friend at work. How come you never remember anyone's name?'

'I've been a bit distracted!' he protests. 'I mean, there's been *quite* a bit going on . . .'

'Well, he's been staying at Prish's but that's just temporary. I said he can come and live with us,' I add.

Frank pales in the early evening sun. 'Oh, really? Did you say that?'

'Frank, I'm *joking* . . .' I place a hand on his thigh.

'Jesus, Carly.' He shakes his head and laughs, and then he kisses me lightly on the lips. 'I wouldn't mind, you know. It'd be okay . . .'

'No, honestly, it's just me and you now. If you can bear it.'

He looks at me and smiles. 'I can more than bear it. But actually, it's not just us, is it?'

'Well, me, you and Badger.' I nod. When Frank moved back home it didn't feel right to leave the cat roaming around the scrubby waste ground, perhaps looking for him. Because they'd grown close while Frank was living in the truck.

He leans down and picks up a smooth, worn pebble and rubs his thumb over it. 'I want to tell you something,' he adds.

'What?' I watch him, fixating over the pebble.

'Remember when you were going to Suki's cabin?' I nod. 'I didn't care that you'd bought champagne because of the cost, you know,' he adds. 'I thought you were trying to impress her and her friends. And you don't need to do anything special or different to impress anyone, d'you realise that? You can just be yourself, because you're wonderful as you are.'

My eyes mist and my heart seems to swell. 'That's a nice thing to say,' I murmur, reaching for our cool bag now, and lifting out the bottle of white wine. I fill two paper cups and hand one to him. 'Here we are,' I muse, 'drinking on the beach like teenagers. Like we did when we first met, remember?'

'Of course I remember,' he says softly. I watch him as he takes a sip. My darling Frank, who would do anything for me. He moved to Scotland for me and he loves us all.

All those nights he spent in the shed, he was doing the only thing he could think of, in order to be useful with

Eddie and Lyla's baby on the way. He was designing and building a wooden cot for the baby. Not just any old cot but a beautiful object which rocks on its stand. It's hand-carved and is now embellished with her name, and it's perfect. With Grace's early arrival they hadn't got around to buying one yet. Suki had offered, of course – virtually from when the pregnancy was announced. But Lyla, who's turned out to be impressively strong-minded, wouldn't be rushed.

We're going to visit them all in Edinburgh tomorrow. Eddie has promised that he'll treat us to lunch at Bracken – so maybe he's not so ashamed of us after all. 'Of course I want to take you there,' he insisted, and I pictured my boy as a teenager, charging ahead whenever we were out in public together, terrified of being spotted with us.

'I'm just amazed you'd let us go to your restaurant,' I explained.

Eddie laughed then. 'Well, I do get a massive discount,' he admitted.

'So, what are you thinking?' I ask Frank now.

'About what?' He turns to me.

'About us and what's next . . .'

He smiles. 'Surely you've consulted that book of yours? About what our next chapter should be?'

'Yes,' I say. 'We could move house, maybe? Is Kilmory Cottage too big for us now?'

'Maybe.' Frank nods thoughtfully. 'We could get married? How about that?'

I take his hand and squeeze it tightly. 'We could do that. But d'you think we're rushing into it?'

Frank grins and sips his wine. 'Or we could travel and have adventures?'

'Yes, we could do all of those things.'

Or, I think, *we could stay right here, in the place we love.* We finish our bottle of wine, not minding that it's no longer chilled, or that our town is faded and the pastéis de nata craze has yet to arrive in Sandybanks. I glance up as starlings swoop above us in a glorious cloud. And then Frank's hand folds over mine, and my heart soars like a bird as we turn back towards home.

ACKNOWLEDGEMENTS

Huge thanks to Caroline Sheldon and all at Avon, especially Sarah Bauer and Emma Grundy Haigh. Special gratitude to Helen Huthwaite – for all the chats, lunches, parties and wonderful support over many years. I do hope our paths cross again! Thanks to Helena Newton for excellent eagle-eyed copyediting and to Shima Banks for inside info on the workings of a library. All my love to Jimmy, who helped me to crack my deadline by taking over virtually all kitchen duties, and to my fantastic readers for your morale-boosting feedback every time a new book of mine hits the shelves. Your loyalty and messages make writing a real joy – thank you! Xx

Being married to a comedian is no joke.

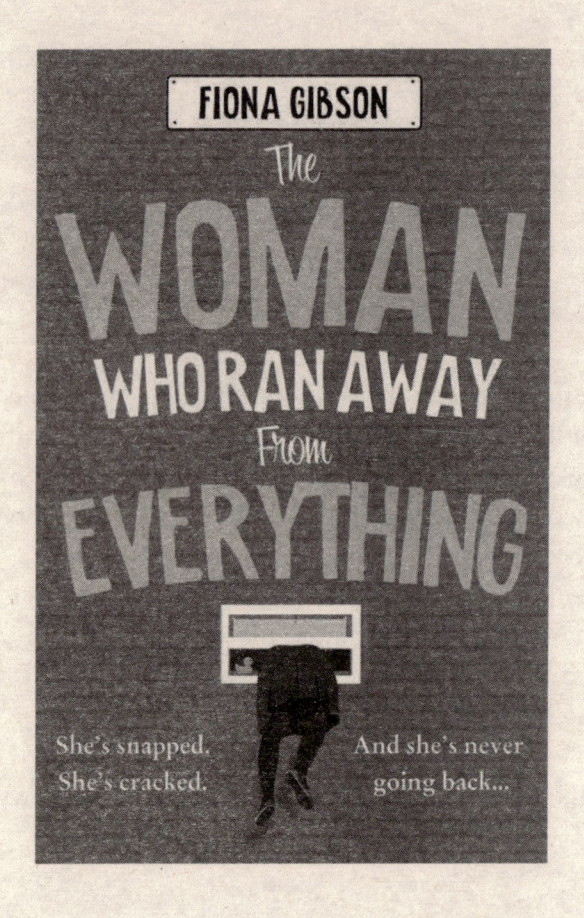

FIONA GIBSON
The WOMAN WHO RAN AWAY From EVERYTHING

She's snapped. She's cracked. And she's never going back...

A hilarious and heart-warming tale of a woman who has had enough, perfect for fans of Sophie Kinsella and Jill Mansell.

Is he just a summer fling? Or the one she's been waiting for . . .

FIONA GIBSON
The MAN I Met on HOLIDAY

Is he just a summer fling? Or the one she's been waiting for...

A hilarious and heart-warming tale of second chance love, perfect for fans of Sophie Kinsella and Kristen Bailey.

**Meet Jen. Flight attendant.
Mum to a grown-up daughter.
Permanently single . . .**

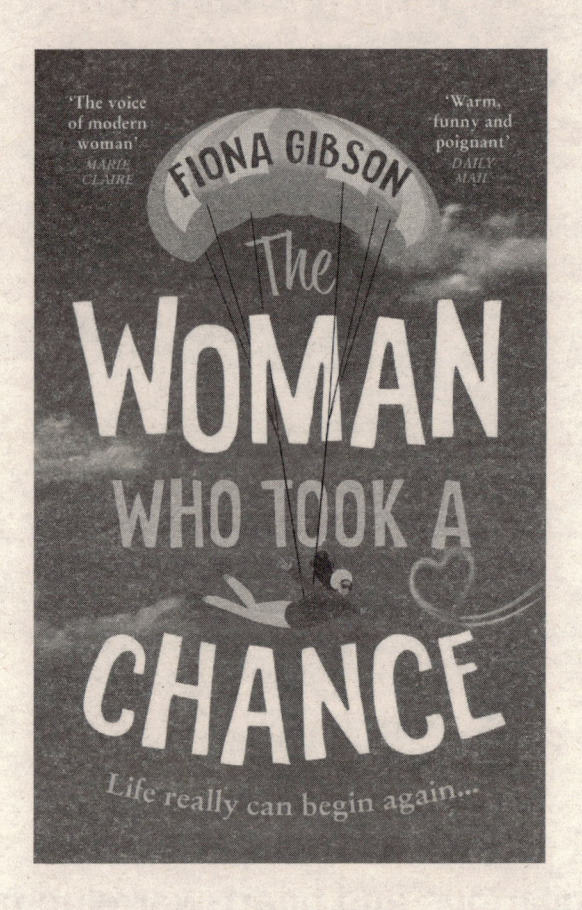

FIONA GIBSON

'The voice of modern woman'
MARIE CLAIRE

'Warm, funny and poignant'
DAILY MAIL

THE WOMAN WHO TOOK A CHANCE

Life really can begin again...

A hilarious novel that proves age is just a number and it's never too late for a second chance!

Suzy Medley is having the worst day of her life when a shabby terrier turns up at her door...

FIONA GIBSON

The DOG SHARE

Two strangers. One dog.

It's complicated!

Can one unruly dog change her life forever?

Sometimes life can be bittersweet . . .

FIONA GIBSON

WHEN LIFE gives you LEMONS

...just add gin and tonic!

When life gives you lemons, lemonade just won't cut it. Bring on the gin!

When the kids are away . . .

> 'Warm, funny and poignant' *Daily Mail*

THE MUM WHO GOT HER LIFE BACK

An empty nest has never been so much fun!

Fiona Gibson

A gloriously uplifting and laugh-out-loud novel from the *Sunday Times* bestseller!

Everyone has a last straw . . .

THE MUM WHO'D HAD ENOUGH

Everyone has a last straw . . .

Fiona Gibson

A hilarious tale perfect for fans of Milly Johnson and Jill Mansell.

What happens when The One That Got Away shows up again . . . thirty years later?

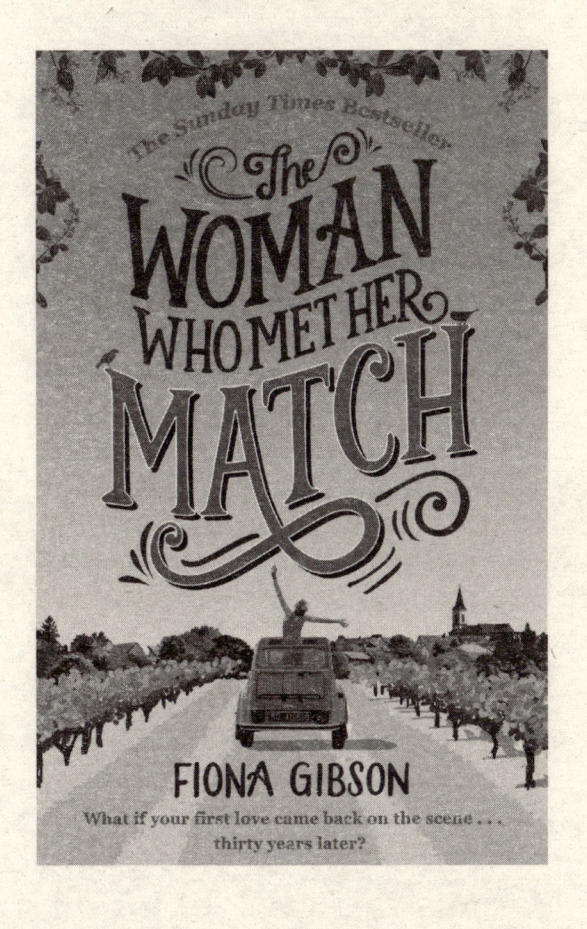

The Sunday Times Bestseller

The WOMAN WHO MET HER MATCH

FIONA GIBSON

What if your first love came back on the scene . . . thirty years later?

An unmissable novel from the voice of the modern woman!